THE LIFE AND DEATH
OF MY LORD
GILLES DE RAIS

THE LIFE AND DEATH
OF MY LORD
GILLES DE RAIS

ROBERT NYE

HAMISH HAMILTON · LONDON

HAMISH HAMILTON LTD

Published by the Penguin Group
27 Wrights Lane, London W8 5TZ, England
Viking Penguin, a division of Penguin Books USA Inc.
375 Hudson Street, New York, New York 10014, USA
Penguin Books Australia Ltd, Ringwood, Victoria, Australia
Penguin Books Canada Ltd, 2801 John Street, Markham, Ontario, Canada L3R 1B4
Penguin Books (NZ) Ltd, 182–190 Wairau Road, Auckland 10, New Zealand

Penguin Books Ltd, Registered Offices: Harmondsworth, Middlesex, England

First published 1990
1 3 5 7 9 10 8 6 4 2

Printed in England by Clays Ltd, St Ives plc
Filmset in Monophoto Baskerville

A CIP catalogue record for this book is available from the British Library

ISBN 0-241-12964-8

CONTENTS

PART THREE

PROLOGUE

Last night, once more, I had to go back to the castle. I rode down through the forest and out over that desolate plain. It was bitter cold, it was winter, and darkness was falling. I spurred my horse on, in a foolish sweat to be with my master before night overwhelmed me. But the jade would go no faster, and the moon was up when at last I reached Tiffauges.

Nothing had changed. The castle, that outpost of hell, was just as I remember it – spires, watch-towers, donjons, thick ramparts of granite rising sheer from the foul sluggish waters of the moat. In the moonlight I saw his banner stream above the battlements, a sable cross on gold, with the lilies around it. The great drawbridge had been lowered, as if my lord awaited me.

Dismounting in the courtyard, I ran up the flight of stone steps which leads to the iron-studded door. That door swung open on its hinges before I set my hand to it. Far off, from the forest, I heard a wolf howl, then another wolf-voice joining it. I crossed myself. I entered once more that dark and glittering spider's web which, waking, I have prayed never again to see, far less get caught in.

Corridors, passages, staircases, galleries, all were ablaze with torches and those hanging silver lamps I know so well. I recognized every tapestry, of course, each vaulted and fretted ceiling, the armorial trophies rattling as I strode past them down chill familiar pavings of black marble. Door after door I opened, room after room I passed through, stair after stair I climbed. But he was not there. My lord and master seemed nowhere to be found.

Yet the place was in good order, and gave every sign of recent habitation. In the library his illuminated manuscript of the *Lives of the Caesars* by Suetonius lay open at the usual page on the brass lectern fashioned like an eagle with spread wings. Tall black beeswax candles burned in his robing room. And when I reached the banqueting hall the oak table was spread as if for a feast, while on the hearth a fire of logs flamed and flared, sending a hollow roar up the wide chimney.

Then I heard music. I left the hall. I climbed the twisting stair which leads to the chapel of St Vincent. As I neared the top I could hear his choir singing, those boys' voices of pure silver that still sting my heart and send shivers of impotent pity down my spine.

Laudate pueri Dominum, they sang. *Laudate nomen Domini*. Praise the Lord, ye children: O praise the name of the Lord ... It is the liturgy for the Mass for the Feast of the Holy Innocents.

My old well-hated vestments lay spread out for my use in the sacristy: white linen alb and amice, a maniple of heavy silk, the crimson stole and chasuble embroidered with rubies that gleamed in the candlelight like drops of warm red blood. I stared at them, God help me, with revulsion. I did not put them on. I could not touch them.

The choir had just started the *Gloria* – vile Rossignol's treble as always outsoaring the rest – when I passed into the blaze of light that is the sanctuary.

And there they all stood, ranged along the golden rail, his principal creatures: the magician Prelati, gross Griart, de Bricqueville, Poitou. They were as they had been in the days and the nights of their infamy. They stared at me, but I knew that they could see nothing. Their eyes were dead in their hellish corpse-blank faces. I saw them and I knew them all, each one. Did I pray for them? I hope I tried. I don't know. The words would not come. The responses got stuck in my throat. I prayed for the Holy Innocents, as usual. It is always the Feast of the Innocents when I go back to Tiffauges. And all other times it has ended in horror, murders, blood.

Last night, for the first time, it was different. When my master appeared he was kneeling in front of the altar, dressed as at the beginning of his trial in pearl-grey silk with white boots and a crimson belt, his whole person sparkling with jewels. There was a woman, too, kneeling beside him, a woman clad from head to foot in white. She turned her face as the music stopped and she looked at me. I never saw a look so beautiful. And yet the woman now looking at me was not beautiful herself. She was short in stature, snub-nosed and pale-complexioned, with dark hair cropped close and ugly like a herald's. She smiled, and beckoned. My master turned. He was laughing out loud with delight, and suddenly the air was full of butterflies: black and red and golden butterflies flying and falling everywhere about us like a whirling painted snow. Then I knew what I was born to do, and for what reason I'd been summoned. I took his left hand in my right hand and her right hand in my left, so that the three of us made a harmonious circle, and I celebrated the marriage of Joan of Arc and Gilles de Rais.

To trust a dream, one must be morally certain of its divine origin. Attempting to obtain insight into the future from the stream of thoughts and fancies that flows through the mind during sleep is otherwise an act of superstition. That God has sometimes taught by means of dreams, however, is clear enough from Holy Scripture, and I can count it no accident that on waking this morning the first news I heard was that the appellate court appointed by His Holiness Pope Callixtus III has just declared Joan of Arc innocent of all those crimes for which she was burned to death at Rouen some twenty-five years ago. A formal Sentence of Rehabilitation has been passed upon that soul. So she wasn't a witch and a heretic, after all. Well, who ever thought she was, apart from her bought judges, and the English?

3

Gilles de Rais, though, must be admitted to be a different matter, if not quite a different story. The nature of the difference and the sameness of the story is the burden of my dream and the present narrative. I want, if God will grant me grace to do so, to make sense of the two of them together, both His creatures, the probable devil as well as the possible saint. I cannot revoke or rehabilitate, nor would I wish to, but I am impelled by some power beyond myself to remember and to record that remembrance. I have no other motive but to seek to exorcize the ghost of Gilles de Rais by the act of recounting and understanding what I alone of all men living have been given to know about him. This is a tale like no other I hope you will ever read, for it is the tale of a man so dedicated to evil that hearing his confession the judge stood up and veiled the crucifix.

I, Dom Eustache Blanchet, the author of this work, am a person of little importance, a mere priest. But I spent three years of my own life in the devil's service, and have now endured many more years banished as a consequence, during which time of exile I have sought diligently as a penance to gather all the facts together and make sense both of my own experience and of what others have reported to me, so that what I write here you may believe to be no more nor less than the truth of a very strange case. He was once my master, this Marshal of France and terrible artist in blood. I speak, let it be plainly understood, of Gilles de Rais, Baron de Laval, sometime captain-at-arms under King Charles VII in the wars against the English; Gilles de Rais, chosen companion and bodyguard of the most holy Maid of Orléans, Joan of Arc; my lord, the man whom some now call Bluebeard, though his beard was black with just a frost of silver in it latterly, and his poor wife to my knowledge is still living; that same Gilles de Rais who was brought to trial in the thirty-sixth year of his age, charged with witchcraft and heresy,

4

sacrilege and sorcery, the evocation of demons and the practice of unnatural crime against many children of both sexes, ending with their murder for his delight; who was found guilty on all counts after a trial in which he made three full confessions in open court; who was properly sentenced to death by hanging and burning; and who was then duly executed at Nantes, in Brittany, on the twenty-sixth day of October, Our Lord's year 1440.

Pay heed, for this monster was my master and my friend, the wickedest man in the world and my brother in Christ.

PART ONE

I

CHRISTMAS EVE 1437

Of my life before I came into the service of the Marshal Gilles de Rais I will speak briefly. I was born in Ushant, that island like a rock flung by a giant far out to sea from the coast of Brittany. My father was a fisherman, but he was lost with his boat in a storm in the year of my birth. I was, in fact, a posthumous child, and when I was born my mother vowed that I would never suffer the same fate as my father. She gave me to the Church, to the Ark of Christ, rather than to the sea. It is a decision which I have not regretted.

Imagine: it is Christmas Eve 1437. Here I am sitting in the muck and the mire of the road outside the palace of my lord the Bishop of St Malo, with snow starting to fall from a nasty bruised sky and night coming dismally on. I wear the black habit, with leather belt, scapular and hood, of one professed of the order of St Benedict. I am aged thirty-three, not a bad priest but not a good one either, a species of educated fool, a goat in monk's clothing, a misfit, a Breton who never learned to sing in tune in choir with the French, an awkward unbiddable fellow, philosophical enough but feckless and a little too fond of his wine, partial to good cheese when he can get it, and even any old bad cheese when he cannot.

St Malo is a walled island city and sea-port, some fifty miles north-west of Rennes, communicating with the mainland by means of a stone causeway known as the Sillon. Sillon means furrow. I sit here in the winter gloom, half-drunk, shivering, chewing my empty purse, trying to make up my mind as to what I had better do next. I have, so it seems to me, but two alternatives. Either I crawl back into the palace and lick the Bishop's slippers, or else I get to my feet and cross that causeway, follow the furrow through the sea and find out Gilles de Rais in his castle at Tiffauges.

I had, you see, just got myself chucked out on my arse, sacked by my venerable pot-bellied patron, Nicolas Lefumeux, aforesaid Bishop of St Malo, who for the twelvemonth past had employed me, out of the mysterious charity of even the episcopal version of the human heart, as secretary to himself and tutor to his half-wit orphan nephew.

The reason for this sudden dismissal is soon stated. That afternoon, my brain and heart made warm by my Christmas wine, I had again returned ('like a dog to his vomit', as the Bishop so graciously put it, kicking me downstairs) to a previous favourite opinion of mine, first expressed on the very day of the burning of Joan of Arc: namely, that Pierre Cauchon, Bishop of Beauvais, and all her other judges had done wrong, that they were cheap tools of the English, that the Maid was no heretic or sorceress, but innocent, possibly saintly, certainly inspired.

As I say, I first expressed this view, again when my tongue was loosed by wine to the service of truth, some six and a half years before, on Wednesday the thirtieth of May 1431 to be precise, the day of the blessed Joan's burning in the old market-place at Rouen, when I happened to be in that city, not a Benedictine yet, but in the last of my four qualifying years as a Dominican friar in the monastery ruled over by Maître Jean Lemaître, chief of Joan's inquisitors.

I wish I could lie to you, and boast that I saw this dear girl's martyrdom. I might claim, in that case, that I too heard her cry out '*Jesus! Jesus!*' in the flames, or that I stood by the soldier who gave her some twisted sticks for a cross to kiss and put in her bosom between her person and her clothing. But it is not my purpose to lie to you about this, nor any other matter, good or bad. Seek simplicity and mistrust it, that's my motto. I never saw the Maid of Orléans. I was twenty-seven years old when she perished in the fire, studying as I say to be worthy of that order founded by St Dominic in 1215 for the salvation of souls, especially by means of preaching. I knew that Joan wasn't a witch. So did others, including to my knowledge Guillaume Manchon, chief of the notaries who questioned her during her trial, and Thomas de Courcelles, one of her assessors, who later was responsible for translating into Latin the official text of her trial. These men, and others, great and small, were prudent; they kept their mouths shut. My grave mistake, as on lesser occasions, was to give voice to what wise men merely thought, to shout out loud what the judicious only whispered.

Well, the error of my ways being indicated to me, I prostrated myself before my superiors, and was generously pardoned after spending a mere year on bread and water imprisoned in my cell. The Church is an amiable mother. Yet I could never quite put it out of my mind that there were those in that same monastery with me at Rouen who saw and knew Joan and comforted her secretly during her trial and in her last terrible hours, and that these men shared my opinion of her sanctity, as they were prepared to make plain by nods and winks and handclasps when Lemaître was not looking. They were wiser than me, as I have remarked, in the ways of the world and of Christ's bride, as St Paul calls the Church. They knew that bride as a body that gives birth to the truth in her own good time. My sin was always impatience aspiring to importunacy, which too often has misled me into *saying* what had better been left unsaid for the time being. But I only did this in those days when I was drunk.

Granted an indult then to change my monastic direction, I moved to the Benedictine Abbey of Saint-Pierre de Seuilly, near Chinon, in Touraine, just after Easter 1432. Lemaître, of course, was glad to see me go, and these events are now sufficiently in the past for it to be admitted that it was his unswerving self-rectitude and inquisitorial grand manners that finally convinced me I could never be a good Dominican. I served my span at Saint-Pierre as a novice, and was eventually professed, all without incident. But about the beginning of my last year, in the early summer of 1435, I saw in Orléans the pageant-play *The Mystery of the Siege of Orléans*, and all my old obsessions came flooding back.

This play, which began each day at dawn and ran till dusk, was unlike any other play I ever saw or heard of. It was, in effect, a total re-enactment of the relief of the siege of Orléans accomplished exactly six years before by that victorious army led by Joan of Arc. Written in rhymed octosyllabic verse, more than 20,000 lines of it, the play contains 140 speaking parts and employed more than another 500 extras for the crowd scenes in the three performances I witnessed. Fresh costumes were provided for each performance, and all these robes were to my eye of such striking richness and beauty that I cannot imagine any of them to have been fashioned in the usual stage counterfeit. Even the rags worn by the defeated had been created by the slashing of fine cloth. The action, which began in England on the eve of the Orléans campaign and ended with Joan's delivery of the city, took place around and about and above the spectators on a series of open-air stages. Those stages were never empty, and sometimes different scenes would be proceeding on several different levels at the same time. In a cave under the main stage were stored barrels of hypocras and fine vintages for the refreshment of performers and audience alike. Admission was free to all performances, and as you can imagine every available hostelry in Orléans and the surrounding district was taxed to its capacity to provide accommodation for the crowds that came. The play was a vast banquet for all the senses. It was said to have cost more than 80,000 gold crowns to mount, and in Orléans none remembered, or ever expected again to see such superfluity of theatre, excess of art, unreasonable expenditure on spectacle.

To one spectator, though, it was not the crowding ambition that impressed. What struck me more than dumb was the play's story, its careful but passionate pursuit of the exact sequence of events in Joan's career. The scenes include the vision of Joan while tending her sheep and her first interview with the Dauphin. Another is laid in England, as I mentioned, showing the enemy preparing for their expedition against France, followed by scenes of the relief of Orléans and the return to the city after the victory of Patay. The verse, no doubt, displays neither literary quality nor dramatic interest, but just as the rest of the audience found such defects of minor importance in a spectacle so gigantic, so I found them irrelevant to the authenticity of this pageant-play's portrait of Joan. She was there at the heart of all the action, shining and saintly, a peasant girl to whom each grand lord bowed his head, addressing her invariably as a queen:

> *Aussi moy, Dame, ne doubtez;*
> *Faire vueil ce qui vous plaira . . .*

'As for myself, Lady, have no doubts; my wish is but to do your will.' These, now I come to think of it, are the only lines I can remember from this prodigious *Mystery of the Siege of Orléans*. They were spoken at a key point by the man who of all Joan's captains seemed the most faithful and valiant: the Marshal Gilles de Rais. As the play made clear, this man had been her personal escort and bodyguard, obeying her commands without question, upholding her divine mission, treating her always with a deference and respect that amount to love. Joan is a saint and Gilles is her most devoted servant. That's how the play presents it, and how I took it in. Of course I was also aware, squinting up at the ermine and the swords, watching these brilliant figures that seemed on their tiered stage to outshine the sun, that the Marshal de Rais was responsible for the whole production. He was, as they said, the richest man in France, and alone he had commissioned this great saintly entertainment and paid for everything to do with it.

Thus, I confess, began a second obsession. My belief that Joan of Arc had been innocent of all charges of heresy and sorcery became compounded or fortified by a related conviction that the Marshal de Rais – who appeared to me splendid both to have put on such a festival celebrating the Maid of Orléans, and for his direct and intimate part in her story – that this illustrious Marshal of France could *do* something towards her rehabilitation. Not that I had any reason to suppose that he would, apart from the fact of that play which was so overwhelming that it seemed to take place in some theatre of the soul itself. Concerning the Marshal, I knew little beyond his honourable role as Joan's captain. He was Lord of Champtocé, Tiffauges, Pouzages, Machecoul, St Etienne-de-la-Mer-Morte, Pornic, Grienne, and other places, but a man is not to be defined in terms of his estates, else Dives had been canonized. I learned that he kept a personal army of more than 200 soldiers, whom he equipped with the finest horses, and that like the King himself he appeared to spend his days moving from one of his castles to the next, keeping open house to nobles and commoners wherever he went. It was reported that the Marshal was no less extravagant in his religious observances. His ecclesiastical household numbered over eighty persons and included clergy, chaplains, cantors, clerks and numberless choristers. At Machecoul, quite recently, he had founded his own chapel, dedicated to the Holy Innocents, already one of the wonders of Christendom, organized as it was on a scale that made the cathedrals of France look mean and shabby. All this impressed me, yet none of this impressed me. No one could miss the rich external trappings of the Marshal Gilles de Rais, nor the swathe he cut through his times like a bright sword. But what interested me was the absolute nature of the obedience he had paid to Joan of Arc. He had been her chosen one, and fought by her side as her friend and champion. At the least, I suppose I now stored it in my heart that one day I might learn more about the real Joan of Arc from the lips of Gilles de Rais.

Whether all this pother interfered with my vocation, or at some profounder level was a part of that odd pilgrim's progress, only God can know for sure. Suffice it to report that drinking my wine and nibbling my cheeses I gave voice to some of these speculations and opinions from time to time, so that before too long the Abbot of Seuilly was moved to recommend me to his friend the Bishop of St Malo for a more secular employment than the monastery could offer. Absolution for breaking my monastic vows was not difficult to come by, and the St Malo post seemed agreeable at first in that it left me with a little free time to work at my Greek and my Latin, to botanize in field and forest, to drink up the wisdom of harbours and markets and taverns. Latin and flowers I love, and I like to drink. As to my character, in those far-off days I was perhaps two men. When sober, I was mild and no more than commonly foolish; drunk, I returned always to this obsession with the holy Joan of Arc. Yet even that is not unique perhaps. We Bretons have a weakness for making saints.

So, here I am at the turning point in my life, a priestly scarecrow sitting in the road outside the Bishop's palace that had briefly been my home, my handful of belongings in a bundle at my feet, my head aching, my teeth chattering, expelled if not from paradise then still from the only shelter I had on earth, thirty-three years old, Our Lord's age at the time of His crucifixion, grateful I suppose that Nicolas Lefumeux was at least not coming in pursuit of me with his silver crozier, to beat me in full view of the passers-by.

I suppose I had better confess that it is true that early on that crucial Christmas Eve, the year of man's redemption 1437, I did sing drunk in choir at the cathedral of St Malo. Drunken carol-singing, however, was not the cause of my dismissal. The cause of my dismissal was the cause of my drunken carol-singing: namely, my excitement over a tale just told me by a pardoner, that Joan of Arc was in fact *alive*. Whether she had escaped the flames, or whether she had been restored to life again, I cannot now remember. The pardoner had one blue eye and one brown, which for some reason made his story the more plausible. Joan, so he told me, was now once more at Orléans, where she had been publicly recognized by her own brothers, and was in process of being fêted by the municipality. She rode everywhere on a white horse, he said, and there was this blazing light about her.

Suicidally injudicious, as ever, I repeated the pardoner's tale to my pupil, the Bishop's nephew. That little rat lost no time at all in scuttling to his uncle with the latest heresy according to Dom Eustache. Summoned to the episcopal presence, I was theologically excoriated, mocked, and fired on the spot.

No doubt I deserved no less. But in condemning my gulli-bility, the Bishop also made it quite clear that he considered me half-mad, at best. Then, under his breath, he added something about another in similar state.

'Who, lord?' I queried, hardly able to credit my hearing.

'I said the Marshal de Rais,' the Bishop explained. 'You are mad as de Rais is.'

For a moment I thought I was witness to the birth of a proverb. Then, rather tediously, the Bishop went on further to explain that he considered the Marshal Gilles de Rais to be another driven mad on the subject of the girl Joan. Witness, he said, the waste of so much money on that unintelligible pageant. And had I not heard that the Marshal's own family had appealed to the King, and that a royal edict had been proclaimed, describing Gilles as a spendthrift and forbidding him to sell off any more of his estates to finance his insanities? And that Gilles' own wife had left him, taking their only child, a daughter, with her, since evidently the Marshal preferred the ghost of an apostate witch for company?

It was at that instant, standing before the Bishop on his throne, that it fell into place in my head that my destiny was somehow crossed with the destiny of the Marshal Gilles de Rais. *Dies infaustus.*

An unlucky day, indeed. And what should I do next, sprawled here in the mud of the public highway, but determine and make a vow to myself that I would go now on foot to Tiffauges? I reasoned it thus: whatever might befall me, the worst had surely befallen. (Well, little did I know . . .) Besides, I was now quite without employment in the world, arrived at what I took to be my lowest point, beyond ambition or much hope, beyond prayer almost. This realization was so dire it made my heart leap in my breast, as if that organ were suddenly without any weight of cares to it. I had no money, no resources, no desires. Everything that was expected had fallen from me. There were, thank God, no expectations left.

Added to which, the weather was bad, and the night gave every promise of being a cold one. Snow, as I think I may already have mentioned, was pouring down thickly now from a darkening sky. I was homeless, I was friendless, I had crabs. I was the happiest man alive.

I resolved then to walk to Tiffauges, begging my way, and that when I got there I would throw myself upon the mercy of the Marshal Gilles de Rais, Baron de Laval, Count of Grienne, and so forth. I would seek employment from him, either as a cleric attached to his private chapel or in some such secretarial capacity as I had served the Bishop of St Malo. Alternatively, if the Marshal could not or would not give me a position in his household, then perhaps he might take pity on a fellow student and follower of Joan of Arc, and act the part of an indulgent patron, finding me a substantial cure somewhere in the countryside that belonged to him, a parish where I might be considered the secular priest while I pursued the common practice in such cases and paid a needy vicar to take my place.

For if that happened then I would indeed be free. And I think, in that moment, in the roadway, that Christmas Eve, at the pivot of my life, I desired above all things to be free, free at all costs, free of irritable abbots and bombastic bishops, free of nephews and nepotism, free of lice and itchy feet of course, free of copying encyclicals, free of this, that and the other, but above and beyond all free of the implications of my own eccentric and truth-telling tongue. I could again appeal to the Pope for an indult, and this time there would be no need of a pardon for breaking monastic vows, no *absolutione ab apostasia*. Complete freedom of thought is plainly a nonsense. Where there is certainty then there has to be determination of the intellect. No one can be free of the laws of logic or free of truth: a wise man cannot believe that the moon is made of green cheese. Neither can anyone who hopes to attain and sustain truth be free of authority; life is not long enough, for one thing. Notice, therefore, that I was never an idle dreamer. Even at this point I did not entertain wild notions of pursuing my studies at the university of Paris, or studying medicine perhaps at Montpellier. I am for ever a priest, I am forbidden other callings. And even as a wandering scholar I knew that I would have small chance of an honest life unless I could discover the protection of a patron.

I read somewhere of a man who once was awarded, undeservingly, a bottle of wine so fine that even a short sight of the seals on it made him drunk. That's how I felt in that moment when I said aloud to myself the name of the Marshal Gilles de Rais as my salvation. Perhaps, it occurred to me, I had even been born to serve him. And this was not so fanciful or incongruous a thought as you might suppose. I had discovered, you see, that we had been born in the same year, myself and this man who had wished for nothing else but to do Joan's will, who had fought by her side, who had taken Orléans with her, and who had gone back to Orléans to make that play which was like history held for ever in the mystery of art. And if Joan *was* alive, as the pardoner said, and ranging abroad, where else would she be going now but to seek out her best companion, that *gentilhomme vaillant* as they called him in the play?

I got up then and went across the Sillon. I walked all night and kept walking all Christmas Day.

II

TIFFAUGES

I must confess that my heart sank when I first set eyes on the castle of Tiffauges. From the outside it resembled a fortress, dark and forbidding. Fifty miles south of Nantes, it stood at the centre of those waste lands where Poitou, Anjou and Brittany all meet. Here was a melancholy world of scrub and stones, sparse verdure, clumps of gnarled and blasted oaks, pools choked with reeds. The castle itself was perched on a great rock commanding two ravines where rivers ran, the Crûme and the Sèvre. Buzzards wheeled above it, in a sky the colour of slate.

I had begged my way hither, on foot, through winter weather as harsh as any I could recall. Consequently, I was sober as the day I was born that memorable morning when I first entered the castle. Once within its walls, though, what met my weary senses made me wonder if I wasn't drunk without benefit of wine.

Here was a paradise concealed in a purgatory. Grim and impregnable from the outside, with massive donjons and thick ramparts guarding every angle of attack, Tiffauges glowed inside like a series of magic caskets packed with jewels and seemingly fitting one within another to infinity. The interior walls were covered with cloth of gold, the floors paved with white marble and jade, the ceilings decorated with paintings which dazzled even my unsophisticated eye as indubitably the work of some Italian master. I was escorted to a chamber with a roaring fire, and invited to sit down and have my feet washed by manservants who bore ewers of silver, embossed after Grecian designs, and filled to the brim with *mélisse* and rose water. After I had rested, I was bidden to restore and refresh myself at the banquet table before being quizzed as to my business with the Marshal. There were pastries of beef, a pie of leveret heavily spiced, lampreys, and a salad of briony and mallow sprinkled with mace. I think I also tasted caraway and hyssop, probably poppy seeds, certainly ginger. The drinks were dry wines, and hypocras, beer and fermented mulberry juice. Musicians played in the gallery, *jongleurs* tumbled, and a boy with yellow hair juggled with three swords. By the end of this feast, I was ready to fall asleep.

Perhaps I did, and thus dreamed what I think happened next. Yet it seemed to me that I was ushered into a library where a man sat reading a book at an oaken table. He glanced up as I entered, and greeted me pleasantly, announcing his name as Messire Roger de Bricqueville. He was the cousin, he said, of the Marshal Gilles de Rais. The Marshal was elsewhere for the time being, but if I would state my devices and desires then he, Messire de Bricqueville, would endeavour to do his best to satisfy me. He smiled courteously as he said this, and then he stood up. He wore no garments and his virile member was erect.

You must understand that I intend to tell you this story just as it happened, without fear or favour, prevarication or untruth. Whether de Bricqueville received me for this original interview in a state of nakedness, or I merely imagined that he was so in a dream or a vision, I do not know and thus cannot say for certain. There will be other points in my narrative where a comparable incertitude clouds the facts of the case; all I can promise is that nothing I tell you will be fiction, and that when I am not sure of the reality of a thing then I will say so. Concerning de Bricqueville here in the library, unclothed and with his organ of generation engorged, I may observe that the shock of the image is so much at one both with the general feel of Tiffauges as I came quickly to know it, and with particular vile matters later to be discovered, that whether it happened or was imagined is almost irrelevant. What is important is that I thought or believed that it happened. As to its being an imaginative vision, if it was so then that would not lessen its force. Such was the angel who appeared to the blessed St Joseph. These extraordinary favours are neither to be desired nor asked for, since they are quite unnecessary to perfection; yet bear in mind also that visions can be counterfeited by the Devil. Tiffauges, as you will see, was a place where that spirit was rampant.

'*Devices and desires* . . .' The strangeness of Messire de Bric-queville's phrase has remained in my memory. In truth, did I come to the castle with either devices or desires, wishing to devise anything against the Marshal or desiring anything of him? I think not. And it is precisely because I think not that I am just disposed, on balance, to assume that my naked welcomer was not a dream or a vision. For had he been so, then his locutions would no doubt have been shaped and given substance by my own hysteria, whereas here in this strange fall of words seems evidence of quite another intelligence than mine – the real de Bricqueville's mind, in fact, as I would come to know it in the days and nights that followed, the mind of the Marshal's steward, a Norman mind, cold, politic, self-possessed.

Quite how I answered him I do not know. Either at this time or at some other equally early, I must have given my name and stated my business. I must have told them my story, and declared my passion for Joan. Perhaps I did ask for employment along the lines I had intended? In the time that now followed the exploration of the chapel looms large, as though de Bricqueville or one of the other disciples took seriously my hope to be employed there, and showed me around, and allowed me to believe that in due course, when the Marshal came back, he might well have work for me. I remember noting that reciting the sevenfold daily office in choir Gilles' chapter wore mozettas trimmed with fur, a distinction I had never seen before and later learned was supposed to be reserved to the canons of St John Lateran. I remember admiring a particular cope of crimson brocade figured in green and powdered with golden birds . . . But I am loath to go on in this vein, providing evidence of my own priestly vanity and very little else.

Enough to say that either as a result of that rude interview in the library with de Bricqueville, or other interviews, or none, I found myself accepted at the castle as not exactly a guest or a visitor but rather as one waiting on the master to return. My interest in Joan was known, and my faith in her innocence, as also the way in which sundry intempestive declarations of that faith had served to knock my life this way and that, blowing me finally here to the gates of Tiffauges. I was, in this regard, treated a little like one given sanctuary, though I understood that in some manner not specified that sanctuary was not unconditional and might yet be put to the test. I was accepted, in short, as a sort of fugitive from the world; but made to understand that I had not yet been granted immunity to remain in this castle that was somehow not quite of the world.

And what sights and sounds I saw and heard there! In those early days, far from being the prison which it later became for me, Tiffauges seemed like a feast, a festival. Peacocks strutted on its lawns, spreading the fans of eyes which were their wings, indifferent to the falling snow. I stood on the tower with the wind blowing my robe and watched a hawk stoop while through the open door behind me came the music of rebecks and citholes. I knelt in the chapel measuring my prayers by candles mirrored in shrines of pure crystal and gold. I dabbled with my fingers in the fountain that played all the time in the walled garden. Most things within that many-towered massy castle seemed peace and light to my first innocent eye.

It was the library which interested me most, and where I spent much of my time when there was no one to talk with. This was a long high room panelled in Irish oak and cypress, lit by thirty chandeliers and a single huge silver lamp in the shape of the full moon, with gilt-trellised shelves and oaken presses. More than 1,000 manuscripts reposed there, most of them vellum bound in embossed leather with clasps of gold and ivory. Apart from the usual selection of the Fathers of the Church, a number of Books of Hours, many missals, manuals of devotion, and commentaries on the Scriptures, I turned the pages of volumes on heraldry and hawking, the art of war and the craft of music, the Latin grammar of Aelius Donatus, the *Doctrinal* of Alexandre de Villedieu, a rhymed Priscian and that charming *Opus Tripartitum* by Gerson. These last titles suggested to me that the Marshal's education had started early, and been orthodox and thorough in its progress. I leafed through lighter volumes, too, from his later days: the *Roman de la Rose*, the *Chanson de Roland*, the *Chansons de Geste*, the *Cantilène de Sainte Eulalie*, and Rutebeuf's *Théophile*, as well as translations of Boccaccio and *The Golden Legend* of Jacopo de Voragine. If thumb marks in the margin were anything to go by, then the books which the maker of the library had read most were without doubt a copy of Ovid's *Metamorphoses*, bound in vermilion leather with silver-gilt clasps, and an equally ornate copy of St Augustine's *De Civitate Dei*.

I had never hoped to encounter such a library in private hands. I sat reading until the candles guttered out.

Gradually I got to know my way about the rest of the castle, and grew acquainted with its other occupants. The place was a bewildering labyrinth of rooms and galleries and corridors, some of them underground, like the oubliettes below the level of the moat. I was allowed to wander at will, wherever I wanted, from the cream and gold of the high chapel of St Vincent down to the hot and spicy fug of the enormous kitchens. I encountered no obstacle anywhere I passed, my principal problem being merely to find my way back to the library which was my favourite abode for study or contemplation, or to the snug oak-raftered chamber where I slept. After a few experiences of being lost, I contrived a simple plan of gauging all space and distance in the castle from the resonance of the chapel choir. As I have remarked, its choristers and singing men, under the tutelage of an apple-cheeked hunchback, were both diligent and punctual in performance of the daily office. If lost in some twist or cranny of the network of apartments that comprised Tiffauges, I had therefore only to wait until the moment when that choir started up for Prime, Terce, Sext, or whatever was the hour, and then pursue the singing sound until I found myself in the glory of the chapel and could fulfil my obligations.

Though I have said that I could go wherever I wished to go, I must add that there was this one far tower, tall and dark, apparently to be entered only by a single door at the top of a steep flight of stone steps, which I found it impossible to visit. That door was always locked, and no one seemed to go there. Nor, looking across from any of the other turrets, did I ever see lights in the casement windows of this dark tower at night. At the time, in those days of blessed innocence, I did not wonder about it much. What was one dark tower in a world of such grace and colour? It seemed to me that I had passed from the darkness of monasteries and the mean confines of episcopal palaces into a brilliant if often dream-like heaven of bright lights, sweet scents, and long-linked musical sounds. Tiffauges was all opulence and magnificence, an open house fit for some great prince, an imperial court thronged with what seemed to me like ghosts with jewels at their throats, tinted hose on their legs, and pointed shoes of a fashion I had never seen elsewhere on their feet that bore them up and down and round and about in the castle. I felt like a mole that has burst out of the earth into sudden incredible sunlight.

I was not yet to see that this sun was satanic and unreal, a false painted disc in the sky, and this brilliance just the flickering of the flames of hell. I ask the reader to bear patiently with the distance between what is observed and what is understood in these initial chapters of my story. No doubt I was a fool to take Tiffauges at its face value, but as you will learn my ignorance was never quite invincible.

Concerning the other occupants of the castle, I learned their names and faces soon enough. Apart from Roger de Bricqueville, the Marshal's cousin and controller of his estates during his absence, there were three principal persons seeing to the management of affairs. The first of these, Henriet Griart, was a gross, effeminate fellow. He seemed to be some kind of bodyservant, yet he had neither the manners nor the appearance of a servant and I took something of a dislike to him and a disgust at his fat presence from the start. He chewed upon comfits and marshmallow a great deal, in an effort to sweeten the stench of his breath and his rotting teeth. This trembling jelly of a man was accompanied much of the time by his physical opposite, one Etienne Corillaut, known for some reason I never was told as Poitou (probably he came from that province). Poitou resembled nothing so much as a pair of scissors; he was spindle-shanked, thin, and dry. From a chance remark he once made, I deduced that he had originally been employed as a choirboy in the chapel, and that from this he had graduated to being the Marshal's page, no doubt when his voice broke. Poitou seemed now more secretary than page, but again there was that which struck me as ambiguous and ill-defined about his role. All that was certain was that he and Griart were usually to be found together, the fat one sucking his sweets, the thin one coughing. You might catch a whiff of Griart's bad breath in the corridor, but then turn a corner and bump into Poitou first. Or perhaps I would hear Poitou's distinctive bark of a cough behind me, only to spin on my heel and surprise Griart leading his inseparable companion by the hand. I got used to Griart and Poitou, but I may claim that I always mistrusted them.

The third of the Marshal's disciples was Messire Gilles de Sillé. I gathered that de Sillé, like de Bricqueville, was a cousin of de Rais'. Like de Bricqueville, he had red hair and blue eyes and was courteous in style and correct in speech. Unlike de Bricqueville, he never appeared to me even in sleep or delusion without his clothes. Both the cousins dressed particularly elegantly, favouring silken doublets with puffed sleeves and short gowns of brocade, damask, and velvet. Both affected a somewhat melancholy humour, but whereas de Bricqueville was saturnine in expression, de Sillé smiled even as he sighed. An eccentricity of this second cousin's was that often he was to be seen with a little bird in a cage. The bird was some quite unremarkable type of thrush, so far as I could tell, yet the cage had silver bars. Messire de Sillé wore silver cage and thrush dangling from his left wrist like a bracelet.

Apart from Messires de Bricqueville and de Sillé, and Griart and Poitou, I should mention also that the merry-cheeked humpback in control of the choir was called Dean de la Ferrière, and that I soon learned to recognize the voice of one boy, nicknamed Rossignol, the nightingale, whose piercing solo treble soared above all the others and the chapel organ too. He had been a member of the choir of Poitiers cathedral, so the dean told me, before Gilles de Rais had engaged him for the chapel here, compensating his parents with 300 gold crowns and promising Rossignol himself an estate at Machecoul which would bring him 200 livres a year. I must report that I was impressed by this evidence of the master's generosity.

And so I found myself a witness to this eccentric coloured whirl of carnival that was Tiffauges, a world of feast and folly, wit and flattery, a perpetual rich banquet of learning and music and religion and art. If there were shadows there I did not notice them. I saw only what I suppose I wanted to see:

the peacocks strutting on the lawns, the crisp bright flicker of the candles in the chapel, the winter sunlight making the Marshal's private army look like guardian angels with swords of fire as they drilled each morning in the outer courtyard. I entertained no suspicions that all this was devilry.

Yet why had I been admitted to the castle? Even in those heady early days, this question occasionally vexed me in the nights. When it did, as surely as Griart followed Poitou, that image of Messire Roger de Bricqueville naked and ithyphallic would also loom up in my mind and prevent me from sleep. Thus, I have now some comfort from a retrospective analysis which permits me to assert that I was not quite utterly taken in. Yet, even when I wondered at my being at Tiffauges, I fear I passed too swiftly to wondering at the wonders of the place instead of examining with proper critical address the whys and wherefores of my having been given admittance thereto. For the most part, I was content to suppose that I had fallen by good fortune into a pot of honey. I was in a never-ceasing stupor of pleasure, with as much to drink as I could take of wines finer than any I had ever tasted before, as much to eat of seemingly heavenly food as I could manage, and as much to read in sumptuous manuscripts as my brain could absorb or my eyes feast upon. God forgive me, I soon began in my stupidity to fancy that what I had entered here at the castle of Tiffauges was perhaps some man-made ante-room to heaven itself, or if not that then most assuredly a court being got ready for the earthly entertainment of some saint. And when this final thought occurred to me I remembered that rapt devotion of Gilles to Joan at the still heart of his pageant-play *The Mystery of the Siege of Orléans*, and I found myself sometimes standing tiptoe on one of the battlements looking out over the plain half-expecting to see the Marshal returning to his home in company with that holy girl in white armour.

This standing on the battlements must have begun about the start of my third week at Tiffauges. It was towards the end of that same week that I realized my concern was changing to something of an obsession with the Marshal's absence. Why was the Marshal not here? Where was he? When would the Marshal return? Where had he been, and why? I started to ask these questions, first of myself, then, since of course such askings could find no answers, I began to ask them of de Bricqueville and de Sillé, of Griart and Poitou. I asked them at first diffidently, then with a steady purpose of persistence. But all my queries were met with smiles and bows and a little fluttering wave of the two hands in an outward circle, the fingers stiff, which I had come to notice was a somewhat common sign among the several guardians of the castle.

'Our lord will be with us soon enough,' de Bricqueville told me.

'Be sure, you shall see the Marshal,' de Sillé said.

I had grown accustomed by now to less in the way of verbal courtesy from the two servants, Griart and Poitou, yet they also proved patient and polite in the face of my enquiries. Griart, oozing sympathy, proffered me an atrocious sweetmeat. Poitou clucked his tongue, then beckoned me to follow him into the library. Once there, he opened a drawer I had never before noticed, extracted a small scroll of parchment, and unrolled it for my inspection. The document itself, some sort of legal pact or receipt, was of minimal interest, as Poitou made apparent by directing my attention immediately to the signature at the foot of it.

'There he is,' he said.

Did the Marshal's secretary mean thus drily to mock my faith in books and writing? He must of course have noticed the inordinate amount of time I spent poring over the manuscripts in this room. His method of referring me to the Marshal's signature, as if the mark *was* the man, might well have been a way of laughing up his sleeve both at my love of literature and my declared desire to see the Marshal in the flesh. Certainly he turned on his heel, like one who has done his duty by effecting an introduction between two strangers, and left me there in the library alone with the handwriting.

What I saw was a bold clear Gothic autograph, a civilized and cultivated piece of pencraft which suggested both a good sense of form and a masterful grasp of the art of the quill. The G was decorated with flourishes at the top, the remainder of the six letters plain, the whole name underscored with a jagged line flowering at its end in an emblem of loops and dots which more or less mirrored each other. What I saw was this:

Inspecting those loops and dots that made a droll flower to the right of the name, where the hand that signed the paper had rested for a moment, I found myself reciting an ancient axiom favoured by the mystical school of alchemists: *What is above is as that which is below, and what is below is as that which is above.*

Truth to tell, I had no great interest in alchemy. But the subject was on my mind since just the day before de Sillé, setting the little silver cage down on my pile of books, had stopped on his way through the library to ask me, tickling his thrush through the bars as he did so, 'What is your opinion of Avicenna on alchemy, Dom Eustache?'

To which question, I was able to answer that I had no opinion of the Arab doctor on that subject, never having read him, but that my view of alchemy was perfectly orthodox: namely that while the Church in her wisdom has not discouraged scientific research, and even in this particular field Aquinas draws a sharp distinction between the alchemist and the quack, I hold fast myself to the old belief that the only thing the alchemists ever succeeded in turning into gold was gold.

To which Messire de Sillé said nothing, snatching up his thrush and trotting out.

Still, I recalled his curious question as I sat examining that first signature I ever saw of the Marshal Gilles de Rais. Why should my opinion of an obscure treatise by a drunken Arabian philosopher be of any consequence? Were the two occurrences – de Sillé's question and Poitou's directing me to the signature – indeed related, or was I simply growing edgy and suspicious of all that happened to me? Sitting there in the library, I began to wonder if I was being tested, studied covertly by the others, scrutinized by invisible eyes to see if I was worthy of a place in this peculiar household. Yet, apart from de Sillé's sudden question, would it not be true to say that what distinguished the attitude to me of the Marshal's satellites was a quite remarkable *lack* of curiosity? I could not understand it, any more than I could work out their relationship to him by trying to make sense of their relationship to one another. Messires de Bricqueville and de Sillé, with all the advantages of gentle blood and breeding, and despite the fact that they had been set in charge of the castle during their cousin's absence, seemed often to let Griart, a mere body-servant, dominate with his sallies of obscene wit the dinners we all sat down to share. And I had seen the secretary Poitou strike de Bricqueville himself across the cheek with his open hand, and then both of them burst out laughing, when I was behind a screen and they thought they were unobserved.

Waiting now until I was absolutely sure that *I* was unobserved, I traced the Marshal's signature so that I could keep it, secreting the tissue later in the hem of my black robe.

I don't know why I did this. I felt compelled to. I daresay already I'd fallen under his spell.

The very next night I was awoken from sleep by the clatter of hooves upon the cobbles of the courtyard. I leapt from my bed, convinced for some reason that this noise betokened the return of Gilles de Rais. The time was just before dawn, when the night is always darkest. I heard shouts from below, and the sound of soldiers marching. But when I looked down from my window I saw in the light of flaring torches held aloft by the guards that the horse which had galloped up was riderless. Nor was it saddled or caparisoned in any way for the use of a rider. So I went back to bed, said my prayers, and fell asleep again only idly wondering at the strange behaviour of the watchmen in admitting a riderless horse.

That morning, shaving my face, I was suddenly overcome by a conviction that there was someone behind me, someone whom I would see in the steel looking-glass if it had not been fogged with perspiration from my steaming bowl of water. My hand shook, I cut my chin, but when I summoned up sufficient courage to turn around there was no one there, though I swear that I had heard a floorboard creak behind me.

Then, three nights later, as I was at my prayers alone in the chapel, I opened my eyes at the last amen and there was a figure kneeling before the high altar. It was a man dressed from head to foot in black velvet. He was not praying. He turned his head and looked at me and I knew at once who it was. Though the castle of Tiffauges contained to my knowledge no portraits of its master, and I had only ever seen him impersonated by the actor who took his part in *The Mystery of the Siege of Orléans*, I knew in that moment without a shadow of a doubt that I was face to face with Gilles de Rais.

III

THE BRAQUEMARD

'Consider,' he said. 'I am a perfect Christian.'

I did not understand him. I said nothing in reply.

The Marshal Gilles de Rais was tall and graceful, with great breadth of shoulder and a body that seemed both lithe and perfectly formed. His features were noble and handsome, his eyes blue, large and liquid, his hair black, thick and curly, with an olive skin and a smile of becoming frankness playing about his full red lips as he looked upon me there in the candlelight. Only from his cheekbones, which were somewhat high and crooked, could his descent from Breton pirates have been guessed. I knew that his grandfather, Messire Jean de Craon, had once been convicted of banditry, after waylaying Yolande d'Aragon, Duchess of Anjou, and stealing her rings and her horses. This ungovernable old villain, I should say, had also been guardian to Gilles, bringing the little prince up when his father and mother died young. There was royal blood in those veins, but then there was robber blood too. Not that a single vein showed on the Marshal's temples, and I observed as he picked up a wax taper and lit a candle to burn before the statue of Our Lady, all without removing his gaze from mine, that his hands were surprisingly small and soft and white.

He was dressed, as I have remarked, in a suit of black velvet, with boots of creased black leather on his feet and a sash of crimson silk about his waist. I saw before me a martial, comely figure, with an expression of masterful intelligence. His voice was sweet and low, and he had spoken to me gently, yet all the same there was that in his tone which warned me that for some reason he was on the edge of anger. I did not know why, any more than I understood the words he had said. Yet it seemed to me then that it was right that the subject of his discourse was perfection. I considered this man to be the most perfect being I had ever seen. The angel Lucifer, I thought, must have looked like this when he was God's favourite, in those days before his infernal pride pitched him headlong out of heaven.

'You are a priest,' he said.

'An imperfect one,' I replied.

'That is impossible,' he said. 'When Benedict XII consecrated his bishops, it was not the drunkard who laid his hands upon them, it was the Pope.'

I understood this. When I was still a novice I had once received the sacrament at the hands of a Franciscan celebrating Mass by the wayside during one of those *pardons* which are plentiful in Brittany. The priest was drunk and unshaven, and his hands shook as he held the Host aloft. Yet he said the words properly for the appointed miracle, and I knew that what I ate was the Body of Christ no less than if the celebrant had been a saint. From that day I had never had difficulty in distinguishing the office from the man. Without such mercy, I could never have managed myself to be a priest.

'You wish to be my man?' the Marshal asked.

'I am given to God,' I answered. 'But if He wills it, then I would serve you.'

My interlocutor nodded impatiently, as if only half-satisfied by this response. Again, I had the impression of a fury in him, though this was quite at variance with both the style of our interview and the gentleness which possessed his hands as he now unlocked a compartment in the altar, drawing out a short, thick, double-edged sword, a braquemard, which he laid on the altar-cloth for my inspection. I saw that the braquemard was chased with a series of seven engravings. Smiling kindly, the Marshal de Rais invited me to interpret them.

I began with the scene in the point of the blade. This showed a woman standing naked in a fire, a cross in her right hand, a sword in her left. The nakedness was abhorrent, but I took this to be Joan of Arc in the market-place at Rouen.

To the right of this, the same woman figure was depicted holding a crown above the head of a man enthroned, while beside him other men were standing uncrowned. I said that in my opinion this must refer to Joan's first audience with the King at Chinon, when they sought to put to test her claim that by divine power she would know him in the crowd.

In the next engraving, the woman rode a tall horse into battle, advancing towards a city of many towers. I thought this must be Joan at Orléans.

The fourth scene showed the woman and the King together. They both wore crowns and held swords erect in their hands. This puzzled me, but I ventured to suggest that it represented King Charles VII in his temporal glory, and the blessed Joan in some eventual after-life crowned with bliss.

Next, both the woman and the King were pictured playing upon pipes, with a line of little children dancing behind them. I considered this a reference to that terrible crusade in which so many innocents perished, but was at a loss to find any connection with Joan of Arc.

In the sixth scene, the woman appeared at the heart of a golden rose, attended by the King and eleven robed female figures, one in each petal. Somewhat ingeniously, I read this as an emblem of Joan's examination for virginity by the ladies of the court.

The woman did not feature in the final engraving. This showed the figure of the King hanging from a gallows tree, with a fire below him. Shaking my head, I confessed after long deliberation that I could not relate this fatal picture to the other six.

The Marshal Gilles de Rais did not correct or contradict me at any point during this exposition, but when I failed to

interpret the seventh engraving on the braquemard he withdrew the weapon from my sight and returned it to its secret
drawer in the altar. I supposed that I had failed the test, and
was taken aback when he spun on his heel to congratulate me
upon my powers of observation and promise that I should
enter his household here at Tiffauges once I had performed
for him two small errands. 'You are,' he said warmly, 'a man
after my own heart.'

Just to write these words down now causes me to shiver and
feel the gorge rise in my throat. At the time of hearing them,
however, I was absurdly honoured. The reader must appreciate that in the recitation of my story I labour to avoid
any blunting of its moral purpose by the endowal of myself
with a true understanding of what the Marshal was about.
Not that in every item I comprehend this even now. In the
case of the seven scenes on the braquemard, for example, I
might claim that I came in time to grasp the meaning of all of
them rather better than I did when I offered him those
interpretations which he pretended to find cogent. But it is
best that I leave the reader to ponder these matters without
authorial interference, to reflect upon the distance between
what I saw and what I understood, and to discover as
gradually as I did myself the true and terrible significance of it
all. Sufficient to say that this same braquemard must come
out of its hiding place to figure appallingly later on, somewhere
near the dark heart of my tale, and that even now I cannot
understand how the final scene depicted on it could so
accurately have foretold the Marshal's end.

These were my two tasks, upon which my employment
depended. First, I was required to journey to the prison at
Angers, some fifty miles to the north, bearing with me a book
on alchemy which the Marshal assured me was the property
of a soldier whom I would find languishing there under
sentence of death. This I did. The book itself I did not
examine, having found long ago that suchlike writings only

serve to make me feel sick. Why the Marshal was so anxious for the borrowed book to be returned, I never discovered; but then neither was I ever curious to know. I supposed at the time that my possible master wanted merely to see if I was willing to risk falling foul of ecclesiastical authority in doing his dirty work for him. Possession of the text was hardly a capital offence, but I imagine that if I had been caught with it in my bag the Bishop of St Malo and the Abbot of Saint-Pierre de Seuilly, not to speak of Maître Jean Lemaître, would all have found themselves confirmed in their worst suspicions regarding my orthodoxy. As for the soldier, he was executed the day after getting his book back. I cannot say that he was glad to see it, but then by the time I gave it into his hands the poor fellow had already arrived at a point of general indifference to such things.

My second errand was rather more peculiar. I was despatched to Poitiers, as far to the south as Angers had been to the north, and required to bring back from that city a doctor, one Jean de la Rivière, who was said to be an adept of the white magical arts. Whether or not this was true, I have no opinion. I must tell you only what ensued, which I may say that I saw with my own eyes. The Marshal bade us all travel together to his other castle near by at Pouzages. There, one starless spring night, the sorcerer, dressed in a white cuirass and armed with a sword and other weapons, led the Marshal, and Griart, and Poitou, and myself, to the edge of a certain thick wood, not far from the castle. Leaving us, he passed into the even denser darkness of the trees, in order as he claimed to make the necessary evocations. After a little while, a great clanging was heard, the sound of steel on armour. Frankly, I reckoned that this was the noise of Dr de la Rivière beating his own cuirass, but all things considered it seemed to me best to hold my tongue in such company. It was the first time, after all, that I had ever experienced magical operations. Before long, Dr de la Rivière emerged from the wood, running and shouting. The Marshal de Rais seized hold of the sorcerer, and asked him if anything important had occurred.

'Lord,' cries the doctor making as though he were afraid and greatly troubled in his mind. 'Lord I just met the demon Beelzebub in the shape of a leopard!'

'Beelzebub,' Gilles marvels. 'What did he say?'

'Nothing,' says the doctor. 'He was a leopard.'

None of the others appeared to find this comical. That surprised me somewhat. I had assumed that Poitou was possessed of the beginnings of a sense of humour: witness his directing me to the Marshal's signature when I grew restive in spirit at never having met the man.

Dr de la Rivière then announced with much knocking together of his knees that Beelzebub the leopard had passed close by him in the wood, disdaining to look him in the eyes or say anything at all. The Marshal, losing patience, demanded to know the magical reason for such behaviour, and in my opinion began to lose faith when the sorcerer could not give him one.

We returned to Pouzages, where we dined well. The next day, de la Rivière approached the Marshal and announced that the trouble was that he lacked certain magical accessories essential to success. Gilles tossed him twenty gold crowns and advised him to obtain whatever was necessary for the undertaking, and then to return without delay. Whereupon Dr de la Rivière, promising all possible diligence, vanished from Pouzages and to the best of my knowledge was never seen again.

Now, after these two events, it was apparently adjudged – despite the soldier's execution and the silence of the leopard – that I had succeeded in carrying out the tasks required of me. I was then formally admitted to the Marshal's service, and given my own permanent chamber in the castle of Tiffauges.

It did not take long for me to deduce that since the time of the staging of *The Mystery of the Siege of Orléans* Gilles de Rais had found himself in financial difficulties, comparatively speaking. I learned that he had been forced to sell the towns and seigneuries of Confolens, Chabannis, Châteaumorant, Fontane-Melon in Anjou, Grattecuisse, St Aubin de Fosse-Louvain, Voulte, Sénéché, d'Auzence and de Clone, as well as the castle and lands of Blaison, the castle and lands of Motte-Achard, the castle and lands of Prigne, and half the forest of Brécilien.

By this time the Marshal's relations were up in arms against what they regarded as the dissipation of the family inheritance. They had tried peaceful persuasion in the past, but when they learned of his intention to dispose of the rich revenues of Champtocé and Rais for the benefit of establishing a foundation in honour of the Holy Innocents at Machecoul, they could restrain themselves no longer. The fact that he had a particular devotion to those children murdered by the order of King Herod (as recorded in St Matthew's gospel ii, 16–18) meant nothing to them. It must have seemed to them that Gilles, not content with ruining himself with one religious folly, had decided to impoverish his heirs and successors for all time with another. A formal protest was presented to the King. The prime movers in this action, so far as I could make out, were my master's estranged wife, Dame Catherine, and his younger brother René de la Suze, who had never shared or had sympathy with Gilles' tastes in art or religion. Poitou informed me that the meanest details of the Marshal's fortune had been set out for inspection in this complaint, with an equally comprehensive statement of what was called his riotous extravagance. Amongst other sins against prudence, the domestic arrangements at Tiffauges had come in for spiteful criticism. 'Some eighty persons eating and drinking, including the chaplains and singers of the chapel,' Dame Catherine gave witness against her husband. 'More lavish a household and more talked about than the King's,' his brother sneered.

His wife's and his brother's opinion of Gilles de Rais as *a*

39

perfect Christian was there in a pungent sentence in the testimony set before the King: 'All this is nothing but vanity without devotion, and in defiance of good order.'

The result turned out to be just as the Bishop of St Malo had informed me: Charles VII, by an Order in Council, had now taken steps to check his prodigal subject, and a royal interdict had recently been issued prohibiting the Marshal de Rais from selling or mortgaging any more lands, incomes or properties, and forbidding any person to contract sales or loans with him. The captains and guardians of all castles remaining to Gilles de Rais were warned under heavy penalties not to deliver any of these establishments to strangers, or suffer them to be delivered, until the Council of State had granted its consent. One effect of this measure was to put an end to our master's plan for a foundation in honour of the Holy Innocents, Dean de la Ferrière told me, all the beneficiaries being prevented by law from taking part in the project. The interdict had been proclaimed by a royal herald throughout the territory belonging to Gilles and subject to the King's writ.

God forgive me, but in that first spring and summer at Tiffauges in the year of our salvation 1438 I considered this fiasco rather glorious. Had not my new master run through much of his fortune in mounting *The Mystery of the Siege of Orléans*? Was the glittering spendthrift splendour of his court not fashioned in preparation for the possible return of Joan herself? Did not his whole life and being, like the seven scenes on the braquemard, revolve about that woman sent by God?

I was ready even to turn a blind eye to his obvious passion for alchemy. The King having prevented him from raising further money by conventional means, was it unreasonable that he should dream of finding some other source for whatever he might need to spend in Joan's service? As to whether there was anything to find, I was prepared to keep an open mind on the subject.

To be sure, when I asked him any questions about Joan of Arc – was she truly still alive? if so, where was she? and when would she come hither? – then the Marshal waxed more radiant than coherent. He expressed his devotion to Joan, calling her always the Pucelle, the Maiden, in much the same terms and with many of the phrases which had been put into his mouth by the maker of the pageant-play. He spoke of her devoutly, with reverence and awe, sometimes as though he had loved her, sometimes as though she was the gold never quite attained in some past alchemy of the heart. Such talk dazzled and bemused me. When my master talked to me like that I even fancied that I perceived an odour of sanctity about him, a scent of the sharpest and sweetest of violets lingering on the air. So vivid was this impression that I imagined I could almost see them: violets in a dark wood, fragrant and blue, a most penetrating perfume. Was this a delusion? That delicious odour seemed even to cling to my habit, so that surreptitiously I would sniff my own sleeves while Gilles spoke to me of Joan. And other times it was another smell, more bracing, the scent of light summer rain on the rocks and the biscuit-smelling heather of Ushant when I was a boy there. I could not relate this magic to anything save Joan. Gilles spoke of her as a portent sent from heaven, as an angel who had fought by his side, as the finger of God. I found his allegiance and delight in her deeply beguiling. And yet, while he spoke of her always *as* alive, I could not help observing that he did not say categorically that she *was* alive, so that it was impossible to know for certain what he believed in this strange matter.

Meanwhile, back in the world of coin and ruin, it soon became apparent that the King's writ was not absolute in Brittany, nor could it do more than momentarily stun my master. Our Duke, Jean V, had his own designs on his chief vassal, being particularly determined to gain possession of the great fortress of Champtocé, looming over the Angevin border, commanding the Loire, a highly valuable frontier post. Duke Jean of Brittany, as I say, had long coveted Gilles' estates and contemplated absorbing them into his own domain. Neither did he relish the King's attempt to interfere in what he regarded as a matter for his own jurisdiction. Duke Jean bided his time, playing a deep game. His son was sent to Niort-sur-Erdre to obtain the King's permission for him to continue his negotiations with Gilles for the remainder of his lands. Charles refused. Our Duke, in high dudgeon, thereupon swore that he would not allow the interdict to be published in any town in his duchy. All this encouraged my master to go his own way almost as if that edict had never been issued. He continued to fling good money after bad, seemingly confident of very soon finding his own private mint, the philosopher's stone, a way of transmuting base matter into gold.

Here is all I could ever find out about my master's wife. Her name was Catherine de Thouars, daughter of Milet de Thouars and Béatrice de Montjean, and her dowry enriched him immensely. They were distantly related, fourth cousins in fact, but sufficiently close to infringe canon law on consanguinity. Gilles and his ruffian grandfather kidnapped this girl. They carried her off to a chapel where the two sixteen-year-old cousins were married by a monk in waiting. Later, Jean de Craon, in accordance with custom, deposited a large enough sum of money in the coffers of the Vatican to see the union regularized. One child – a daughter, Marie – was the only fruit that came of it. I would guess that once the excitements of the kidnapping had cooled down, Gilles was bored and indifferent regarding his bride. It was a union as incongruous as the mating of a lion and a lamb, and Gilles tired of married life almost before it had begun.

I caught one glimpse of Dame Catherine. This was at Pouzages, at the time of the unspeakable leopard. My master usually arranged matters so that when he was in one of his castles, his wife would be in residence at another. On this occasion, though, the time I saw her, they found themselves together under the same roof. It was at Mass, the only time I saw her. Her face, moon-shaped, was also as pale as the moon. She knelt before the housel-cloth by the light of two thin candles, her child fearful and a-fidget at her side. I remember the lady joined her hands and stuck them up before her, so that the tips of her fingers, pointing upwards where her thoughts would fly, were level with her chin. She remained thus, frozen in prayer, throughout the consecration; nor did she relax or alter her posture when at the elevation of the Host her husband the Marshal bowed himself to the paving stones. It seemed as if she took, bearing it between her hands, her own heart, lifting that organ up for sacrifice. I remember the lady made her communion with much modesty, and the Marshal watched her feed sans a twitch of his lips. But when the Mass was over and there was thanksgiving to be done, Dame Catherine got up and hid herself away from her husband in the shades of the chapel. It was as if she felt safe in his presence only when they were both of them in the presence of the Presence. There she lurked darkling, behind an arch, and he, lunging out suddenly from where he had stood, swept with his sword's point the furthest edge of her gown. He trod like a cat. But I think she must have felt him touch her with the sword, for she shuddered then although her eyes were closed.

One other thing I learned that time at Pouzages. It was as I returned with him to the castle on the night of the leopard. As we passed into the chamber, I tripped in the hem of my gown, stumbled, and fell against him, grabbing at his arm. The Marshal's recoil was instant. He stood there shivering, a spasm in his cheek. I had surprised this morbid horror he had of being touched.

IV

RAIS LE HÉRAUT

Within three full moons of the night of the leopard – in fact, about the middle of Holy Week 1438 – I witnessed something which seemed at first even more defiant of any rational understanding.

I was gazing down from my casement window when I saw the Marshal de Rais standing atop the rocky eminence below which the river Crûme ran in a silver torrent. The wind was in his hair and wrapped his cloak about him. As I watched, he raised both his hands slowly in a strange hieratic gesture, as if to curse or bless. Yet there was nothing in the prospect before him worth cursing or blessing; only the river and the rocks and the familiar bleak terrain that stretched as far as the eye could see beneath a pouring sky.

Believing for a moment that the Marshal's gesture might be one of greeting, I allowed my gaze to wander away from his figure and out across the waste lands. There was nobody there to be seen, just a few buzzards wheeling, and shadows chasing across the desolate plain as the wind blew clouds between Tiffauges and the sun.

My eyes came back to the rock. But the Marshal was gone. Then a trumpet sounded. I looked up. There he was again, high on the battlements, his banner in his hand. Be sure, I nearly toppled headlong from my window. It was all of half a mile from the great rock to that flag tower, yet he had flown there in the time that it had taken me to turn my head!

This little experience shook me to the roots. Night fell. I locked my chamber door. For the whole night I sat up by the light of my candles, praying, distraught, shivering at the thought that what I had seen must be the outcome of some black magic, clear and terrible proof that my master Gilles de Rais was at best a warlock.

First thing the next morning, I sought out Griart where he dipped his fingers in a vat of soup in the kitchens, breaking what for him was never a serious fast. I described exactly what I had seen, inviting his opinion. No doubt but that the fat man loomed in my mind as the most solid and substantial of the denizens of the castle. Therefore, if there was reason to be had, this Griart would provide it.

My hope was soon disjointed. Smiling horribly, Griart said, 'Our lord is everywhere and nowhere, like the Holy Ghost.' Then he licked his fingers, and went back to work on the soup.

Just for once, Poitou's proximity to his fellow servant proved to my advantage. Emerging from the kitchens, I bumped into him. He listened to my story and then laughed. It was a kind of laughter I longed to hear: frank, sceptical, amused at my foolish superstition. I received from the secretary a thoroughly reasonable explanation for what I had seen. The Marshal had completed his household with a facsimile of himself, he informed me. A servant had been taken into his employ purely because of his close resemblance to Gilles de Rais. This man, renamed Rais le Héraut, the herald Rais, was always dressed in precisely the same clothes as his master, right down to identical buckles on his shoes, and thus equipped would strut about the castle with a comparable magnificence. His sole purpose, so it seemed, was to offer the Marshal de Rais a sort of walking mirror of himself.

I came to the conclusion, hearing this, that what I had seen the previous afternoon must have been the Marshal on the rock and then Rais le Héraut up on the tower, or possibly the other way around, but it didn't matter which. The vital point was that there was no taint of witchcraft to my experience. All the same, when I said as much to Poitou he just shrugged and spat.

I began at this time to put together information about my master's childhood. From the beginning there had been something fatalistic in his life. He was twice betrothed early, first at the age of thirteen to Jeanne, daughter of Foulques Peynel, Lord of Hambuic and Briquebec, and then a year later to Béatrix, daughter of Alain IX, Viscount de Rohan and Count of Porhoët. By a tragic coincidence, both the selected brides died. How Jeanne Peynel died I never discovered, but Béatrix de Rohan was pricked by a poisoned rose. Messire Roger de Bricqueville told me this. He had been Gilles' companion from the earliest days, a youth of his own age, in every way the antithesis of the tiger cub but apparently valued the more because of that. For his part, de Bricqueville said, he had gone in terror of his cousin from the beginning. I did not understand this remark, but I stored it in my heart, noting secretly that the fellow was not the most wholesome of witnesses, and it was at least plausible that any malign influence had been the other way about.

Gilles' father Guy died when he was nine years old, gored by a wild boar while out hunting, and when his mother Marie married again, her second husband being Charles d'Estouville, Gilles and his brother René de la Suze were entrusted to the care of their maternal grandfather, that already mentioned villain Jean de Craon. So many pretty names, but so few of them important, alas, to my tale. The mother, for instance, disappears from Gilles' life when she makes her second marriage. I confess that I have wondered about this. Was Marie an unnatural mother, or was she merely callous in the extreme? We do not know. Only that she never had to do with Gilles again, neither in his moments of glory nor in those of his darkest defeat. Nor was she even mentioned in the legal wrangles over family property after his disgrace and execution; so the probability is that she was dead by then.

René, the younger brother, resembled the mother's line, and he was the one more favoured by Jean de Craon. Gilles, as de Bricqueville told me, drifted soon into a habit of solitude which darkened and distorted his whole vision. And yet, again according to his cousin's word, his first years at Champtocé were taken up with study and with field sports. He showed early an unusual proficiency in every pursuit which he undertook, quickly outdistancing his tutors and relying on his own appetite for knowledge and capacity in acquiring it. Already there was a smell of honey and sulphur about him.

Jean de Craon was too advanced in years to be equal to the task of disciplining Gilles, whose temperament made him as intractable as he was self-centred. Roger de Bricqueville became a more convenient target for the grandfather's whip. The cousin was Gilles' whipping-boy, punished for Gilles' misdeeds in his stead. As for Gilles, he was the heir to vast wealth and estates, and his knowledge of the fact only served as a spur to his inherent pride. In mind and body he was far in advance of his years. In spirit, self-admiration became a vice, and from the habit of basking in his own reflection the young Gilles developed an arrogance that would brook no restraint. He began early to exhibit a spirit of revolt and to impose his will on those around him.

Now, the best writers teach that pride is a capital vice opposed to humility, and that it consists in excessive love of one's own excellence, commonly exhibited in three ways: first, contempt for lawful authority – which is a mortal sin; second, contempt for equals and inferiors – which may be mortal or venial according to the depth of the contempt; third, desire to surpass one's equals – which is venial merely. St Thomas Aquinas and many other spiritual writers have put pride in a class by itself as the most deadly and devastating of all vices, and instruct us that pride has its part in every sin of whatever sort, that is committed; for every sin is in its degree a contempt of God, and often of our superior or neighbour as well. Pride

feeds and thrives on itself. So it was with Gilles. Pride stirs up
the mind and the will to rebellion against the laws of God and
man. So it was to be with Gilles. But I must not rush on too
far ahead of my story. Patience, my readers. Patience is not
the opposite of pride, yet I may say that you and I would do
well to possess what we can of it. For patience is surely a sweet
fruit of the spirit, strengthening the soul to bear the trials of
this life with proper resignation to God's will. Gilles had little
patience. We must have much of it. Gilles had pride overmuch.
Let us strive to have none of it.

Picture Gilles de Rais first at the age of fourteen, in his
castle of Champtocé on the borders of Anjou and Brittany.
Suppose it to be growing dark perhaps, though the wind is
full of snow and nothing distinguishes where the sun sets.
Look, Champtocé itself is ablaze with lights. In the Black
Tower of this castle our hero was born, maybe in November,
most miserable and merciless of months, assuredly in the year
of Our Redeemer 1404, which happens to be the year of my
own birth also.

Gilles is standing at a twist of the great stair, a jewel-
encrusted mirror in his hands, and he is laughing. He is tall
and graceful, with a lithe body, which conceals uncommon
strength; he has dark hair, blue eyes, and an olive skin. Has
he ever been innocent? His laughter sounds to the rafters. At
the moment of his baptism, of course. The candles flicker.
Already he regards the world as nothing but a dictionary, and
considers that those who have no imagination merely copy
this dictionary, which results in a very brutal vice, the vice of
banality.

For from the start has there not been some dark angel
lurking, attendant on the young lord's life, twisting the path
of fate this way and that to suit his charge's wayward tumbling
steps? For the fact, as I say, is that this sweet youth in the
milk-white cloak studded with diamonds, ermine-collared,
scarlet silk lined, has been twice betrothed yet has twice

escaped the marriage he does not desire. It is the circumstance of the second escape that delights Gilles now. The marriage contract was signed at Vannes on the twenty-eighth day of November, the year of the Only Begotten 1418. And now, within the week, Béatrix is dead, killed, so they say, by pricking her thumb on the thorn of a poisoned rose. She lies at Porhoët in the bridal gown that must serve now for burial, while the boy who never wished to be her husband stands smiling at himself in a little silver mirror backed with pearls. Gilles' lips open softly. 'Death,' he whispers, and then again 'Death', watching his hot breath kiss and cloud the glass.

I confess I like this present indicative tense, but still I think that I must use it sparingly. Otherwise it imparts too sharp an immediateness to the page, like a taste of quinces. The result of that would be a two-fold danger: first, of making Gilles come too close to the reader, presenting him almost sympathetically in all his evil glamour; second, of letting Gilles come too close to me again, than which fate anything might be preferable. For these good reasons I shall write the rest of this chapter in a more historical manner, though reserving the right to revert to the style of present images when theme or occasion so press.

Gilles' physical environment was not without effect on his disposition. Raised on a rock, overlooking the right bank of the river Loire, the castle of Champtocé was a prison of pillars and ramparts, with subterranean galleries leading to its defence works. A turgid moat above the level of the river washed the gaunt granite sides of the towers. Although it was the smallest of my lord's castles, a regal state, of which this lonely lad was the pretty centre, had been established and was maintained at Champtocé. Cribbed and cabined, he lived here in a hell of one soul only: himself, and his imagination which as the Omnipotence once remarked is evil from our youth (*Genesis*, viii, 21). Introspection and morbidity became the forerunners, no doubt, of a dark interior life given over to

sickly speculation. Now by reason of its immediate end, knowledge can be said to be either speculative or practical: the first
stops at knowledge, the second applies it to some action or fit
conduct. Speculation rules practice, and the latter is therefore
subordinate to the former. I hold these truths to be elementary,
having learned them long ago myself in Lemaître's monastery.
In the case of Gilles de Rais, however, I fear that the speculative pursuits of his childhood led not so much to knowledge as
to *accidie*, that capital sin of spiritual sloth, or regret for one's
spiritual good. Such sins are not uncommon in childhood, and
might be regarded as venial at any time. Whether Gilles'
accidie led him later to the mortal sin of regretting the love of
God, that is a subject that will keep.

After his mother's second marriage and her disappearance
from his life, the boy Gilles seems to have been quite cut off
from all womanly influence, and in this unfortunate isolation
there was none near him sufficiently comprehending to gain
his confidence or his sympathy; that is, until the advent of his
cousin Roger de Bricqueville, whose companionship was in
any case more baleful than benign. The two seem to have
been the victims of their own delusion in an intense game of
king and slave, though by degrees de Bricqueville was able to
reverse the order of the attraction by trading upon his cousin's
susceptibility. Here, though, to a large extent I have to take
Messire de Bricqueville's word for it, and it is a word which
for reasons yet to be divulged I am not well inclined to take.
All that can be said for sure is that the two boys were
companions in the castle of Champtocé, playing out their
games in corners where the grandfather did not go. When old
de Craon *did* go there, and there was whipping or other
justice to be done, then de Bricqueville was always the one
whose buttocks knew about it. Such immunity from punishment can have done Gilles de Rais no good.

Allowing for these factors, all of which played their part in
the moulding of his soul, the taint in Gilles' blood still seems

to me to have been self-germinated, a poison from the heart that he was born with. Yet the virility of his adolescence craved action and impelled him with the desire to live the future in the instant. Hedged round with natural restrictions and conventions which served to limit the scope of his efforts, the life of the mind was the obvious highroad of escape, and he turned to his books like a drunkard to his bottle, or more precisely like a boy who has discovered the genie that inhabits his magic lamp, and now cannot stop rubbing the vessel to summon up the spirit again and again. He read Valerius Maximus, and Ovid's *Metamorphoses*, and the *Annals* of Tacitus, and St Augustine's *City of God*. Each of these texts left its mark upon him, the last-named not enough. But it was a critical moment for the young Gilles when he first took up the *Lives of the Caesars*, a finely illustrated manuscript of the account by Suetonius. The cruelties of Caligula, the obscenities of Tiberius, and the despotic sway all the imperial Roman line wielded must have had for him the strongest and most perilous fascination. Here was his own heart revealed in its future putrescence. This was the man he would be: a king, a tyrant, a monster ruling by fear rather than by affection, bending his subjects to the inexorable power of his will. The rapture of the pictures left him breathless, so that he would be compelled to fling the book aside and mount his horse to ride, or plunge into the river to swim, all and anything in order to cool for a while the fever that these wicked fancies aroused in him. And he went back again and again to this strange salacious history until it became an obsession. Many years later, at his trial, he admitted the deadly effect which it had had on him. But this and all such matters, I am glad to be able to leave for a later chapter.

The death of the soldier at Angers, the night of the leopard, and the seeing of the double or *doppelgänger* of my master continued to return to worry now and again at my mind in the weeks that followed during that slow-footed spring of

1438. Truth to tell, I found my duties in the chapel of St Vincent hardly onerous or exhausting and thus I had rather too much time in which to fret. I found myself praying that the first two events – in particular, the death of the soldier – would turn out to be as innocent and as possible to wrap about with my reason as had the business of the *doppelgänger*.

Yet to my discomfort I could not help but perceive that both the book I had been required to bear back to the soldier and the figure or fancy of the leopard had alchemy as their common signifier. It worried me that the Marshal was quite definitely committed to alchemical experiment himself. There was that tower, black and gaunt, which was always locked. One morning in March I saw a great eruption of smoke from this tower's chimney; it hung in the air for hours, like some earth demon released from shades of underground to haunt and harass the castle. I found that cloud oppressive. Even when it was gone, I was sure I could still smell it. I asked de Sillé if it meant what I thought it must mean, since he had been the first one to mention alchemy to me. He put his head on one side and made a noise that mimicked his wretched little thrush. This I took to mean that if I wanted to know anything about alchemical procedures at Tiffauges, I had better ask the Marshal.

So I did. And found Gilles all charm and reason on the subject. At first he appeared put out that I had been disturbed by the smoke from the dark tower, but then, smiling, peeling a grape fastidiously with his teeth, he confessed to dabbling in what he called *the art*. Did I consider such pursuits heretical? he asked. I fell back, as usual, on Aquinas; but Gilles could see I was uneasy. 'Dom Eustache,' he said, 'I have a treat for you.'

It was a splendid cask of burnt brandy-wine. I had never tasted anything quite like it, that *eau de vin* which is an *eau de vie*, itself an alchemy, an elixir, *eau d'or*, *aqua auri*, the golden remedy for conscience in any of its guises. Drinking those goblets of brandy-wine was like drinking the sun. I got quickly intoxicated, while the Marshal sat watching me, just picking at his bunch of grapes, not once joining me in a measure. I remember thinking what an agreeable master I had found, a gentleman of taste and refinement who could not endure any sort of coarse wit or jesting. I remember thinking that there was a definite illumination about him, a blaze as of jewels; just as the castle, within, was like a Book of Hours come to life, a page of pictured manuscript opened and all the people and creatures and flowers and trees in it sprung suddenly and wondrously to life, so did it seem to me that the Marshal Gilles de Rais had to be *known*, as it were inwardly, for his many fine moral and spiritual qualities to be seen and appreciated. Well, I shudder to set this down now, but of course it was for the most part the brandy-wine which had flooded up into my brain to make me think such quite incredible manure, just as it was the same booze talking when I spoke in flattered agreement with all he then said. What did he say? My memory is blurred, but no more than my wits were blunted at the time. I am convinced that it was during this well-oiled interview that he told me it was necessary for him to find gold wherewith to provide for Joan of Arc's renewed mission. Yes, he said, Joan was alive all right. Alive and coming. Coming here to Tiffauges, he said. In her own time, at the right moment, but that was what his court was *for*, for her, the living Joan, not for anything else.

Reader, you may imagine how happy this made me. We had this glorious passion in common, for Joan, the Marshal and I. Nothing else seemed important, and everything else paled into insignificance beside the fire of it. Two goblets more of that burning brandy-wine and I was even prepared to believe Gilles was a hero because he was pursuing science (though he kept calling it *the art*) even to the point of risking serious trouble with our mother the Church. Not the Church in her eternal and incorruptible wisdom, that is; rather the Church in her temporal local mistakes and abortions, such as Lemaître, the Seuilly Abbot, and the Bishop of St Malo, not to speak of those spiritual mercenaries who butchered Joan for the English.

'There is no Papal Bull forbidding alchemy,' I said. 'It is not science the Church opposes, but trickery and black magic.'

Gilles rolled another grape upon his tongue, then swallowed it. Joan, he instructed me, had sent word that she could not come to Tiffauges until all was made ready for her. It was up to him, Baron de Laval, to make all ready for her in this world, and that did not just mean Tiffauges. And as for me, Dom Eustache, presbyter, had I not been sent hither by God to help in this holy mission? Together we would mount the *Mystery* again, in Joan's honour, here, at Tiffauges. And then, perhaps, at Orléans, before the King . . . But first there was an errand I had to perform.

When I woke the next morning my head hurt horribly and my throat was parched and foul. For a few minutes I lay on my cot in my chamber going over the content of what my master had told me. When I got to the ultimate point, the errand which I had to perform, the errand which in my drunken bliss I had *agreed* to perform, I cried out to God to forgive me. My only hope was that this was a joke, or that I had dreamed the demand, or that it had not been Gilles all along, but Rais le Héraut. It was not a joke. I had not dreamed it. And of course it was not Rais le Héraut to whom last thing last night I had given my word that I would go to Italy in quest of a real alchemist.

V

FRANCESCO PRELATI

The best alchemists in the world, my master assured me, were to be found in Florence. To Florence then I came, in that long hell of a summer. And in Florence I found what my master thought he wanted. But before I speak of the magician Francesco Prelati I want to tell you here about a small adventure that befell me in Tuscany on my way to Florence. Strictly speaking, it is part of my story, not the story of Gilles de Rais. Yet although I could not say why, I know it is not irrelevant to his story. Besides which, my story is his story, and his story mine. How many stories do you think there are to tell?

One evening in Siena, then, because of the noise and heat of the city, I had wandered up to the great half-forsaken church of the Servi di Maria for the sake of the silence and the wind. It was the hour before the sunset. Before me stretched the *contado*, that restless country of uptossed tawny hills. And over this arid world, where the little walled cities burned like precious stones, hovered Mont' Amiata, not too near, not too far away, faint in the heat, the last outpost of Siena looking towards Rome and the sea.

I sat in the shadow of the cloister, my cloak across my knees, and from my pocket-housewife I selected a needle, and fitted it with a long thread of brown wool. I had torn the cloak on one of the thorns in the rose tree which spreads its branches over the apse of the chapel, and was determined to repair the great three-cornered rent before descending again to Siena and continuing my journey. First I drew the jagged edges of the tear neatly together, then I darned with my needle to and fro, following diagonally the ribs of the cloth. At intervals I allowed myself a moment's relaxation when my eyes rested on the greenness of the grass, or on the red and white roses tapping against the stained-glass windows, or higher still on the faraway blue and white sky. There a range of before-sunset clouds offered a spectacular and satisfying pageant. They stood shoulder to shoulder, one exactly similar to another, close together but with a hand's breadth of blue between each; and scarcely moving at all, they were drawn in long-linked loveliness right across the heavens from east to west. I cannot say what a relief this aerial prospect afforded me, after the slate-grey skies and desolation of Tiffauges. The upper edges of those Tuscan clouds, crisply curved, showed white as Alpine snow against the blue, and their intense lilac shadows and sun-saturated heights offered contrasts of colour which made the soul ache. Each time I looked up my gaze rested longer on these clouds than on the roses or the grass, and when I brought my eyes back to my needlework I remained dazzled for a while, and could see nothing.

I continued in this routine for some time, now bent to my task of darning the cloak, now considering the clouds, when all at once, in a moment of losing the dazzle and finding focus again on the thread of brown wool in my needle, I was roused from my stupor of delight by a sense of danger in the air about me. I could not trace this perception to any obvious source, to any blossom in view or scent upon the breeze; the olive trees were no different from the trees of a minute ago, nor was the grass more or less green; the change was too subtle for the ordinary senses to discern, or perhaps for the signs of the world to record or represent. It was everywhere, and yet, when I sought for it, it was nowhere. It wrought upon my tired nerves like a tonic.

I put away my needle and my thread, and waited. This is something I have learned to do. I might even claim that I have grown quite good at it. Not for long, however, did I have to wait, for almost immediately the silence of the hilltop was broken by the tolling of a bell. Now, the church of the Servi di Maria is used only for festivals, and this day to my knowledge was not a feast day of any sort. Besides, the tolling of the bell was most irregular, and somehow it did not sound as if it could be occasioned by human hands. Even more peculiarly, the nearby bell-tower was broken, in a state approaching ruin, as I had earlier observed for myself, with the frayed rope and the cracked bell still intact but the masonry fallen away in so many places that it stood open to the air and to my gaze from where I sat. The tolling, or vague tintinnabulation, persisting, I looked up at the tower then and was astonished to see the cause of this small commotion. A long black snake was winding its way slowly down the bell-rope, and with each tight undulation of its slender cylindrical body the rope received a shake, none of them sufficient in itself to ring the bell, but the cumulative effect of several of them such that the disturbance travelled up the rope, the clapper was scraped against the split iron sides, and the rasping ringing sound which I had heard was made again.

My first thought was to pitch a couple of stones at this sinister apparition, which I did, the second stone dislodging him from his purchase upon the rope. However, the weight of the snake's body caused the rope to swing out as he unwound from it, and he fell to the ground not more than a few yards from where I now stood in the cloister, my cloak draped over my arm, all considerations of its mending quite forgotten. The creature seemed not in the least stunned by his fall, if fall it had been, for truth to tell, and however fanciful this may sound, it had appeared to me that in parting company with the bell-rope the snake had come thrashing or *flying* towards me through the evening air, an impression in any event not so easily to be discounted since, after all, the bell-tower was not situate directly above where I had been sitting. Fallen or not, able to fly or not, he came to a sudden halt as my shadow crossed his body, his black forked tongue flickering in and out as he raised his head and fixed his eyes upon me.

I think I must have supposed that if I advanced the snake would scuttle backwards, and I was on the point of moving forward when to my horror, instead of retreating, he began to sway his head to and fro horizontally, at the same time coming towards me by imperceptible degrees, using as points of support the slightest projections in the ground, drawing his ribs closely together on alternate sides thereby producing bends or twists of his body until he lay poised with his fangs within striking distance of my legs. I cannot account for the feelings which then took possession of me. I believe I had a natural desire to retreat – I had only to go back a pace or two, after all, and I would have been in comparative safety – but for the life of me I could not do so. Let it not be thought that I was immobilized by fear, notwithstanding the fact that I sensed that a single bite from this creature would mean certain death. My chief sensation was that of wonder at the serpent's behaviour, fascination with his appearance, and a consciousness of my own inability to move amounting to a minor species of paralysis.

As for the reptile, after remaining thus poised for some time, he drew his length by slow degrees into a huge coil, his transverse belly-scales making a gritty, hissing sound as he dragged them over the stones and cracks of the cloister. Then the snake gradually raised his head about twelve inches above the centre coil, a gesture achieved with such grace that my heart bowed down before it, and I have a distinct recollection, however absurd this may sound, that even as a cold sweat broke out in the palms of my hands my only thought was regret that there was no one else present to share with me the beauty which the black snake served and showed forth at that moment. I wanted, as it were, to publish the serpent, to call the world's attention to this, its own wonder: his polished jet-black skin; his diamond eyes without eyelids; the furrow beneath his chin; his poison-glands; his teeth; the lovely tints of his belly that flushed and glowed from bright crimson to rosy pink; above all, the eternal licking and flickering of his long, forked tongue, quivering back and forth an inch or two away from me. After a time my attention grew fixed on that black tongue alone, and as I watched its incessant rapid motion, in and out, I felt so thoroughly helpless, yet so conscious of that helplessness, without, I maintain, the slightest approach to fear, that I wondered how it was that the snake could disdain to destroy me. I did not know then, and I do not know now; this story has no moral or spiritual purpose, nor any other save my need to tell it.

Yet disdain to destroy me is just what the black snake did. I know now that his venom, introduced into my skin, or worse still injected directly into one of my veins, would have killed me almost on the instant. Yet that infernal, eternal, ever-restless tongue did not even touch against my damaged cloak as I turned my back upon the snake and walked away. My adoration of the serpent's beauty, I should add, stayed with me only for a few strides once I could no longer feast my eyes upon it. Then I was possessed by panic, and fled headlong down the hillside, not ever looking back.

The hillside down which I hurried was burnt up with heat and the ground was veined with tiny fissures, like pottery spoiled in too fierce an oven. Of what did I think as I ran? I thought of other illuminations experienced by simple-minded men, such as a story I had read somewhere of an anchorite who saw God and likened Him to 'a quantity of little pears'. Why I should have remembered this I have no notion. I thought of my encounter with the snake as a meeting with a story which could not tell itself. That the snake was speechless and that I had words struck me then, as it does now, as something not too far from the heart of the matter. That is, if there is any matter at all.

The narrow streets of Siena with their many windings and steep ascents were curiously silent and vacant when at last I returned to them. In fact, at first the only creature I saw was a yellow cat which, stretched upon the black and white marble steps of the cathedral, lay napping lightly in the twilight, his limbs loosely apart. I took crumbs from my pocket, the remains of my alfresco supper up at the Servi di Maria, and scattered them on the cathedral steps. Sparrows came first, a cheerful and impudent crew, with finches watching them from coigns of vantage, gargoyles and the like, tiny heads on one side, bright eyes fixed on this crumb or on that. When the finches swept down they carried away easily the coveted tit-bits from between the sparrows' feet. Almost before I could regret this, two robins appeared. I watched them fight each other after they had driven off the sparrows and the finches and finished every crumb. They stabbed with their beaks until the blood ran down their breasts. Then the cat woke and the robins flew away and night fell and I wrapped my half- mended cloak about me and went on my way by mule to Florence, having made up my mind to give Mont' Amiata a miss.

Sufficient remained of the funds which the Marshal had given for my journey for me to put up at one of the better Florentine hostelries, and then spend freely in a bid to attract the attention of the right kind of people. I must say that I enjoyed the city. And it was, of course, also a great honour that I, a mere fisherman's son from Ushant, should find myself there at the moment when so many princes of the Church were assembled in Florence for the oecumenical council. This was the one that discussed the double procession of the Holy Ghost: that is, whether the Holy Ghost proceeds from the Father alone, or from the Father and the Son. I saw Bessarion, the Archbishop of Nicaea, who delivered then his famous discourse *Oratio Dogmatica*, in which he endeavoured to prove that the double procession is taught more or less explicitly by both Greek and Latin Fathers, and thus that the

Greek Church has never denied that the Holy Ghost proceeds
from the Son. Purgatory and the use of unleavened bread for
the Eucharist were also discussed, and the council later effected
a reunion not only with the Orthodox but also the Armenians,
the Copts, and some of the Syrian Jacobites, though alas even
at the time of this writing it has still not become operative
among most of our separated brethren. Bessarion himself was
an impressive figure, with a long flowing beard such as one
imagines on any of the prophets of the Old Testament. I saw
him once in the Piazza del Duomo scraping dog shit from his
shoe while talking with much magniloquence of Plato. His
shoes were silver; Constantinople work.

My immediate business in Florence was a little less elevated
than the *Filioque*. And I had what you might call luck, though
that does not match the manner in which I now view it.
Anyway, soon after my arrival I fell in with agreeable company at table, one Guglielmo di Montpulciano, one Nicolas
de Medicis, one Francesco di Castellane, and two or three
other cultivated Florentines were among my new acquaintance. These were all pleasant and free-spoken companions,
worthy heirs of the city of Boccaccio, and as interested as I
was myself in religion and art, literature and good talk. They
were also lovers of wine, and introduced me to Vin Santo, a
sweet white concoction made of ancient dried-out grapes
which was so strong they said it had the power to bring the
dead back to life. It was towards the end of a long evening
spent drinking several firkins of this stuff that my good friend
Guglielmo introduced me to an amiable young tonsured clerk
– that is to say, a man in minor orders, like all Italian
university graduates, but not yet a priest. His name was
Messer Francesco Prelati.

Prelati, that first time I saw him, looked like one just come
fresh from a hot bath, his cheeks pink and glowing, every pore
opened and every muscle soothed. He had a baby's face, but
an old man's eyes. The room where I sat with my companions

was crowded and smoky from rushlights and guttering tallow candles, which made the newcomer's scrubbed appearance even the more remarkable. I saw before me a young man, about twenty-five years old, with curls that glinted like burnished gold upon his high white brow, rich cherry lips proudly smiling, and eyes which in their peculiar mixture of softness and shadow resembled the grey vair that trimmed his collar. Those ancient eyes were his single most extraordinary feature. They never left mine as he told me about himself, and their gaze was cold as it was unwavering. There is nothing, those eyes said, which we have not seen, and nothing you could show us which would surprise us. And yet, as I remarked, the face in whose sockets they were fixed was innocent and shining, quite unpunished by experience, the face of a virgin cherub.

Messer Francesco Prelati came from Montecatini, near Pistoia, so he told me. He claimed to have been lately attached in some capacity to his reverence the Bishop of Mondovi, with whom he had come to Florence for the council. He was a scholar, an earnest enquirer after truth, a seeker on the way. He smiled as he said all this, as if inviting me to criticize either his apparent modesty or his somewhat ill-concealed presumption.

I said nothing. Whereupon Prelati continued: 'Truth. I said truth. Does it taste? Has it neighbours? Who has lived it? I am its fugitive student, no more. I say it tastes of eternity, I believe it is neighboured by the now, and I boast that it has been lived by a score or more strict rascals before me. That is all.'

He recited this curious little speech as if it were some lines of verse which he had learned by heart, yet the way he said the words made them sound more like a prayer or a rubric. I did not dare to ask him what he meant. Instead, I remarked that I had come to Florence in the service of a great lord of France, and that my mission was to find the philosopher's stone.

To which Prelati gave me reply that in this sense the word stone was about equal to the word substratum, which is compounded of the Latin *sub* and *stratus* (spread-under), the latter being related to the verb *stand, stood,* and meaning 'something on which the experiment stands'.

I stared at him. We *know,* said those eyes of vair.

'The philosopher's stone,' Prelati said, 'is, in fact, a red powder or amalgam to drive off the impurities of baser metals.'

I confess that I was impressed, even if at the same time there was something both in his manner and in his very definitiveness that repelled me. He spoke Latin and Italian words alike with an extreme purity and elegance, and as I found later his French was also quite correct. Considering it politic not to discuss my master's business in front of the others, I contented myself with noting aloud that Messer Francesco was possessed of a proper passion for science, and arranged to meet with him privately the next day.

Our second interview went even better. Prelati lost no time in conveying to me the information that he was not merely skilled in the theory of alchemy, but a serious research worker on its forbidden side. (All this done with hints and whispers, as we leaned together on the Ponte Vecchi, for fear that some police spy of the Singoria might be hovering.) Prelati, I gathered, had dabbled in the commerce of demons, and with some success, if his word was to be believed. I plied him with plenty of Vin Santo for his supper. Truth, he told me, was a country not metaphor of but metaphorically tangent to his own thought. The most reliable alchemical treatise was the *Asch Metzareph* of the Hebrews. The work of the alchemist was to take a dead thing, impure, valueless, and powerless, and transform it into a live thing, invaluable and thaumaturgic. He had himself made contact, so to speak, with a powerful spirit named Barron. He had raised this Barron, he claimed, in the company of a Dr Giovanni Fontanella, a leading

Florentine adept, with the sacrifice in prescribed form of a hen, a pigeon, and a pregnant turtle dove. (I baulked at this, though something told me Gilles de Rais would not.) 'Have you truly set eyes on this Barron?' I asked. 'Or spoken to him?'

Now this, as the reader will see, was a singularly stupid question, since any fool may speak *to* a supposed demon, and the real test is surely whether the demon has *answered* you with a single word of sense. However, I stress that I simply did my master's business.

In any case, oh yes, *certo*, Prelati told me in his slightly mincing way, heralded by a silent flight of ravens, the spirit Barron had materialized before him in the form of a handsome young man, and very amiably agreed to a pact of reciprocal service. Henceforth, Messer Francesco and the demon were firm friends and collaborators.

My secret attitude to what this magician was telling me was quite complex. I suppose I half-believed that he was mad, half-wondered if there might indeed be some kind of allegorical truth to be learned from his story, with through all this a fear of my master and a desire to please him paramount. My main feeling, I might admit, was relief that my quest was at an end, especially since I'd considered it a fool's errand, and dreaded above anything else the prospect of returning to Tiffauges with either no alchemist or one as impotent as Dr de la Rivière. Even to a sceptical eye, Prelati looked the goods. Even to my ear, much that he said was impressive.

'Can you transmute base matter into gold?' I asked him bluntly.

'I could transmute the seas,' Prelati said, 'if you found me enough mercury.'

Did this mean that he *would* do it? Or just that he was aware of the correct procedures? I advised him that my master was a very wealthy man, therefore there would be no shortage of mercury. Prelati smiled, but his eyes were pure grey fur. He refused to be more explicit.

I think that he mistrusted me because of my clerical garb, and possibly – to put it no higher – because he detected in my own thought a certain bedrock of faith and orthodoxy which cancelled out his talk of preternatural powers. Even in drawing him out to declare his occult interests and expertise, I took care to refer only to the narrative of the witch of Endor (*1 Samuel*, xxviii, 7–25) and the condemnations of witchcraft in the Old and New Testaments (particularly *Galatians*, v, 20–21) in revealing my own view of the subject. I think it was for this reason that he chose to remind me that Tertullian and St Augustine had believed in witchcraft. Assuredly, he was displeased when I responded by reminding him that St Hippolytus, St John Chrysostom, and St Caesarius of Arles had not.

Still, my master had asked me to find him a real magician, and here, so far as I could tell, was the finished article.

'Will you come with me to France?' I said. 'The Baron de Laval has need of you.'

Eyes like furred poison, Prelati agreed to come.

VI

THE FALSE PUCELLE

There is nothing like watching a man be sea-sick for getting to
know him. Since I had enough money left, I elected to avoid
the wintry terrors of the Mont Cenis by taking ship from
Leghorn to Marseilles. Prelati and I shared a cabin. Unfortunately, storms blew up, and we spent much of the passage
mewing and spewing, bent exhaustedly over buckets. I was
pleased to find my alchemist was no coward. It alarmed me,
though, that his vomit was no different from my own.

We rode into Tiffauges on Ascension Day, having journeyed
up through Provence and Languedoc and the Limousin, on
horse-back and mule-back, in litter and by barge on the rivers.
I had sent letters full of enthusiasm on ahead. The Marshal,
as a result, knew something of what wonders to expect.

He was not disappointed. From the hour of his arrival,
Prelati dominated Gilles de Rais. The magician's manners, his
poise and his charm, the range of his occult scholarship, and
his elegant knowledge of Latin, all this enabled him quickly to
establish a complete ascendancy over the household. He soon
realized how much he was needed, and that none of the other
denizens of the castle would be able to call his competence
into question. Messires de Bricqueville and de Sillé might be
jealous of the glamorous young Italian, but there was nothing
they could say that would discredit him. As for Griart and
Poitou, they plainly resented the upstart's presence, and
disliked having to devil for him in the alchemical work which
now began daily, but Gilles' passion for the alchemy and
infatuation with the alchemist made it impossible for them to

fall out of line. I was unhappy at what was happening, but for the time being I held my tongue.

While I was away in Italy my master's finances had been replenished by the receipt of 100,000 crowns from Duke Jean V of Brittany as part of the purchase price for Champtocé. His need for the manufacture of gold from base metals might thereby have been expected to be reduced, yet on the contrary his enthusiasm was at white heat. I fear that my foolish reports of the marvels of which Prelati was capable had given his hopes a new lease of life.

What happened next? I can hardly say, let alone understand it. The truth seems to be that though Francesco Prelati was a villain and a charlatan, it might be that on several occasions he succeeded all too well in his invoking of the demons. I will set down what I know without more fuss.

At first only Gilles and Prelati were present during the ceremonies. A room was set aside (not in the dark tower). Gilles used to go to this room with Prelati, sometimes during the night, sometimes during the day, sometimes even at cock-crow. Whenever this happened, the one sure thing was that none of the rest of us was permitted to interrupt them. Once, as I passed the door of that room, knowing them in it, I overheard Prelati say 'Come then, Satan'. On another occasion, the same formula, only I believe that this time the words were being repeated over and over, with the Marshal adding 'to our aid' as an antiphon. Whether Satan came or not, I don't know. I do know that shortly after I heard them chanting a cold wind blew suddenly through the castle, extinguishing every candle in the place.

These were what I would call the minor evocations. The major ones began one evening after supper in the great hall. This time, as well as the Marshal and Prelati, Griart and Poitou were invited to participate, for what weird reason I was never told. It was from Poitou that I heard what happened.

First, Prelati made a circle on the paving stones with the point of his sword. Then he made crosses, signs and characters ('like armorial bearings', Poitou said) in the four extremities of this circle. Griart was sent to fetch coal, incense, a magnetic stone, an earthen pot, torches, candlesticks, firebrands, and other accoutrements, which Gilles and Prelati arranged in the circle to their own pleasure. A fire was lit in the pot which had coal in it. Then Prelati made other signs or characters, still like armorial bearings, on the four walls of the hall, and in the angle of the door, lighting other small fires beneath each sign. Immediately after that, he opened all the windows. Gilles and Prelati then stepped into the circle, and the magician threw magnetic powder, incense, and aloes on to the coals in the earthen pot, so that a stinking smoke filled the hall. Gilles and Prelati stayed in the circle, sometimes standing, sometimes sitting, sometimes kneeling, for almost two hours. Gilles said nothing, according to the frightened Poitou, but Prelati every now and again recited the following formula: 'I conjure you, Barron, Satan, Beelzebub, Belial, in the name of the Father, the Son and the Holy Ghost, in the name of the Virgin Mary and all the saints, to appear in person, to speak with us and do our will.'

This confusion of demonology and piety struck me as a peculiar revelation of the contents of Prelati's mind. Still, I did not comment, merely pressing Poitou to continue. Unfortunately, neither he nor Griart had been invited to enter the circle, and round about the time of the twentieth invocation, when the coals in the pot burned blue, and the wind came howling in at the opened windows, Prelati commanded both the servants to leave. Although they had then left the hall, excluded from the ceremony, they crept back to listen at the door. They could hear Prelati's voice droning, but could not distinguish precisely what he was saying. Then they heard, according to Poitou, 'a noise like that of a great four-legged animal walking on the roof'. I asked the secretary if he thought this could have been a cat. He answered that it was more likely Dr de la Rivière's leopard!

I doubt if these things could have bothered me much in themselves. But coupled with Prelati's talk I found them disturbing. On one occasion, at supper, he leaned across the table to ask me directly, 'Dom Eustache, does not the Mass itself consist of taking common things, transmuting them into things divine, and then consuming them?' The ingenuity of this argument in defence of his black art struck me as quite appalling, not least because I could think of no ready answer with which to dismiss or deflect it. Another time, Prelati said: 'St John was an alchemist. He transformed the pebbles by the sea into gold.' And then again: 'A child could make gold if he knew what to do. The *prima materia* is everywhere. Children play with it in the lane.' I dared to query what he could mean by this last remark. 'Living gold engenders gold, as corn engenders corn,' was his whole reply. This made no sense to me, yet it sounded beautiful and chilling. His attempts to provide a philosophical basis for the idea of transmutation were hardly logical or convincing, but I was worried that somewhere under the tissue of humbug was a grain of reality. Two other of Prelati's sayings stick in my mind: 'In the alchemist's work, the first stage is decay' and 'Nature, which tends towards perfection, wants only to produce gold.'

What did the Marshal think on these dangerous topics? He said little enough for himself, preferring to sit and stare at Prelati as if the young Italian were an oracle. To be sure, I do remember that when the alchemist pronounced that dictum about Nature tending towards perfection, Gilles remarked, 'But we must start with putrefaction to reach perfection?' (I provide the question-mark since he said it in the tones of one seeking spiritual guidance.) To which Prelati said: 'My lord learns fast. Lead, copper, iron and other metals are miscarriages of Nature.'

The reader who considers all this black drivel has my

sympathy. I do not approve or condone it, and my function in repeating it here is purely historical. At the time when Prelati dazzled me with his questions, I had no answer to him. Yet I then felt the way that I think about it now – that is to say that I knew, though I lacked courage or conviction to declare so, that his hermetic wisdom was spurious, his mix of Christianity and magic a poison porridge, his ideas not gold at all but an alloy of contradictions. At best, I suppose, his error was the same as that of the Gnostics: wanting not to believe in God, and love and adore and serve God, but to *know* God, understand God's nature, finally even be 'like' God in power and glory and effect. This masks a grave and sad sin, a Luciferan pride. For the wise, on the other hand, it is not knowledge that is blessed; *faith* is blessedness. And even holy ignorance, acceptance of the limited nature of man, seems better to me now than Prelati's vain and wicked over-reaching.

I daresay it was my scepticism regarding his pretensions that made Prelati keep me, literally and metaphorically, outside his circle. But gradually all the others were drawn in. Matters came to a head on the night de Bricqueville and de Sillé were included, when the lot of them assembled at midnight, surrounded by all the trappings of high ritual magic. Gilles was already in the circle when de Sillé lost his nerve, refusing to obey Prelati's injunction to join him. In such circumstances, I imagine, fear is contagious. For whatever reason, Gilles tried at that point to make the sign of the cross, but found his hand was suddenly paralysed. So he prayed aloud the *Alma Redemptoris* instead:

> *Alma Redemptoris Mater, quae pervia coeli*
> *Porta manes, et stella maris, succurre cadenti . . .*

'Out! Out of the circle!' shrieked Prelati.

The rest may be told in Gilles' own words, spoken later on oath at his trial: 'I heard voices which were not human and I was afraid. I left the evocator to himself, closing the door of the room upon him, whilst Gilles de Sillé fled by the window. As for my cousin and the servants, they fled too. But when we came back later to the door to listen, we heard that someone was beating the evocator, even as one might beat a feather bed. I drew my dagger. Gilles de Sillé drew his dagger. Then we opened the door to see what was the matter. What we saw was the evocator lying on the floor outside the circle, as if he had been thrown there through the air. He was moaning and weeping, covered in blood. He had this great wound upon his forehead. I feared that he might die.'

The Marshal took up Prelati in his arms and carried him to his own bed. For seven days the Italian lay there at the point of death, Gilles nursing him until he began to recover.

Was this fantastic play-acting, or hellishly real? Prelati could have beaten with his sword upon a cushion, and then wounded himself. That, to the sceptical intelligence, is more readily to be believed than the alternative: that he had been spurned and attacked by the spirits he had succeeded in summoning up. I would favour the sceptic's opinion myself were it not for one thing. This is that when Prelati lay there in Gilles' bed in a pool of his own blood, apparently *in extremis*, the Marshal sent for me, demanding that I shrive him. I could not refuse: the worst of Christians facing death has a right to the sacraments. The point, though, is that I then heard what could well have been Prelati's last confession. Without breaking the seal of the confessional, I can say that either he compounded his other sins by lying to me, or whatever he was guilty of it was never attempted self-murder. I don't think he lied to me. And what else he said would have made such a lie quite senseless.

Still here I was weighed down by Prelati's confession. It pressed heavy upon me as the clay upon a coffin, though I may say that it did not yet reveal to me the worst that was to be known about my master. But it did not take the worst to chill my blood. Sometimes I think that this summer of 1439 was the most difficult time of all, for there I was oppressed by nameless dread, never quite understanding what was going on around me in the castle, helplessly observing these only half-known figures like one trapped in a dream one knows to be a dream yet cannot wake from, full of shadowy apprehensions of the horror and the hopelessness to come. It must have been in the June of that year that Rossignol claimed to have found overnight a red-and-white rose growing by the fountain in the walled garden of the castle keep.

A red-and-white rose (red petals and white petals grown on the one green stem) is of course *contra natura*, an impossibility. Yet I saw with my own eyes the red-and-white petals the chorister placed in the hand of Gilles de Rais, and I heard with my own ears Prelati declare that this was what he called 'the union of irreconcilables' and so much to be desired. Certainly, also, it was during that August that I overheard my master say, in his cups, 'It is always by way of pain that one arrives at pleasure.' The sentence sent more than a shiver down my spine, though at the time I did not understand what he could mean by it. I repeated the remark to Poitou. That dry knave just rolled his eyes, grinning horribly, but when I bored him by dwelling upon my own lack of comprehension he jerked his thumb in the direction of the dark tower. Later that night I came upon him talking to Gilles on the steps to the chapel, and I knew at a glance that he had betrayed my confidence, and that the two of them found my ignorant fear amusing. The Marshal, even drunker by now, roared with laughter as I passed hurriedly by them, my hands clasped in prayer. Then he said, almost shouting, in a voice that mocked with his intention that I should hear but not understand every word: 'The most infamous, the most forbidden – that best arouses the intellect and the blood! That is what always causes us most deliciously to discharge!' I ran to my room and locked my mind fast in its devotions. At that moment, I suspect, some listener in my heart saw through the mask of Gilles' drunkenness and perceived in him an evil mix of cold logic and terrible passion. And yet I could not grasp what it was that my conscience was telling me. How could this same drunkard be the man I had first met, that *perfect Christian*? Sober, he still talked much about perfection, the search for it, even if now such talk, redirected by Prelati, always ended in nonsense about alchemy and gold. I was thoroughly confused, and I was scared.

And then, one autumn morning, the trumpets sounded. A small troop of cavalry was admitted to Tiffauges; riding at their head was a woman in white armour. When she removed her helmet I saw that she was handsome, with jet-black hair and a skin as white as whey. Her bearing and her beauty were remarkable. The Marshal welcomed her as Joan of Arc.

From the first minute of the lady's visit, I did not understand this. For I, who had never in my life set eyes on the living Joan, knew instantly that this person was an impostor. To be sure, she spoke often of campaigns and visions, of this day at Orléans and that night at Patay, of the siege and the Dauphin and the fire. Yes, she even dared speak of the flames in which she was supposed to have perished at Rouen some eight years before! Whether she claimed to have escaped from the scene of her martyrdom, or merely to have risen later from the dead, I never bothered to determine. Let me say straight out now that this young woman's name was Jeanne des Armoires, known as *La Pucelle Sauvée*, the False Pucelle, ever since that moment a year later when King Charles VII exposed her as a fraud, she having betrayed her imposture by being unable to repeat the secret the true Joan had revealed to him ten years earlier at Chinon. Before this, she fooled not only the Marshal but the citizens of Orléans and her own brothers, presumably on the strength of what must have been a close personal resemblance to the original Joan. But who can say why my master was so taken in? Did he suffer this counterfeit for the sake of his memory of the real? Was he hoping perhaps that even a false Joan might save him, by awakening what was left of the good in his soul? I can find no sense in his hospitality otherwise, and in any case it is hard to credit that his own evocations of old times did not trip up the False Pucelle at their first banquet. Yet there they sat at the table, laughing and drinking, night after night, Gilles de Rais and this counterfeit creature. And some nights he would send Rais le Héraut to entertain her in his stead, so that a false Joan was falsely served by a false Gilles . . . It was all lies, and I detested it. So did Prelati, who viewed this rival charlatan as a dangerous intruder. He scowled and gnawed his fingernails when he heard the Marshal offer this woman command of his military household. The wound in his forehead glowed red when it was further suggested that 80,000 crowns might be needed to provide for a series of performances of *The Mystery of the Siege of Orléans* in the precincts of Tiffauges. If this ever came to pass, then I know that it was Gilles' declared desire that he would play himself to this false creature's Joan. But when it happened I was not there to see it.

The advent of the adventuress proved too much for me. I was now in a downward whirl of alarm and disenchantment. Prelati, because he was clever, I found it possible at least to fear, and fear is a kind of respect. But Jeanne des Armoires was not even a decent actress. I found her presence in the castle an affront to reason. So my master was going mad. Did I have to follow?

Consider. I had come here because for some years past I had believed Joan's story to be a true miracle sent from God. I had desired to serve the man who had been her closest companion on earth, and so learn more about that maid and her holy mission. But such knowledge had not followed from my sojourn at Tiffauges. Instead, I had been sent to Italy in search of a magician; I had been compelled to endure the company of cynics and brutes; I had been mocked and abused by this master who seemed hellbent on reducing himself to the swinish condition of a drunkard; I had been forced finally to stand and watch while thus reduced he consorted with a whore dressed up to resemble a saint. The only thing even remotely to do with Joan that Gilles de Rais had revealed to me was that braquemard with the seven engravings on it, and I could no longer be sure of the safety of my interpretations of these. Just the other morning I had observed the false Joan play a flute while children came dancing in behind her across the drawbridge, as if drawn hither by the music. That reminded me of the fifth scene on the sword – the one which I had taken as a reference to the children's crusade. Now I wasn't sure about anything. Why had the children followed her, when her playing on the flute was full of wrong notes? I was tired of such puzzles. I was sick of all mummery. I was exhausted both by Tiffauges and the shadows who lived in it. The coming of the False Pucelle showed up the sinister falsity of the whole.

The final straw, for me, came on All Saints' Day. Gilles de Rais ordered the celebration of a solemn Office of the Damned in the chapel of St Vincent, a blasphemous idea which seemed only to confirm that he might be mad. Prelati laughed. Jeanne des Armoires indulged him, smilingly. They and the other henchmen were apparently prepared to take part. I was not. I was not even going to pretend to. I picked a quarrel with the false Joan's squire, one Robin Romulart, a surly fellow, as to whether a litany addressed to Satan might be necessary for such a service.

'It is,' said he.

'Sir, only the damned would think so or could say it!' said I.

Then, in half-simulated fury, I swept out of the castle, taking care to make my exit when Gilles was engaged elsewhere.

VII

AT MORTAGNE

I found lodging in the village inn at Mortagne, five miles away from Tiffauges in the same valley of the river Sèvre. From my window there I could just make out the towers of the castle, pale in the distance across the plain, like horns on a snail. Darkness was falling, so I lit my lamp, then recited Psalm 109 with more feeling than usual, pausing to meditate upon its twenty-third and twenty-sixth verses in particular: *I am gone like the shadow when it declineth: I am tossed up and down as the locust . . . Help me, O Lord my God: O save me according to thy mercy.* That done, I ate my crust and a little mouldy cheese, then called for a bowl of hot water and set to work to shave my upper lip and chin. With a ragged shawl over my shoulders and a candle beside the looking-glass to make a double flame (the blind being carefully tucked against the window), I scraped away for ten minutes with some attempt at patience. I always find shaving a soothe.

Whilst I shaved I reflected upon my relations with the Marshal. It occurred to me again that all we had in common was Joan of Arc – which was why his present allegiance to her counterfeit was so distressing. All I had ever sought from him was some understanding of the divine mystery that was Joan. But had he understood her? He talked of her little, and obscurely. Yet it seemed that in the first place he had employed me because of my interest in her. Or was it just my innocence he had wanted? As well, of course, as the use and usages of a working priest, with some knowledge of science and medicine, Latin and Italian. I had been useful to him. That was undeniable. Why then did I feel so unclean?

I cut myself, mopped the cut, and put on a piece of spider's web to stop the bleeding. It is precisely for this purpose that I never forbid spiders to spin in one corner of any room I occupy.

My shaving at an end, I drank some wine, and finished off the meat from a pork bone. Then I took off my boots, blew out the lamp, and resigned my mind to sleep.

The dream began with me walking along a crescent of sand that curved at the base of a cliff. As I went the water welled up in the slanting hollows left by my feet, and when I looked up it was to see the fat, evil-smelling leaves of the cliff plants glistening with moisture from the spray. Even the swollen fingers of the marsh samphire, which seemed to point at me as I passed, each bore a tremulous drop at the tip. I was back in Ushant again. At the end of the little beach I stopped, and turned to gaze out to sea, balancing myself on a slab of shiny wet granite, where cone-shaped shellfish clustered and from which long green seaweed floated out and in on the heave of the tide. There was a dark thing that was bobbing up and down in the curdling foam. At first I thought that it might be a dolphin. A stinging scatter of spray blew into my eyes, blinding me, and when I looked again the dark thing had come nearer, and I saw that it was the body of a man caught in the ratlines of some shrouds that the sea's action had lapped around the mast they had once supported. Were it not that the man's chin was hitched over the ratlines, so that he was borne along with his face – a pale blot among the paler blots of the foam – rigidly upturned, he would doubtless have sunk, for he was not lashed to the mast in any way. A huge foam patch had formed in the web made by the tangled shrouds, so that his head and shoulders showed clearly against the creaming halo, on which his long hair, dark with wet and released from its queue, lay streaked away from his tilted face. I called twice to the man; then, since even if he still lived he was past consciousness of doing so, I kept my energies for the saving of him. Wading in as deep as I dared – not more than up to my hips, for even then the heave and suction of the water threatened to knock me off my feet – I clung on to a ridge of rock with one hand, and, leaning forward, made snatches at the spar whenever it surged towards me.

The next thing was that I saw to my dismay that with every heave his legs must be catching against some rocks, for his head began to sink away from the supporting ratlines, and when at last I caught one end of the spar I only succeeded in drawing it away from him. The man's head disappeared; for a moment the black hole in the midst of the foam circle held, then it broke and was overrun quite as the whiteness closed upon it. But the very next minute a surge of undercurrent brought the body knocking against my legs; I just managed to hold on with one hand while with the other I plunged down at him. My fingers met the cold sleekness of his face, then caught in his tangled hair and, drawing myself up backwards against the rock ledges, I pulled his body with me, step by step. A few moments more and I had staggered up the narrow slip of beach with my burden dragging from my arms. Tumbling him along the drier sand at the cliff's foot, I knelt beside the body and with hands trembling from the strain that had been put upon their muscles, I pulled apart the clinging shirt which was so sodden it seemed to peel from off him like the skin off an over-ripe plum. I felt at his heart, then laid my ear to the pale glistening chest where dark hair was matted to a point between the breasts. I beat that pale chest with my hand until at last I saw faint red respond to the blows.

Meanwhile, out over the sea, the sun was sinking. The sky was no longer an intense midsummer blue but fast becoming the colour of green emeralds. The hosts of the clouds still poured out of the west but these Atlantic regiments were not clothed like their predecessors in white and gold but wore more sober uniforms of mauve and brown, the colours of the Duke of Brittany. And in that moment light broke upon me.

A wave of horror and recognition turned me faint. My whole body was aglow with a raging heat, then as quickly fallen again to the temperature of ice. Of course, it was my father I had rescued from the sea!

My father spoke then. His lips moved in his corpse-blank face, though I noticed his eyes did not open. 'Woman has no opposite,' he said.

Then in my dream I fell to the ground like one struck by lightning. But presently, when I had lain still for some time in the clutch of this strange revelation, my brain rioting like some machine gone out of control, I rose to my feet and began to walk down into a dark valley. I was moved by some incomprehensible but definite impulse. It seemed that there remained something I had to do. I walked forward but felt like a child who is led by the hand. This sensation of guidance and companionship grew upon me. *Someone* was walking by my side, keeping step by step with me, imitating my gait, and leading me in a certain direction. I found myself casting sudden furtive glances over my shoulder, and I had the impression that my companion was always just whirled away out of eyeshot. Once I thought I caught a vague shape like a shadow or a blur of smoke . . . And a little later, so strong was this feeling of haunting, I stopped dead and spun round quickly, sweeping all sides with my eyes; but everywhere the moors rolled away as bare and empty as the palm of my hand. It was only when I looked straight before me, making no direct attempt to see this phantom, that the latter became half visible out of the corner of my eye; and then at one time it seemed to me that it was my mother who walked with me, and at another it was my father, while again the face that I almost saw would be the face of some radiant and lovable stranger.

For a moment I wondered if I was going mad, and the thought frightened me but my fears soon left me again when I realized how welcome this invisible presence had already become. The sense of companionship was real and pleasant; and I who had never known a friend had some conception at this, as it seemed, the extremity of my life, of the beauty of friendship. My spirit was warmed and comforted as by a fire. My hunger seemed to have been satisfied, my weariness dispelled, the very veins of that hard-used and abused shell, my body, filled with some new, invigorating fluid, something better than blood.

Yet I knew well enough by now whither I was being led. I was no longer in Ushant. Tiffauges lay before me at the heart of this place of desolation. I did not know – in the dream I did not want to know – what fate or fortune awaited me there in the castle. I only desired to hurry on, to get things finished, to be at rest at last. And so I trudged forward vigorously, singing, looking now neither to left nor to right, caring little about anything but content with my strange mother-father companion, and as I journeyed the sun sank lower and lower in the sky, the shadows lengthened and thickened and filled up hollow after hollow, and the hurrying clouds grew ever darker of hue.

It was night when I and my companion passed into the castle. The wind was rising, so that the torches flickered, while overhead a wrack of shapeless cloud was driving athwart the stars. It seemed to me odd, even in the dream, that the place should smell of home. For the smell of brine was strong in the air, and mingled with it there swept by now and again those other odours which belong to places given over to ships and the sea: odours of tar and paint and hemp and sail-cloth. These familiar scents caught me by the throat and filled me with delight and sadness, although as I say even in my dream I knew they did not belong here, but rather to the world of my childhood. My companion hurried me on.

Looking up, I saw lights in the tower.

Dreaming, I saw lights in that tower where waking I never saw any. Now I went up the stone stair to the door that was always locked. It was not locked now. My companion knocked three times upon it, and we went in.

The first thing I noticed was that the tower was full of smoke. It seemed to belong to the brutish old days before we had proper grates and chimneys. Foul smoke hung everywhere on the air, and collected in my lungs, and made me cough. It stung my eyes, making it hard to keep tears away. Yet although it was vile there was sweetness in it too, that sweetness as of the scent of violets which once I had thought I could detect on my sleeves from the Marshal's presence. The tower was full of this cloying and terrible smell. It made me feel sick, yet I forced myself to go on.

At the top of the first flight of the winding stair I found a kind of chapel. There was a cross upside down on the wall, black candles, wands, chains, pantacles, and cups. On the altar a white rat sat watching me, its whiskers twitching. I hurried on, knowing great evil here, and on the second floor I came into a room laid out with furnaces and retorts, alembics, charcoal, all the apparatus of an alchemist. My heart was pounding in my chest as if it wanted to get out. Shaking with fear, I ascended the winding stair to the third and final floor.

And found myself in a chamber as white as alabaster, a simple place, where the violet fog was vanished. It was well-lit by a series of seven silver lamps hanging from the rafters, and warm from a fire of oak logs blazing beneath the copper canopy of the hearth. The floor was marble-paved, spotless. There were red roses and white roses, freshly picked, full blown, arranged in ivory vases along the walls. And in the middle of the chamber stood another vessel, whether of gold or burnished copper I could not tell, wonderfully polished and shining, glowing indeed, so that it seemed itself to emit sparks or flakes of light to add to the general glory of illumination. I approached this vessel. But with each step I took I saw a shiver run down through it, almost as if it were a living thing, and fearful of my coming, and cracks appeared in its sides, and multiplied quickly, and the whole vessel shook where it stood. I grabbed it in my hands in its moment of breaking, driven desperately to seize it through desire that I might stop its self-destruction. Yet I felt like a murderer. And the vessel burst apart as my fingers closed on it, exploding softly in all directions like the head of a dandelion blown by a child to tell the time.

I woke then, crying out with pain and anguish and disgust, for I think I had found the vessel to be full of blood, and imagined in my dream that I was bathed in it. You will understand even more my horror then, when I felt in the darkness of my lodging that my hands were indeed covered with some warm and sticky liquid of unknown origin. I fumbled for a light. It was blood all right. Yet here, if you require it, is a reasonable explanation for that: the cuts from my shaving had opened again in my sleep, perhaps as a result of my scratching at them in the dream's turmoil. I washed myself thoroughly. I did not go back to bed.

Instead, I sat thinking for some reason first of the children's crusade, then of the real motive behind my decision to absent myself from Tiffauges. Regarding the former, I suppose the subject had been floating in the back of my mind ever since that day when Gilles de Rais invited me to interpret the engravings on the braquemard, and certainly I had been reminded of it recently by the sight of the False Pucelle playing the flute at the head of a crocodile of dancing children following her into the castle. As a matter of fact, though, this story of the children's crusade was something that had horrified and fascinated me for as long as I could remember; my interest in it dates back at least to my time in Lemaître's monastery near Rouen, where I had taken the opportunity to study a manuscript history of this pathetic event which was kept in the library. I knew therefore that the crusade had been led by a shepherd boy, Stephen, who claimed to have seen in a vision the deliverance of Jerusalem from the infidel by an army of children. Stephen gathered together some

30,000 followers, boys and girls of from ten to sixteen years old, and with them set out in June 1212 from Vendôme for Marseilles, in defiance of the King, to capture Jerusalem and restore the holy land. At the same time, another 20,000 children, many of noble birth, led by another shepherd boy, called Nicolas, set out from Cologne in Germany on a similar mission. And yet another body of children traversed Suabia, with the same purpose, to go south through the St Gothard Pass. They were joined by small numbers of adults, but it is well-attested that all three expeditions were led by children, and consisted for the most part of boys and girls who believed that they would pass dry-shod through the seas to the holy land.

Stephen's army embarked from Marseilles in seven merchantmen; some perished at sea and the rest, through the treachery of the shipowners, were captured by Barbary pirates and sold into Egypt as slaves. Those under Nicolas lost half their number in the snows on Mont Cenis; the rest were pillaged, kidnapped, beguiled, drowned, died of hunger and weariness; until Pope Innocent III turned the remnant back home without dishonour. The third party, similarly reduced, did get as far as Brindisi, where the local bishop dissuaded many of them, but many others were given free passages on ships – and sold as slaves or captured and killed by the Moors. Altogether, as my manuscript said, this children's crusade was an extraordinary and disgraceful occurrence. It should never have happened. Parents and priests ought to have prevented it. The children themselves seem to have been possessed for a while with a fever which none could explain. One boy, who came back because he lamed himself, said later that it was as if he heard music play and he had to follow it. The pathos of this story haunted me.

Yet still, as I say, what on earth did the children's crusade have to do with my nightmare of returning to Tiffauges? Thank God I did not then know the answer to this question. The reader, be sure, will be told it soon enough.

Whether by some process of intuition or by pure chance I could not say, but immediately after sitting in meditation upon the children's crusade there in my lodging at Mortagne I started up from my chair with a shout, slapping my forehead with the heel of my hand as the real reason why I had run away from the castle burst in upon me. I had imagined that I picked that pointless quarrel with Robin Romulart because I was exasperated by Gilles' belief in the False Pucelle. Not so. His tolerance of an adventuress was an irritant to my self-esteem, but no more than that. No, the true cause of my need to fly was that I had to remove myself from the scene of what I now sensed to be a very great evil. I did not have to believe that the dark tower contained such black magical and alchemical furniture as I had seen in my dream. It might well contain it; or it might contain nothing. It was enough that the door was locked, that the place was forbidden me, that there was some vital and sinister *secret* there, shared by the others, relating to the Marshal, kept out of my knowledge and my care. Why should this be so, unless it was wicked? That tower *was* Gilles, and it was Gilles that I had run from.

I remembered Messire Roger de Bricqueville at our first interview, how he had seemed suddenly naked to my eyes. What else was that but an early intimation of the same evil? I remembered a dozen occasions when I had come across Griart and Poitou, or the foppish de Sillé with his bird-cage, or the choirboy Rossignol, gathered in twos or threes in some corner of the castle, engrossed in discussing something evidently so private and dangerous that the moment I appeared they would stop talking. I remembered Prelati – well, those vair eyes had looked on things considered too dark for my seeing, and by that I do not mean demons. I recalled his confession. I recalled that so far as I knew the Marshal de Rais had never once communicated at any celebration of the holy sacrifice of the Mass while I had been at the castle. To communicate it is necessary to confess. Did he not communicate because he had that to confess which he knew to be too terrible for confession? And what could that be? Was there such a sin? I knew of one sin only which is beyond forgiveness, the sin of blasphemy against the Holy Ghost (*St Matthew*, xii, 31–32). I once asked Maître Lemaître what that great sin was. Maître Lemaître was burning hot on sin, but even his ingenious inquisitorial manners and procedures seemed not to have succeeded in rooting this one out. The six sins of despair, presumption, envy, obstinacy in sin, final impenitence, and in particular, deliberate resistance to the known truth (so he told me), may be regarded as specially directed against the work of the Holy Ghost in the soul; generally (he added), they so harden the soul to the inspirations of grace that repentance is unlikely. End of sermon. I was not convinced. Could it be (comforting thought!) that only those few *capable* of this sin against the Holy Ghost would ever know what it was? And was the Marshal one of those few since the world began? And was that what he meant by calling himself a perfect Christian?

I breathed a sigh of relief at having escaped from I knew not what. I flung open the window, to welcome the new day. Below, in the inn's yard, a boy was drawing water from the well. 'Good morning,' I called out. The boy looked up from his labours. He saw who had greeted him. Instead of answering me, he crossed himself. He knew where I had come from.

VIII

A TRAVELLER'S TALE

I had been at the inn at Mortagne for about one week only when the first of the Marshal's creatures came out after me. It was a rare bright November morning, with frost on the grass and robins fighting for crumbs of flour outside the bakery, and I was standing in the courtyard watching children play at Hoodman Blind. This is a simple game, common in those parts and for all I know elsewhere. One of the players is blinded by his *capuchon*, or little hood, being turned back to front. Then his fellows, holding their own hoods in their hands, try to hit him without being caught themselves. Sometimes the hoods are twisted and knotted, so as to give the Hoodman a sounder smack. The game I was watching was a rough affair, with much thwacking and shouting and tumbling, but the children seemed to like it.

I stood apart, by the ale-house door. It had been made plain that the villagers wanted nothing to do with the priest who had come from the castle. In vain I protested to the innkeeper that I had fled away, that Tiffauges was no longer my home, that I was not going to return there. That surly fellow looked at me askance, said nothing in reply, but took my money. His servants shunned me, leaving my meals hot on the table but refusing to get nearer than that. If it had not been for my clerical garb, and no doubt most of all my small bag of gold crowns, I think I would have been refused a room. These dislikes and suspicions preyed upon me. I felt like an outcast, and broken down. However, I had not decided where I was going to go, and my main desire was merely to clear my head.

86

Here at Mortagne at least I had found refuge while retaining a vantage post from which to try to make sense of the life I had left. I suppose I still hoped to collect and collate the local gossip about the Marshal de Rais and his reign over this countryside, though as yet not a word of that had reached my ears.

So there I stood, watching the children play. And all at once a shadow fell across the yard, and turning I saw the thin outline of a cloaked man in the archway between us and the sun that hung low in the sky like a dangling crab. The man coughed. Shielding my eyes, I looked into the light and saw that it was Poitou.

The children ran away shrieking as he advanced upon us – with the exception, that is, of the unfortunate boy who wore the hood. This boy, hands stretched as he groped forward blindly, calling out in his bid to discover why and where his friends had gone, went running straight into Poitou's arms. Poitou stopped then. He held the poor lad clutched to him, his skinny hands clenched about the neck of the *capuchon*, preventing its discard. The boy roared. Poitou laughed. Then, slowly, with a skilled solicitude terrible to see, he raised the boy from the ground so that he was hanging from those hands about his neck. The child kicked and fought. But the man held him out at arm's length, and would not let go.

'Poitou!' I shouted. 'Stop that! Poitou, you will kill him!'

I ran across the yard, fists up, God forgive me. But before there was need to strike him, Poitou flung the child away. That little body went flying through the harsh November sunlight, turning over and over, to land with a crash on the cobbles. There it lay still a moment, so that my heart missed a beat. Then, howling, the boy sat up, snatched the hood from his head, took one terrified look at the two of us, leapt to his feet, and ran off.

Poitou coughed again, then spat on the ground.

'These brats,' he said shortly, 'they take a lot of killing.'

He was wearing one of those hats fashionable at that time, with a stiff circular brim rising to a crest and a long tail of stuff called a *liripipe* hanging down at the back. Poitou, though thin, was tall, yet this *liripipe* was so long that it still trailed the ground behind him. He kicked at it irritably now as he sidled across to me, more than ever resembling a walking pair of scissors, I thought.

'Dom Eustache,' he said, 'I have a message for you.'

'Go away,' I said.

Poitou smiled nastily. 'Dom Eustache,' he said, 'I shall pretend I did not hear you say that. I bear a message from our master. You must come back with me to Tiffauges.'

'I think not,' I said, hands on hips, favouring him with more defiance than I felt. In honesty, I was scared. Yet a glance down the road reassured me that Gilles' secretary had been sent on his own. Was my lord so accustomed to having his wishes obeyed that he thought there was no need to despatch a small troop of his soldiers to enforce them? Or perhaps he believed me to be so thoroughly under his spell that a single emissary beckoning with crooked finger would call me back?

'I do not understand your answer,' said Poitou. 'The Marshal wants you. You have to return with me.'

'No,' I said.

'No?' snapped Poitou. 'What do you mean: no?'

'I mean,' I said, 'that I am not coming back. I am not coming back – and there's an end to it.'

I turned on my heel and hurried into the inn, going straight to my room where I slammed the door shut and then dragged the bed against it. However, Poitou made no attempt to follow me. I heard him shout up from the courtyard: 'Dom Eustache, you may be sure that this is *not* the end of it!' I lay low. I waited a long while. All was quiet. The children did not return to continue their game, judging from the silence. When at last I looked down covertly from the window, Poitou was gone.

But this was only the first messenger sent by the Marshal. The next came two weeks later, when I had almost begun to think I might be free. I was saying my prayers in my room when a knock disturbed me. This was so unusual an occurrence that I opened the door. There in the passage stood Griart. He seemed exhausted.

'Dom Eustache,' he said, 'how glad I am to see your honest face again! May I come in?'

It was a long and complicated spiel he offered me. All to do with a toothache which required some oil of cloves. That toothache I could credit: Griart's teeth were soft and rotten from a lifetime spent indulging himself on sweetmeats. The smell of his bad breath lingered in my chamber long after he had gone. His approach had been conciliatory, where Poitou's was peremptory. The Marshal *needed* my assistance, he implied. Christmas was coming, and there were not enough priests to serve the chapel. Would I not, please, consider returning and resuming my spiritual duties? My fit of pique regarding Robin Romulart could be overlooked.

'And what about that Office of the Damned?' I asked the fat man.

'What Office of the Damned?' Griart replied.

This made me feel quite mad, for my visitor then denied that any such blasphemous travesty of real religion had ever been proposed or carried out at our master's bidding. Yet just three weeks past, on All Saints' Day, he had been one of those who raised no objection when the service was mooted. Now, sucking on a stick of cloves, clutching his jaw, moaning softly like a plump unpleasant turtle-dove, Griart changed the subject. Prelati's operations were proceeding well, he told me, and they were hopeful of a satisfactory result. Yet our master felt that sometimes the alchemist went too far along what you might call the sinister or left-handed path, and then he missed the restraining and orthodox influence of his revered friend Dom Eustache. Added to which, there was still the plan to mount a new production of *The Mystery of the Siege of Orléans* in the grounds of the castle, probably early in the year of our Salvation 1440, and the Marshal de Rais would welcome a little literary revision of the text of this pageant-play by the aforesaid clergyman, his most respected critic. And so on and so forth, all interspersed with small belches and yelps of pain, as Griart alternately stuffed his face with comfits and comforts of medicine. At last I took pity on him, and pointed him back to Tiffauges.

'Have you some word I can give him?' Griart begged, as he sank into the cushions of his cart.

'No,' I said. Then, noticing the tears of self-pity which started to his eyes at the prospect of having to report this to our master, I added: 'You may tell my lord that his friend Dom Eustache says no. Not that he has no word to say, do you understand? But that he has a word, and the word that he says is: *No.*'

The cart creaked off, with Griart groaning in it.

I stood and watched them disappear down the road, reflecting on what a complicated issue my flight from the castle had become. The interesting thing was Gilles de Rais' unease at my continued absence. Why should that bother him? Why did he really want me back?

A few days passed without incident. There was no sign of any further emissary from the Marshal. I sought with quietness to impose some order upon my own ruined soul. I prayed much, and I fasted. I managed to abstain from wine. This was not so difficult, the wines at the inn tasting foul after the rare nectars I had found in the Marshal's cellars. Yet also I was helped to my abstinence by a memory of Gilles de Rais himself: his bouts of wild drunkenness. What did it mean – that a man should get drunk like that?

I read somewhere that drunkenness can be a distemper of the spirit, the soul's natural thirst for God being waylaid or perverted into this lust first for excitement and then for oblivion. I had seen Gilles drink like a man possessed. Was it the demon of the wine itself that possessed him? Or was he driven to allay and satisfy some deeper inward devil with the remedy of wine? I had witnessed his drunken ravings, and then his remorse and his anguish. But I did not comprehend the reasons for any of this, if indeed there were reasons to comprehend. My own love of wine seemed different, not merely in degree but in character. All the same, I valued my present sobriety.

Now that I had my wits about me, I began to grow aware that I was under observation by the Marshal's agents. Strangers would appear in the inn's yard, note my presence by checking with the landlord, and disappear again without comment. The few of these whom I saw I did not recognize, but then Tiffauges was in certain respects like a little city, thronged with retainers and soldiers, and it would have been impossible to have remembered every face even if I had seen them all. These enquirers appeared to be sent out from the castle to determine that I was still at Mortagne. As for me, I hardly dared to talk to anyone in the village, and none of them wanted to talk with me, now that they all knew who I was and where I was from.

Then, a few days short of Christmas, a traveller turned up at the inn. I remember that it was on the twenty-first of December, which is the Feast of St Thomas Didymus. This traveller's name was Jean Mercier, and he had journeyed here from Nantes, though his home was at La Roche-sur-Yon. He was by trade a milliner, and a maker of chaplets, but like others of that kind I have known he could also turn his hand to barbering. Jean Mercier's own haircut was remarkable, for he had allowed the hair to grow thickly on his crown, but cut it round his head above the ears, leaving the parts below shaved bare. I do not know why I bother to tell you this, unless I am motivated by a desire to recall his reality and present him indubitably before you. What Jean Mercier had to say was, as you will hear, fantastic.

The people of Poitou are taciturn by nature. When you add to that the fact that the villagers were scared of me, and shunned my company, you will appreciate that after all these weeks of eating my meals alone and in silence I welcomed this traveller's company at the dining table. We were left to ourselves, two strangers, to share a dish of *mortrewès* for our supper. This consisted of chicken and pork hewn small and ground to dust, mixed up with breadcrumbs, yolks of eggs, and pepper, then boiled with ginger, sugar, salt, and saffron. I remember telling myself this local mess seemed nicely apt for Didymus Day.

Like all barbers and hatters, Jean Mercier turned out to be a great talker. Our repast begun, he asked me who I was and what I was doing here. I gave him my true name, but defined myself evasively as a priest from St Malo. I don't know why I took this precaution. Perhaps I was tired of the way any mention of Tiffauges caused conversation in these parts to stop dead when it had hardly begun. At all events, Jean Mercier was not much interested in me. But, after a little desultory talk about fashions in headgear, the correct procedure for ridding the hair of lice, and other trivia, he suddenly embarked upon a topic that *did* interest him.

'Have you heard,' he said, 'of a man called Gilles de Rais? He is a mighty lord. He lives in this great castle not five miles from here, somewhere out in the mists and fogs of that damned heath.'

Something in the way he had broached this subject made me hesitate. I took a look around, but there was nobody near to hear us, or to inform him that his companion at supper had only recently been eating at my lord de Rais' table. I did not need to lie, only to say nothing, making my excuse an obstinate mouthful of *mortrewès*.

'This Gilles de Rais,' said Jean Mercier, 'I have heard strange tales about him. All the way from Nantes, I've met people who tell me the same thing. They say he is a magician, and consorts with witches. They say that he learned the black arts from that woman the English burned at Rouen. They say he was the master of her coven.' He paused to scratch his ridiculous haircut. 'What was her name? You must remember it, father?'

'Joan of Arc,' I said. 'Called the Pucelle.'

Jean Mercier crossed himself, nodding grimly, wiping saffron dribble from his chins. 'That's a joke,' he said. 'The bitch was no virgin. I met a man from Domrémy, and you know what he told me?'

My look must have warned him that I did not want to know anything whatsoever to Joan's discredit told him by his Lorraine scandal-monger. I held up the silver cross about my neck to remind him of my office. Jean Mercier blushed. 'Forgive me, father,' he went on. 'It's probably lies, and not important anyway. What *is* interesting, though, is that I've met plenty of folk who still want to think that woman was some sort of saint sent by God, if you'll pardon my saying so. Of course, they've got it wrong. But isn't it incredible? There's Joan of Arc – that idiots think was so good. And there's this Gilles de Rais – she chose him out of all the King's court to be her right-hand man, the captain of her captains – and now, here we are, just a few years after he gave the crazy farm-girl a bit of military credibility, and what are they saying about *him*?'

I had lost all appetite. I sat staring at this traveller and wishing he had never come. I wanted my old lonely silent meals back. But I heard my own voice speak as if from a long way off: 'What are they saying about him?'

'Why, that he is a magician,' Jean Mercier said. 'All across the countryside I've been hearing the same story. That the Sire de Rais has sold his soul to the Devil. That things happen in his castle at Tiffauges that it does a Christian no good to think about.'

'What things?' I said.

'Murder,' said the traveller. 'They say that he has murdered many children. The children go to his castle and they don't come back. Nobody ever sees them again, they say. I can tell you every village round about seems to have at least one such story – of a boy or a girl who was lured to the castle of Tiffauges and never seen again. They say that the Sire de Rais kills the little children. They say he needs the blood of little children for the writing of his book.'

'What book?' I said.

'His black book of magic,' Jean Mercier answered. 'They say that it is because of this book that no harm can befall him, and his castle is impregnable to others. You understand, father? His book is written in the children's blood!'

I had heard enough. I retired to my room in horror and despair, and sat all night in tearful vigil before the crucifix. Could such things be? Could I believe there was truth in this traveller's tale? In the morning, Jean Mercier was gone, with his hats and his haircut (which now it occurred to me might very well have been a wig). I wished that the images he had fed into my head were as easy to dismiss as his faithless person. But they were not, and I would never have opportunity to question him further.

At noon that day I received my third message from the Marshal. This time it was Gilles de Sillé, wearing a fine golden surcoat, mounted on a prancing dapple grey. He did not bother to get down as he commanded me to climb upon the other steed he had brought along with him.

'Never,' I cried. 'I can never return to Tiffauges.'

As usual, de Sillé kept smiling as he gazed down upon me. He enquired with much politeness why I could not, and asked what had applied the spur to my obvious vehemence. I was in a panic, but that did not alter my resolve. I had heard rumours, I told him, which made it impossible that I would ever go anywhere near the castle again. I valued my immortal soul, I think I added. Certainly in a whisper, foolishly en-

94

couraged to frankness by de Sillé's smiling, I urged my visitor, if he knew such rumours to have any foundation in fact, to try to persuade the Marshal to abandon his criminal folly.

De Sillé's smile froze in his eyes, though his lips kept it up. 'What crimes do you speak of, Dom Eustache?'

I shook my head then, scuffing my shoe in the dust. I was not going to repeat what I had heard. It was enough that I had heard it.

De Sillé sat playing with his horse's mane and staring down at me for a long minute. Then he spun his mount in a fury and rode off. I was left standing by the roadside, half-convinced that I must be an utter fool to have listened to a traveller's tale, let alone given credence to it. But I would never go back to Tiffauges. I was sure of that.

IX

THE HOUSE OF PERROT CAHN

All my life, I will confess, I have lacked what the world calls common sense. I know those things necessary for salvation, but as for saving myself from my enemies that is a different matter. Sometimes I think that I was born without some important instinct of self-preservation which everyone else seems to have the use of. If I had possessed either that or any common sense, I would surely at this point have run far away as fast as my legs could carry me, and hidden myself in some dark corner of a monastery. The truth is that my present situation was perilous, but I did not realize the fact. I had made it clear to Messire de Sillé that I knew *something*, and I suppose it must have occurred to me that he was bound to report my knowledge to the Marshal, yet still it did not sink in to my foolish head that this would make me too dangerous to be allowed to roam at large.

Remember that I was hanging on to reason only by my fingertips. There were days at Mortagne when I struggled to keep sane, sitting with eyes fixed on the crucifix, walking up and down reciting my prayers, lying on my bed without any hope of sleep or rest or release from the hellish prison of my thoughts. Had I or had I not *seen* anything at Tiffauges which suggested that there could be substance to Jean Mercier's story? Had I not rather *dreamed* that it might be so? But where did such dreams come from, if not from reality? I was able only to be sure that I would not willingly imagine these things out of nothing. For the rest, I was not sure. I knew nothing definite. Yet in my stupid way, had I not been convinced that something terrible was going on behind the scenes of alchemy and worse? Had I not been driven to escape by a feeling that Tiffauges contained a secret I must not share? Again and again I went over in my head all my time at the castle, reliving in imagination that series of events which still had some significance I could not grasp. I had gleaned hints at times from furtive looks, from scraps of conversation overheard by chance. I had heard little unexplained noises at night. I had seen lights where there should have been none, and noticed rooms in darkness where candles were called for. There had been goings to and fro more mysterious than might be ascribed to the doings of Rais le Héraut. There was the dark tower. There was the smell of burning on the wind. *Anything*, I concluded, could have been happening in a castle that size, behind tapestries concealing thick stone walls or masking doors that led to staircases and corridors and galleries and secret apartments I had never visited. But 'anything' did not necessarily mean the horror spoken of by Jean Mercier.

In an effort to discover for myself whether the milliner had been telling the truth when he reported that the local populace accused my lord de Rais of murder, I tried once more to engage the landlord of the inn in conversation upon the topic. This proved useless; he shut his mouth like a clam. When he was busy in the cellars, though, his wife told me a story which she said was the first thing she had ever learned about the Marshal when she married her husband and moved here from Cravant. It was a sort of fairytale, she said, and I was not to think that she believed such stuff. All the same, this was what people said of him round here, so if I was really interested, and promised that no harm would befall her for telling me . . . I gave her my assurance as a man of God, and she told me as follows.

Weary of making war against the English, said the inn-keeper's wife, Messire Gilles had retired to his castle at Tiffauges. All his time was spent in feasting and pleasure. Then one day a knight, Count Odon de Tréméac, lord of Krevent and other places, rode by his castle on his way to Morlaix, with at his side his betrothed, a beautiful young woman named Blanche de l'Herminière. Gilles de Rais invited them both to rest at the castle and drink a goblet of hypocras with him. The travellers were anxious to pass on their way, but de Rais was so pressing and so friendly that evening came and still they had not departed. Suddenly, on a sign from the master of the castle, a body of archers marched into the banqueting hall, seized Count Odon de Tréméac, and threw him into a deep dungeon. De Rais then begged the lady to forgive this trifling discourtesy and accept him as a substitute in marriage. Blanche wept and refused to be pacified. De Rais brushed aside her opposition and her tears, dragging her to his chapel. A thousand candles glowed on the altar, and the bells rang a nuptial peal. Blanche was as white as a lily, and she was trembling. My lord de Rais, dressed all in gold and with a magnificent red beard, came and stood at her side.

'Quick, master Chaplain, marry us,' cried the impetuous wooer.

'I do not want my lord for my husband,' cried Blanche de l'Herminière.

'Marry us! Marry us!'

'Do not do it, sir priest,' the young woman begged, sobbing.

'Obey me! I order you.'

Then, as Blanche tried to fly, Gilles seized her in his arms. 'I will give you everything,' declared he, passionately. 'I will give you my castles, my lands, my jewels, my gold.'

'Let me go,' the woman cried.

'I will give you,' said de Rais, 'myself, my body and soul!'

At this declaration a change came over the fair Blanche.

'I accept! I accept! Do you hear me, Gilles de Rais? I accept you, Lord of Tiffauges, and henceforth you belong to me.' At the same instant the beautiful Blanche became a blue devil, with a voice like thunder, who now stood at the baron's side. 'Gilles de Rais,' the demon said with a sinister laugh, 'God has grown tired of your sins. You belong now to hell, and from this day forward you shall wear its livery.' As he uttered these words, the demon made a sign and the beard of Gilles de Rais changed from red to the darkest blue. 'You are Gilles de Rais no longer,' the demon said. 'Henceforth you are *Barbe Bleu*, the most terrifying of men. Your name will be accursed for all ages, and after death your ashes will be cast upon the winds, whilst your wicked soul goes down to the depths of hell.'

Gilles begged for mercy, but the demon only laughed. Then the demon spoke of the corpses of the seven wives which lay in the cellars of the castle. 'The Count Odon de Tréméac, whom I rode with under the guise of Blanche de l'Herminière, is riding here at this moment at the head of a band of knights. They come to avenge the deaths of all those you have killed.'

'Then I am lost?' cried Gilles de Rais.

'No, not yet,' said the demon, 'for your hour has not struck.'

'Who will stop them?' asked Gilles de Rais.

'I will,' said the demon.

'Why will you do that?' asked Gilles de Rais.

'Because,' said the demon, 'I have need of you. Alive you will serve me a thousand times better than dead. And now farewell, Gilles de Rais, and remember that you belong to me body and soul.'

Then the devil disappeared in a cloud of sulphur. But from that time, said the inn-keeper's wife, the beard of Gilles de Rais had been blue. The demon had stopped the Count de Tréméac from avenging the dead, and the castle of Tiffauges was still protected. But one day the devil would return and claim the soul of Gilles de Rais. That was what she had heard, my host's wife said. She might not believe it herself, for she was from Cravant where people took such superstitious stuff with a pinch of salt, but this was the tale as she had been told it when she came to live in these backward parts.

I set this story down here, just as I had it from her lips. To me, it was worthless even as an antidote to the perhaps more credible horrors I had heard from Jean Mercier. Yet I suppose it told me something of the mixture of terror and awe which the mere mention of the name of Gilles de Rais inspired in the Poitou peasantry. And this story may still be the source of his being called Bluebeard by many. (Though I need hardly remark that my lord's beard was not blue, and indeed it had never been red.)

Having learned little of merit from one of the parents, I turned then to the children. What did the children of Mortagne think of Gilles de Rais? They ran away from me, hands over their ears; they would not answer my questions. But later I watched and heard them play a game which told me all.

Their game was called Sheep, Sheep, Come Home. All the players were sheep except two, one of whom was a shepherd and the other one a wolf. The shepherd left the sheep and went to the far end of the patch where they were playing. Then the wolf hid somewhere between the sheep and the shepherd. The shepherd called: '*Sheep, sheep, come home.*'

> The sheep replied: We are afraid.
> Shepherd: What of?
> Sheep: Gilles the wolf.
> Shepherd: *The wolf has gone to Machecoul.*
> *He won't be back for seven years;*
> *Sheep, sheep, come home.*

The sheep ran towards the shepherd. The wolf waited until they were near him then sprang out and tried to catch one of them. Any sheep caught by the wolf had to pretend to be killed and eaten. And thus, innocently, did the children of Mortagne play out a horror they knew but could not explain to themselves. I admit that to tell of this game still brings tears to my eyes.

I was listening to the same children at their wassailing on Christmas Eve when the wolf came for me. There was a clatter of hooves on the cobbles of the inn-yard, then a thunder of shod feet upon the stair, and the door of my chamber burst open to admit all three of Gilles' henchmen who had previously come as individuals to my importuning, that is to say Gilles de Sillé, Griart, and Poitou, plus one Jean Lebreton, known for his skill with the whip. The party were armed to the teeth, and addressed me in a manner which allowed no room for disagreement. Lebreton fitted a horse-collar about my neck. Then they bundled me downstairs and trussed me to a hurdle set across their cart. Only when the knots were tight enough to satisfy Griart's warped sense of humour did we set off, a sinister band of wassailers indeed, down the road to St Etienne-de-la-Mer-Morte.

The night was sharp with sleet. I was very frightened. Poitou and Griart taunted me as we drove on over the plain, and their ominous jests and threats, and de Sillé's grim silence, convinced me before we had gone a mile that St Etienne was to be the home of my grave. It did not occur to me to wonder why they were bothering to drag me all the way there before killing me. I was to hang on the gallows at St Etienne, that's what Poitou said. I begged them to have mercy, shouting and screaming, drumming with my heels upon the hurdle. At first, they took no notice, saying what a fine sight I would make when hung up in my cassock for the crows to eat my eyes. There was plenty more in this vein, most of it more obscene than I care to repeat. I lay soaking wet in the bottom of the cart, gnawing at the ropes that bound my wrists, but my teeth made no impression. In vain I kept on roaring out in protest at the injustice of it all. 'I am loyal! I know nothing! I know nothing! I am loyal! Why should my lord have commanded you to kill me? Have pity on me! Have mercy! I am a man of God, a simple priest . . .' Yes, it shames me now to remember the things I said, but this book would be no true record if it contained only the matters I can be proud of.

They let me suffer all the way to La Bénate. Then I realized that we could not be going to St Etienne. If we had been going to St Etienne we would have taken the Legé road. Even at the time I was not fool enough to believe that it was my begging which had made them change their minds. We had never been going to St Etienne. There had never been any serious intention of stringing me up. Don't ask me how I knew this; I just knew it. Once I realized that we were not going to St Etienne, I knew that they were not going to kill me. What they *were* going to do with me, I had no idea; but it was not to be St Etienne and the gallows. I lay silent and exhausted once I understood this, listening to the sound of my teeth a-chatter in my skull, now glad to feel the rain fall on my face. Whatever this night was to bring, it was not going to be my death.

Dawn broke as we came down to Machecoul, in the west of the Pays de Rais. I knew, of course, that my master had a castle here. But from something that passed between Griart and Poitou I gathered that it was not to the castle that we were going. We were going to the house of Perrot Cahn.

The name meant nothing to me. The house of Perrot Cahn lay back from the road outside Machecoul, a plain stone structure, a square box like a child's drawing of a house, flat-roofed and stumpy. The front was relieved only by the projection of a porch, equally dour and squat, with two dumpy, bulging columns supporting a weak entablature, some horrible misconception of the Doric order. The road itself was deserted, no more than a track. Both house and surroundings seemed part of a painted scene, as if one approached a pictured nightmare of no real substance. I was worn out in both body and mind from that terrible journey. Yet I swear I did not dream what happened next.

First I was washed in hot water and given several draughts of good strong ale to drink. The tub that I bathed in was set before a great fire, with a Yule log blazing in the heart of it, and the room in which I found myself was festooned as if for Christmas with bay laurels, mistletoe, ivy and holly berries as red as drops of blood. There were rushes strewn on the floor, but it was all very tidy. While I scrubbed myself, Griart remained with me, pouring fresh water over my shoulders now and then from a big earthen pitcher. His presence alarmed me, but he performed this duty with a kind of indifference that recommended itself before long. The ale, as I say, was powerful, and this also proved a benison. I lay back in the tub, soaking and quaffing, hardly knowing what to think. No doubt I was so relieved to be alive that I enjoyed more than usual the particular joys of that moment.

My ablutions over, I found fresh clothes set out for my use. Nor was I required to don secular apparel. Whoever had selected and laundered and prepared these garments was fully cognisant of what my monastic office required. Never, I think, did St Benedict's simple black wool seem so sweet to my senses as when I donned my habit that Christmas Day.

De Sillé and Poitou and Lebreton then reappeared, also newly apparelled, and we all sat down to table like old friends. Not a word was said about the night's adventure. Looking back on it now, I find this extraordinary, but at the time I cannot remember remarking it. The power of the ale, the warmth of my bath, and my gladness at being alive left me sleepy and content. Nothing much was said. I recall that de Sillé returned with his thrush in its cage and set this beside his place at table, and that he fed the bird with titbits throughout the meal, sometimes addressing it with remarks of a perfect banality, such as 'There we are, my pretty one,' 'Who likes his frumenty, then?', and so forth. Only in recording this now does it occur to me as strange that the bird was there. Had my lord's steward borne it hither with us through the night? While not impossible, I may say that I consider that unlikely. Yet the bird was there by de Sillé, however inexplicable its presence.

Our meal was served by a man whose skin was black. He waited on table excellently, but without a word. None of my companions ever addressed the black man by name, yet I knew this was Perrot Cahn. He wore a hood of white silk and a white tunic, and he went barefoot over the rush-strewn floor.

The main item of our meal was a boar's head. Perrot Cahn carried this into the room on a silver platter. The boar's head had been roasted well, and there was a lemon thrust in its mouth, and it came decorated with rosemary, bays, and laurel, in accordance with Christmas custom in those parts. We ate without talking to one another. For myself, I declare that the events of the past twelve hours had left me with little to say. Griart belched a lot when his eating was finished. Poitou played with a piece of burnt crackling. As for Messire de Sillé, he sat at the head of the table, watching the rest of us all the while with the usual humourless smile at work about his lips. He stuck his little finger between the bars of the bird-cage, and let his thrush peck at it.

It was all very strange and slow and dreamlike, that dinner at the house of Perrot Cahn. Had it not been for the weals upon my wrists where the ropes had bitten, I think by its end I would not have believed how I was brought here.

I remained for three days at the house of Perrot Cahn. On St Stephen's Day, Francesco Prelati joined us. He was the only one of our party ever to ask me any questions regarding what I might have learned to the Marshal's dishonour either during my time at Tiffauges, or later when I ran away to Mortagne. His verbal inquisition, now I look back on it, was gentle, subtle, thoroughly indirect. He was concerned to discover (and report back to our master) exactly what I knew, or thought I ought to know. I contrived to allay or blunt suspicion with my answers. It might have been better to have blurted out Jean Mercier's words, or the words of the children's game.

Had I done so, would the Marshal's men have killed me then and there? Why was I not taken to St Etienne-de-la-Mer-Morte in the first place? Could Gilles have been so well pleased by the prodigal's recapture that he declined to destroy him? Even now, I do not really know the answers to such questions. It is possible that my lord may even have hesitated at the sacrilege of murdering a priest. It is also just possible that he already perceived some bond between himself and me, and was unwilling to break it. I cannot know. These problems tease and torment me. The reader will have to appreciate that there are many possibilities which lie behind the story I have to tell, things which I still turn over in my mind, trying to understand them. This book itself is an attempt to know what happened.

Once Prelati had satisfied himself that I knew next to nothing, I was allowed out to walk about the village, though either Griart or Poitou always dogged my footsteps as I did, and often both of those grim rascals together. Thus I was able to notice that Machecoul, like Mortagne, was a place of fear. Nor is this surprising. These were *his* villages, after all. Doors would be barred hurriedly and shutters drawn as any of us who were in the Marshal's service passed down the streets. If there were curses muttered, then it was in private. That Christmas I never saw anyone who even dared to weep in a public place.

So much for these things. But does my account of the house of Perrot Cahn make it seem like a habitation of some pleasantness? Well, that Christmas fires burned in it for my pleasure and comfort, and I was made welcome to a certain degree as a guest as I have told you. But you should know that before Christmas came again to the house of Perrot Cahn the ashes from human bones and a child's bloodied vest would be discovered there.

X

HOLY INNOCENTS' DAY

I am writing this book at the monastery of the Sacro Speco, near Subiaco, some fifty miles east of Rome. I was Keeper of the Archives here, before my sickness. Most of my writing is done by day in the monastery garden, on the side of the hill that looks down towards the river Anio.

Sacro Speco means the sacred cave. It was to a cave in this hillside that St Benedict retired as a hermit in the year 494, founding the first of his twelve monasteries here about ten years later. The chronicles state that the principal monastery, where I am, was devastated by the Lombards in 601, and rebuilt in 705; but there is little foundation for these statements. Our church, dedicated to St Scholastica, St Benedict's sister, was erected in 981, according to an inscription belonging to a later date, but which I found carved upon a slab decorated with reliefs of the end of the eighth century, or possibly the beginning of the ninth. Our cloister is a fine Romanesque arcaded court with twisted columns and mosaics, the south side of which was constructed by Lorenzo, the first of the family of the Cosmati, early in the thirteenth century, while the other three sides are due to his son Jacopo and Jacopo's sons Luca and Jacopo, who worked here over 200 years ago in the time of the abbot Lando (1227–1243 of our Redemption).

Subiaco itself was anciently called Sublaquem – no doubt from its position under the three artificial lakes constructed in the gorge of the Anio in connection with the aqueduct of the Anio Novus, which had its intake at the lower end of the lowest of them (the *Simbruina stagna* of Tacitus). These lakes gradually ceased to exist owing to the action of the Anio, the last dam being washed away in Our Lord's year 1305, according to the chronicles.

Here then, between water and rock, I live out my days. I sit under the olives in this garden, and I write down his story. Have I not chosen the brightest hillside in all Italy for my work, no doubt because his story is so dark? Sometimes I shake as if with cold under the noonday sun, but that might merely be the course of the leprosy.

It is not the monastery that holds me, so much as the sacred cave. I have discovered a spring near it, and like to believe that this was what first held the blessed St Benedict himself. It must come from deep down, a long dark way down, that water, from under the rock. It must start hot down there, but by the time it comes out in the hillside, in this place I have scooped clean and keep filled with white pebbles, it is cold and good. My sores need it. For some reason the birds keep clear of this place and do not peck about or upset the water. I am grateful. I keep this place decent and pick out any leaves that happen to drift in while I am not here. I have to have a certain degree of this water every day, to keep my sores cool, and heal them. This morning, Holy Innocents' Day, when I knelt and drank from the spring there was a skin of ice upon it. I bit this ice between my teeth and it tasted of the water and the rock. It did not taste of the earth, there was no taste of earth or death to it. I liked this ice the more for knowing that the spring will never freeze right through no matter what, that the water comes up too fresh and fast for this spring of mine ever to freeze right over so that I would have nowhere to sup cleanness in the world. I eat the little bits of ice and I drink the water. Each is so cold it warms me.

My disease has not yet reached the final stage. When that happens I know I shall look like a lion. There is nothing magical about this, it being due to the thickening of the skin of the face. All I have so far are these coppery patches on my feet and on my chest and on the backs of my hands. My ears and my nose are not yet much thickened or enlarged and my eyebrows have not fallen off. I have much to be grateful for. It could take years before this leprosy kills me. I give thanks also that I suffer in enlightened times, and times in which my disease in general has undergone a remarkable diminution. A century ago, at this stage, I would already have been confined to a leper-house.

I have tried a large number of internal remedies with varying results, the best being arsenic and chaulmoogra oil. As to externals, nothing surpasses the water of this spring at Subiaco.

So it was precisely seventeen years ago today, on the twenty-eighth of December 1439, that I was brought back to Tiffauges by the Marshal's henchmen. Prelati had warned me of the summons the night before. 'Our lord has need of you tomorrow,' was what he said. How could I possibly have resisted him? Prelati sat watching me attentively, eyes furred with malice. I knew that if I now betrayed the least reluctance to return to the castle it could prove my death-warrant.

We rode through a melancholy landscape that bitter winter's day. I remember the misery of our horses as we thrust against the wind. The sky loured ahead, a wrack of low black cloud seemed always to drive towards us where we galloped, and when we reached the plain a heavy rain of sleet began to fall, increasing almost immediately to a furious hissing downpour. My companions cursed as they rode. For my part, I felt too deep a despair to give utterance to anything. And the castle, when we reached it, looked like a palace of the dead.

Once within its walls again, however, the old original glory came flooding back. It was in vain that I kept telling myself all this was spurious. Minstrels played, candles blazed by the thousand in every room and corridor, everywhere was the scent of rich rare perfumes. Not for the first time I thought of

Tiffauges as some wondrous Book of Hours come to life, all dusty and forbidding when you considered its exterior, but intricately illuminated and ornate when you opened it up. A feast had been prepared for my return. The Marshal, dressed all in gold, seemed in careless high spirits.

The False Pucelle sat at the table by him, a silver chaplet crowning her jet-black hair. Rais le Héraut was also present, and Prelati, and de Bricqueville and de Sillé. Rossignol sang madrigals, standing with his back to a fire of chopped logs of pine and elm which blazed and crackled on the hearth, sending long dancing shadows across the cloth. It was only when the meal was ended that Gilles turned to me.

'Here is Dom Eustache back,' he said, 'although I do believe he doubts our orthodoxy.'

I think I must have blushed, for the Marshal burst out laughing. 'Come, priest,' he said, 'confess it! Did you not consider it a blasphemy when I pretended on All Saint's Day that my chapel was to be used for an Office of the Damned?'

In vain I looked from one face to another about that table. Would none of them admit that the Office had been real? Yet even before I looked, I knew the answer.

'My lord's wit is another perfection of his understanding,' I said abjectly. 'And I am witless, for I misunderstood him.'

Gilles seemed satisfied, or he was pleased to pretend as much. But then he said: 'Tell me then, priest, what day is this?'

I had been dreading such a direction. Hoping against hope that he was not about to suggest what in my heart I knew for sure was coming, I replied, 'Why, it is the third day after Christmas Day, my lord.'

'And what dear day is that?' asked Gilles de Rais.

'It is,' said I, 'the Feast of the Holy Innocents.'

Then my master pronounced the reason why he had wanted me back on this particular day. It was so that I should don the purple vestments and say for him the Mass of those poor infant martyrs, murdered in Bethlehem by order of King Herod long ago. Their number is not known, but it cannot have been large, legends to the contrary notwithstanding. The Church from early times has regarded these little ones as the first martyrs, and the festival of their massacre is commonly known as Childermas, of course. I might add that this day is a day of ill omen for reasons which have nothing to do with Gilles de Rais, and so even then, before I knew all that there was to know about my master, I regarded the Feast of Childermas with abhorrence. In the first place, there is the widespread feeling (crass superstition, I grant you) that Holy Innocents' Day is so black a day that none should contract a marriage upon it, and so doomed a day that whichever day of the week it falls on can be counted as the unlucky day of each week in the year that follows. In the second place, there are the abuses and follies which have been associated in the past with Childermas, when sometimes boy-bishops were permitted into the pulpits to preach mock-sermons, and there was a Feast of Fools and other gross nonsense. Parents used temporarily to abdicate their authority on this day, and in nunneries and monasteries the youngest nun and monk were for twenty-four hours allowed to masquerade as abbess and abbot. These mockeries of religion were condemned and anathematized in 1431 by the Council of Basel.

Such mockeries, however, were far from my master's mind that day at Tiffauges. He wanted the whole and proper rite for Childermas performed in the chapel of St Vincent. He needed me there at the castle for this high specific purpose.

Now, Gilles de Rais had many other prelates, and any one of them would have served as well. The fact is, I have to point out, that in the circumstances my lord derived cruel pleasure from getting me back within his walls in order to command me to celebrate that particular Mass. I knew this, and I think he knew that I knew. And thus was his pleasure compounded, and my fear begun freshly, and worse. For, as you will appreciate, I had no choice but to comply with his commandment. In fear and trembling, voice failing, tongue cleaving to the roof of my mouth, I said the Mass for Holy Innocents' Day.

That Mass has a certain Gospel reading in it, which is as follows: '*Vox in Rama audita est, ploratus, et ululatus multus; Rachel plorans filios suos, et noluit consolari, quia non sunt . . .*'

Which, if I may translate the holy text, can be seen to be St Matthew's transposition of a verse in the prophet Jeremiah: 'In Rama was there a voice heard, lamentation, and weeping, and great mourning, Rachel weeping for her children, and would not be comforted, because they are not.' (*St Matthew*, 2, xviii; *Jeremiah*, 31, xv).

When I arrived at these words, as you may imagine, I felt as though my own throat had been cut. To this day, I do not know how I managed to say them aloud. In the back of my head, also, must have been the knowledge that the selfsame text was being recited at the same time in village churches in Mortagne and Machecoul and up and down the length of the Pays de Rais. If there was truth in that traveller's tale told me by Jean Mercier, what would the parents of those lost children be thinking at this moment? The traveller's words came back to me like an echo from the recesses of the chapel as I pressed my lips to the book: 'They say that the Sire de Rais kills the little children. They say he needs the blood of little children for the writing of his book. They say his book is written in the children's blood!'

Other words and images came flooding through my memory in the wake of these. Nor is this necessarily to be taken to my detriment – I mean as a sign of what an inadequate priest I must be. I am, God knows, not a good priest, but for other reasons. This matter of the mind's attention during celebration of the sacrifice of the Mass is something that interests me deeply. Is it because here we are concentrating on the most important subject for thought and action which God has given us, that all manner of *other* mental flotsam and jetsam comes floating to the top? I cannot believe that such memories are sent us by the Devil, or belong simply to that category of irrelevant intellectual interruptions he devises to spoil our prayers. Rather, it seems to me, might the words of each Mass said be like magnetic stones that draw out meaning from the mess of living, or if that is heresy then might not the divine deed of the Mass itself be considered as an incidental stirring up of this and that from the very depths of our minds and hearts? Not a lodestone, but God's rod probing the pool of half-forgotten thoughts and feelings, reminding us what we should remember, awakening us from our habitual sleep? This might overstate the case to the point of unorthodoxy, but the basic simple truth of it remains. I have often thought that if I were a poet I would make a work consisting only of what has passed more than once through my mind and my heart at the deepest moments of my concentration during Mass. Such a work, I am sure, would touch on matter common to us all, but not the less rarely to be prized for that. Such a work could not fail to illuminate the way, and might at best be a true evangel for others serious in the profession of holy living and holy dying.

Not that the images which came to me there in the chapel at Tiffauges as I celebrated the Mass of Holy Innocents' Day can be placed in this high category. Yet nor were they irrelevant to my thinking about the story of Gilles de Rais. I thought of that book which they said he was writing in blood. I thought of that image carved upon the braquemard: of a man and a woman pictured playing upon pipes, with a line of little children dancing behind them. I thought of the eyes of that snake which had disdained to destroy me. I thought of those red-and-white rose petals in Rossignol's hand. I thought of my father's drowned corpse saying 'Woman has no opposite', and I thought of that burnished gold vessel which had burst in my hands. I thought of Prelati's confession as he lay in the Marshal's bed, the sheets stained with his blood, and I remembered the children at Mortagne crying, 'Gilles the wolf.' I thought of the smoke that came from the dark tower and hung over the castle like a cloud, and the image of Béatrix de Rohan buried in her bridal gown came into my head so fiercely and suddenly that for a second I imagined I could smell the wet clay of her grave and hear the rustle of her dress as the earth came down on her. I imagined Roger de Bricqueville naked again, with his member erect, and I thought of my master kneeling before Joan in the mystery play:

> *Aussi moy, Dame, ne doubtez;*
> *Faire vueil ce qui vous plaira . . .*

I thought of other words then, when these faded from my head. I thought of the demon saying, 'You are *Barbe Bleu.*' I thought of Poitou with the little Hoodman in his stranglehold, how the boy had fought and kicked, and Poitou had said only, 'These brats take a lot of killing.' I thought of the white rat twitching its whiskers on the altar and the sound on the roof which they said was de la Rivière's leopard. I thought particularly of Gilles' first words to me: 'I am a perfect Christian.' Did that mean anything? What did it mean? God is perfection, and there is no other. God is the limitless sum of all perfection of being. All perfections of creatures are mere analogues of the perfections of God. I remembered the words of St Thomas Aquinas on the subject: 'The perfection of a Christian life consists essentially in charity, primarily in loving God, secondarily in loving one's neighbour' (*Summa Theologiae*, Prima Secundae, II, clxxxiv, 3). When a man loves God with his whole heart, soul, mind and strength, and his neighbour as himself for God's sake, then is he perfect. Was that Gilles de Rais? No, that was not Gilles the wolf. 'You are *Barbe Bleu.*' But I thought of the smell of violets.

Gilles did not communicate at that Mass. As I think I have already had occasion to observe, in my experience of him since I had come to Tiffauges my lord had never made his communion, though his degree of religious observance was otherwise admirable and I believe I hardly ever celebrated the holy mysteries without him being present in the chapel of St Vincent, an attentive and devout participant in all but the central mystery. He would march in as though he owned God's house, and stand right below the altar, and say the responses in a loud clear voice. I never raised the Host but that he bowed down, and when I held aloft the cup in which the wine had been changed into the Blood of Christ he would prostrate himself full-length upon the marble floor, for all the world as if enraptured. Nor did these devotions strike me as insincere or theatrical. Gilles might not be a perfect Christian. But he was without doubt a true believer.

My Childermas ended. I blessed my congregation and bade them depart in peace. It was only afterwards, saying my private prayer of thanksgiving, that I fell to wondering about the sum of those images and thoughts and remembrances which had flowed through my head so copiously during the service. It was then that I knew for a certainty that I had not been summoned to return to the castle simply for this. Whatever Gilles de Rais might require of me, it had not yet been asked. Whatever Gilles de Rais planned as a fate for me, that had still to be performed. I thought of that red-and-white rose, and I knew he was a murderer.

Next morning I was awoken at dawn by the sound of a woman screaming. I looked down from my window. It had snowed in the night, and the ground was white and new. There below me in the courtyard went the Marshal Gilles de Rais and the False Pucelle. My lord, in black armour, had the braquemard in his right hand. The false Joan, naked, was running away from him. As I watched I saw Gilles strike the impostor three times across her buttocks with the flat of that sword. She ran wailing, plainly in terror of her life.

It was as plain to me that he could kill her. His blood was up, and the marks on her flesh burned red. Suddenly, the false Joan stopped and sought to embrace her pursuer, as if she thought that lust might save her from death. Gilles cast her away from him. She fell face-down in the snow.

The false Joan lay so still that for a moment I thought she was dead. Then she scrambled to her feet, and ran away as fast as she could, falling down again in her panic to be gone, through the gate, over the drawbridge, out into the snow now whirling thick in the wind that blew across the plain. Her squire Robin Romulart ran after her, trying vainly to hide the lady's nakedness with his cloak.

I heard my lord laugh softly. Then I must have made some sound that betrayed my presence. Gilles de Rais looked up. When he saw me he raised the braquemard to his lips in a kiss of salute.

PART TWO

XI

THE DAUPHIN'S CALL TO ARMS

I was now a fly deep-embedded in the spider's web of the Marshal's life at Tiffauges. Unlike the other flies I was not required to take part in the continued experiments in alchemy, and as you will learn there was another dark corner of the web which I never visited, but in all other respects I could be counted my master's man.

Regarding the alchemy, Gilles chose to believe that I had picked that quarrel with Robin Romulart, and removed myself from the castle, because I was appalled by the idea that Prelati was working with devils. Perhaps, to do my lord justice, this might be regarded as some small oblique expression of the respect he felt for my priesthood if not for me. It was as a priest that I was excused from having to participate in the Italian's new method of invocation. This involved, as I understood it, a crested bird and a certain dyadrous stone, but as the stone was not obtainable they had to abandon the idea. Prelati then suggested that Gilles himself was the reason for the failure of their work. I gathered that he had tried to get the Marshal to sign some pact or *cédule* to please his spirits, but the spirits did not like the wording of it. When I enquired what Gilles had promised, Prelati said that the formula had been thus: 'Come at my call, and I will give you what you will, *except my soul and my life*.' If that was true, then it seemed to me that my lord thereby showed himself to be marginally more sensible than his alchemist, but Prelati's view, expressed with a vehemence I should call Florentine if not infernal, was that the spirit world does not like loopholes.

Since Gilles was not willing to commit himself utterly, without the reservations concerning his soul, there was no further purpose in his attending the experiments, Prelati said. Indeed, he said, Gilles' presence might well be a hindrance.

My master, besotted, accepted this spiritual criticism, and withdrew. Whereupon, naturally, the demon Barron appeared twelve times to Prelati 'in the form of a handsome young man of about twenty-five, wearing a red or violet cloak'. On the last of these visits the demon was kind enough before he vanished to indicate to Prelati a pile of gold ingots lying in a corner of the room. Prelati ran to get the Marshal, but when they returned together and he opened the door the Italian leapt back, having seen, as he said, a big black snake coiled on the floor, 'thick as a dog'. Crying 'Keep out! I see a great serpent!' Prelati fled for his life with Gilles at his heels. The Marshal went back after supper, having drunk in my company another keg of brandy-wine. He wanted to take with him a relic of the True Cross which had been in the Laval family for centuries, but Prelati dissuaded him. When Gilles entered the room, it was empty. No Barron, no serpent to be seen. But there, in one corner, he told me, was this small heap of what looked like gilded leaves. He touched it, and the whole heap fell to dust.

Was Prelati a charlatan? I hope that is all that he was. It would be better for him, and for the Marshal, if that were the truth. I found out a thing or two about Francesco Prelati when I fetched him from Italy, and now the pattern of my days and nights back at Tiffauges allowed me some leisure for the finding out of more. What I learned I set down now here, for the first time. That is to say, I shall reveal a little more than I had to reveal at his trial, which was also the Marshal's trial, and mine. Prelati, on his own description, had come into this world well-equipped for a black life, having been born with four little hairs curling from left to right in the exact form of a swastika upon the skin over his heart. His parents

helped him to be a warlock, too. They subscribed, so he told
me, to some minor heretical sect which forbids itself, apparently, even the saying of the Lord's Prayer, regarding it as
'vain repetition'. What else should a lad of imagination do
then, but learn not only to say it, but to say it backwards?
Amongst the suffocatingly pure, no doubt, to try to be evil is
to aspire to be human. Yes, I can understand the whited
sepulchral forces that made Prelati the black fool he was, and
sympathize with him in his predicament. But it would be
more sensible to withhold sympathy from the vanity and ignorance that made him persist in his rebel way for the rest of his
life. For that, I believe, is what Prelati was, beneath the
handsome mask and his alchemist's cloak: a reactionary rebel
with a second-rate mind and a taste for obfuscation. He never
grew up or calmed down, and he never forgave first his father
and then Gilles for dying when he needed them. He said to
me once, as an excuse for cutting a dung-beetle in half with
his dagger, 'Dom Eustache, I am anxious to distinguish myself
by the sins that I commit.' The reader will forgive me my
disdain, but this is an old and boring story, of far less import
and interest than the story of Gilles de Rais. That the two
men were charged with and convicted for the same crimes is
no reason why we should confuse them. What Gilles was I
must try to say when the time comes, and may God help me.
But here and now I say that Prelati was just another of those
pathetic little necromancers who have sat brooding down the
centuries in the lavatories of the spirit, trying constipatedly to
figure out for themselves exactly what the sin against the Holy
Ghost is, so that they might commit it, never be forgiven, and
become immortal as some kind of saint-in-reverse. And unless
the sin against the Holy Ghost is banality then it seems to me
impossible that Prelati ever committed it.

Some of the other flies in the Marshal's web now began to
seem to me more interesting. I looked with new eyes at de
Bricqueville and de Sillé, following my return. Gilles' cousin

Roger, in particular, I had underestimated. He was far less the Marshal's creature than I had supposed. The tokens of his independence were trivial, yet the wonder was that they had passed unnoticed before. He had this deliberate habit of being always a few minutes late for any meal, coming to the banqueting hall perspiring profusely and with his face covered with cobwebs. He had an elaborate, awkward way of strolling in, saluting everybody with a wave of his hand, and then of giving the edibles a close inspection. If there was meat, he would pick up a bone and sniff it; or he would dip the ladle into the big pot and try a mouthful of soup, smiling suspicion. He was like a fine bloodhound, Messire de Bricqueville, his nose to the ground all the time. I realized that what this behaviour indicated was that he viewed the Marshal and his doings from a certain critical distance, and what is more he wanted the rest of us to know it. He looked at Gilles with no anxiety to please, and at Gilles' satellites as though he was not one of them. This was unusual among the Marshal's followers.

De Sillé, on the contrary, was a perfect whore. He might also be my lord's cousin, but there was never any sense that he was his equal. I came to think of him, in effect, as Gilles' pet thrush. Just as that little tiny bird lived in the silver cage that dangled from de Sillé's wrist, so did de Sillé himself live dangling from the Marshal. I perceived that behind the nobility of his gestures there lurked the spectre of the ridiculous: Gilles de Sillé might behave sublimely, but he was absurd.

It will be remarked that my temporary escape from the castle had enabled me to obtain another perspective on its occupants. I was no longer dazzled, and I was the less bemused. As to my lord himself, I was struck even more forcibly by his descent into drunkenness, for it seemed to me now that he was seldom to be seen without a goblet of some fine fiery wine in his fist. He walked straight and erect, but I was well enough acquainted with the shadow of the vine to

understand that he walked *too* straight and *too* erect, with the
fierce attention to port and carriage which alcohol breeds in
the drunkard brain. Griart and Poitou drank with him, but
where their drinking was gluttony, his was not. It must have
been at this time that I dared to say to him, 'My lord, in the
name of God, why do you drink so much?' Gilles de Rais
laughed. 'Because I am thirsty,' he said. 'My lord,' said I,
'what are you thirsty for?' 'Death,' said Gilles de Rais, 'I am
thirsty for death.' This exchange seems to me to have its
comical aspects now that I come to write it down, but at the
time I can assure you I did not smile. 'Hola!' Gilles shouted.
'Bring me a pot of nothing! Extinction is in the cup – and I
would drink it!' *In vino veritas* . . . but I did not understand.

One day in January there was a brief respite from the
round of alchemy and alcohol, drunkenness and remorse,
Gilles' spinning and his playing poison spider with the rest of
us. Rais le Héraut came running down the staircase from a
turret. He had seen the *fleurs-de-lis* on pennons streaming
across the plain at the tips of lances held aloft by a great host
of cavalry. It was the Dauphin, and soon he was at the gate,
demanding entrance.

Gilles, the worse for wine already, although it was not yet
noon, seemed thrown into a state of consternation by this
news. He roared at Prelati to go and conceal every least bit of
alchemical activity or optimism before the Dauphin was
admitted. The Italian ran about screaming and waving his
hands as a consequence, kicking the dogs and barking at the
lackeys. I gathered that there was panic in one particular
tower, with the magician and his acolytes working in a frenzy
to destroy two furnaces, wash the pentacles from the floor,
and let loose all the turtle-doves from a window. Feathers
were still falling like magic snowflakes from a clear blue sky as
Gilles came out to welcome his royal visitor.

I was aware, of course, that it was the Dauphin's grandfather King Charles VI who had established a total edict

against alchemy. That was still in force these many years after its issuance. But observing Gilles' panic I wondered if a rats' nest of sorcery was *all* that he had to conceal. The Dauphin, if he looked anywhere, was highly unlikely to look everywhere, and even if he found the unfindable dyadrous stone there was little chance that he would know what it was for. And yet, as I say, my master's guilty conscience was unmistakable, and his anxiety infectious. He was beside himself with a fear of being found out.

Picture this meeting of the Dauphin and Gilles de Rais. The sixteen-year-old visitor was an ungainly figure, with rickety legs, a twisted torso, and one shoulder higher than the other. His eyes were keen and piercing, but a long hooked nose gave grotesqueness to a face marked with cunning rather than with dignity. His ugliness was emphasized by the old felt hat he wore – its sole ornament the leaden figure of a saint. The Dauphin dressed habitually in pilgrim grey (and still does, so I hear, now he is King Louis XI). He talked rapidly and much, and most indiscreetly. I watched the Marshal summon all his wits to answer.

'Where is the woman pretending to be Joan of Arc?' the Dauphin began. 'We've ridden here from Angers after her. Our father wanted to employ the whore to direct the defence of Languedoc against the English. Now in his wisdom he's realized that even the damned English wouldn't believe in her. We have an order to put down brigandage, and arrest the bitch.'

'Gentle Dauphin,' Gilles said, 'she has fled.'

Hearing this, I had to turn aside to hide my face, so sharp was the remembrance of the false Joan's blushing naked bottom as she ran away through the snow. Only later did it occur to me that this manner of address ('Gentle Dauphin') was an echo of the style always used by the real Joan when she had spoken to this prince's father (then King Charles VII) in the days when *he* was the Dauphin. I feel confident that the Dauphin Louis did not appreciate this; in which case, did Gilles do it for my benefit? or to signal to a ghost across the years?

Spiced wine was provided for the royal guest. He sat dabbling his spiky fingers in the silver cup, but did not drink from it. 'Fled, you say, Baron. Where has she fled?'

Gilles shrugged his shoulders, then disguised the obvious indifference in a little cough as soon as he registered the Dauphin's displeasure. 'Gentle Dauphin, I could not say. She did not tell me, and I do not know.'

'Did she take soldiers with her?'

'Soldiers, highness?'

'I think you understand us well enough, Laval. Did the woman leave here with a company of men? Did you equip her out for brigandage?'

My master was sweating. But I sensed his great relief when he heard this question. So *that* was what the visit meant, I could imagine him thinking. The Dauphin was sniffing out brigands here, not alchemists. 'Gentle Dauphin,' said Gilles de Rais, 'I can assure you that the woman left with less than she had when she came.'

Louis flicked wine with his forefinger and thumb. 'Yet you gave her house room?'

'She interested me,' Gilles said simply.

'You did not believe in her?'

'She is not Joan,' Gilles said.

'And you knew that from the start?'

'At first she interested me,' Gilles said, as if admitting something with reluctance. 'But she is not Joan, gentle Dauphin.'

Their exchange is burned upon my memory for a reason I cannot understand to this day. At the time, as I remember it, I put down my master's repetitions to the fact that he was intoxicated, and therefore teasing out his thought with difficulty. Now it occurs to me to wonder if he did not pose as drunk in order to cover the complexity of his feelings. My reason for wondering this will be made apparent when I get to that part in my story where I found out more about what Gilles really thought of the Pucelle.

For the moment, here is the Dauphin taking off his hat and fiddling with that holy medal which adorns it. 'We saw her once,' he said. 'That was at Rheims, at our father's crowning. She stood near the altar, on the Gospel side. A very awkward creature, wasn't she? But there she was, gripping her battle flag, wearing this suit of white armour, and the tears rolling down her cheeks like little gooseberries. We remember that quite clearly, and the trumpets. And you, Laval, when you came riding up the steps of the cathedral on your horse, one of the guard of honour escorting the holy ampulla of coronation. Four of you holding the canopy that day: the Marshal de Boussac, Admiral Louis de Colan, the Sire de Granville, who was master of the crossbowmen, and you, Laval. And then you were one of the twelve peers of France there too, grouped in a ring around our father, elevating and placing the crown on his head with your outstretched hands. Oh yes, shall we ever forget it? But mostly it was that weird little female from Domrémy tripping over her own banner, and you coming right down the nave of the cathedral on your horse.' The Dauphin's face was shining at the memory. 'You dismounted at the gates of the choir,' he said. 'And then your horse pissed.'

Gilles, who had been visibly shaken by this speech, now burst out laughing. 'The Dauphin has a passion for truth,' he said.

'We were a child,' said Louis. 'We were only six years old. When you are only six years old and sitting on a hard seat at a coronation that goes on for hours and hours that is the bit that you remember – the black horse pissing! That and Joan of Arc with the gooseberries running down her face!'

Gilles poured himself another goblet of wine. His hand was

shaking, but lifting the drink high he said in a firm voice, 'Prince, the future of France is secure if it rests upon such memories.'

My own opinion is that the Dauphin Louis quite deliberately demeaned his remembrance of his father's coronation for two reasons. First, he had been dazzled as a child by this single sight of Joan of Arc and Gilles de Rais, and now in seeking out the man who had been to him like a figure in a dream he was concerned to some degree to *reduce* him, to render him less fabulous and more real. Second, he desired by this stratagem also to put Gilles at his ease and to induce his confidence, for now, still talking rapidly and disjointedly in that insinuating nasal whine, his legs in their mud-splattered hose and riding-boots stretched out to the blazing logs, he abruptly switched the subject of their discourse.

The theme was all at once not Joan but soldiering. We were to understand, from hints and nose-rubbings and direct indiscretions, that the unfilial Louis was hatching a plot, assisted by the Duke of Bourbon, to hasten his progress to the throne of France by the removal of his father. Georges la Trémouïlle, that unsleeping cynic, was also involved in the conspiracy, of course; so was Duke Jean V of Brittany. These were all powerful men, as the young arch-conspirator reminded us, and la Trémouïlle was the Marshal's cousin besides, and the Duke Jean his liege lord. It would be as well to be on the same side as such notables, would it not? Above all, was it not always good policy to be at the side of the coming king? One way or another, he, Louis, was on the road to such a crowning as he had witnessed that fine day in Rheims, and when that happened, when he was King Louis XI, why then he would be in an even better position, would he not, to save the Marshal Gilles de Rais from his fate?

My lord knocked over his goblet. 'What fate?' he said.

The Dauphin sat there rubbing at his nose with his skinny forefinger. 'Our father has not employed your very great talents, Laval. Do you not waste your life here, idling on your estates, in some disgrace that no one understands, ignored by your King?'

'Gentle Dauphin,' Gilles said, with a sweetness which seemed to my ear frankly to acknowledge his relief at the discovery that his visitor had meant no more than a life of idleness when he spoke of a fate, and intended nothing else but a simple call to arms to save the idler from it, 'You may be sure of my loyalty when the time comes, gentle Dauphin.'

Louis must have recognized this for the mere diplomatic formula it was. He stood up. He put his hat on. 'Damn you, Laval,' he said. 'We offer you nothing less than your soul back as a soldier.'

My lord bowed, icily polite, though I noticed beads of sweat on his brow as he came up again. 'It's not my soldier soul that I need now,' he muttered. Then, as if realizing that he had spoken aloud a thought that had better stayed private, he said in a voice which sought to bring this duologue to an end: 'I rot here quite satisfactorily, highness, as you see . . .'

The Dauphin shook his head, baffled; then he held out his hand for Gilles to kiss, and took his leave.

XII

LA MEFFRAYE

There was a woman here now called La Meffraye. I did not understand her presence in the household. Her role seemed ill-defined; what did she do?

La Meffraye means 'the bird of prey', and it was not long before I gathered that this was only the woman's nickname. Her real name was Perrine Martin, and she came from either St Etienne-de-Montluc (which was what Griart told me) or Port-Launay (according Poitou). Perhaps it does not matter which provenance you believe, yet it strikes me as cogent to credit that she came from *somewhere*, since in other respects she bore about with her an air of unreality, floating through the castle as unpredictably and insubstantially as any ghost. She was an old woman – smiling, soft-footed, motherly. She had these rosy red cheeks, like the russet skin of certain kinds of apple. Whenever I saw her, indoors or out, she would be poorly dressed in a grey wool gown, with a shawl of tattered white lace over her shoulders, and a black velvet hood drawn tight about her head. Her face she invariably kept half-hidden under a veil of bunting. There was something both cronelike and deathly about La Meffraye.

The oddest thing – which I would be prepared to swear on oath – is that this creature had not inhabited the castle before I ran away. Yet when I asked Poitou where she had come from, and when, he looked at me as though I must be mad. 'Why, La Meffraye's always been here,' he said. 'You must have overlooked her, that's all.' Now, although Tiffauges was large and commodious, I consider this nonsense. The

Marshal's world had been almost exclusively male, and as someone susceptible to womanly presence and influence, I know I would have noticed if La Meffraye had indeed been there from the start. The fact is that when I took flight to Mortagne there was only one woman at the castle: that False Pucelle, the Dame des Armoires. I knew it; I was sure of it; no question. Yet, like several other such matters, this remark of Poitou's served to unsettle me, leaving me compelled to doubt my own perceptions of the reality of what happened at the castle. It made me feel mad, or as if in a dream. For in dreams, of course, people can come and go suddenly, without explanation or reason, appearing and disappearing so fast that there is hardly time to notice them. Then there you are, in another part of your dream, and it all slows down, and you see this one or that one, some figure that you know was always there, though up to now transparent or unfocussed. That is precisely how I felt about La Meffraye, after worrying about the secretary's insistence that she was not a newcomer. However, I must also put this remark of Poitou's in a category with one once made to me by Griart. I had reported to the fat man something said to me by our master when he responded flatly, 'The Marshal would not say that.' 'What do you mean?' said I. 'He *did* say that. I'm just telling you what he told me.' Griart shook his jowls and spat for luck. 'In that case,' he growled, 'you must have been talking to Rais le Héraut!' Well, the mere suggestion stunned me. *Could* some of my later conversations with the Marshal have been in fact with his double? I think not. I pray not. I am very nearly sure not. But it seems only right to mention here the dubiety put into my mind by Griart, though the actual colloquy referred to did not happen until later.

Returning to this time when I first noticed La Meffraye, and asked about her, I recall another exchange that took place with Poitou. We were standing together on one of the towers, when I saw the sinister figure of that old woman pass over the drawbridge and set off down the road, walking with quick little birdlike steps, a stick in one hand, a covered wicker basket over her arm.

'What does La Meffraye do?' I asked Poitou.

'She scours the country places and the moorland,' he replied.

'To what purpose?' I persisted.

Poitou coughed in his hand, then played with the cough with his finger. 'You could say that she catches butterflies,' he said.

'What does that mean?'

'It means,' said Poitou, 'that La Meffraye is a collector.'

'A collector,' I repeated. 'But what does she collect?'

I have never forgotten the look which Poitou then fixed upon me, his mouth an uncouth droop, his eyes red-rimmed. 'Father,' he said, 'she collects pretty children.'

The Marshal's secretary had this long thin scar on his left cheek. It stood out angrily now, as white as a bleached fish-bone. Flexing his wrists with a crack, he blew his nose and looked in his handkerchief. 'She makes up to certain sorts of children,' he said. 'Boys herding sheep and cattle. Girls picking fruit.'

I said nothing. I did not know what to say.

'Boys performing errands,' Poitou said. 'Girls begging alms. Boys and girls playing in the street. Boys and girls going to school, or on their way home from school.'

I was afraid. I could not look at him. I watched La Meffraye where her shape was just a sharp black dot in the distance.

At last I managed to speak again. I said: 'What happens to these children? Tell me that!'

Poitou shrugged. 'She flatters and caresses them. She brings them to the castle.'

'And then?' I demanded.

'Then our master is pleased,' said Poitou.

He strolled off, yawning. I knew he would not then have told me more, even if I had been able to ask him. I stood and drank deep draughts of the rising wind, my hands as cramped with cold as a scribe's in winter.

Soon after the Dauphin and his troop of cavalry had gone jingling away in the direction of Poitiers, the Marshal decided with rare prudence that Tiffauges had become an unhealthy place. I suspect, but do not know, that Prelati influenced him in this decision. The Italian was always a suave villain, and enjoyed being seen as such, and certainly he had not relished those moments of panic when Gilles had ordered him to destroy the alchemical furnaces. Prelati's dignity was at stake, and he favoured a removal from Tiffauges now that he had so nearly been caught there, so to speak, with his black magical breeches down.

Gilles also, once he had taken in the full import of the Dauphin's visit, came quickly to the view that we needed a change of scene. Tiffauges, as he remarked, had served its purpose. As I say, Prelati might very well have assisted him in his impetuous arrival at this conclusion. However, the choice of Machecoul as the place that we must now all inhabit was without doubt the Marshal's own. As it happens, I had not previously seen his castle there, but I was aware that he considered it the equal of Tiffauges, and that therefore it was his other favourite residence. As soon as we were removed to it, I saw why. Machecoul was in many respects a mirror image of the castle I knew already. The countryside round about was identical too – the same heathland and bogs, the same blasted trees, the same miles and miles and miles of desolation. We came there from Tiffauges at the end of January, on a raw sunless day, with three horses killed under us on the way. This last ill omen was entirely the product of my lord's insistence that we make a race of it – wilful and wild, that command, for a day of foul storms.

Before we left Tiffauges, I seized the opportunity to ask

Prelati if he had been much incommoded by the loss of those furnaces (having by this point decided that his work was a waste of time).

'Not at all,', the Florentine responded 'The alchemist's true furnace is his laboratory, his *laboratorium*, and that is in a sense indestructible.'

'What sense is that?' I asked.

'In the sense of prayer and work,' Prelati said. 'Come, Dom Eustache, surely I do not need to teach you Latin? *Labor* is labour, *oratorium* as you well know is prayer. Thus is my laboratory to be found wherever I work at my prayers.'

'Or where you might pray for work?' I interjected politely, although I fear he missed it.

For Prelati was in full rhetorical flood, and not to be dammed by either my scepticism or any small regard for etymology. 'Perhaps I could again suggest to you,' he declared, 'that as a priest ordained you would make the ideal alchemist? It is the same trade, when you come to understand the fundamentals. I have my transmutations, and you have your transubstantiations. What is it that you do daily in the Mass but take the *prima materia*, the base matter, bread and wine, and then turn them into the gold which is the sacraments?'

I bit my lips, first the upper one, then the lower, in chewing over this dangerously dubious theology. It seemed to me that the singularity of the eucharistic conversion lies in the un-doubted change of the *whole* substance, matter and form, and that to this there is no parallel in nature, and assuredly none in magic. The miracle, in any case, is God's, else the priest were a conjuror. But I said nothing.

Unfortunately Prelati did not need my assurance to keep his argument running. Face scrubbed and shining with his own peculiar self-generated soap of enthusiasm, he went on: 'In this world the most perfect substance is imperishable gold. Can we not start from that?'

'Maestro, I thought the idea was to *end* with it,' I said.

'Besides, what do you mean by "perfect"? It seems to me sometimes that there is a deal of perfect nonsense being talked about perfection, that is all. And what good does any of it do us? Better, I'd say, to accept our imperfections, and perhaps strive to make sense of them.'

But Prelati ignored me. Wetting his fingers on his long pink tongue, he proceeded to smooth his collar as though he considered I might concern myself with how he looked. That done, he said: 'The transmutation of base metals into gold is only part of the story, of course. What we are really talking about is the transmutation of man. The seven steps or stages of the alchemical process are at the same time seven steps or stages on the human path to blessedness.'

'That's good to know,' I said. 'But what exactly do you mean by blessedness?'

'Knowing God,' said Prelati. 'Man's ultimate happiness is to see God.'

'Through a dyadrous stone?'

'You are dry, father,' Prelati scolded. 'God is not mocked. God is perfect happiness. God is gold.'

I invented a sudden attack of dysentery to save listening to any more of this. Seated on the jakes I reminded myself of all that it is necessary now to remind the reader of: namely, that God is neither gold nor happiness, but the supreme spirit, who alone exists of Himself, and is infinite in all perfections. He is utterly distinct in reality and essence from all other things that exist or can be conceived, all of which, if they exist, get their existence from Him, the first cause uncaused. God is *eternal*, without beginning or end or succession; *all-knowing*, even of man's most secret thoughts; *immeasurable*, being at once in heaven, on earth, and in all places that are or can be; *just*, rendering to everyone according to his due, in this world or hereafter; *almighty*, for He can do whatever He wishes by the simple act of His will; *merciful*, for He wants the sinner not to die, but to be converted and live. God is *all-good*, untouched by the breath of any evil or imperfection, and His *beauty* is the cause of the being of all that exists.

That, I trust, is sufficient in the art of homiletics to undo any little knot tied in the reader's brain by Prelati's heresy. I might claim that he never convinced me with any of his nonsense for longer than it takes to say the *Credo*. Whether he influenced or corrupted the Marshal is another matter.

Winter died late and massively at Tiffauges, and nor did spring come early to Machecoul. The pattern of my existence was much as before, with daily recitations of the Divine Office, additional labours on high days of festival, attendance on the Marshal whenever he called. In the performance of my religious duties I was always punctilious, and perhaps never more so than at this time when anxieties about what was secretly going on behind closed doors began to obsess me. There were days at Machecoul, when first we removed there, that I spent in a swivet of fear for the soul of Gilles de Rais.

Not once did we visit the house of Perrot Cahn, and nor did the black man himself come to dance attendance on Gilles at the castle. That dinner and the terrible night which had preceded it seemed more than ever now like things in a dream.

Then, oddly, the name of St Etienne-de-la-Mer-Morte again cropped up. This, it will be recalled, was the place where de Sillé and the others, including Jean Lebreton, had threatened to take me, on the night that they kidnapped me from Mortagne. I knew that the Marshal had another castle there, with important dependencies. Now he announced that he was disposing of these, selling both castle and lands to Guillaume le Ferron, treasurer of the Duchy of Brittany. Le Ferron, I gathered, was acting merely as intermediary for the Duke. When I expressed surprise at the fact of the transaction, Prelati declared with bitterness that our master had announced that there was to be no more alchemical work. At first I did not see the connection, then I did. Since Gilles no longer had

hope of relieving his financial distress by the manufacture of
gold, he had elected to sell castles to replenish his coffers. I
might add that as before at Tiffauges there was never the least
prudence in the manner that money was spent at Machecoul.
The opposite, indeed, was about the case. I doubt if it once
crossed my lord's mind that he might save money by being
less lavish, say, in his entertainments, or by ceasing to maintain
a small private army, or by cutting down on the number of
priests and choristers in his train. At Machecoul, simply, there
was to be no more alchemy. The castle of St Etienne had
therefore to be turned into gold.

This decision and transaction were to have the most desperate consequences in due course. It is not too much to say that
if Gilles had never sold that castle to le Ferron, and perhaps
even more pertinently if le Ferron's brother Jean had not been
in minor holy orders, the Marshal's crimes might have gone
on and on, without discovery, unpunished, for years innumerable. As it was, this year of God's mercy to us in the person of
Jesus Christ 1440, which began with our removal to Machecoul and the sale of St Etienne-de-la-Mer-Morte, was to see
an end to the evils, their horror revealed, and the Marshal
brought before first an earthly and then the divine judgement.
But I must not run on ahead of my own story.

Gilles' decision to abandon alchemy must have been taken
during a short spell of sobriety which occurred in this beginning time at Machecoul. It was then, sobering up, that he
also took the opportunity to confide in me (or so it seemed)
that he now perceived the whole business of the visit of the
False Pucelle to have been a nonsense, a drunken delusion, a
self-indulgence in wishful play-acting along the same lines as
his pageant-play but far more reprehensible in that by welcom-
ing the Dame des Armoires to Tiffauges, and permitting her
to stay there, he had been guilty of insulting the glorious
memory of Joan of Arc.

I found this moving, and perhaps was mistaken in letting

my lord know it. I say mistaken because immediately he realized that his words had been believed by me, he began to deny them. Now, shifting his ground, he claimed that he had known all along that the Dame des Armoires was an impostor, but that he had admitted her quite deliberately to Tiffauges, playing along with *her* dream, allowing her to think that she was fooling him to the top of his bent, even letting her believe that she was improving her own act of imposture by extracting from him intimate details of the real Joan's life – how she walked, how she talked, the substance of her visions, what her 'voices' told her – all this done with conscious cunning and delicacy, since it had been his ambition to persuade or compel the woman to play the part of Joan in a new perform-ance of *The Mystery of the Siege of Orléans* in which he had intended to play himself . . .

I found this less than moving; cynical, in fact. However, I was even more mistaken in letting my lord see that reaction. He flew into a fury, cursing me for what he termed my lack of subtlety. And then, with scarce a pause for breath or thought, he launched upon yet a third explanation of his behaviour in the matter of being host to the False Pucelle. By this account, if I understood him right, we had been visited by a minor demoness. The creature I had seen riding up on a white horse, and then eating and drinking in his company, finally running away thrashed and naked in the snow, had been (he said) a spirit called forth by the invocations of Prelati, summoned to assist him in the recovery of certain immortal memories of Joan and her mission.

Well, I found this deeply shocking. 'Do you say,' I asked him, 'that the creature came from hell?'

'Not at all,' said he. 'She was an earth-bound spirit.'

Not for the first or the last time, I found myself even more confused by my master's explanations than I had been by his mysteries. Which version, in any case, was I really supposed to believe? The truth, so it seems to me, is that Gilles had that in his mentality which never could bear it when his words were believed. If I had not accepted and been moved by his first declaration that he had been deceived by the False Pucelle, and felt he had thereby dishonoured Joan of Arc, I doubt if he would have had the need to invent the alternative stories. There was that in Gilles de Rais which abhorred simplicity. Which is perhaps to say that there was that in Gilles de Rais which adored untruth. This makes my task the more difficult as his chronicler. Still, I set the man down as I knew him, with all his contradictions and deceits.

La Meffraye came with us to Machecoul as well. It was not long before I stood on a new tower that was just like the old, and saw her pass by on the road below, the black veil over her face, as usual.

XIII

THE APE BEGINS TO CHATTER

My master's newfound sobriety did not last long. Within a week of his command that Prelati should abandon the alchemical work, and the three contradictory accounts of what he thought of the False Pucelle, I saw the bottle again in Gilles' left hand and the goblet in his right. This drinking would start in the morning, and then go on all day. It was not often, as I now began to notice, that I ever saw him at night. In my innocence, therefore, it was possible for me to suppose that drinking was his lust in the night time too. Notice that I say lust, and could not say pleasure. Gilles drank like a man enraged, as if there was some fire deep in him blazing that only wine and more wine could put out. He drank, in other words, to blot out knowledge. His tragedy was that wine made the fire burn more.

There is a Talmud parable which says that Satan came one day to drink with Noah, and slew a lamb, a lion, a pig, and an ape, to teach Noah that man before wine is in him is a *lamb*, when he drinks moderately he is a *lion*, when like a sot he is a *swine*, but that any further excess makes him an *ape* which senselessly chatters and jabbers.

This is a parable I have often called to mind when thinking over the way the relationship between the Marshal and myself now deepened and intensified in those first few weeks of our coming to Machecoul. While outside the confines of the castle Gilles was becoming involved in a wrangle with Guillaume le Ferron over the sale of St Etienne, within the walls of Machecoul the central play of what I take to be his cat-and-mouse game with me became predominant.

Briefly, I have to suspect that my master now supposed that I knew something of his hideous secrets, and that probably it had crossed his mind to kill me. That he did not kill me may have been just my good luck. Alternatively, it could be that Gilles desired not so much my silence as my understanding. For whatever reason, and most certainly because the wine made a chattering ape of him, he fell into the habit of calling me to him in his cups. Because I was required to drink whatever he poured out for me, I cannot have absolute trust in my memory of these sessions. Yet in those days my stomach was good, and I could drink as long as any. Perhaps here is another reason for my lord favouring a simple priest with the confessed complexities of his heart? He had established I could hold my liquor, and that even when drunk I was willing to do his will. I should say also (though it hurts to say it) that in my opinion it was my innocence that made him confide in me. He needed to reveal and conceal even in the act of revelation. What better person to whom to tell your secrets than one of virgin understanding?

'Nero never wore the same clothes twice. Did you know that, Dom Eustache? Nero never wore the same clothes twice. I read that in Suetonius.'

Gilles sat by the fire, with his legs stretched out to it. The wind roared in the chimney. His eyes were like a robin's for their brightness. Yet I thought that he looked terrible, impure, a little sore on his lip as if his blood must be unclean. He was glaring at me now, very blue-eyed and fierce.

'Caligula drank pearls dissolved in vinegar. I found that in Suetonius too, you know. And when his guests wanted gold, he gave them bread and meat of gold to eat. Imagine that! Picture the greedy ones trying to swallow it whole! Picture the other guests who dined with Tiberius. He used to fill them up with enormous quantities of wine and then tie strings about their genitals so that it was impossible for them to urinate. He thought nothing of executing twenty people a day. Nero's

very mules were shod with silver, and his muleteers wore
priceless Carnusian wool.'

Much of this made little sense to me. I sat and cradled my
cup, and watched my master. He was grinning with a complete abandon that made him look sometimes like a satyr, but
from certain angles of the candlelight like something more
sinister. It was a dark day. Rossignol had been instructed to
light the candles early, singing as he did so. Rossignol had
always to sing, whatever he did. He was a blond, wizened
creature; a once-pretty castrato.

These titbits from the *Lives of the Caesars* by Suetonius were
Gilles' route, round and about, to his childhood. He spoke at
length of his grandfather, old Jean de Craon. He had taught
the boy in his care that he was not truly subject to the laws of
God or man. The young Gilles had revelled in imagined
omnipotence. Had he not been the heir to three vast fortunes?
Was he not Caesar, Nero and Caligula in one body, outstrip-
ping his own monarch in wealth and power? The world was
his, and he was born to enjoy it.

All this poured from that drunken mouth where the sore
bled like a crushed raspberry. And the wind whistled in the
tapestries along the walls, and Gilles spoke of the luxury and
vice of his boyhood. He had grown up to become the perfect
egotist, charming when he felt like it, brutal and cruel when
he did not. He had waited until he was twenty before asserting
himself. Then, he said, looking at me slyly through his fingers
the while he said it, then it had been his grandfather's turn to
feel the backlash. Then he had taken upon himself the admini-
stration of all his lands and estates and used them as he
wished, taking no advice from his grandfather and no account
of anything he said.

'No doubt,' I said, 'he loved you.'

Gilles shivered like a dying dog. 'I think it is time you said
your prayers,' he said.

Next day there was more of the same, about the angelic

glory of his childhood, though it sounded like a little hell to me. Again he spoke of de Craon, and of how the old man 'felt the backlash' when it was Gilles' turn to assume the upper hand. Blue eyes flaring, long legs straddling apart, my master demanded to know what I thought of this. I felt hypnotized. I did not feel capable of discussing it. Making a quick, crooked smile, I asked for more wine.

'He taught me to drink,' said the Marshal, seeming pleased to oblige me. 'He taught me early pleasure in small cruelties. Nothing extreme, do you understand? Nothing beyond what other men have thought, or felt, or fancied, even done . . . Then he taught me how to soldier.'

I am setting this down exactly as I remember it, with every ellipsis and diversion. Even at the time I wished that my lord had pursued that line about his grandfather having tutored him in small cruelties, but he was off now in a different direction altogether.

'Consider,' he said. 'If I kill one man I am a murderer. If I kill one hundred men, then I am a soldier. But what if I kill *everyone*, every soul that lives – what am I then?'

I shook my head, baffled.

Gilles laughed in my face.

'Why, *God!*' he shouted, slapping his thigh with his hand. 'You, little priest, you of all people should know that one. A man may kill many, but God is the one who kills us all!'

I considered this vile blasphemy, but held my tongue. Then I asked him to tell of his early campaigning as a soldier. Gilles spoke with insouciant candour. At the age of sixteen he had won the esteem of our suzerain, Jean V, the Duke of Brittany, by his courage and skill in the campaign which ended the ancient rivalry between the houses of de Montfort and de Penthièvre. At twenty-two, following the Duke's brother, the Constable Arthur de Richemont, he had entered the desperate service of Charles VII, with a troop maintained at his own expense, and distinguished himself in what at first seemed the hopeless resistance to the English arms. When Joan of Arc appeared he was charged with the special duty of watching over her personal safety, and, from the relief of Orléans to the repulse at the gates of Paris, he had been ever at her side. In the coronation ceremonies at Rheims he received, though but twenty-five years old, the high dignity of Marshal of France, and in the September following he was further honoured with permission to add to his arms a border of the royal *fleurs-de-lis*. There was then no dignity beneath the crown to which his ambition might not aspire, for he maintained himself so skilfully between the opposing factions of the Constable and of the royal favourite, la Trémouïlle, that when the latter fell, in the year of grace 1433, his credit at the court was unimpaired.

A pale, tragic resignation fixed Gilles' face like a mask as he recited all this for my benefit. Outside, I knew, a yellow fog had come seeping up from the river, and the castle drifted in it like some shipwrecked hulk. I heard the hoarse crying of kites where they swooped beyond the window-slit. The flames roared and struggled upward in the hearth.

My master poured himself more brandy-wine. On these occasions he always dismissed Griart and his other bodyservants, seeming to prefer it that we were alone together. A curious, impersonal light gleamed in his eyes.

'When I first saw her,' he said, 'she looked like a white flame. It was at Chinon, towards the evening, on the twenty-third day of February, 1429.'

I hardly dared to breathe. At last, the moment I had been waiting for! Inspired by reminiscence of his soldiering, my lord Gilles de Rais was to tell me of Joan of Arc.

'She had arrived for an audience with the Dauphin. Jean de Metz accompanied her, and Bertrand de Poulengy. She wore a black doublet, with grey tunic and trunk-hose, and her dark hair cut round at the neck as a boy's would be. I remember that hall was filled full with the people of the court, all splendid, each in the robes of his order and the jewels of his estate. Light shone from their silks and from their velvets, and there was light from fifty cressets on the walls. In that hall stood Regnault de Chartres, Chancellor of France and Archbishop of Rheims, and that big-bellied cousin of mine Georges la Trémouïlle, then the man who had most power with the King, and Raoul de Gaucourt, who was master of the household. In that hall were full three hundred lords and knights close crowded, all full of talk and moving till she came.'

Gilles sipped his brandy-wine. He sat staring for a minute into the fire, his eyebrows like black rainbows in its glow. Then he fixed me with a shrewd, far-distant look, as a hawk perhaps looks far down in his search over open country. 'When I first saw her,' he said, 'when she came walking into that great high hall at Chinon, something dropped away from my soul – some crab, some cancer. She was short and sturdy to see, strong of body and clear of mind, as anyone would know from her way of walking. Simple and straight in her carriage, she was. It was Louis de Bourbon, Count of Vendôme, who led her in.'

He fell silent, poking at logs with the tip of his boot. There were questions I would have liked to ask, but I knew better. Holding my breath, I waited for him to continue. And, before long, he did.

Gilles said: 'There were some there who had heard how she had said that she would know the King by divine power. They said to her, "Look, there is the King!" and pointed to another as she passed. Or again they said, "Look, that's him, over there!" The King, you see, to test her, had taken care to put on no mark of rank, and did not stand apart or look for deference. He was dressed as any other might be, and mixed in with the crowd in that bright assembly. She went straight through them like a sword through water. She went straight up to him, without halt or turning, and knelt down at his feet, and bent her head. Then, looking up into his face, she said,

"God give you long life, noble King." Charles said to her: "I am not the King." She answered: "In God's name, sir, you are the King, you and no other!" Then she demanded troops to relieve Orléans, promising that when that was done she would guard him to Rheims to be anointed and crowned. All this, she told him, was the will of God.'

I crossed myself. Gilles smiled. His eyes were watchful. He was pouring himself another drink from the bottle. When he had finished, he said, 'Tell me, father, you believe in the Devil, don't you?'

'I never met him,' I answered, as evasively as I dared. 'But yes, I believe in him, of course. It is of divine faith that the Devil and his wicked companions were created by God, that they were good and by their own fault fell into sin, that the Devil tempted man to his fall, and that he and the other fallen angels still tempt and persecute mankind.'

Gilles nodded. 'It is certain, then,' he said, 'that the Devil is a pure spirit, and as such he must have an intelligence of a very high order?'

'And a will now obstinately bent to evil,' I reminded him.

'Evil,' said Gilles. His voice possessed a sing-song note of deep indifference. He sounded like a man who talks in his sleep. 'What is evil, father?'

'Evil,' I said, 'is a negation of good. It is the absence of a perfection that is due. In one word, a privation.'

'Is it not real then, evil?' Gilles de Rais demanded.

I answered him with care, remembering my training. 'My lord, Aquinas assures us that it cannot be real in itself. Evil is only real in so far as it presupposes the good which it limits. Evil, you might say, is founded on the good.'

Gilles was frowning horribly. 'What then of the Devil?' he persisted. 'Is he not the supreme evil and the cause of all evil?'

'No,' I said. 'That is Manichaeism, and quite wrong, and I do not claim merely that *I* think so; rather, I tell you that the Church knows so, and has taught us clearly in the matter for a thousand years. Think of it this way: since evil is a privation, a total privation would be absolute nothing. This notion of the Devil as the supreme evil, and the cause of all evil, is not of our faith. The Devil does not sit on the left hand of God!'

My master seemed to dislike my orthodoxy. He stuck his black-booted foot in the fire and kicked the logs till they blazed. He said, petulantly: 'So God causes evil?'

'Not so. God permits evil that good may ensue.'

'But God causes sin!'

'My lord, God is not the cause of sin. God permits sin that human free will may be safeguarded.'

Gilles sighed, and slumped into silence, wriggling his boot in the fire as if his foot were some offending member he would like to burn off. He continued in this dangerous game for some while, apparently undismayed by the heat of the flames. When he tired of it, he turned to more brandy-wine.

'From the start,' he said suddenly, 'I was her friend and her champion. From the moment she came into that hall, against the scepticism of the Dauphin and the court, I insisted on my belief in her divine mission. My cousins, Guy and André de Laval, the Count d'Alençon and Dunois, the Bastard of Orléans, all of them followed my lead.'

This habit of disjointedly going from one theme or story to another was something I learned to grow used to when my lord was in his cups. It worried me that I could not find connections perhaps apparent to him. On the other hand, the Joan theme interested me so much that I was invariably grateful and newly attentive whenever he came back to it.

I could wish that at this point he had seen fit to speak of that sign which Joan is known to have given to the Dauphin at Chinon, whereby his mind was changed so that he knew she was from God. I have heard that this sign consisted in her knowledge of a secret prayer which the Dauphin prayed, a prayer known only to him and to God before that day, but which Joan then told him of, having had word of it from her kinsmen in paradise. Alas, this was not of import to Gilles de Rais.

'Four things she promised. These were those four things: first, she would make an end of the siege of Orléans; second, she would crown the King in Rheims; third, Paris would come back to its true king; fourth, the Duke of Orléans, captive in the Tower of London, would come home.' Gilles had been counting out this catalogue on his fingers, with all the pedantry of the drunken ape. 'That was the order she gave these things to come. That was the order in which they came to pass.' He drank deep from his silver goblet. When he glanced at me now, a smile creased his face, showing the strong white teeth. 'I gave her a sorrel mare,' he said, 'lovely in colour, and well-made, with a powerful broad neck and the hollow back that betokens a swift runner. And I had made for her, in Tours, by an armourer of that town, a suit of white armour. Its plates were thick and heavy, and the helm with its visor was stout – the whole almost impossible for a woman to wear. She wore that impossible suit, and she wore it well. And she had a standard made, of fine white linen, with emblems upon it described to her by her voices: the lilies of France sewn there, and a painting of Our Lord with the world in his hand, and on either side angels adoring, with the motto *Jesus, Mary*. She bore that standard herself, on its long staff. As for the blazon on her shield, which was blue, that was a white dove with a scroll in its beak, and written on this scroll the words: *By command of the King of Heaven*.' Gilles smacked his lips over the inscription. His eyes were blazing. As he went on I noticed again – yet for the first time this particular day – the sharp sweet scent of violets on the air. 'It was the end of April when we set forth. She rode at the head of the army, between me and Jean d'Aubon, her squire. And a week before we rode she made this prophecy: that Orléans she would save, and the English put to flight, and that in that saving and putting to flight she would be wounded by a shaft and yet not mortally. You believe in prophecy, Dom Eustache?'

'I do,' I said. 'It is a gift of God, an extraordinary grace which may be bestowed upon anyone.'

Gilles nodded, though I think he was hardly listening. 'Remember her words, then. She said she would be wounded by a shaft before Orléans, and yet not mortally. She told this to the King, and many others. Before we rode, she had a sword found too. She instructed the priests at the shrine of St Catharine of Fierbois, a day's ride beyond Chinon, that there by the altar they should dig and they would find buried in the earth an old sword with five crosses graven on it. That sword was found, and it was hers. She had a strong sheath of leather made for this sword, and kept it at her side whenever we rode. But though it was often in her hand, it never drew blood, and only once did I ever see her strike a blow with it: that, when she used the flat of it to drive out a whore from our camp. Her sword was for her a signal of command. With that sword in her right hand, and that standard in her left, she would stand in the heat of the battle crying *"Hardi!"* to her own. Of all which own, there was none that was more dedicate than I. Well then, now then, what was I telling you, father? Ah yes, that April day we rode forth from Blois, and the banks of the river Loire were broidered with violets –'

XIV

THE APE CHATTERS ON

'Violets!' I cried. 'My lord did you say *violets?*'

'I did,' said Gilles de Rais. 'And what of that?'

Little dagger-points of light gleamed in his eyes as he looked at me, drinking, over the tilted brim of his silver cup. The stone pavings of the floor felt suddenly insubstantial below my feet. I thought of that yellow fog swirling outside, its lapping at the towers of the castle, and this, combined with my master's drunken stare, made everything seem to spin into a dream. For a moment, I swear, I heard music play, although there were no minstrels in the gallery. Then, again, I suffered the distinct impression that the castle was some vast ship, torn from its moorings in space and time, adrift in a limitless, fog-enshrouded ocean of pure nothingness. I could hear the creak of timber, and sea-gulls calling. Then a fresh log fell forwards into the fire, with a crack that brought me back to our reality, and I knew that what I had heard was not the remembered gulls' crying from Ushant but the sound of the kites where they circled about Machecoul.

'It is nothing,' I said. 'Pray continue, my lord.'

'We came to Orléans,' Gilles said. 'We went by the southern bank, to her displeasure. She wanted to go by the north, and come straight on the town. She was angry when she found I had misled her. Her idea of military strategy was naïve. She intended to march straight at the English and attack immediately while our soldiers were full of enthusiasm and fresh from the confessional. I thwarted that plan. The enemy held Beaugency and Meung on the northern bank, and their main

camp was there outside the western gate of the city. The only
gate that was open was in the east, the Burgundian gate. My
intention was to march past Orléans on the south side, cross
the river and enter by this gate. This we did, although she
told me nevermore to go against her, for she had better guides
than me, in heaven.' Gilles smiled, and bit his lip ruefully, so
that the little sore bled anew. 'I can never forget the moment
she told me that. A strong wind was blowing down the river
from the east, making it impossible for us to get our boats
across to Chécy village with their cargoes of provisions for
Orléans. As she spoke her anger with me, she held up her
hand. That east wind fell, then it started to blow from the
west. So strong the wind blew that each barge under sail
could tow two others. I was frightened. I never again went
against her.'

This sounded to me like the rankest superstition, since
Gilles was giving credit for the wind to Joan. Yet I was sure
that the Maid herself would have given all credit to God, so I
said nothing, being anxious to hear my lord continue. Which,
fortified with more brandy-wine, he did, as follows.

'She came into Orléans like an angel of God. It was at
night, on the Friday, the twenty-ninth of April. The people
came rushing out to meet her, lighting her way with burning
torches, shouting, women and men and little children surging
against her stirrups to touch and kiss her mail. A flame from
one of their torches caught her standard, setting it on fire. She
extinguished it like one who had served long in the wars,
turning the staff down to let the burning flag touch the
ground and riding her horse over it to crush out the flame.
When she raised it again, she looked like God.'

I could not let this pass. 'You say too much!'

Gilles leapt to his feet. He lurched angrily towards me. 'I
say what there is to be said, no more, no less.' He seized me
by my scapular and shook me as a dog might shake a rat it
holds in its teeth, then let me fall back in my high-backed

chair. 'God save us from His holy priests,' he muttered. Then falling back in his own chair and drinking now directly from the bottle, he launched into a monologue I could not claim to understand, though its wild weird words are burned upon my memory, and having made note of them upon the day in question I am enabled now to set them down here with some hope of accuracy, though any meaning they may possess continues to elude me.

Gilles de Rais said: 'In her presence, for that brief while, going in the company of God, *killing* for God's sake, my will subsumed in hers, my trouble left me. I was, for that shining span, no longer at the mercy of the evil of the imagination of my own heart. Was I not *her* heart, this woman who was so soft a kiss would bruise her? I worshipped what I thought I knew in her. I mean – not carnally; not the girl who would eat strawberries all day long, and filled her trunk-hose oh so prettily. I mean what moved in her, and lived, and had its being. I was her man. I desired her to triumph utterly. I tore myself from my shadow at her behest. I tell you, father, this was more than love. She was in spite of lovers. She was the dark. And I was her fool – fool not to know what knowledge is, pretending to partake of it, to eat and drink its accidental sacraments.' He fell silent for a moment. Then he said querulously, 'What filled that suit of white armour so that it looked to me like an empty fury, and she stood exhausted, leaning on her sword, like another woman ravished by the Holy Ghost?' He had asked this question, I need scarcely add, of himself, for by now my lord was oblivious of my presence. I thought, in fact, that he had fallen asleep, but he suddenly said one more thing. 'I was her mirror,' he whispered. 'Who looks in me, sees her.' That said, he slept.

The next day was a day of storms. Calling me to him, Gilles resumed immediately where he had ceased.

'I desired her to triumph utterly,' he said. 'I wanted to die in her service, perhaps in the last moment of her taking Paris.

That was my soul's secret prayer. Was this wicked, Dom Eustache?'

'Suicide is a mortal sin against the fifth commandment,' I replied. 'But to hope for death in a just war is perhaps a different matter, and not dishonourable.'

I watched the Marshal pour out the brandy-wine into two golden chalices. These chalices were huge, with ornate handles like wings, but he intended us to drink from them. I sipped at mine slowly and with difficulty, while he gulped his wine down wholesale. Outside the castle I knew the clouds must be fuming up from the horizon as if breathed out from some gigantic cauldron of ice and fire. Even inside the turret where we sat the air smelt steely of the rain. I heard the storm at the windows and I shivered. 'Will you tell me more, my lord, of the siege of Orléans?'

'What more is there to tell?' said Gilles de Rais. 'Orléans was not important. *She* was the miracle. The war was just what happened where she was.'

I must have frowned at this, for his own brow blackened. 'Consider,' he said. 'Out of all men, she chose me to be the captain of her captains. Twice I carried her in my arms from the battle when she was wounded.'

'So her prophecy came true,' I said, without surprise.

'On that Saturday, the seventh day of May,' Gilles said. 'During the action against the forts of St Augustine and St Jean le Blanc, at noon, an English crossbolt thick as a man's finger struck right through the white shoulder plate over her left breast, and she fell. In the panic that followed, she was deserted by all but me. I dressed her wound with oil, and before the reddening of the day she had returned to battle. Again she fell wounded, and I sucked out the bad blood from her wound. Night was falling, and we heard the Bastard's trumpets sounding the retreat.'

'The Bastard?' I queried.

'Dunois,' Gilles explained. 'Bastard of Orléans, half-brother of the Duke who lay prisoner in England, and uncle of Alençon's witch of a wife.'

'Why did he sound the retreat?'

'He believed in her,' Gilles said, as if this was an answer, 'but he did not believe in her enough. She gave him and others meaning, but with me alone she made sense. Well, that is vainglorious, no doubt. I tell you, father, she shone with such sense, that woman, there was so much light about her, such illumination, that it drew out sense from me, who am unmeaning, and she lightened my darkness, and set fire to it. That night before the forts, with darkness falling, even as the Bastard's trumpets wailed retreat, she got up from her second wounding and she seized her standard in her bloody hand and commanded me to make the counter-attack. We were to go straight against the enemy, she said, one last advance, and when her flag touched against the ramparts, then all would be ours! "Lady," I said, "where you go, I will follow." And so she rode forward, and I rode at her side, and when the white tip of her standard touched the walls where the English were, then their defences crashed to the ground and our assault poured in! The English host withdrew from the forts remaining. Orléans was free. The siege had lasted for eight months. She relieved it in eight days. There, priest, I have told you its story.'

My master was in the vilest of tempers that day. He sucked brandy-wine from his chalice with the sullen application of a pig. It was a while before he reached the ape-jabber stage, as a result. During his brooding and drinking, he answered just a single question of the several I put to him.

'What do you recall of the morning *after* the battle which won back Orléans? What did you see when the sun came up?'

'I saw a horse,' said Gilles de Rais. 'I saw a dead black stallion. It lay in what had once been no man's land, its throat-vessels rat-ripped, the cage of its skeleton smashed, flaps and patches of flesh hanging loose at its neck and at its quarters, its knotted veins like red string in the dirt . . . That's what I remember. I never saw blood flow but that it made the hair rise severally upon my head.'

I had expected an image of a more triumphant character. Perhaps it was that day's storm of wind and rain which made my lord so quickly morbid.

Either for that or for some other reason, when the liquor inspired him again to eloquence he had little to say of his further military exploits with Joan of Arc. It is probable that he was bitter about the matter. I have learned since from other sources that after the victory at Orléans the success of their campaign was greatly hindered by lack of the resources of war. Joan had less material assistance from the Dauphin than is commonly supposed, and again Gilles stepped into the breach. With his cousins the Lavals, he mortgaged some of his estates to increase the personnel for the attack on Jargeau, where Suffolk and other English nobles were captured. Nor, when my lord again addressed me now on this day of storms, did he have anything to say regarding that time a few months after Orléans when the King was crowned at Rheims and he was made a Marshal of France and given, like Joan herself, royal letters patent authorizing him 'in recognition of his glorious service' to show in his coat of arms a bordering of *fleurs-de-lis*. Since he had no self-esteem in this matter, perhaps I may be permitted to comment that my lord was barely twenty-five years of age when he thus attained the summit of his ambitions, and it seems to me a striking commentary upon the manner in which those ambitions had been realized that he reached fulfilment through humility and the surrender of his will to a higher purpose. This, I take it, was the true moral burden of what might otherwise appear to be his idolatry in what he had to say to me of Joan.

Throughout these intimate speeches on this subject, I believe I noticed, not once did my master use Joan's name. *She – she – she* – It was always 'she' – like an impersonal force, or a progeny – never Joan, or the Maid, or even the Pucelle. This

refusal to name the most important personage in his life, or
perhaps just careful or instinctive avoidance of invoking her
by name, struck me as very curious, if somehow right. I did
not understand his reasons for it, and the passage of the years
has failed to clarify the matter. One other minor critical
observation which it occurs to me to offer here in commentary
is that while the Dauphin Louis had said that as a child Joan
had appeared to him both awkward and uncomely, my
master's adult view seemed rather the opposite. Perhaps she
was a vision differently apprehended, thus to be variously interpreted?

I should say that by the time that Gilles resumed he was
quite drunk; drunker, indeed, than I had ever seen him
before. The storm raged overhead, and about the castle, with
thunder and lightning now, while my lord sat playing with
the crown wheel and the hands of his balance clock. Instead
of reciting the success of the royal armies in marching on
Paris, he spoke suddenly of Joan's capture and her martyrdom.

'It was the archer of a captain who served that one-eyed
lord, John of Luxemburg, Burgundy's right-hand man, who
caught her by the coat and dragged her from her horse and
took her captive. One year later she was burned to death. She
who had been a flame was turned to ashes. How is this
possible? tell me that, priest! *How did God allow this to happen to
one of His saints?*'

There was such anguish in Gilles' voice that I found it more
than usually difficult to attempt comfort by means of the
formula offered by our faith: namely, that God's plan is
mysterious, and it falls to us only to know that He draws
ultimate good out of every physical evil. My master would not
even let me finish the sentence. He snapped the hour hand
from his balance clock. 'You know the crimes they found her
guilty of? You, monk, you know what they called her? Sorceress, divineress, false prophet, witch, and heretic! She was

declared apostate and blasphemer. They said she rejoiced in bloodshed, and that she was indecent.' Gilles spat out the words, stabbing at me with the snapped-off hand of his clock to emphasize each filthy epithet. 'This was the Church said this,' he reminded me. 'This was not just the English, or the Burgundians. Nobody need care what the English thought about anything. The Church called her witch and whore, and then God let them burn her. Is this not insupportable, Dom Eustache Nobody? Heaven turning a deaf ear to one of her own? The world is mad, where truth and purity are burned at the stake in the market-place, and evil triumphs. When I learned of her burning I knew malevolence at the heart of all – a deep and a fetid and a dazzling darkness. I saw the dark face of God, then. And it peeled away. And there was nothing there. Nothing.'

I feared my lord would fall down and dance like St Vitus in his spiritual fury. He was shaking with rage as he butchered that expensive little clock. The other hand was wrenched off in a single savage gesture. Then, drawing his dagger, he plunged it deep in the works. The crown wheel shattered, the escarpments came tumbling out and fell chattering across the floor like broken teeth.

'My lord!' I cried, then prudently held my tongue.

I was very scared. But Gilles, once the clock lay broken at his feet, seemed exhausted and content just to drink brandy-wine to assuage his despair. Lightning lit the darkening chamber from end to end before he spoke again. Then, watching it stab the gloom, he said: 'In that same year she burned, my grandfather died. She was ashes, he was clay, and anything became possible. I turned my back on military glory. That, like all else, left only the taste of excrement in my mouth. I retired to my estates. I swore defiance. I made a pact, priest; do you understand me?'

'With the Devil?' I said.

'No, with God!' said Gilles de Rais.

He never explained this remark, and I have never understood it. It is my belief that in that year of grace 1431 my lord may well have fallen into a state of mind akin to madness. The world, by his own account, then suddenly seemed to him random, meaningless, and empty, all its purpose drained or withdrawn like a tide going out never to return. We can imagine with what saturnine gibes of defiance, almost in the spirit of a monstrous metaphysical jest, he swore to his Maker that henceforth he would serve evil alone. As he had been linked with Joan in all that had been glorious and noble, so would he take upon himself actually to commit those crimes laid to her account which he knew existed only in the imagination of her judges. He would blaspheme, evoke evil spirits, deal in sorcery, rejoice in bloodshed and indecency. Is this, perhaps, what he meant by 'a pact with God'?

'I made curious machines,' he told me now. 'Clockwork nightingales that sang. Automata. I had gardens laid out for my pleasure; mazes, fountains. Ah, I see by the stupid ignorant light in your eye that you approve all this . . . Do you suppose I indulged in a taste for art to keep my hand in touch with grace and order? Fool! Know, then, that I only made these things to destroy them! Sooner or later, one day, I would smash them. Ah, a broken automaton is so much more amusing. And then the pleasures of the hunt became the final pleasure you can imagine . . .' He looked at me keenly, biting the sore on his lip until it bled. 'Little fool, you cannot imagine it, can you? That's why I like you, that's why I let you live!'

I dared not speak. I counted the seconds between the bolts of lightning and the thunder, to determine how near we were to the heart of the storm. Not more than a few miles, by that reckoning. But Gilles' lips were working; my master was talking again.

'All I wanted, Dom Eustache, was to understand God's meaning by joining in His game with us. There, surely, you must see that my purpose was theological at bottom? I found the way. Isn't that what we have to seek? I found the way even to wed my earlier dalliances in lust, my wasteful little luxuries of the flesh, to this profound vocation. Not vice, you must understand, but infinite evil. The infinite and eternal evil of God Himself!'

I am forcing my hand to record this, even as I compelled my ears and my brain to hear and absorb it that black day at Machecoul. The storm raged over the castle, thunder and lightning in the same blink of the eyes, as my master reached his drunken climax.

'She was holy innocence itself,' he said. 'And that sweet holy innocent had been cruelly done to death. Had I killed her, father? In my secret heart: did I desire to abominate her body, and to murder her? Well, I will admit to you now that perhaps I could have saved her from the fire. I had the men and the means. I lay at Louviers, just sixteen miles from Rouen, with two armed companies. La Hire and d'Alençon would certainly have helped me. But I did not save her. I did nothing. I did not act. That vacillation which was always at the root of me, my most grievous fault, ruling my soul from the start until I found a purpose and a direction in her strong bladed will, that same terrible vacillation of spirit came to paralyse me utterly in the hour of her greatest need. Be sure, I hated myself for her burning. But then I hated her more for mine.'

Gilles drained his chalice and hurled it at the wall as thunder and lightning together made the tower shake. Then, in a halting, strangulated voice, he said: 'It began, I must tell you, when La Meffraye brought me the brother and sister on their way to their first communion. I had them dressed up in little black doublets, with grey tunics, and pretty trunk-hose . . .'

He could not go on, thank God. My lord Gilles de Rais either could not or would not spell out the vileness of what he had done. But throwing himself on his knees before me, and clutching at my robe with wine-stained hands, he begged me to hear him as soon as possible *in sacramental confession.*

XV

SACRAMENTAL CONFESSION

The sacrament of penance was instituted by Our Lord Jesus Christ. In it, by the absolution of a priest, acting as judge, sins committed after baptism are forgiven to a person who confesses them with sorrow and a purpose of amendment The sacrament is in the nature of a judgement, in which the priest is the judge and the penitent is the accused and self-accuser. It is an article of faith that this power was given to the Church in the circumstances related in *John* xx, 21–23: 'Receive ye the Holy Ghost: Whose soever sins ye remit, they are remitted unto them; and whose soever sins ye retain, they are retained.' The confession of sins is ordered in *James* v, 15–16, and in *John* i, 9; and the exercise of the discipline in the earliest days of the Church is referred to in *1 Corinthians* v, and *2 Corinthians* ii, 5–11, as well as in *Galatians* vi, 1. The governing principle is laid down that the sin of the member affects the whole body, and therefore that society is bound to deal with it both from pity for the sinner and for the sake of its own purity. Though penance means *poena* (i.e. punishment), and it was apparently the doctrine of the early Church that sins must be atoned for in part by the punishment of the sinner, on the ground that it is better to endure the punishment in this world than in the next, still the kinder modern view would have it that penance is a 'heavenly medicine', which heals the wounds inflicted by sin.

Now, I had no doubt that my lord Gilles de Rais was spiritually sick unto death, and therefore in the gravest and most urgent need of such heavenly medicine. At the same time, I have to tell you that I refused point-blank to hear him in confession. My reasons for doing so, which will soon become apparent, may only serve to demonstrate my continued insistence that I was never a good priest, yet might I invite the reader to stand just for a moment in my sandals, confronting all the perils as I saw them. Honest reader, what would you have done?

At first, I sought by stratagems to avoid or evade the issue. I was deeply disturbed by what I knew already, and even more frightened at the prospect of what further horrors would lie in wait for me, face-to-face with the Marshal in the confines of the confessional. I urged him to pray and fast, saying that I would do the same, for guidance. Gilles may have prayed, but I beg leave to doubt his fasting; he returned to me, drunk, the next day, again saying that he required me to hear him in confession. I offered him exorcism instead. He refused the rite haughtily. He was neither insane nor possessed, he insisted. He was an ordinary sinner, and only the extent and the intensity of his sins made him in any way extraordinary. (I must say that I now agree with this, having had the intervening years to consider his horrible crimes in the context of his whole life and death. But at that point, when he laid drunken hands on me, it was not mere cowardice which led me to wonder if what I was hearing could be the importuning of a man with seven devils.)

Exorcism rejected, we now fell to arguing as to whether I had any power or right to refuse him. It transpired that Gilles believed that any priest was bound to hear confessions on demand. In this, I pointed out as tactfully as I could manage, my lord was mistaken. In the year of all our absolution 1215, the council of the Lateran, while decreeing that confession should be made at least once a year, stipulated that such confession should be made 'before a parish priest, or some other priest with the consent of the parish priest'. Gilles said that such legislation was for peasants. Had I not been given the keys of heaven and the power of binding and loosing sins with my ordination? he demanded. I replied by telling him that although the *potestas ordinis* of every priest includes the power of granting absolution, according to the established discipline of the Church, yet no priest can be a confessor without a special faculty from his bishop. In short, I said, I was not licensed by the bishop to hear confessions. At which my master smiled terribly, and reminded me that I had heard Prelati's.

I had better come right out with it, and admit that I feared both for my own skin and my own sanity should I have to bear the burden of listening to the Marshal's confession in detail. Unable of course to say as much to him, I next feigned illness for a few days, and pleaded my incompetence when he came back to me with all the unquenchable enthusiasm of a relentless despair. I claimed that I considered myself somewhat tainted by our involvement in alchemical activity, even if I had only watched the experiments from the sidelines. The alchemy, Gilles responded, was of little importance, especially when compared with certain other pressing sins which he had it upon his conscience to confess. I was by now only too well aware that this must be true. In fact, I wondered privately to myself whether some of my lord's gravest sins – could they even go beyond idolatry, adultery, and murder? – might be 'reserved'; that is to say, so gross and serious that they would have to be referred to the bishop, or even the Pope, before absolution could be given.

This was, of course, a thought I should never have had. It did no credit to my cloth to have it. Even more cravenly speculative was another thought that immediately crossed my mind: What if the Marshal's mercurial moods should drive him to regret the confession and to kill his confessor because he knew too much? I remember that the moment I thought this, I very nearly despaired. For how, in these circumstances, could I refer Gilles to any alternative confessor? To do so might be to condemn that priest to death!

My master's drunkenness made such a future course of tragedy not impossible. Worse, it occurred to me, there was the presence of his henchmen to consider. Once they saw Gilles slinking off to the confessional, they were bound to feel endangered by the priest who knew too much. If they were all of them accomplices in his guilt – and I was now reasonably certain that not one of them was innocent – then any of them might feel obliged to slit a priestly throat to ensure its owner's respect for the secrets of the confessional. Worse yet, had the less Christian and over-zealous agents of the Inquisition no means of compelling or persuading any priest to reveal such secrets, when the highest authority demanded it? The fact was, surely, that Gilles' confessor might as well be dead from the moment that Gilles knelt down before him. As for me, I simply could not live with such definite knowledge of evil, and I knew it. Nor was it my skin only for which I was fearful. Truth to tell, I suspected that my shaky leaky faith could be utterly undermined and then destroyed by what the Marshal would have to teach me of the depravity of his soul.

I prayed for release and guidance. And my prayers were answered. Visiting one day in Lent the church of the Holy Trinity down in Machecoul, I noticed the priest spit blood, and learned that he was dying. This priest's name was Dom Olivier des Ferrières. I wish I could say he was saintly, but I fear that he had the pox. The important thing was straight-forwardly that he was dying. Here, therefore, I had found the ideal confessor to whom Gilles could unburden his soul. In that act, in essence, the penitent addresses his truth-telling recital of sins to God, while the penitentiary overhears him. What better, for everyone's sake, than that my lord's confessor should go soon to God after overhearing what I was convinced would be a catalogue of sins that stank to hell?

I waited for the right moment to recommend to Gilles that this plan was heaven-sent. Persuasion was not difficult, I discovered. As soon as he heard that Dom Olivier was at death's door, he perceived the wisdom of the procedure. Accordingly, on the twenty-seventh of March, Easter Day, 1440, I can say that I witnessed my lord Gilles de Rais and the said parish priest of Machecoul, Dom Olivier des Ferrières, retire together behind our Lady's altar in the church of the Holy Trinity, and that I had every reason to believe that Dom Olivier there heard the Marshal's confession because immediately afterwards Gilles emerged to receive the Blessed Sacrament at the high Mass of Easter in company with the poor parishioners of that place. These common folk, when they saw their seigneur among them at the altar rail, wished to rise up and go elsewhere, but he would not permit it. Did they act thus because of his nobility or because of his notoriety? I have never been able to determine.

And did Gilles spell out all his crimes in private to Dom Olivier? If he did not, his confession was valueless, and 'perfect Christian' that he was, he would have known it. Worse, it would have *added* to his iniquity if he then made a sacrilegious confession, wilfully concealing mortal sins of which he was conscious, or having no real contrition or purpose of amendment or intention of making satisfaction. By so doing, Gilles would have rendered null and void the sacrament of penance, nor would absolution have taken effect even for those sins which he did find courage in him to confess. However, I have no reason to suppose that his confession was not full and proper. I know for certain that he proceeded thereafter to Mass in the manner described, and received the Host then, making his communion for the first time in my experience of him, which sacrament he was given at the hands of Dom Simon Loisel, priest, then serving at that church.

For some days after Easter, the Marshal may well have been at peace. I hope so – but have no sure means of telling. When I saw him he looked stunned, or even wounded, walking about the castle in a trance. But for the most part, in those few still and sunlit late-March days, my master avoided me;

and I may say that I was glad to avoid him too. Dom Olivier des Ferrières I also avoided.

It was at this time, standing one morning on the tower to take the air, I saw a wolf padding across the frozen river down below. He stopped half-way across, and then looked up at me. Why was I spellbound by this? Reason tells me that he could not see me there against the sky, or that distance made my presence quite irrelevant to him. It is something deeper than reason which instructs me that the wolf stood looking at me for a long strange time. That moment is a sinister stillness at the heart of a brief interlude which seems in retrospect all still and sinister: a single frozen picture from a Book of Hours. The wolf looked at me, I looked at the wolf; time stopped. At last I clapped my hands, and he loped off. He moved on the frozen river like a grey ghost. When he reached the far bank he passed into the darkness of the woods as softly as the wind.

I spent hours during this interlude meditating upon one of the things which my master had told me in his drunken confidence. Gilles had said that he could have saved Joan. Is this to be taken seriously? I suspect not. I believe that some of the things he said to me were said at best to tease and at worst to mock. On the other hand, I believe that he may well have felt guilty that he had not even *tried* to save Joan. I was later to put together much about his life in the years before I knew him, but there was a period about which I could discover nothing. To be specific, this period ran from just after he led the attack at Paris on the Gates of St Honoré, in company with Joan, on September the eighth, the year of Our Lord 1429, to that day after Christmas 1430 when as he had told me he turned up at Louviers. During this period, Joan of course was captured. And when he was at Louviers, she had just been brought to nearby Rouen under English escort. However, I have to say that his assertion that it was merely indolence which prevented him from marching to her rescue does not square with the facts as I have unearthed them.

What Gilles was really doing at Louviers was buying a horse for one of his men, and borrowing money to do it. I have seen a bill made out to one Roland Mauvoisin, acknowledging that my master owed him 160 gold crowns for the purchase of a black horse, saddles and bridles. Nor can it be imagined that this horse was intended for the use of a rescued Joan of Arc, since on the back of the bill was scribbled 'a mount for Michel Machefer'. I do not know who Michel Machefer was. I do suggest that whatever was occupying Gilles' mind just then it was not Joan of Arc.

Rachel weeping for her children ... Those words which had struck my heart from the Gospel reading for the Mass for Holy Innocents' Day came back to me now, for it was at this time also that I first heard the rumour that the Bishop of Nantes, Messire Jean de Malestroit, was being prevailed upon, by one desperate secret implorer after another, to bring the Marshal Gilles de Rais to justice. The Bishop, as I learned later, had been at first inclined to dismiss the allegations as wild gossip. It was only when the vague charges were supplemented by the disappearance of a nephew of the Prior of Chermère, who had been taken into our choir to be taught singing, that he decided that there was at least some sort of a case for enquiry. Preliminary investigations must have filled him with a grave disquiet, but there would still have been lacking sufficient direct evidence to warrant him bringing such serious charges against a person of my master's eminence. The Bishop of Nantes began then a series of episcopal visits over the areas from which the majority of the complaints had come. Wherever he went, I imagine, he was overwhelmed with revelations of Gilles' infamies. With the Church on their side the people were no longer afraid to speak plainly. All the same, a man might not be arraigned on the words of a children's game, and much of the evidence amassed must have been hearsay and surmise. It was to be Gilles himself who enabled the Bishop to take decisive action against him.

But the story of what Gilles did to incur this must be kept for my next chapter. Meanwhile, be sure that when I heard the rumours of these stirrings of the coming retribution I was frightened. I trembled, both for my master and for myself.

Others now heard the same rumours, but reacted differently. On the third Wednesday after Easter, the feast of the Solemnity of St Joseph, Prelati and the others got Gilles drunk. I heard Rossignol singing in the banqueting hall: that lacerating soprano that caused crisp flames to go through my veins whenever I listened to it. Then, to my horror, I heard the Marshal's voice as he tried to join in. The canary and the screech-owl: which was more vile?

Fear as well as prudence made me pause in the doorway. It was then that I overheard de Bricqueville say: 'That priest is a spy and a fool, and I reckon you should get rid of him.'

There came murmurs of agreement and approval from the others, but from Gilles himself a shout: 'God's spy! That's all Dom Eustache is. God's spy, that's all!' My master's voice was thick with brandy-wine. My heart sank. What were they celebrating? Whatever it was, I felt sure it was not St Joseph.

Prelati spoke next. I knew he had never liked me, but the depth of his malevolence still came as a shock. 'He is not to be trusted. You cannot afford to let him live. He tricked you into going to public confession . . .'

'My dear François, what nonsense!' Gilles interjected. 'You know as well as I that it was not public. And did I not make it clear to you: the confessor is as good as dead?'

'As good as dead's not good enough,' said Griart. 'I say that we should cut his throat for him. Yes, and we should cut Blanchet's throat as well!'

De Sillé spoke next. With several obscenities and blasphemies, he gave it as his opinion that my throat should have been cut in the house of Perrot Cahn. What Gilles thought of this, I have no means of knowing. I was cowering back into the shadows, and had no wish to read the hate I am sure must have been written on their faces. Rossignol sang on through all this grim incitement to my murder, coupled with recommendations that the parish priest who had heard Gilles in confession should be finished off with me. Not a single voice was there to speak of mercy or justice. I even heard Prelati urging Gilles, if we were not to be killed, to give him permission to cut out our tongues and then cut off our hands so that we could not write down anything we knew.

I was frozen with fear. I thought that my hour had come. Then I heard my master say: 'Not a hair of God's spy's head is to be harmed, do you hear me? I need Dom Eustache Blanchet! He is my man!'

I hurried then to the chapel, on tiptoe, without betraying that I had overheard them. I spent the rest of that day in prayer, begging St Joseph and Our Lady herself to protect me through whatever trials the future was to bring. As to what Gilles meant by declaring that he needed me, and that I was his man, I did not then understand these remarks. However, he was himself to say something else along these lines, directly to me, on the very night that we were taken to Nantes as captives, and then I believe that at last I *did* understand. Since that night is now not so far off in my narrative, I must ask the reader's patience, for all will then be revealed.

The day after St Joseph's feast, I hastened to see Dom Olivier. I fancy I had some ill-conceived notion of warning him that men would be coming with an intent to murder him, but one glance sufficed to tell me there was no need. Dom Olivier was dying; he was almost dead. I prayed with him. I gave him the oil of unction. He lay on his cot by the wall. I comforted him.

Perhaps I should not have troubled his dying hour with mention of the name of the Marshal-Baron Gilles de Rais, but my own fear was such that I could not resist it. In fairness to myself, I will add that mention is all I did. The name made Dom Olivier shiver. His right hand twitched as he sought without success to bless himself. I performed that office for him. He sank back, grateful. 'The Marshal de Rais...' Dom Olivier was trying to say something but the words would not come, or he had not the breath for them.

I should not have spoken further, but I did. I said: 'You heard his confession. Do you think my lord the Marshal must go to hell?'

It was then, even with the death-rattle starting in his throat, that Dom Olivier summoned all his faculties and put me to shame with an answer of perfect faith and orthodoxy. Hell, he said, might well be empty save for the devils. The Church in her wisdom has never named a single human soul that is certainly in hell. Not even Judas Iscariot...

He died as he said this, and I knelt for a long time beside him, and prayed for his soul. It is my experience, and that of many others in all ways my superiors, that such prayers after death can help to bring peace to the dead one. But even when I closed Dom Olivier's eyes, I do not think I could claim that he looked at peace.

XVI

SACRILEGE

From Easter to Whitsunday it is always fifty days. It had been on Easter Sunday itself that Gilles made his sacramental confession to Dom Olivier, and it was at the Feast of Pentecost (commonly called Whitsun) that he blazed into that paroxysm of rage and folly which eventually delivered him up for justice.

As to whether my lord's confession to the dying priest had been full and sincere or not, I still have no sure means of knowing. What is certain is that the Marshal relapsed into his former vicious life from that time when Prelati and de Bricqueville got him drunk, and I overheard the party of conspirators urging him to kill me. As to my working knowledge of his vices: I can repeat here what I said on oath before the Bishop of Nantes, namely that I knew of the murders only by hearsay, and of the gross impurities that preceded and sometimes followed them I knew nothing at all. I had been told by the traveller at Mortagne that Gilles de Rais killed little children in order to employ their blood in the writing of a book of magic which was supposed to make him invincible. While I did not ever quite credit this, my master's superstitious indulgence of alchemists and his willingness to excite his imagination with heretical thoughts, made it (as I supposed) not impossible. As I told my spiritual lord of Nantes, it was during these fifty days before Pentecost that I saw him once or twice reading from a book in which the letters were written in red. That book had disappeared by the time of the trial. My fullest understanding of its nature, after many years' worrying at the subject, is that it was more likely some disgusting catalogue of his victims, than a manual of magic. As to whether its ink was their blood, or just innocent cochineal, that lies thankfully beyond my knowledge.

Perhaps it was an awareness that the Bishop of Nantes had begun to heed the horrible stories about him, and was already in process of collecting evidence to back the complaints, that caused my lord's relapse to be so severe. His drunkenness and his rages became ever more crazy and uncontrollable. He alienated, I think, even some of his closest accomplices. I saw Griart one morning with his fat face all covered with bruises, and Poitou with his doublet slashed as if by a dagger, and when I asked them if they had been waylaid by brigands they replied separately that they had not left the castle all night, that they had been drinking in company with the Marshal, and that he and he alone must be held responsible for the condition in which I found them. Yet, be it noted, the villains might have mocked me with such moaning. It was not Griart and Poitou who ran away before justice sounded the trump at the gates of Machecoul.

My master's drunkenness might make a swine and then an ape of him, but it never quite sufficed to blot out his baptism. One noon I heard Prelati urging him to close down his chapel and renounce Christianity altogether in order to gain the ear of hell. Gilles replied that this was witchcraft. Then the smooth Florentine launched upon a wickedly learned and clever speech, larded with complicated irony, in which he suggested amongst other things too evil to remember that the very word *witch* corresponded to the German *hexe* and the Latin *lamia*, and that these were names not originally applied to human beings at all, but to *child-devouring demons*. Gilles laughed most horribly when he heard this stuff, but still refused to shut down either his chapel or his intelligence. He picked the petals off a rose as he harangued Prelati. The alchemist had to stand and grin, shifting from foot to foot, abashed and irritable. For him, no doubt, the final indignity came when Gilles noticed me half-hidden in the arras, and called me to join them, and made Prelati kiss my crucifix. Perversely, at this time, my lord insisted that each of his grosser servants treat me with increased respect, although there was no more talk of him making his confession to me, or again communicating. I was instructed to go on saying Mass daily, and told that prayers for my master's soul were unfailingly to be prayed with each Mass offered.

Gilles, drunk, would lie prostrate upon the pavings of the chapel during some of these services. On one occasion, which it is gall itself to recall, so pitiful and terrible are the implications now, he shouted out to me that we were to pray for the souls of Jean Jeudon and Jean Roussin. Then, another time, he handed me a tiny folded piece of parchment with the names Colin Avril, Guillaume le Barbier, Kerguen and Aisé written on it in his own hand. These were souls to be remembered, he said, when I prayed for the faithful departed. I believe that it was on the Feast day of Saints Philip and James the Apostles that he required me to remember in my prayers Edelin, and Chastelier, and Guillaume Delit. And from other times I find the names Fougère and Loessart, Perrot Degaye, Bouer and Olivier Darel, Jean Toutblanc, Jamet Brice, Lavary, Sorin, Jenvret, Jean Degrepie, Jean Hubert, Sergent, Jean de Lanté, Eustache Drouet, Guillaume Hamelin and Robin Pavot all inscribed upon and never to fade from my memory. I prayed for these persons then, and I pray for them now. Then I did not know who they were, but now I know well. All these names were the names of children who were to be mentioned at his trial as his known victims. Sometimes I think that any one of these names is more worthy of my prayers than was Gilles de Rais. Often I wish that it was possible to spend my days remembering and reconstructing the few years it was given to Guillaume Delit, say, or Robin Pavot, to pass in this world before meeting my lord they met death. Is not any one of the infants slaughtered by Herod to be preferred before that base king in our pity? Not just that, but would it not say more for a man's own soul, and better serve his immortal health, if he should give his attention to the innocence of the victims rather than to the guilt of the criminal hand that slew them?

I know these questions well, for I have lived with them and heard them not only in the doubtful antechamber of my own heart but from the lips of my pastors and masters in God. Nor have I easy answers to any of them. Yet it could be claimed that an understanding of the motives of King Herod might not be irrelevant to salvation, and that in order to come to the good it is necessary to pass through the truth, however contemptible or disgusting the details of that truth might sometimes prove to be. To the reader who declares that in the last analysis he or she would rather hear the story of Robin Pavot, and not the story of Gilles de Rais, I can say only that I do not know the story of Robin Pavot. I can assure such a reader that the time is long past when I ever found Gilles de Rais, his evil, or evil generally, worthy of much interest. I am telling this tale because I have to, not because I want to.

The problem of whether it is morally reprehensible to dwell upon Gilles' story is more interesting than the man. As a matter of opinion, I would say that it might be better to forget him if it were not for Joan of Arc. If all that we had here was an account of a life given up to vile enjoyment of the kind of depravities common to the worst of the Roman emperors, then he would be an object fit only for contempt, or at best pity, and the account should be made in such a manner that he would be soon forgotten, for the good of all. I say that it is because of the great mystery of Gilles' love for Joan that he is worth our study. Is his evil to be explained as a dreadful No of an answer to her goodness? Or, as in some moods he sought over-simply to explain it to me, as an act of revenge against God for allowing her death? Gilles was a spoiled child swayed by pride, and just as a man in church is tempted most easily to imagine orgies on the altar, in the holy of holies, so his expression of rebellion against God by the mere satisfying of fantastic lusts need not too much surprise us. It is in the coincidence of Gilles and Joan that the mystery lies. Only when I imagined their marriage did I start to tell his story.

Often during those fifty days before Pentecost I thought of fleeing, but I was now a prisoner in the castle, more or less. Worse, I reckon, I was the prisoner also of an acceptance of being part of a drama that was not of my making, for I had come to believe that my fate was now bound inextricably with that of my terrible master. I went creeping about Machecoul, my feet almost refusing to move. It began to seem as if *I* deserved whatever retribution was coming one day soon for the Marshal. Nor was my guilt in this merely a matter of complicity; it reached too far back for that: as far back as Ushant. It had lain dormant all these years, but it had been there, and now it arose to confront me. I looked with sick eyes upon the April sun, shining through the white foam of the fountain in the inner court (here, as in so much else, Machecoul was the mirror image of Tiffauges). I gazed on my own face in the pool with a malignant hatred. In my brain, at that time, a single text from the apostle Paul reverberated: 'It is a fearful thing to fall into the hands of the living God!' (*Hebrews* x, 31).

I came later to see what my master did that Pentecost as an act either God-directed or an expression of the Marshal's will calling down divine vengeance or justice upon him for his hideous crimes. Retribution is punishment inflicted by God on the sinner in the form of suffering or misfortune. If patiently borne it may cleanse the soul from all the effects of sin and so take the place of purgatory. According to Aquinas, the punishments of this life are medicinal rather than retributive (*Summa Theologiae*, Secunda Secundae, lxvi, 6). I do not say this would be sufficient for Gilles. I do say he acted as though asking for the punishment he got.

The act which my lord chose was sacrilege. This is how it came about that he committed it, and what he did, and my part in it. As I have already remarked a while back, upon our removal to Machecoul he had sold his property at St Etienne-de-la-Mer-Morte to Guillaume le Ferron, the treasurer of the Duke of Brittany. Possession of that castle had already been taken by le Ferron's brother Jean, a priest. Some difficulty over payment had arisen, and either for that cause or in a fit of drunken petulance, Gilles had demanded the place back. The two brothers le Ferron flatly refused him. Gilles could not believe it. He was used, of course, to his wishes being obeyed without question. Beside himself with rage, that morning of Whitsunday saw him select sixty of the best soldiers from his private army, parade them rigorously beneath the towers of Machecoul, and then ride off at their head across the Breton border and into Poitevin. I tagged along, trying vainly to persuade my master of wiser counsels.

We reached the outskirts of the village about noon. The place was deserted, with only cats and dogs in the length of the street. It did not take more than two minutes' sucking on his wine-flask for Gilles to work out where everyone had gone. High Mass of Pentecost was being sung in the parish church, and the entire local population was assembled for it. In that congregation, as Gilles shouted for our instruction, his enemy Jean le Ferron was certain to be found.

Now I should explain that the mere act of riding across the border at the head of a band of armed men was bad enough. This constituted open revolt against the Duke and against the King, the pair of them having jointly forbidden the levying of forces without special authority. No doubt the King was aware of his son's impatience to succeed him, and in any case the Duke must have long been weary of rival seigneurs taking advantage of the unsettled condition of the country to raid each other's estates and settle their private quarrels by a resort to arms. For whatever such reason, very heavy penalties had recently been framed for those who rode out with private armies behind them. However, what Gilles did next was worse than banditry.

Jean le Ferron was not merely a member of the congregation in the church at St Etienne. He was, that Sunday, the officiating priest. Even when Gilles found this out, he did not hesitate. Posting his men in the wood that surrounded the building, he marched with his bodyguard straight up the steps and down the central aisle of the church. He brandished a double-edged battle-axe in his hands as he came. The dozen soldiers who accompanied him had all drawn their long swords on his orders.

Mass, thanks be to God, was drawing to its close as they burst in. I cowered in the doorway, peering through the clouds of incense, unable to do anything to check my master's folly. I saw the heads of the people in the church jerk up, disturbed in their devotions by the tread of the armed men marching.

Buffeting his passage through the throng, Gilles advanced straight upon Jean le Ferron where he stood. The priest had his right arm raised. He was offering blessing to his congregation in the last words of the Mass: '*Ite, missa est . . .*'

Before a voice could cry out *Deo gratias* in response, Gilles was upon the priest, roaring, swinging his battle-axe.

'Out! Out! Out of this church or I kill you!'

Seizing the priest by the hair, he dragged him down. Women screamed. Men shouted that this was blasphemy. Most of the choirboys ran. Not a single person dared to intervene, for the armed bodyguard ranged themselves along the steps of the chancel and turned to threaten the onlookers with their weapons.

Le Ferron was down on his knees, and begging for mercy.

I was doing the same, only doing my begging to God. When I got to my feet it was because I heard Gilles' voice once more roaring:

'Thief! Scum! You have robbed me! You have beaten my men and had my money! Out! Out of the church or I kill you!'

This was pure nonsense, so far as I know. The priest had not robbed Gilles, nor had he beaten Gilles' men. Nor had his brother, nor had the Duke himself. Perhaps it is of some small interest that in his frenzy of intoxicated excitement my lord attributed his own crimes to someone else. Le Ferron could be forgiven for finding it crazy. He called out to Messires de Bricqueville and de Sillé, members of the bodyguard, to protect him from this madman. Both looked unhappy and uncomfortable, but neither made the slightest move to help. People were now fleeing wholesale, and in all directions. It seemed certain there must be murder done in the church.

I wish I could claim that I saved le Ferron's life. Let the reader decide, for myself I could never determine. When I saw him there on his knees, begging for mercy, and Gilles towering over him, battle-axe in hand, I threw myself down beside my brother priest, and clutched at the axe blades with my naked hands. My palms got cut, of course, and the blood ran down my vestments. It splashed on le Ferron's robes too, and some fell upon his face. Gazing down at two bloody and frightened priests before him, Gilles de Rais threw back his head and laughed.

He laughed long and hard, so that the whole church rang with it. It was a vile sound, with no one joining in. I never heard laughter like that before or since.

Then Gilles cast the axe away, and dragged Jean le Ferron out into the sunlight. His accomplices assisted him in the task of trussing up the priest, and throwing his well-roped body across a horse. Then they all rode singing and whooping to the castle of St Etienne, where le Ferron was chained up in a dungeon below the moat. Gilles left de Bricqueville and de Sillé in charge of his reclaimed estates. The rest of us returned with him to Machecoul. He was in high good spirits, and sang the whole way home.

Would my lord de Rais have killed that priest in front of the altar if I had not intervened? I do not know, but I must beg leave to doubt it. Perhaps the truth is that my intervention afforded sufficient diversion to allow le Ferron himself to be dragged from the church. Gilles had not said that he *would* kill the priest, either inside the church or when they got outside. What he threatened was that he might kill him if le Ferron would *not* come out. But here I am clutching at straws, and be sure I know it. What my master performed that black Whitsunday at St Etienne was a most appalling act of sacrilege, even if (thank God) for one reason or another, or none, it fell short of murder. Sacrilege is a grave enough sin against the virtue of religion. Gilles had done violence to a cleric *in* a church, and while that cleric was still in the last stages of celebrating the Mass. By marching armed into that church he had violated ecclesiastical property, and by then imprisoning that priest he had broken canon law. Also, by dispossessing Guillaume le Ferron of the castle of St Etienne he had committed civil crime against a member of the Duke of Brittany's household. In short, by a single act of quite primitive rage and stupidity, my master had transgressed against the laws of both Church and State in a manner at once beyond pardon and impossibly provocative. Duke Jean V and the Bishop of Nantes, Jean de Malestroit, could now bring him to trial whenever they wanted.

These realizations burned in my brain on the long ride back. That night Gilles drank in triumph at Machecoul, seemingly unaware of any of the implications of what he had done, or careless of the doom he had invited down upon his head. I heard Rossignol singing, and the shrill birdlike cries of Prelati. I sat far from the banqueting hall, up in my room with my old cloak stretched across my knees, unpicking with shaking fingers the stitches I had put in the garment that evening above Siena so long ago. When I had opened the wound I began to mend the tear again. The thread snapped.

My hand faltered. I heard a sound in the distance like the beating of muffled death-drums. I went to the window of the turret. I *could* hear the distant beating of drums in funereal rhythm and beyond them, far beyond, a vaguer sound still, now growing, swelling, rumbling in the distance like the pounding of surf upon the rocks of Ushant, now like the surf again, receding, growling, menacing. Then it was gone: there was nothing upon the wind.

I washed the blood from my vestments before I went back to the mending of my cloak. I worked until it was dark and the moon came out. When I looked again from the turret window the very sky appeared disgraced to me, though the noise of Gilles' revelry still came up from the banqueting hall.

XVII

GOD'S SPY

That night I dreamed I saw Gilles and Joan ride together to the attack on Paris. Joan was struck in the thigh by an English arrow. She fell from her horse, and Gilles carried her from the battle in his arms. He set her down gently under a tall white tree with many green leaves. Then he washed and dressed her wound. When he had finished, Joan kissed his hand that had washed her and comforted her. Then she sang a song. The words of the song were these:

There was a man of double deed
Sowed his garden full of seed.
When the seed began to grow
It was a garden full of snow.
When the snow began to crack
It was a stick across my back.
When my back began to smart
It was a black knife in my heart.
When my heart began to bleed
Then it was death and death indeed.

I woke with the words of Joan's song to Gilles still ringing in my head. When I closed my eyes I could see again that white tree in its green dress. I recognized the words of the song as something like a nursery rhyme which I had heard long ago in Ushant. The meaning of this dream is quite beyond me.

Why did I dream this? Why do we dream at all? I believe that it was Democritus who held the cause of dreams to be the simulacra or phantasms of corporeal objects which are constantly floating about the atmosphere and attack the soul in sleep – a view hardly to be distinguished from that Gnostic nonsense which would have it that the phenomena of animal life are produced by an immaterial *anima*, or soul, distinct from matter. I think that I prefer the teaching of Aristotle, who refers dreams to the impressions left by objects seen with the eyes of the body. Plato, also, connects dreaming with the normal waking operations of the mind. All the same, in that case how did I know to dream that Joan was wounded in the thigh before Paris? It was only when I mentioned this dream to my master that he told me it had been so. Pliny seems to have taught that all dreams are supernatural in origin, with the exception of those which take place after meals. Hippocrates was disposed to admit that some dreams might be divine, but held that others were premonitory of diseased states of the body. Since I had not eaten before dreaming my dream of Joan and Gilles, and it was a long time after it that I first suffered any ill health, I may be excused for trusting that this dream of mine was sent from God.

God sends us such dreams, but we may not always interpret them. No doubt we should cleave fast to the experience of the dream, even when we cannot comprehend. I have told you my dreams, in order, as they happened, throughout this book. It has seemed to me important to do so, although I could not say why. Perhaps all that I am trying to tell you is itself a dream. That may be so, but then this dream's not mine.

The day after the sacrilege at St Etienne, there was a dinner to celebrate the affair. Gilles' feast, as you may imagine, was a matter of roaring spirits and self-congratulation, with lashings of the good wine of Arbois – scented of raspberries – and Aunis flowing. The table was loaded with roast goose, and there was interminably more of the laughter and song which I had heard from the banqueting hall the night before. I ate a little larded capon, but I soon felt sick. Hypocras, spiced with cinnamon and ginger, failed to fog my brain as sufficiently as it seemed to fog his, and Prelati's, and Griart's, and Poitou's. Sober or drunk, I knew that my master was done for. His mad rage of Pentecost must give the Bishop of Nantes the signal to proceed against him now.

At that feast, drunk, Gilles said again to me: 'You are God's spy!'

What did he mean by this? Perhaps that I was sent, in his opinion, to act as witness to his life and death, and then to bear the burden of his story for the rest of my days, which burden the writing of this book may lighten. Perhaps that my function was as a sort of conscience for him. Perhaps that in my innocence I possessed a gift denied to his other companions, all of whom knew things about him which I was spared from knowing until his trial. My lord de Rais might have meant all these matters, or none. *God's spy*, he called me. It is a title I honour. I would rather be *God's spy* than *a perfect Christian*.

I had better explain. By now, by the time when I sat across the table from him at his joyless feast, I was able to appreciate that there might indeed be a sense in which Gilles de Rais could be said to be 'a perfect Christian', at least in his own mind. This had nothing, of course, to do with beauty of faith or the performance of good works. It was just that Gilles was locked into a pattern of good and evil which undoubtedly owed everything to that understanding of fallen human nature which is afforded us by our mother the Church. Gilles was perhaps more truly a son of the Church than I would ever be. In his pursuit of extremities of thought and feeling, he was like a figure from some dark parable. He lived and moved in a world that was blazing black and white. Compared with this, my world was a shadow-world of greys. I was, indeed, an imperfect Christian; perhaps not even much of a Christian at all, which was why I needed my prayers and the prayers of others and even the crutch of my vocation. Yet looking at Gilles where he splashed and roared in his cups across that table, I saw at once the merit of imperfection, and the horror

– moral and otherwise – of the perfect ones. I had been variously impressed by Gilles' person, which seemed at moments to give off an odour of sanctity, and then again I had been plunged into hell in his company, when he gave off a stench of uttermost evil. Neither heaven nor hell, extreme good or the vile profundities of evil appeared wondrous to me now. If I had any stance, it was that common human decency set me against all notions of perfection. I did not want to be gold. I rejoiced in my own base matter.

Prelati fell asleep in a pool of his own vomit. Griart and Poitou stuffed their faces with so much wine and so many little fishes that I thought they would burst, but they did not burst, only slipped down from the bench and rolled on the ground in each other's arms until they also slept. Then my master beckoned me close to him, and while Rossignol sang in the gallery he spoke drunkenly again to me of Joan.

'It was for heresy and witchcraft and blasphemy that she was tried,' said Gilles de Rais. 'It was said that the Devil was her power, and for five months the case proceeded against her, with Cauchon and the Vice-Inquisitor Lemaître her judges and summoning to their court more than forty bishops and abbots and doctors of Church law for assessors. First they gathered testimony, questioning her, and sending to Domrémy itself and to all places where she had been and where their ministers might have access, putting together all that she had done, and the marvels to show that they were done by witchcraft. Then they held public session in the castle chapel at Rouen, forty-two of them, with Cauchon presiding, and questioned her with every trick they could. They chained her at night in a dungeon, chained her by the neck and both hands and both feet in a narrow dungeon, with common grooms of Warwick's garrison to watch her. These mocked her and jeered, and made her nights a hell. It was in dread of these guards and their lechery that she kept her man's clothes and would not take a woman's.'

This thought went home to me like an everlasting responsibility. My lord sat drinking in the most floridly elegant
manner now, although well into the ape stage of his drunkenness. His eyes held a grey dawn of contempt in them as he
considered me across the board.

'They did not torture her with racks and screws,' said Gilles
de Rais, 'though they debated on it. They wore her down
without recourse to the rack. At last – it was in Whitweek, a
year from her capture, and after four months in the dungeon
– they got a little weasel priest to persuade her to sign a piece
of paper. This was a list of her errors and crimes of heresy
and witchcraft, and her abjuring such wrong-doing. They
promised her that if she signed, and then put on woman's
clothes in proof of her repentance, they would take her from
that abomination of a prison and remove her chains and keep
her where she would be tended by women only, as the law of
the Church requires, as you well know, father.'

I felt tears start to my eyes. Gilles' face was a crumpled
mask of intoxication. He poured himself more wine with a
careful hand.

'They could not conquer her,' he said, 'however much they
violated her. Because her spirit was hard and flawless as a
diamond. They could not conquer her, so they shattered her.
When the multitude saw that she had signed the paper of
abjuration, some, who pitied her, were glad that she had
escaped the fire; and there were others, fit but few, who knew
her to be holy, and they grieved; but the many, and especially
the English lords and their soldiers, were angry to madness,
supposing she had escaped them. Then Cauchon broke his
word. He did not take her to a Church prison, where she
might be unchained, and with women to tend her. He had
her returned to the castle dungeon, and the chains again
applied to her neck, hands, and feet, and with those grooms in
attendance through horror of whom she had signed. Only
now there was this difference: they dressed her in woman's

clothes before the chaining. You understand me, father? I think that you do. She was chained there, at the mercy of those grooms.'

Gilles' hand, dropping idly between the goblets, beat a sort of vague but persistent rhythm in time to his words. Rossignol's cap, with a blue feather stuck in it, had been cast down upon the table before he ascended to the gallery to sing. Now my lord took up that cap in his left hand, caressed its velvet, and rubbed the feather softly against his lips. He had this wolfish look between his brows.

'Two days and nights she lay there, chained, in woman's dress. Then, on the third day, they took away her dress and brought her those boy's clothes she had worn before her abjuration. Since she was naked, she was bound to put them on, being in the company of such men. But on the next morning, eight of her judges came and asked her why she had again put on boy's clothes, and when she told them that it was for modesty and because of the outrages attempted upon her person by Warwick and his grooms, they scorned her explanations and abused her and called her a witch and a whore and said this was to be seen as a sign she had now relapsed into her heresy. So, on the Tuesday, Cauchon put on his cap and condemned her to be handed into the fire.'

In truth, my lord de Rais was well informed, and his account of the last days of Joan of Arc was in most points sounder and richer in detail than any which up to that time I had heard. As to whether he was correct in stating that her English guards essayed to rape her, I do not know; the important thing, perhaps, is that he believed it to have been so. Now I saw the ghost of Joan's terrible martyrdom in his face, and suddenly I was terrified, though not for my own life.

'They dressed her then in a long white dress,' said Gilles de Rais, 'and they took her in a tumbril into the market-place at Rouen. In the middle of the square was a stone with a tall stake standing in it, and faggots piled around it. They chained

184

her to that stake, and the torch was set to the faggots, and she was burnt.'

There was a silence.

Then I said: 'I have heard that an English soldier gave her two sticks bound together for a cross.'

Gilles shrugged. He was still teasing his lips with the blue feather. His eyes suggested the eyes of a wild cat peering intent from under the darkness of some bush where it lies unseen.

I said: 'I have heard also that in the midst of the smoke they heard her praying to God, and calling out the holy name of Jesus.'

Gilles had picked the feather from the cap with his teeth. He held it for a moment between pursed lips, then quite deliberately spat it at me. I felt his boundless anger and contempt.

'They threw her ashes in the river Loire,' he said. 'Only her heart had not been consumed by the fire. So they scooped up her heart and threw that in the river too.'

There was a dead silence. Then Gilles rose slowly to his feet and came at me. I was transfixed with terror. The back of his right hand struck me across the mouth, and my head went back and smashed against the wall. I fell from the bench. He was towering over me. I stood crouched against the wall, my mouth open and bleeding. Gilles stood leaning forward across the table, eyes glazed with wine, his breath coming from his nostrils with an animal sound. Then he shook his head as if to clear it, brushed the sweat from his brows, and sank back heavily in his chair. 'Dom Eustache Blanchet,' he snarled. 'Dom Eustache Blanchet. God save us all from Dom Eustache Blanchet.'

Mechanically, I was wiping the blood from my mouth. It did not seem to me I was much of a threat. I felt that nothing would prevent him if he rose again to his feet to kill me. A weariness came over me. I wished that I had never left

Ushant, never become a priest, never heard of Joan of Arc and Gilles de Rais. I could feel the hot tears trickling down my cheeks.

'My lord,' I said, choking.

Gilles waved me from his presence. I was glad to go. But as I passed out of the chamber, La Meffraye came in. The woman gave me a startled glance, no doubt noticing the blood upon my face. She held a little blue-eyed girl by the hand. I never saw that child before, or again.

Within a week we had word of the ducal retribution. For the whole of that week, my master seemed determined not only to be drunk but to celebrate the sacrilege done in the church at St Etienne with every resource of feasting and folly known to man. Fortunately for me, that blow he had struck after telling me the story of Joan's burning seemed to have left him with feelings of shame and nausea in my regard. Either that, or he was just sick of the sight of me. I made my excuses; he did not summon me further to the celebrations.

This was the punishment imposed upon my master by the Duke of Brittany: Gilles was ordered instantly to return the castle of St Etienne to its rightful owner, to release Jean le Ferron from imprisonment, and to pay a fine of 50,000 gold crowns into the bargain. This last was a crippling imposition, as well as an insult. Gilles could not possibly pay such a sum without recourse to the sale of other castles, which needless to say was a procedure without appeal for him. Yet if Gilles did not pay the fine, according to the rights of feudal possession his property would in any case be forfeit to the Duke. All the lands he had regained through the sale of Champtocé would again be lost. He would have nothing left but Tiffauges and the smaller fortress of Pouzages, which belonged in title to his wife. All else that he had inherited had by now been lost.

News of the Duke's justice reached Machecoul on the day of the Feast of St Mary Magdalen, the twenty-second of July, Our Saviour's year 1440. I heard the trumpets of the heralds, and I heard my master's roar of fury when Jean V's order had been read to him. The immediate effect of that order, indeed, was to drive Gilles half-demented with a passion to ignore it. He instructed his bodyguard to seize hold of Guillaume de Hautrays, who brought the order to him as legal officer for the Duke, and to bundle this poor fellow into the same dungeon where the manhandled priest was already languishing. Then, riding out himself at the head of another little troop of cavalry, Gilles succeeded in capturing Guillaume le Ferron as he went about his lawful business as the Duke's treasurer. This Guillaume he threw into prison alongside his brother Jean. Instead of releasing the one man wrongfully imprisoned, Gilles had provided him with two companions to share his fate. The dungeon beneath the moat at the castle of St Etienne must now have stunk to high heaven of injustice and the shit of the innocent.

Next move in this appalling end-game was down to the Duke. He despatched his sergeant-general Jean Rousseau to serve Gilles notice that all three prisoners must be released forthwith, and St Etienne restored to the le Ferrons, and of course the 50,000 crowns paid. Rousseau arrived at Machecoul one fine morning mid-way through the last week of July, accompanied by a band of soldiers to assist him in the collection of the money. Gilles had his own men beat up and expel this band without too much difficulty. Then he sent Rousseau to add his innocent shit to the others'.

I prayed in the chapel. Day after day the coloured sunlight dipped from the painted window across the chancel, and passed away; day after day I watched it, and prayed, and begged God to put an end to this. I knew now that my master's inconsequential passion was all of a piece. He was behaving like a crazy Caligula, only of course he did not have Caligula's real imperial power. All the same, it was plain that Gilles had gone irrevocably over the edge, and that now he inhabited a world of violent public fantasy quite beyond reason. Just as he had struck me, in his cups, without any cause, so he was striking out at each and every face that passed before him. Nobody dared to oppose him, or even question his actions. Griart and Poitou, along with Prelati and the other toadies, might perhaps be as terrified as I was, for fleeting moments, when they woke up in the morning with sore heads and remembered what extra lunacy had been added the day before to the general madness. Yet for the rest of the time they were part of the wine-soaked pattern, joined with the Marshal in his drunken fugues, incapable of offering advice or restraint. I prayed for an ending. I prayed for the little blue-eyed child. Concerning that, you may know that I prayed for peace and justice for her soul, being wise enough now to be sure that she must be dead.

The desire to inflict just punishment for an offence committed is quite lawful. The sin of revenge is committed only when the desire is to inflict punishment beyond what is deserved, or on the wrong person, or from a motive of hate. I did not hate my master Gilles de Rais, but as a murderer he deserved the punishment of death. According to St Thomas this penalty is lawful not only because the criminal has by his crime become a destroyer of the common good but also because, by choosing to fall from the order of reason, he partakes in some measure of the state of slavery of the lower animals which are ordered only for the use of others. Only the due punishment of death, by giving Gilles an opportunity to restore the order of reason in himself by an act of conversion to his last end, could enable him to recover his dignity as a human being. I prayed for the dead child, and for Gilles to die.

XVIII

A CASTLE KEPT BY DEMONS

So I lie here like Lazarus at last. I suppose I should be grateful that the dogs have not yet come to lick my sores. *There was a certain rich man, which was clothed in purple and fine linen, and fared sumptuously every day* ... That was my master Gilles de Rais when I first met him. *And there was a certain beggar named Lazarus, which was laid at his gate, full of sores* ... This must be me, perhaps then and most certainly now. Luke alone tells the story, which has struck me as curious for three reasons this morning: first, because it does not appear in the other gospels; second, because in no other of our Lord's parables is a name given to the central character; third, because by extension this name of Lazarus has come to stand for any poor and diseased person, especially a leper, and here I am, suffering from that sickness, not yet in the lazar-house, the lazaretto, but undoubtedly bound for it when I grow too ill for my fellows to countenance my continuance here at Subiaco.

It is my habit to read a little of the holy scriptures each morning by the spring in the sacred cave, and this morning that tale of Lazarus and Dives has beguiled me with its parallels to my tale of Gilles de Rais. Not that the Marshal was exactly Dives, or indeed that anyone ever was, since we get this name of Dives only from the Latin word which means 'rich'. *Quidam dives*, which is to say 'a certain rich man'. In other words, Dives cannot be taken as a proper name from the parable, but then if *any* rich man is indicated it could most certainly be construed as Gilles, in my opinion.

Very well, amen, so let us look a little harder at that story which you will find in *Luke*, the sixteenth chapter, verses 19 onwards:

There was a certain rich man, which was clothed in purple and fine linen, and fared sumptuously every day:

And there was a certain beggar named Lazarus, which was laid at his gate, full of sores,

And desiring to be fed with the crumbs which fell from the rich man's table: moreover the dogs came and licked his sores.

And it came to pass, that the beggar died, and was carried by the angels into Abraham's bosom: the rich man also died, and was buried;

And in hell he lifts up his eyes, being in torments, and seeth Abraham afar off, and Lazarus in his bosom.

And he cried and said, Father Abraham, have mercy on me, and send Lazarus, that he may dip the tip of his finger in water, and cool my tongue; for I am tormented in this flame.

And so on, with of course the rich man being admonished by Abraham and told that between heaven and hell there is a great gulf fixed, so that while Lazarus is comforted the rich man must be everlastingly tormented. So what am I trying to say? What did I perceive here this morning, sitting beside the spring where it comes bubbling up out of the rock? Perhaps that my book is this single act of charity: that before I go to Abraham's bosom it has been permitted me to dip the tip of my finger in the water of truth, and cool my lord's tongue where he is surely now tormented in the flame. My writing is that finger. Sitting watching the beads of water throb up from the rock in the sacred cave, that is what occurred to me this morning. But then my eye fell upon the second verse of the very next chapter in Luke, where our Lord says to his disciples (regarding the sins of some great sinner such as Judas): *It were better for him that a millstone were hanged about his neck, and he cast into the sea, than that he should offend one of these little ones.*

You will see why my Bible reading today has put me in

mind of my master. Perhaps it would indeed be better if I tied a millstone about the neck of my memory of him, and cast my book into the sea, or at any rate the river Anio, and forgot him. But when this thought comes, as soon do I recall that it is the mystery of where Gilles stands in regard to Joan of Arc that gives my tale significance and weight beyond itself. I cannot hope to comprehend that mystery, or even wrap it round with the words of my commentary, and yet I come back again and again to this attempt at some clear representation of it. There is some truth here which, though it is not *against* reason, so far transcends it that I suspect that no created intelligence could ever discover it. Even if this truth were revealed, it would be in its nature impenetrable. That is what I mean by calling the matter a mystery. Like a mystery proper, such as for instance the mystery of the Holy Trinity, its existence is known only by faith, and its nature is never completely to be known in this world. Yet it is not without spiritual profit, for some knowledge of it is available by analogy with things of sense and by the light of faith. Those are the reaches and limits of what I have wrought. I tell you one story in hope that you will glory in another.

Of course, if Joan had been what her accusers said she was – only a witch – then there would be no mystery, therefore no story worth the impossible telling. But Joan was not a witch; and Gilles wasn't a devil. He tried to raise devils, no doubt, but that's a minor matter. The major matter is what may be almost unsayable. Namely, that he once held her in his arms, in those same arms that later held those children. Lord Jesus Christ have mercy, it doesn't bear much thinking about. That's what I have to think about, O God.

Sometimes I wonder if I have not gone mad with the burden of it. Why else do my brothers leave me so much alone? It might not only be my leprosy that makes it so. For whatever reason, I am the only one set to run and catch the leaves here. I sweep them together with my heavy broom and then I shovel them into the cart. Of course, I do not really have to catch them before they touch the ground; that is my game. When I was a boy in Ushant we used to say that the leaves were wishes, and if you could run and catch one before it touched the ground then what you wished would come true. Now, alas, even if I could run, such antics would be beyond me; and even if they were not, I know that what I would wish could not come true. I would have names for the leaves, you see. Each leaf would be a soul and I'd wish them back for a long and happy life: Robin Pavot, Jean Roussin, Guillaume Delit, Colin Avril, Bernard le Camus, Kerguen, Aisé, Edelin, Chastelier, Sorin, Jenvret, Jean Degrepie, Fougère, Loessart, Perrot Degaye, and the others, all the innumerable and unnamed others.

And yet, yesterday, so uncritical can be the compulsions of memory, I found myself singing as I shovelled up the leaves; and the song that I sang was a favourite of my master's, the song which Rossignol used to sing with his back to the roaring fire:

> *Water benefits all creatures.*
> *Water does not quarrel.*
> *Slake your heart, your idle heart,*
> *For can you speak of ice*
> *To a summer insect?*

I would give quite a lot to be able to forget that song. No doubt I will forget it in the lazar-house. No doubt I will have no memory of anything then. My face will be a lion's and my arms will be a crab's. I shall be swathed in bandages through which matter oozes the colour of rust. Am I not already well on the way to becoming what Prelati called the *prima materia*? I am decaying, to prepare myself for heaven: putrefaction for paradise, rusting to be fit to be turned into gold. The old Greek writers called this *elephantiasis*, I believe, and the Arabs *lepra*. The skin, the nerves, the mucous membrane and the lymphatic glands are the structures most affected. Well, thank St Lazarus, the patron saint of lepers, I am able to observe the progress of my own disease scientifically, with detachment and interest. As yet I do not find it difficult to swallow or retain the Host, which I am told is often the most distressing symptom of the later stages.

Knowing the progress of your own death within you is not necessarily a limiting thing. For instance, while I am aware that the condition of the inner chambers of my nose means that I will never again breathe freely the free air, yet I can welcome this and other such slow processes of decay as a means to the wished-for end of being free for ever from the bondage of my flesh. As for death: the extinction of life in the body, through the departure of the soul, is but a step towards the sure and certain fact of the resurrection to come. That re-animation of the bodies of all men, whether saved or lost, will take place on the last day. 'Man will rise again without any defect of human nature, for as God made his nature without defect so will He restore it; and human nature will be brought by the resurrection to its state of ultimate perfection, in that youthful age at which the movement of growth has ceased and the movement of decay has not yet begun' (St Thomas Aquinas, *Summa Theologiae*, Tertia Pars, lxxx). Aquinas himself was poisoned at the age of forty-nine by order of Charles of Anjou. The end of that angelic doctor came not so very far from where I am: in the Cistercian monastery of Fossa Nuova, in the diocese of Terracina. His mortal remains lie now at Toulouse, and in his works.

Not that I wish to live in these words I write, either. To live in words were foolish, and I no longer consider myself a fool. To let words live in me, that is my task so far as these pages are concerned. I will not pretend that the page is not a friend to me, and the words my lively enemies. It is costly to the spirit to spill oneself in this manner, but I do it. This is the full extent of my weakness, and of my ambition. I do not talk to you out of any feeling of being alone, or with any hope of striking an answer from the reader. I have no questions left to ask of anyone but God.

As to the principles on which my writing rests, they are these. I hold that there are two sources of knowledge: the mysteries of faith and the truths of reason. (The distinction between these two is made emphatic by Aquinas, especially in his treatise *Contra Gentiles*, which speaks of each as a distinct fountain of knowledge, but of revelation as the more important fountain of the two.) Revelation is, in this view, a source of knowledge, rather than the manifestation in the world of a divine life. Its chief characteristic is that it presents us with mysteries, which are to be believed even when they cannot be understood. I follow Aquinas in my view of reason too. Reason is not the individual reason, but the fountain of natural truth. What this means, in practice, is a two-fold vision of the world as a place where truth may be found, either through God's grace or as a result of our own striving. Which is all very well, until you hit on Gilles and Joan, a shadow of pure black and a shadow of pure bright pursuing other shadows into the heart of darkness.

And here I notice a sadness in my method, and am moved to ask the reader's forgiveness for it. Only twice in this book have I dwelt on the fact of my leprosy, and sunk back into the irrelevance of where and how I am writing. That was at the start of my tenth chapter, and then at the start of this one. Why did I do so? I have just this moment realized the reason. At the end of my last chapter I dwelt on the blue-eyed child I saw La Meffraye procuring for my master's evil pleasure, and at the end of the ninth chapter I spoke of the child's bloodied vest that was found at the house of Perrot Cahn. In both cases, I suspect, I have been guilty of recoiling into my own disease, and withdrawing from the actuality of his *then* into the similarly noisome but much more tolerable actuality of my *now*, in those pages which immediately followed. I note the practice, and will not repeat it. I shall not speak again of my present decay. As to the Marshal's: the reader had better be warned that some of the chapters to come must contain far worse than leprosy.

It was Gilles himself who decided to quit Machecoul. At least, the ultimate decision was his, proclaimed in the court-yard one morning on his return from hunting, though I suppose that it is possible that he amused himself by listening to Prelati along the way. The Italian diabolist appeared to be losing his nerve. Perhaps he had heard more than rumours of what the Bishop of Nantes was up to; perhaps the full force of Gilles' sacrilege at St Etienne and subsequent maltreatment of officers of the law had sunk into that pretty Florentine skull, and he feared for the civil consequences; for whatever reason, he spoke incessantly of the advantages of Tiffauges. 'Once over the border,' – I heard him telling Gilles – 'and the lousy Duke of Brittany cannot harm you.' This did not sound to me like black magical advice, but no doubt it contained a small nugget of some more than alchemical truth. Duke Jean V would not send a brigade of his soldiery into another province in pursuit of a renegade. His edicts remained powerfully in force, no matter where Gilles might choose to locate himself, but indubitably there was some sense in a removal to Tif-fauges.

Not that sense had much to do with my lord's decision. I have reason to believe that he favoured Tiffauges because he considered himself invulnerable there. Did he really think that the castle was kept by demons? A scrap of curious conversation which I overheard soon after our return there suggests to me that he did indeed. I was in a turn of the winding stair, with the Marshal and Prelati above me; either they forgot my presence, or they were pleased and excited to be back, and content not to care, for I heard Gilles say:

'Death is not lived through!'

And Prelati replied:

'Not at Tiffauges, my lord, especially!'

When I heard these chilling but difficult words, my heart swelled almost to bursting in my breast. I hurried to my cell and sank down at the *prie-dieu*. The crucifix stretched out its arms above me, but the hands for a long blank while seemed to me to hold nothing at all in their embrace. I passed then the most terrible night; it was so special, so dreadful, that I do not remember, in the whole of my existence, to have endured such anguish, undergone such fears. It was an uninterrupted succession of sudden wakings and of nightmares. These night-mares, I might say, overpassed the limits of abomination that the most dangerous madness dreams. They developed them-selves in the realm of lust; and they were so special, so new to me, that when I woke I remained trembling from them, almost crying out. It was not at all that involuntary and well-known act, that vision which ceases just at the moment when the sleeper clasps an amorous form; it was as and more complete than in nature, long and accomplished, accompanied by all the preludes, all the details, all the sensations, and the orgasm took place with a singularly painful acuteness, an incredible spasm, like a kiss of fire. A strange fact, which seemed to point the difference between this state, and the unconscious uncleanness of night, was, beyond certain episodes and caresses which could only follow each other in reality, but were united at the same moment in the dream, the sensation clear and precise of a *being*, of a fluid form disappearing, with the sharp sound of the crack of a whip close by, in the moment of my waking. This being I felt near me so distinctly that the sheet, disarranged by the wind of her flight, was still in motion, and I looked at the empty place in terror. I say 'her', since that is how the phantom seemed to me. I called to mind then stories of the succubus which I had heard in Lemaître's monastery. I had recourse to bathing with cold water in order to recover myself. But when I slept, I dreamed again of the same impurity.

So *was* Tiffauges a castle kept by demons? I do not know. I can only say how it was for me in that night. Real excesses would have exhausted me less than those strange freaks, but what seemed to me particularly odious was the want of satisfaction left by the completed rape of these ghosts. Compared with their greedy tricks, the caresses of a woman diffuse only a temperate pleasure, and end in a feeble shock, I am sure; but with this succuba I remained in a fury at having clasped only a void, at having been the dupe of a lie, the plaything of a phantom, a half-sensed appearance, of which I could not remember the form or the features. Yet that night necessarily brought with it the desire of the flesh, the wish to clasp a real body ... Even now, I have to shake myself to repulse the assault of such foul memory.

Once within the walls of Tiffauges, Gilles without question considered himself safe from harm. He had his prisoners installed there too – the priest le Ferron and his treasurer brother, together with de Hautrays and Rousseau, those two officers who had sought to come upon him in the name of the Duke of Brittany. The deepest dungeon at Tiffauges was as far beneath the level of the moat as the dungeon that they had shared at St Etienne, and I do not doubt that the four of them would have stayed there rotting in their own excrement had Duke Jean V not sent a swift appeal to King Charles VII to despatch his Constable Count Arthur de Richemont to enforce the law.

Now, de Richemont was Jean V's brother. The Duke himself might have no authority outside the confines of his own duchy, but his brother, as Constable of France, had almost unlimited powers of action. The King instructed Arthur de Richemont to act. He rode to Tiffauges at the head of a strong force of cavalry. Not a drop of blood was spilled, however. Even in his drunken folly, Gilles knew better than to try to fight against the King. Forewarned of the arrival of de Richemont, he had the four prisoners scrubbed and ready for delivery that morning in late July when the Constable rode up with his men. Although they were old companions in arms, dating back to the campaigns with Joan of Arc, Gilles himself refused to receive or even see de Richemont when he came to the castle. He sent Rais le Héraut down in black velvet sparkling with diamonds, to supervise the handing over of his prisoners. Whether the Constable was fooled by this deception, I beg leave to wonder. He left with the four released wretches, to all intents and purposes satisfied that part of the Duke's demands had been met at last. There remained, of course, the matter of the fine of 50,000 gold crowns. Worse, from my lord's point of view, there remained the matter of the Bishop of Nantes' secret enquiry into these common cries and complaints that Messire de Rais was a murderer of children. Not the demons of hell could keep my lord from that.

XIX

A DECLARATION OF INFAMY

Did Gilles know? Was my lord aware that the net was closing around him? I suspect that by this point in that long hot summer of 1440 just about all his principal courtiers at Tiffauges had heard the rumours concerning the investigation being conducted by Jean de Malestroit, Bishop of Nantes, and if they had heard the stories then so must Gilles. Yet he did nothing. He sat in the shade reading Suetonius. He went hawking. He licked his thumbs, playing cards with Griart and Poitou. If he did know, then he gave not the least sign of caring. And even if he had cared, where was there for him to hide? I suspect that Gilles knew more or less precisely what the Bishop was doing, but that he considered himself beyond the reach of the law. Had he not got away with his crimes for many years? Did he not inhabit an enchanted castle somehow just over the shadowy border of reality? Was the blessed Joan of Arc not more real and important to him than this pestilential priest collecting gossip? If my lord pondered the problem at all, then I suggest that these are the lines on which he thought about it. But for the most part I am sure that he did not think.

When I recall that time what comes straight to mind is an image of Griart and Poitou in the summer twilight. Griart has a sack across his shoulders and Poitou carries a hoop before him as a servant at table might carry a dish. This hoop is fastened with straps to Poitou's shoulders and around the edge of the circlet sit three hooded falcons fitted with tinkling bells. The moorland is still under its ghostly sheet of mist. Then my lord de Rais rides up on his black horse, Noisette, and immediately those falcons on Poitou's circlet begin to beat their wings and scream.

What else? Another vivid image pressed upon memory like an illumination in a Book of Hours: Gilles beckoning me to him where he sits beneath the oak tree, insisting that I listen while he reads aloud that filthy passage from the *Lives of the Caesars* in which there is description of (as I remember it) the emperor Tiberius swimming and sporting in the sea while a band of little children, called his minnows, dive between the emperor's splayed out legs, sucking with their mouths at the imperial member, and otherwise playing with Tiberius' genitals in the water ... The blueness of Gilles' eyes as they register my reaction. What was it that caused him to care what I thought of such things? My innocence? My carnal ignorance? My celibacy? I cannot forget how he laughed when I blushed and looked away. Is the truth that virginity of any kind aroused my lord, and my cerebral virginity proved of use to him? He was wearing the suit of black velvet, all sugared over with diamonds at the throat, which he had made Rais le Héraut wear when he went down to welcome the King's Constable, Arthur de Richemont. The light on the underside of the leaves was incredibly bright.

When I recall that summer it seems one long procession of swelteringly hot days. The earth about Tiffauges grew baked and cracked. If ever a wind blew, it was full of dust from the parched moorlands. Sometimes there were storms of thunder and lightning, but with very little rain. That weather was sultry and unnatural, like a drawn-out dream of purgatory. Mists steamed up at night from the moat, and from the fens that lay beyond the castle, but they brought no relief where I tossed and turned on my hard bed, still visited by the nightmare of the succuba. The final memory is an auditory one: Rossignol below my window singing that song I never understood, about how you cannot speak of ice to a summer insect. Was Gilles the summer insect? And his coming doom the ice?

The only time Gilles left the castle during that summer was to visit the Duke of Brittany. I confess that I have never grasped the significance of this visit. With the rest of his entourage, I was told that the object of the journey was to collect a sum of money owing to him from the Duke. I cannot believe that anyone was taken in by this story. It would be plausible, perhaps, to suppose that Gilles was motivated by some sense of self-preservation, hoping that Jean V would protect him if the Bishop's investigations ever led to his arrest. However, against this I must point out that my lord's drunkenness had long since atrophied any instinct he may ever have possessed in the order of self-preservation. And it is extremely doubtful whether the Duke of Brittany would have been able to save his vassal from the judicial power of the Church, even had he desired to. In fact, I suspect that this visit was an attempt at conciliation in the matter of the fine of 50,000 *écus* still outstanding. In which case, it proved useless, for the fine was not cancelled.

One small indication of the perilous state of Gilles' grip on the world came out of this visit. The Duke was staying at the time at Josselin, which was not so very far away, nor could the roads be considered more than usually likely to be thick with brigands. Yet Gilles, the night before we travelled, confessed himself terrified. He demanded that Prelati should consult his demon Barron, to discover if it was safe for him to leave the castle, travel to Josselin and see the Duke, and then return. Prelati of course withdrew; then came back claiming that Barron had no objection. They went through the same ritual at Nantes, and then again on their arrival at Josselin, where Prelati made his invocations in a field of poppies. Since Gilles was not present in the poppyfield, Prelati was able to report that Barron had appeared accompanied by a ball of fire, and dressed in a fine violet cloak.

All this nonsense on one side, I may now state clearly what I did not know for certain at the time: namely, that when

Duke Jean was exchanging the usual platitudes of courtesy with my master, *he was already aware of the truth about Gilles de Rais*.

At the time I merely suspected that the Duke knew for certain something which I did not, and that the nature of this something was far worse than the crime of sacrilege. I guessed as much from Jean V's behaviour, even while Gilles swaggered in his court and believed himself 'safe' because of Prelati's promises that they had the favour of the demon Barron.

I remember the Duke received us with few words, and a dead-looking face. There were tense silences after Gilles' protestations of loyalty. Duke Jean considered him with thick black eyebrows cocked up, and his nose and mouth twisted with disdain. I think it was only a morbid curiosity which made him agree to see Gilles at all. He wanted to see what a man might look like who had sold his soul to the Devil. He wanted to examine this criminal against kind without betraying the fact that he knew about his crimes. That would explain the emptiness of their meeting, and its lack of any sensible conclusion. Duke Jean V *knew*. He knew before I did. There is no other way of interpreting the matter. Their meeting at Josselin took place at the start of the second week in August, which means that the Duke had by then received and read a certain 'Declaration of Infamy' prepared and sent out privately by the Bishop of Nantes. Because the Bishop's enquiry was still in progress, and the case for the prosecution not yet complete, this declaration must have had a very restricted circulation. A copy assuredly went to the King, and another to Jean V. This is what the Duke would therefore have read about his visitor just before he met him:

To all those who shall see these present letters, we, Jean, by permission of God and the grace of the Holy Apostolic See, Bishop of Nantes, give greeting in the name of Our Saviour and require you to take heed.

We have discovered, and the depositions of witnesses of good character and discretion have confirmed to us, that Gilles de Rais, knight, our subject and answerable to our laws, has, by his own hand or that of others, slaughtered, murdered, and massacred a very great number of children; and that he has taken with these children pleasure against nature, and practised the vice of sodomy, which he did oftentimes; and that oftentimes also he has made, or caused to be made, a very great number of evocations of demons, offering them human sacrifices; and that he has made finally a pact with the Devil himself. All this he has done apart from other monstrous and numerous crimes against God and man involving our jurisdiction.

On account of this we declare infamous (*diffame*) the said Gilles de Rais. And so that none shall have doubt on the matter, we have written these present letters and sealed them with our seal.

Given at Nantes, on the thirty-first day of July, in the year of Our Lord 1440.

By order of Monseigneur the Bishop of Nantes.

This is the first of several documents which I have to give you. It is my intention for the most part to let these documents speak for themselves, or with a minimum of authorial commentary. Regarding the Bishop's letters patent, however, I must immediately stress again that at the time when I accompanied my lord de Rais on his visit to Duke Jean at Josselin, the contents of these letters were unknown to me. Their circulation, as I say, was limited, and apart from the Duke himself, and the King, I would guess that most of those to whom they were sent must have been higher diocesan clergy whose co-operation with the Bishop's commissaries in outlying districts would have been essential for the collection and preparation of evidence against Gilles. Had I known the precise nature of the charges against my master, I would not have remained another night beneath his roof. And as soon as I did know those charges, I can tell you now, I volunteered to the Bishop of Nantes every single piece of information which I had to give, in the interests of truth and justice, and in order that the culprit should be punished for his crimes.

What else do I recall of the visit to Josselin? The Duke being in an indecent haste to be rid of us; and my master's eyes glittering like diamond points as he bowed and made his withdrawal. Then, on the way home, something else happened. I will describe it first as it seemed to me at the time, then I will tell you the truth of what actually took place. In this way, you will the better see the extent of my ignorance, amongst other things.

We had not travelled far in the direction of home when my master announced that he would like to visit Vannes. From banter between him and Poitou, I gathered that they had a valued acquaintance who dwelt in this place, one André Buchet, sometime a chorister in the chapel of St Vincent, now employed in some capacity by the Duke. Gilles made his horse to dance and prance as he spoke of this fellow. His heart was set on meeting him again, he declared. Poitou and Griart seemed reluctant for a reason which I could not comprehend, but of course they knew better than to cross his wishes.

We lodged just outside the town of Vannes, in a village called La Mothe, in the house of a man named Lemoine, which was not far from the church. There, late at night, I saw this André Buchet for the first time. He was thick-set, energetic, a little bit bow-legged, and he walked with a slight strut. The Marshal spoke alone with him for about ten minutes. Then Buchet hurried away into the night.

Gilles lay on his bed in the lodging house, with a heap of pillows behind him. He called me to his side and asked me to pray.

'Of course,' I said. 'I shall pray for my lord in every prayer which I make. But at the same time, it would be as well if my lord prayed sometimes for himself.'

In the circumstances, this was perhaps a daring remark;

certainly it was somewhat sharper in tone than anything which Gilles had heard all day from his henchmen. He considered me crossly. 'Why do you think you are here?' he demanded. 'Why do you think I employ you? Get to your room and get down on your knees and *work*!'

Does this exchange reveal the true reason why Gilles de Rais needed me by him? Was my function to pray, just as Rossignol's function was to sing? There was that in him which liked lazily to delegate certain responsibilities, and yet I rather doubt it. Not for the first time, I formed the impression that my lord was laughing at me. Griart, spooning honey from a pot, sat in a corner of his room. As soon as I was gone, the two of them would be laughing at my stupidity, the way I did not really grasp what was going on.

Thank God I did not grasp what went on that night at La Mothe! As I crossed the downstairs hall of the house where we lodged, I noticed André Buchet coming in at the door again. He started when he saw me; then shrugged, and strutted the more, as if from defiance. He had by the arm a boy with blond hair, about ten years old perhaps. The boy was wearing a little sky-blue coat. That's all I remember. That's all I experienced at the time.

Later, at my lord's trial, I discovered this: Buchet had indeed been a chorister in Gilles' service, and his own sexual proclivities had saved his life after he had been corrupted. That night at La Mothe he had gone forth to find a boy for Gilles. The poor child in the little sky-blue coat had been taken to Gilles' room, and sodomized. The lodging house, however, did not have a room private enough to kill the boy in. He was therefore taken by Poitou and Buchet to the house of a man called Bretden, where the rest of Gilles' bodyguard were lodged. There the poor child was stabbed, and his head cut off and burned. The headless corpse was then tied up with the boy's own belt, wrapped in the little sky-blue coat, and dropped into the cess-pool behind the house. Unfortunately for the murderers, it was still partly visible. Poitou, being the thinnest, had to be lowered down the shaft of the cess-pool, with considerable difficulty, to stand on the sky-blue coat and tread the corpse under. All this, the odious Poitou swore on oath.

The reader will forgive me the brutality of this telling. No doubt there is a degree to which I am revenging myself for my own crass ignorance. I went to my room in that lodging house at La Mothe, and I prayed on my knees, and I knew nothing of what was going on. Perhaps, had I not been with them, they would have killed the boy there, and there would have been no need to remove him for this purpose to the house of the man called Bretden. I heard nothing untoward. Which is to say that I heard only the usual noises (as I believed) of my lord and the others drinking, and carousing, and indulging in drunken horseplay.

Of course, once I became acquainted with the full appalling facts of that night's work, I began to reach and reckon back in my acquaintance of the Marshal. How many other times had I misinterpreted sounds heard in the castle? How often had I nearly been witness to a murder I did not know had taken place? When I think of these things I think of the thickness of doors and walls throughout Tiffauges. At the same time, I cannot acquit myself quite for not being more curious. I suspect that there was something in me that always knew a little, but never ever wanted to know all. This was my gravest fault, though even had I known I doubt if a single life could have been saved. Had I known definitely of a murder, and had Gilles known I knew, then I would have had my throat cut before morning. The nearest I came to sure knowledge was that smoke from the tower.

Back at Tiffauges, Gilles quickly immured himself in the usual private dream-world, swaggering and drinking, employing brandy-wine to drown his wits. The August weather was intolerably hot. I remember one night when we all repaired to

206

the inner courtyard, by the fountain where the rose-tree grew, and there Gilles chose to act out a number of the scenes depicted in the engravings on the braquemard. At least, this is what I always supposed him to have been doing that hot starlit night. Rossignol, for this purpose, was required to dress up sometimes in woman's clothes and sometimes in the black doublet and grey trunk-hose which according to my lord had been the customary wear of Joan of Arc. I recall in particular their acting out of the second scene on the sword: the one where the woman figure was depicted holding a crown above the head of a man enthroned, while beside him other men were standing uncrowned. For this, Gilles seated himself on a great ebony chair in the courtyard, with Griart and Poitou to each side bearing torches aloft, and Rossignol held the crown above my lord's bare head. Nothing was said. No music played. You could hear the singing of a nightingale perched in the rose-tree. I do not know why I found this scene so moving. Remember, when I witnessed it I still did not know for certain of the children's murders, nor had I read that letter of the Bishop of Nantes'. All through those days and nights of that hot August I watched Gilles like a fascinated, spellbound bird watching a snake dance to a music no one else can hear. By now I think I knew the dangers, but I could not move. I was waiting, like the bird, for the snake to strike and kill me.

Others watched with less fascination and more knowledge. Others knew the sins of the snake, as well as its power. All that August, as I now realize, the Bishop of Nantes and the Duke of Brittany were conducting independent enquiries on behalf of Church and State, and coming to the same conclusion. The Bishop was doing his own work; the Duke's work was done by his chancellor, Master Pierre de l'Hospital, of whom you must hear much more in the chapters to come. Somebody close to that chancellor must have given warning to Messires de Bricqueville and de Sillé. Perhaps they had caught a glimpse of the letters patent? Whatever the fore-warning, they heeded it without fuss. They left suddenly, one night, without word or any other token of intent. The first I knew of it was when Gilles appeared with de Sillé's silver bird-cage in his fist. His cousins had evidently fled in a hurry, no one knew where. Gilles broached a fresh firkin of brandy-wine. He was silent all morning, looking blankly at the thrush where it sat in its cage. At noon, with a crude ostentatiousness, he beckoned me to him. 'Let the bird go!' he commanded. I knew better than to point out that he could do it himself. I opened the door of the cage. The thrush flew away. It did not fly far before one of Gilles' hawks fell on it. I suspect that my lord planned the whole bloody incident, the better to imbue me with some guilt. The flight of de Bricqueville and de Sillé failed to alarm him. He spent the rest of the day listening to the singing of his choir.

XX

ARREST

My lord Gilles de Rais was arrested on Tuesday, the thirteenth of September 1440. In the event he surrendered without a struggle. Prelati, Griart, Poitou and myself were arrested with him. De Sillé and de Bricqueville, as I told you, had already fled. La Meffraye was captured later – caught in the act as she wandered the roads in search of children. She was brought to join the rest of us in prison. But I run on too swiftly with my account of that terrible day. This is how its events fell out, in order.

I awoke that morning with the music of the horn in my ears. That sound ceased as I said the morning office. When I looked down into the court below I saw Gilles stood in the midst of a pack of hounds. A curved horn was strapped over his back, and in his hand he held a long-lashed whip. The dogs whined and yelped, dancing around him in anticipation; there was the stamp of horses too in the yard.

'Mount!' cried Gilles, and with a clatter of hooves Griart and Poitou, with falcons upon their wrists, rode into the courtyard among the hounds. They looked ridiculous. Griart was too fat for his horse, which seemed to sag in the middle as a result of him. Poitou was lean enough, but rode with his long legs twisted round his mount's belly as though terrified that he would otherwise fall off. I would have laughed, had I not known them better. However absurd this pair appeared, there was always something sinister about them. I could not imagine them riding to the hunt. Even the falcons on their wrists seemed unsure about it. Gilles must have pressed his two henchmen to attend him on horseback for the day's intended falconry, perhaps as a result of some wager. As it turned out, they got no further than the drawbridge.

Prelati saw the strangers coming first. For some reason, connected with his magical observances no doubt, the Italian had situated himself on top of the tallest turret in Tiffauges. Now he called down to Gilles in warning: 'My lord, I see a great company of men on the horizon!'

Gilles had been taking his breakfast cup of brandy-wine before galloping off at the head of the hunt. Now he dashed the goblet to the cobbles, where it sparked as it fell, making the horses rear and the hounds yell. 'What men are these?' he shouted. 'Who does your Barron say they are?'

Prelati, shielding his eyes against the rising sun, contrived to dodge the question. 'My lord,' he called down, 'their outriders bear black banners.'

I have never forgotten the way Gilles stiffened and sat bolt-upright in his saddle as he heard these words cried out upon the wind. It was as if in that moment my master knew his fate. No doubt he had been expecting such fatal visitors for many days, weeks, months, years even. The significance of those black banners of the Bishop of Nantes must have gone home to him immediately. He sat straight-backed, immobile on his charger, like a figure in a dream who cannot move. That, gazing out, was how the whole scene looked to me also, in that moment of realization that justice was at hand: we were all of us, the creator and the creatures of Tiffauges, as in one of those direful dreams when the heart strains and the body cannot stir. We were frozen in our iniquity. We were doomed. Only the tinkling of the little bells on the hawks broke the silence. Even the hounds seemed abashed by our master's sudden stillness.

Then Gilles spun his horse.

'Let the hawks fly!' he cried. 'I shall not hunt today.'

Griart tumbled from his horse in his confusion. Poitou did

better, slipping the hood from his falcon's head and casting the bird into the air. When Griart realized what the Marshal wanted he managed to follow suit. The two hawks wheeled and circled, screaming for a prey which was not there. The game was up. Our master was the prey.

Gilles dressed all in red to receive his visitors. He stood in the great hall of Tiffauges wearing a long robe of brocaded scarlet, with dragging sleeves that touched the paving stones. He had upon his head a curious cap that I never saw before: it had twelve pearls about it, and at the front a picture of a black phoenix, only instead of rising from the flames this bird was inverted, plunging down with crippled wings. Gilles never removed this cap throughout the interview that followed. The braquemard hung at his side in a scabbard made of samite. Yet for all this dressing up, my lord seemed to me smaller and more shrunken than I had ever before perceived him to be. His long cheeks were sallow and his eyes had a hollow look, like blue gaps with nothing in them except fear.

The shriek of a trumpet broke the day in two.

The soldiers who marched in were led by a burly little devil of a fellow, with a face like that Greek god Pan. Removing his helmet, he favoured us all with a smile of pale superiority. He announced himself as Jean l'Abbé, captain of arms.

'In whose service?' Gilles demanded.

'Jean V, Duke of Brittany.'

Gilles shook his head. He had plainly supposed that his visit to the Duke at Josselin would prevent anything as bad as this from ever happening. What he did not know, of course, and what I only found out later, was that his liege lord, unimpressed by their meeting, shocked by that letter sent him by the Bishop, had just the week before met with his brother, Arthur de Richemont, to establish that the King would not intervene if Gilles were arrested. De Richemont having assured him that the King was as anxious as anyone to see such a notorious malefactor brought to book, Duke Jean had reported back to the Bishop of Nantes that nothing stood in the way of arresting Gilles de Rais. Thereupon, Jean de Malestroit lost no time in demanding that Gilles should be brought before him to answer all the charges before Monday, the nineteenth of September, which day was the Feast of the Exaltation of the True Cross.

Did Gilles know any of this? It seems not impossible. I suspect that he had heard of the Bishop's intentions, even if not the Duke's. What he said next, while it may only have been a reference to those black banners Prelati saw in the distance, could perhaps be taken to support this small surmise.

Gilles said: 'I was expecting instruction from my lord the Bishop of Nantes, not from some abbot of nowhere.'

This pun upon his name did not much amuse Jean l'Abbé. He motioned with flicking fingers to one of his company, a frail fellow in a dusty black gown, the only civilian he seemed to have brought with him. This, he said pompously, was master Robin Guillaumert, episcopal notary.

'Read him the warrant,' Jean l'Abbé barked. Master Robin Guillaumert stepped forward, bowing, and produced a rolled-up parchment from his scrip. He looked like death; like a risen corpse. His voice was dry and cold as he read from the parchment.

'We, Jean l'Abbé, captain of arms, acting in the name of my lord Jean V, Duke of Brittany, and Robin Guillaumert, lawyer, acting in the name of Jean de Malestroit, Bishop of Nantes, do hereby enjoin upon Gilles, Comte de Brienne, Lord of Laval, Pouzages, Tiffauges, and other places, Baron de Rais, Marshal of France, and Lieutenant-General of Brittany, to grant us immediate access to his castle –'

'Which you already have,' Gilles interrupted.

But Master Guillaumert merely cleared his throat, after the manner of lawyers, and returned to his brisk recitation, with a sidelong glance at the soldiers.

'To grant us immediate access to his castle and to surrender himself our prisoner so that he may answer according to due process of the law to that triple charge which is laid against him this day, the thirteenth of September, the year of Our Lord 1440, by order of the Duke, and of the Bishop of Nantes, aforesaid —'

'What *triple charge* is this?' cried Gilles de Rais. He stood with one hand on the hilt of the braquemard, but whether his bluster was defiance or confusion I would not care to determine. 'What are you talking of? *What* triple charge?'

Guillaumert pursed his lips. They were dry and bloodless. If l'Abbé looked like the Greek god Pan, then this other officer of the law bore every resemblance in that moment to a shrewish housewife.

'The triple charge,' said he, 'of murder, and of witchcraft, and of sodomy.'

The terrible words left silence in their echo. It was a warm day, yet I swear that a chill breeze passed through the hall of Tiffauges now they were uttered. We were all there assembled at our master's bidding: Prelati, Griart, Poitou and myself. Remember that this was the first time I heard directly from any person bearing authority the nature of the crimes of Gilles de Rais. Rumour and suspicion are one thing. They are the stuff of dream and may be dismissed as fantasy by the mind that would prefer not to believe. Now, in a sentence, I was jerked awake. This lawyer speaking for my spiritual lord the Bishop of Nantes had accused my temporal master of murder, and of witchcraft, and of sodomy. All of which made my brain reel, but most of all that calling him sodomite. The name was like a burning coal of fire dropped into my consciousness. I started to my feet, then sank down again with a groan. Griart swore horribly. Prelati started praying under his breath, very fast, in Italian, and crossing himself as though he were scratching a huge wound in his chest and armpits. Poitou had a sickly, meaningless smile spread right across his face.

Gilles said:

'I deny these charges, naturally.'

'Naturally,' the lawyer said.

I sat staring at my master. He would not look at me. His eyes went to and fro, from Prelati to the rafters, from the rafters to Griart, from Griart to the door, from the door to Poitou. He looked up and down the room, and round about, but at me he would not or could not direct his gaze. I felt like crying out to demand his attention. I did not cry out. I sat huddled in my thoughts.

Why did I find it so dreadful, this accusation that my master was a sodomite? I suppose because of all sins that one has always seemed to me the act of most deliberate rebellion against the will of God. St Augustine once defined sin in essence as any thought, word or deed against the law of God. There is therefore a sense in which by any sin a man prefers to choose some self-gratification in opposition to and in defiance of God's law. This particular sin, the pursuit of self-gratification against Nature, *contra Natura*, seems to me Luciferan in its malice, an act of deliberate and calculated wickedness. The soul and the body are good and were made by God who is good, but the body has certain powers which, owing to original sin, incline downwards rather than upwards. The passions reside in the lower part of our nature and these, unless restrained and kept in check by the powers of the soul, drag the soul down. Nothing drags the soul down more than this. It is the sin against Nature, as well as the sin against grace. It is not worse than murder, but it is no better.

I brought myself back from these reflections to the scene before me. Gilles was blustering now. He had launched himself upon some vainglorious speech about his rights as a Marshal of France. Would the King not have something to say about his arrest by a vassal of the crown, a Breton, not in especially good odour as a subject himself? The Duke – had he not been in active sympathy with the Dauphin and the other conspirators? Gilles ranted wildly for a while along these lines. Jean l'Abbé and Robin Guillaumert heard him out politely. Meanwhile, crawling into a corner of the hall, Griart produced a dagger and tried to cut his own throat. He was observed in the deed, and restrained by a pair of the ducal soldiers. This physical diversion served at least to check Gilles in his harangue.

'My lord de Rais,' the captain said, 'will you give me your sword?'

Griart was dragged from the hall, his wrists in irons. Gilles watched him go without interest or compassion, his face a white mask.

'Your sword, my lord?'

Gilles nodded absent-mindedly, then drew the braquemard from its samite scabbard and handed it hilt-first to Jean l'Abbé.

'This is the moment I go to God,' he said. 'I often wished to become a monk, and here is l'Abbé, under whom I must engage myself.'

The captain took the sword.

Then he snapped orders to his soldiers to arrest the remainder of us present. Prelati struggled when the men laid hands upon him, but soon desisted when they struck him about the head and shoulders. Poitou tried to affect a lordly disdain like his master's, though without any conspicuous success. It was only when the soldiers advanced upon me that Gilles intervened.

'This is Dom Eustache Blanchet,' he said. 'This monk knows nothing.'

Guillaumert sniffed. 'We have instructions to arrest you all,' he said. 'See for yourself.'

He handed Gilles the process. Gilles looked it over. 'Why, Dom Eustache,' he remarked, 'here is your name and title after all. It seems our destinies are linked indeed. Did I not always say you were my man?'

He must have seen the horror on my face, that I was now suspected of being an accomplice in his crimes. 'Come, priest,' he murmured, laughing, 'learn a little courage. What is there to fear? The innocent have no cause to tremble, surely.'

Then my master did a strange and baleful thing. Seeing that the soldiers had me in their power, and that as a consequence I could not escape him, he advanced upon me quickly and leaning forwards kissed me on the cheek. It was like being branded by the Devil himself. I shook with fury and revulsion as the soldiers led me from the hall. When I reached the door I managed to call back over my shoulder:

'And you, my lord? Have you no cause to tremble? Are *you* innocent?'

Gilles shouted back:

'I am a perfect Christian! Remember that! Remember to tell them that!'

The five of us – Gilles, Prelati, Griart, Poitou and myself – were led from the castle of Tiffauges, and surrounded by guards, and conveyed at a brisk pace to Nantes. The latter part of our journey took place at night. I remember how dark it was, as though the moon had averted her face and the stars did not want to look down on us. We rode through lands that belonged or had once belonged to the Marshal, yet we now belonged nowhere. We rode in grim silence. I was extremely frightened. I felt sick in my head and in my stomach when I thought of that triple charge: of murder, and of witchcraft, and of sodomy. I knew that my lord was guilty, but how could I prove my own innocence? *Was* I innocent? That was the most horrible thought of all. I had fetched Prelati from Italy. I had done nothing to stop La Meffraye even after Poitou had amused himself by cruelly telling me what her trade was. At every point I had failed to act to prevent Gilles in his evil. Nor had I, a priest of God, done anything to save the soul of Gilles de Rais. All I had done was to listen to his blasphemies and his fantasies, providing him with a corner in which to spin his web of occult verbal memories of Joan of Arc. All I had done, in fact, was indulge him in his passion for Joan because of my own passion for her mystery. And was my passion any better than his? He had used Joan as an excuse for turning his back on God. I had used her as an excuse for turning my back on the most desperate and corrupt soul that I was ever likely to meet, while indulging myself vicariously in that soul's adventures. What a fool and a coward I had been! Well, now I would have to pay the penalty. It would be believed that I was, like him, a murderer, and a witch, and a sodomite. He thought that I was God's spy, but all that the Duke and the Bishop and others would think was that I was the Devil's accomplice. When I should have heard him in confession, I had evaded the duty. At that point, I might perhaps have helped to save him, even stopped him in his evil courses . . . But I knew as I reasoned thus, that the thought was vain and improbable. I could no more have saved Gilles from himself than he could truly have saved Joan from those who would burn her. So, as for me, my wretched skin, my coward soul, did I not deserve to die with him? But was that to be my fate? Was that what was divinely purposed and mortally intended?

Then I remembered my lord's kiss. It had been, as I now saw, a kiss of peace. There was no passion in it, nor affection. It was, if you like, a seal of the bond between us, a mark of recognition. And this bond was not a matter of complicity, but of understanding. I remembered also my lord saying to the others that I was God's spy, and his man, and that they were not to harm a hair of my head therefore, and suddenly I knew that my destiny was not to die with him, but to live to tell his story. I was the one who would tell the Bishop of Nantes the truth. I had been God's spy in the castle of Tiffauges, in the life of Gilles de Rais, and perhaps all along Gilles had known that one day I would be the one to tell the truth about him. If that truth must bring his death behind it, then that was right also, for what else was left to save my lord now but death? Death would provide the only hope he had of repentance, of restoration of his human dignity, perhaps even of ultimate salvation. I was God's spy, and God's spy must now report to God's bishop in Nantes, and tell him all that he knew.

Looking at Gilles where he rode, wrapped in his cloak, I knew that one day I would have to tell his story to others than the Bishop. Did my master know this also? Was that why he had taken me in, and told me that story in the first place? Why else should he have told me the very names of his victims? Kerguen and Aisé, Jamet Brice and Sorin, Loessart and Colin Avril . . . I was to pray for them, yes, for the rest of my days, while there was the slightest breath left in my body. And I did, and do, amen. I was to pray for them, always, but then the difficult particular day would come when I would have to try to make sense of them, and him, and her, and of the whole sad story.

If sense there was to be made. For was it not all wicked nonsense? Sacrilege and sodomy? A dream of darkness, a nightmare of unmeaning? *Contra Natura?* The wasted seed of the man of double deed? A tale of death, and death, and death indeed.

All this I thought as I rode to Nantes a prisoner that night. And as we rode through the blessed darkness the villages of the Pays de Rais sped us on our damned way with yells and with curses, and with bonfires and beacons on the hill-tops to celebrate the capture of the murdering seigneur and his dainty gang of perverts. The curses stopped as we rode into the streets of Nantes, and it was through silent torch-bearing crowds that we came to our final destination. Along with Prelati and Griart and Poitou, I was thrust without ceremony into a dungeon where rats ran. My lord Gilles de Rais was lodged in a comfortable apartment of the castle of La Tour Neuve of Nantes, as befitted a man of his rank and dignity.

PART THREE

XXI

THE TRIAL BEGINS

My home is on this page where my hand crawls back and forth. The movement of hand and pen do not break the silence I have found here, in this garden, by this spring, within my cave; rather the endless scratching is a part of the silence, like the minute dripping of the water or the intricate sound of the wind in the winter trees. So still is the place of truth to those who dwell there, and so crooked the passageways that wind in to it from the hillside of event.

My function for the trial of Gilles de Rais is editorial. I intend to give you all the facts, and to reproduce the necessary documents for your inspection. The story is dire and no story, and I would rather have left it untold, in the darkness to the left and the right of my hand, beyond the margins of saying; but I have no choice. These things happened, and it falls to us to confess and examine them. I must drag this stuff of the final darkness together and make ruin complete.

Gilles, as I say, was lodged in an upper room of the castle of Nantes, comfortable and well lighted, where he was accorded all the privileges properly due to a noble prisoner whose guilt has yet to be confirmed. I have heard it claimed that his trial was unfair in that it followed the usual methods of the in-quisitorial process to extract information from witnesses, but speaking as one of the tortured I have no complaints. The rack was used upon me merely to establish the veracity of what I had already told the Vice-Inquisitor of Nantes, Friar Jean Blouyn of the Dominican Order. The others who were racked would never have told the truth without that assistance. Gilles himself was not put to the Question, but as you will see he came of his own volition in due course to confess all. I have also heard it said that it was an error in law that when the proceedings opened against him certain bereaved parents were admitted to the body of the court, where they were permitted to clamour for justice. But if justice should be done, and seen to be done, should it not also be demanded, and heard to be demanded? I saw no harm in those poor mothers and fathers being allowed their frantic cries. They were present, in any case, only at the preliminary hearing.

Now, in fact, as I think you will see, the methods of the prosecution conducted by the Bishop of Nantes would commend themselves to any judicial authority. There were two tribunals appointed to sit in judgement, the ecclesiastical court, presided over by Jean de Malestroit, and the civil court, with the Chief Justice Pierre de l'Hospital, Chancellor of Brittany, at its head. The Bishop's court, now in session, will try Gilles de Rais for satanism and other heresy, unnatural vice, sacrilege, and the violation of ecclesiastical privilege. Prelati and myself, as ecclesiastics, must come before it. The civil tribunal, sitting concurrently, will deal with the charges of murder and rebellion against the authority of Duke Jean V, trying both Gilles and those of his subordinates concerned. As the charges upon which my lord had been arrested came primarily within the jurisdiction of the ecclesiastical court, so most of the action will be found to take place there, and its findings will necessarily guide the action of the civil tribunal. It is my belief that if I take you step by step through the trial of Gilles de Rais – a trial that was unquestionably fair, and civilized, and Christian – then you will see for yourself that justice was done in the matter. Justice of course is the cardinal moral virtue which inclines one to give whatever is due to God, to one's neighbour, and to oneself. By its extent and implications it is one of the most important and far-reaching of the virtues, for with charity it should govern man's relations with his fellows; it must be distinguished from charity, for justice involves what is *due* to another by right. Gilles, as you will perceive, got his due from the Bishop of Nantes. Justice was done here, scrupulous justice, combined with a charity having one object and one object only in view: the saving of a human soul.

So, after five days' confinement, Gilles is about to be summoned to attend a preliminary examination in the great hall of the castle of La Tour Neuve. It is a vast chamber, brilliantly illumined through windows of stained glass, its floors polished, its rafters lofty, its stone pillars massive. My spiritual lord Jean de Malestroit will sit on the long high dais at one end, with the great crucifix behind him, and beside him his assessors, the Bishops of Le Mans, Saint Brieuc, and Saint-Lô, with Pierre de l'Hospital and other lay assessors in attendance. Already below these judges sit the notaries – black-gowned, skull-capped, ink-horned, with their quills and their snowy tablets – taking down every word uttered during the proceedings. Below these again, to the right, is the red table of the Public Prosecutor, the *promoteur*, Master Guillaume Chapeillon, Curé of St Nicolas, a Canon lawyer, trained in the Sorbonne. It has been Master Chapeillon's task to draw up the indictment against Gilles, under forty-nine heads, of which the first fourteen establish the competence of this Bishop's court and the rest detail the charges. Facing the Prosecutor's table is the witness stand. In front of all, so that he will face the tribunal, with his back to the public in the body of the hall, is the place reserved for the accused and those appointed to guard him. A fine chair, high-backed, oak-carved, waits for Gilles de Rais. As for me, I am kept in a sort of cage beneath the pillar to the left, in company with the cowering Prelati. This means, at least, that I see everything that happens, and hear every word that will be said.

It is Monday the nineteenth of September, the Feast of the Exaltation of the True Cross. The time is approaching the hour of Terce, which is to say nine o'clock in the morning. The public benches have just been filled with some of the great angry crowd milling about since dawn outside in the courtyard. They shouted insults and accusations when they saw the pair of us huddled in our cage. A peasant threw a stone which hit Prelati. Some of the fiercest jibes are directed at me, on account of my monk's garb no doubt. Those few minutes waiting for the trial to begin, while the people of Nantes bayed for my blood as the Devil's disciple, remain in my mind as an image of what an eternity in purgatory would be like. I watched the sand pour through the thin neck of the Clerk of the Court's hour-glass, and in truth it seemed to trickle and then freeze. Time had a stop while those strangers stared at me, and called me evil names, and wished me dead. I could say nothing; I could only hang my head. I knew that in this crowd were the mothers and the fathers of many of the children killed by Gilles. They believed me guilty with him. I would have to prove my innocence, but how?

The hands of the great clock touch nine. The Clerk of the Court stands up, but he waits pedantically for his hour-glass. Only when the last grain of sand has passed through the neck does he reverse the measure, and set it again in clear view on the desk before him. As he performs this duty, the Clerk cries out:

'In the name of God, silence! And be upstanding for Messire de Malestroit!'

I knew the Bishop of Nantes for a noble prelate. He was Duke Jean V's closest friend and adviser, a senior statesman as well as a prince of the Church. In addition to being our spiritual lord, he was Grand Treasurer of Brittany, and President of the Council, and President of the Chambre des Comptes. He was, after the Duke, the principal man in Brittany. Unlike many who rise so high, I never heard a word against his reputation. His life was pure and seemly, his honour unblemished. My lord Gilles de Rais could have fared far worse in the matter of his judge and arbiter on earth.

In his person, the Bishop of Nantes is tall and fat, with a face like a ripe avocado pear turned upside-down. He has watchful grey eyes that water frequently. Observe his carriage now, stately but slightly bent, as leaning on his crosier he approaches the throne on the dais. When he turns to give us his blessing and to declare open the proceedings of his court, you can see for yourself his big slack mouth with the two gold teeth that glint in the early light, his babyish hands and his attitude of unalterable patience. He wears, of course, the purple of his office, with the ruby-encrusted pectoral cross about his neck.

'Call the prisoner before us.'

'Call Messire Gilles de Rais!'

The Clerk of the Court echoes the Bishop's summons. The public benches erupt as the Marshal strides in. White-faced, straight-backed, marching with insolent resolution between two armed guards, Gilles is dressed from head to foot in black velvet. The shouting of the packed crowd he ignores. He stands to attention, saluting the Bishop on his throne. Only those of us who know the Marshal well would perceive anything other than arrogance and rigidity in his bearing. From my near vantage point in the cage I can see, however, a constant twitching of his cheeks below his sunken eye-sockets. This peculiarity, combined with a furtive, almost foxy, slant about the contraction of his eyelids, contrasts disconcertingly with the expression in his eyes themselves. Gilles looks like a man pretending that he has no soul.

The Clerk of the Court is shouting at the public:

'Silence! Silence for the *promoteur*! Silence so that the charges may be read!'

Master Guillaume Chapeillon now rises to his feet and stands leaning forward easily at the red table. Master Chapeillon is tall and sparse. His black silk gown billows as he clasps his wrists under it behind his back. Head bowed, the broad black silk ribbon pendant from his low-perched eyeglasses, he begins to read from the act of accusation. His voice is dry and rueful, like a wasp in a bottle. Now and again, without reference to what he is saying, he smiles to himself. Master Chapeillon's smile partakes of only one side of his face. It creases the arid grey skin below his left nostril. This gives him an air of nausea and sarcasm even when what he is reading appears to lend no cause for it. But his voice does not vary, no matter what his face says. As for my lord, Master Chapeillon has not looked at him. The Public Prosecutor addresses his whole attention to the Bishop.

After a while, I notice my master's features begin to relax. This is because Master Chapeillon's indictment has confined itself to the crimes of heresy and sacrilege. These are offences which do not call for any extreme penalty, and for which Gilles could make full reparation without any loss of prestige. I recognize this at once as a lawyer's trick. By making everything seem slight and reasonable, and by reciting all in a low-key tone, the *promoteur* has given my lord the illusion that he is not an enemy in the way that the howling crowd most obviously is. Now I know I am right to fear the absolute worst. Here is a consummate lawyer. That trouble has been taken to employ him means that Gilles is surely doomed. All very well, you may say, since Gilles deserves his doom. But here am I, reader, inclined to suffer whatever fate befalls him, yet unable to state my case.

The Public Prosecutor concludes his preliminary indictment and sits down. He stares at the rafters, idly dangling his eyeglasses to and fro by the black silk ribbon. A sly sidelong glance assures him that the ruse has worked: Gilles' manner is now almost tranquil. As if it were an afterthought, Master Chapeillon springs back to his feet, half-smiling apology, and passes the papers of the indictment to the Bishop. Jean de Malestroit holds them by a corner between fastidious thumb and finger.

'Messire de Rais,' the Bishop murmurs, 'have you anything to say in response to these grave charges?'

Gilles bows. 'I am quite ready to prove my innocence,' he declares.

Those grey eyes spill their water. Almost you could credit that Jean de Malestroit feels sorry for his prisoner, or perhaps ashamed of the manner in which he has been persuaded to acknowledge the court. 'I am bound to ask you,' he says, with an air of weariness, 'whether you will require the services of a counsel for your defence?'

Gilles bows again, growing in confidence. 'My lord, there is no need for that at all. I am, as you will see, a perfect Christian. I shall take pleasure in proving this myself.'

The crowd howls its anger. Another stone whistles through the air, misses the Marshal completely, goes skittering across the marble pavement to rest by the shoe of one of the notaries. 'The public will not be admitted to our further proceedings,' the Bishop snaps, absent-mindedly.

The Public Prosecutor goes through a little mild pantomime of protest, which the Bishop waves aside. Gilles almost smiles at this. He cannot see that both men are baiting a trap for him.

Then the Bishop says, softly and suggestively: 'Since the charge against you is that of heresy, will you agree that I seek the assistance of a representative of the Holy Office in determining your case?'

'Take me before the Pope!' cries Gilles. 'It is all one to me.'

'Such orthodoxy,' breathes Jean de Malestroit, touching his pectoral cross to his full red lips. 'However, I fear that his Holiness has other things to do. Let it be duly recorded, then, that Messire de Rais has rejected a counsel for his defence, and that he has stated no objection to appearing before the Inquisition. Master Chapeillon?'

Chapeillon pretends confusion. 'My lord?'

'It is your duty,' the Bishop reminds him, 'to nominate a suitable inquisitor.'

The eyeglasses flash. 'Friar Jean Blouyn?'

'Let it be recorded,' declares the Bishop, 'that Messire de Rais is to appear before the Vice-Inquisitor of Nantes, Friar Jean Blouyn of the Dominican Order.' Sighing sweet satisfaction, he considers the prisoner. 'You possess the right to object, if you so wish.'

Gilles shrugs his shoulders. 'I say again that I am ready to prove my innocence of these charges in the presence of any inquisitor whatsoever.'

'Jean Blouyn it is, then.'

'Friar Jean, OSB.'

The Clerk of the Court writes the name on the charge sheet. Chapeillon is on his feet again. 'I would ask that Friar Jean could also hear certain other witnesses in the chapel of your lordship's palace.'

'*Capitula accusationis?*' says the Bishop.

'Naturally.'

'*Recusationes divinatrices?*'

'Let him be asked that now.'

Whether my lord Gilles de Rais understood this exchange between his two principal accusers at the preliminary hearing I have no means of knowing. His face betrayed no particular anxiety, so I suspect that he did not. All the same, I take pains now to explain to the reader that what was being suggested by the *promoteur* was in no wise underhand or untoward. He had requested that witnesses be allowed to testify regarding the charge of heresy against my master. The Bishop had responded by pointing out that the accused had the right to demand a written account of the offences such witnesses might attribute to him (*capitula accusationis*), even while the actual names of the witnesses were withheld from him (this properly in accordance with two bulls promulgated by Innocent IV, *Cum negocium* and *Licet sicut acceptimus*). The effect of this was that Gilles would not know who had denounced him, nor what weight was attached by his judges to the denunciations made against him. The utmost that was to be allowed him was the unsatisfactory privilege of the *recusationes divinatrices*: that is, that at this first examination he was to be asked for the names of any enemies of whom he knew, and the causes of their enmity, so that he had a chance to forswear libel or other malice before it was perpetrated.

All this, I hasten to add, was quite correct and in line with the legal and established procedures of the Inquisition, as expounded by Bernardus Guidonis well over a century ago. To object to it would be to question the principle of the Holy Office itself, and everyone knows that the detection and punishment of heretics and all persons guilty of any offence against orthodoxy has always been a regrettable necessity. St Paul himself 'delivered unto Satan' both Hymenaeus and Alexander, 'that they might learn not to blaspheme.' (1 *Timothy* i, 20.) Our present tribunals for the discovery, punishment and prevention of heresy are based on the principle that truth must be upheld and promoted in the interests of secular no less than divine justice; error must be abandoned or uprooted.

Punctilious now in adherence to the law, the Bishop of Nantes warns Gilles that Friar Jean Blouyn will have power to suborn witnesses to testify against him in all that relates to these charges of heresy and sacrilege. 'We invite you, by God's grace, to name your enemies — that any such persons might be disbelieved.'

Eyes open, proudly, my master steps directly into the trap. 'I have no enemies.'

'None? None who, if found, might speak ill of you? Think carefully, for much depends on this.'

Gilles plainly is inclined to treat the whole matter lightly, so relieved is he to find the more terrible charges against him not even mentioned in the Public Prosecutor's summary of the indictment. Now, however, a suspicion clouds his brow.

'I name my two cousins,' he says, 'Messires Roger de Bricqueville and Gilles de Sillé. It is possible that, if found, they might malign me. They stole money from me some weeks ago, and ran away.'

Master Chapeillon's half-faced smile seems related to something definite at last. He knows, as I know, that it is not Gilles' enemies who will betray him; it is his friends. If my lord had requested a counsel for his defence, that lawyer at his side would have told him to name Francesco Prelati, Henriet Griart, and Etienne Corillaut known as 'Poitou' as witnesses not to be trusted. Yes, and Dom Eustache Blanchet. We are the ones the Marshal should fear now.

It is too late.

The Bishop of Nantes says: 'Let the court record that the witness of Roger de Bricqueville and Gilles de Sillé is to be entered under the heading *recusationes divinatrices*, and any such testimony treated with the gravest suspicion of prejudice. All other witness, male and female, by anyone not here named by the Marshal Gilles de Rais, may be considered on its merits at our next meeting.'

The Bishop of Nantes rises and adjourns the proceedings until such witnesses have been heard. The people, not understanding, shout out in a fury of disappointment. They think that the Marshal might still evade justice. I know better. So does Master Chapeillon, gathering up his papers. So, probably, in his heart, does Gilles de Rais, hesitant for just a moment, casting one long searching look at Prelati and myself in the courtroom cage, before he marches out with his head thrown back.

XXII

FIRST WITNESSES

In the interval of adjournment Gilles spent much of his time hearing Mass, for which permission had been given. I know this for a fact, since I was allowed sometimes to officiate, though I was pledged not to admit him to the sacraments. He seemed thoughtful and devoted on these occasions, but no more than usual. I formed the impression from his demeanour that he had found little enough to worry about in the outcome of the preliminary hearing of the Bishop's court.

The civil court, meanwhile, had begun to sift through the charges of murder and rebellion. This court met in the hall called the Bouffay, about a hundred yards away from where we had appeared before the Bishop of Nantes. The civil court met under the direction of the Chief Justice Pierre de l'Hospital, Chancellor of Brittany. Just as the Bishop had turned over to Friar Jean Blouyn of the Inquisition the task of extracting depositions from all witnesses concerned with the charges to be met in the ecclesiastical court, so Pierre de l'Hospital appointed one Jean de Touscheronde to begin hearing all similar evidence in the matter of the charges applying in the civil court. In effect, Gilles was being attacked simultaneously from two sides. His refusal of the offer of a counsel for his defence, incidentally, reminds me that Joan of Arc took exactly the same course at her trial in Rouen some nine years before his. There, however, all comparison between the two separate trials must end. It is now generally agreed and accepted that Joan's trial was a farce and a travesty of justice. The same cannot be said of the trial of Gilles de Rais.

Before the next public session of the Bishop's court was held in the great hall of the Castle of Nantes, some eighty witnesses were heard by Friar Jean Blouyn on behalf of the Holy Office, with Jean de Malestroit and Master Guillaume Chapeillon in attendance. Many of these witnesses came forward voluntarily to offer their evidence. Others (such as La Meffraye) had been captured and compelled. The deliberations at the first hearing, and the strict procedures of the Inquisition, meant that all this evidence could be amassed against Gilles, and presented to him on demand at a later date, without his knowing who was saying what to his detriment. His sole defence in the process, as I have explained, was that my lord of Nantes had invited him to name those whose evidence might be discounted on the grounds that they were his known enemies, and therefore to be expected to speak ill of him. At that point, Gilles would have been well-advised to nominate his friends and henchmen under the heading *recusationes divinatrices*, so that for instance anything said by those arrested with him as his accomplices would not be allowed to stand in the balance against him. A good lawyer would without doubt have attempted this. On the other hand, so overwhelming was the testimony assembled against my lord over the course of the next three weeks, in regard to both the ecclesiastical and the civil charges, that in my opinion nothing could or should have saved him. There is a sort of justice, also, in that it was pride that pressed Gilles to reject the service of a counsel, so that you could say that it was his most overweening and besetting sin which now left him open to the onslaught of the truth about his life and his crimes. Pride feeds and thrives on itself. In his guarded apartment high in La Tour Neuve of the Castle of Nantes, my lord Gilles de Rais now had no other diet. And, while he paced the floor there, or watched with hungry eyes at each Mass which I celebrated without allowing him access to the Bread of Heaven, the people of the Pays de Rais rose up and damned him with their simple words.

What follows is my selection from among the depositions of the witnesses suborned by either the ecclesiastical or the civil court, or both. All these first witnesses gave their evidence between the nineteenth of September and the eighth of October. For obvious reasons, I was not present when the depositions were made, and since throughout this book I have eschewed invention, it seems to me that the most honest procedure is to give you each statement direct and unadorned, exactly as it was made. Here is the evidence as it was presented before the Bishop when his court met again. It remains for me to say that the Vice-Inquisitor of the city and diocese of Nantes, Friar Jean Blouyn of the Order of St Dominic, seemed to me a man of honour and sagacity, as well as a shrewd man with a passion for the truth. His direct dealings with me were eminently fair, and his questions conformable to the highest standards of the Holy Office. Where torture was employed (as we might well suppose it was in the case of La Meffraye), it can safely be assumed that this was no more than necessary. As I have already remarked, and as you will see in a later chapter, in my own case the rack was brought in merely to verify that I was telling the truth.

Here, then, without more ado, the voices of the first witnesses:

GERARD JEUDON, *labourer, of Machecoul*

In the summer of the year 1432, my only son, Jean, was apprenticed to our local furrier, Guillaume Hilairet. Jean was then twelve years old, a good boy, never blaspheming God nor the saints. He was employed by Hilairet for about two months. Then, one day, Messire Gilles de Sillé, accompanied by Messire Roger de Bricqueville, came to the furrier's and asked Hilairet to lend them my son to go and take a message to the castle of Machecoul. The said Hilairet lent him and sent him to the said castle. Later that same day, when the boy did not return, Hilairet asked Messires de Sillé and de

Bricqueville where he was. The gentlemen replied that they did not know, unless he had gone to Tiffauges. Then, when two days had passed, and Jean had still not returned, I went with Hilairet to the castle of Machecoul and asked after my son's whereabouts. Then Messire de Rais told me that he had sent the boy on a further errand to his castle at Tiffauges, but that no one had seen him arrive in that place. And Messire de Rais said that kidnappers must have carried him off to make a page of him, since he was such a pretty boy. By which I knew that my son Jean must assuredly have been once in the company of Messire de Rais at his castle of Machecoul, but this is all that I knew. My son was never seen again from that day when he left the furrier's at the bidding of the gentlemen.

CATHERINE THIERRY, *of Nantes*

One day in the year 1433 a fine gentleman called Henriet Griart called at the house by the church of St Martin, in the city of Nantes, where I was then living. He told my father (Reginald Thierry, now deceased) that my young brother Bertrand was to travel with him to Tiffauges to become a chorister in the chapel of his lord Messire de Rais. My little brother was then just ten years of age, a good Christian, of simple manners, and well brought up. Because he liked to sing he went with the stranger. None of us ever saw Bertrand again. In the winter of 1435 my father noticing the said Griart by the cathedral at Nantes asked him what had happened to my brother that he never came home to us. The said Griart replied that my brother was dead of a fever.

HAUVIETTE DELIT, *widow, of Pornic*

My eldest son Guillaume went in the first month of the year 1438 to seek alms for our family from the Baron de Laval. My son was twelve years old. When my son did not return from the Baron's castle I asked my neighbour Jean Briand, who was in the Baron's service, what had become of him. Jean

Briand told me that he had seen my Guillaume helping one of the cooks in the castle at Tiffauges to prepare the roast, but he added that he had told the cook it was a mistake to let the boy work there. For myself, I was glad to know that my son was being fed in the Baron's kitchen and kept in the warm in that bad winter. But when May came and I had heard no more of him, I went to Madame Briand and told her what her husband had reported to me, and I said that I was frightened for Guillaume's safety because it was rumoured that the Sire de Rais had small children taken so that he could kill them, and I was fearful since my son had gone to the castle without companion and her own husband had said to me that he had told the cook it was better that the boy should not be working there. Madame Briand reported my words to two of the Baron's men, and they told me that I would pay dearly for them, and so would others. I begged pardon of the servants of the said lord, and left. I never saw my Guillaume again, but Madame Briand told me once that everyone who worked for the Sire de Rais considered it wiser not to think about these things.

SIMONIN HUBERT, *cartwright, of Vue*

I had a fine son called Jean. In the spring of the year 1438 the herald of Messire Gilles de Rais, one Pierre Jacquet, known as Princé, accompanied by a Scottish officer by the name of Spadine, came to my place of work and told me that the said Messire de Rais had noticed my son as a promising fellow, and wished to take him into his employ at the castle of Tiffauges. They made to me lavish promises concerning my son's future. Jean was then in his fourteenth year. He was a good boy, fond of work, and he was never seen idling in the roads, he was more often in the church at prayer. Now I had heard the stories which everyone knows concerning Messire de Rais, and I was fearful to let Jean go into such a man's service. But when I made my excuses to the herald Princé, he replied that Jean need not go into his lord's service, but that he could help him (that is to say, the herald) in his duties. On these terms, I agreed that Jean should go to Tiffauges. He came home only once, about a month later, when he brought with him a big round loaf of bread that had been baked for the table of Messire de Rais, but which he told us the herald had given to him to bring to us. He told his mother that the lord Gilles liked him well, but that he did not care to be in the company of the lord when no one else was near; he did not say why. My son Jean did not much care to return to the castle, but his master the herald Princé came to fetch him back, and his mother said that he should go and that the next time he came home he might bring us a pie from the great lord's table. I thought this foolish, but I saw him go. I never yet saw him return, nor do I know what happened to poor Jean. When six months had passed and there was no sign of him I went to the castle and made enquiries but the herald Princé told me that peradventure the boy had now gone into the service of some upstanding gentleman who would see that he got on. It is my belief that my son never left the castle of Tiffauges after he went to it the second time, and that the Sire de Rais was his murderer. His mother still dreams of Jean's return, but she is a foolish woman, though very charitable and likes to take care of the sick.

PERONNE LOESSART, *wife of Guillot Loessart, of La Roche*
In September of the year 1438 the lord de Rais happened to be staying at the inn owned by Jean Colin which is opposite our dwelling-place. My son Durand, ten years old, was attending school. One morning a man who they called Poitou came to me and said that he had noted Durand for a bright boy, and wanted to take his education in hand. I knew that the man was a servant of the lord de Rais. When I mentioned this, Poitou said that his master would dress the boy well and see that he had every advantage. I replied that I preferred

Durand to remain at school. Poitou then said that there was no reason why the boy could not continue his schooling privately, and that if he passed into the household of the lord de Rais he would have opportunities which he could never have otherwise. Further, this man Poitou gave me 100 *sous* that I might buy a new dress for myself, as a sign of his master's generosity and in proof of his interest in our family. I then allowed the said Poitou to take my boy away with him. And one day I heard the lord de Rais himself when he came from the inn owned by Jean Colin, and he called to the man Poitou and said that my Durand had been well chosen and that he was as pretty as an angel. I did not understand why the lord should say this, except that he was in some way pleased with my son. And certainly it seemed to me that the lord de Rais must have been pleased with him, since only a day after the man Poitou bought a horse from the innkeeper Jean Colin and told him that it was for the boy to ride on. But Durand I never saw again. And when my lord de Rais and his man Poitou returned to the inn before Christmas, I saw another boy riding the same horse in their company.

MICHEL DE FONTENAY, *priest, of Angers*

I had employment at one time as tutor to my lord Gilles de Rais in his boyhood. His other tutor was Georges de Boszac, also a priest with a degree in law, but of his present condition and whereabouts I know nothing. Gilles' mother took no interest in her son, and in his infancy he had been given into the charge of a wet-nurse, Guillemette la Drappière, a respectable woman, of the district of Champtocé. This woman's own child — my lord's *frère de lait* – was named Jean, and he later became a priest and a chaplain to my lord. In mind and in body the boy Gilles seemed to me far in advance of his years. Instead of a gradual development of gifts and talents, Gilles possessed a mature and fully developed mind of unusual brilliancy. He was a genius who was too conscious of the fact.

Perhaps because no one understood this complexity of character, self-admiration became a vice, and from the habit of basking in his own reflection the young Gilles developed a haughty pride and arrogance that would brook no restraint. He began early to exhibit a spirit of revolt and to impose his will on those around him. I have to say that while he received the necessary instruction for the salvation of his soul, his mind remained to my reckoning subtle and crafty. He was very subtle with the subtlety of a woman, as I consider, and more lavish than sincere in his acts of devotion. From an early age I detected in him a condition in which the instinct was both stimulated and gratified by the infliction of pain or cruelty upon others. It was not always necessary that this pain should be inflicted personally; it was enough for him to see the pain inflicted by another, or even to read or hear of its infliction. Gilles to my certain knowledge then took delight in the reading of stories of tortures and executions. But at this time I do not think that his viciousness was otherwise indulged in actuality. Later, when he became a soldier, he would have found a use for his lust for blood.

Gilles was married at the age of sixteen. He had no affection for his wife, with whom he cohabited for only a few months, the result being the birth of a daughter, for whom also he showed little love and no care. I do not think that his grandfather, Messire de Craon, who arranged the marriage, was aware of the boy's vices – though I did hear once, from Georges de Boszac, that it was discovery of Gilles and a certain page in bed together that brought about the old man's death from apoplexy on the fourteenth day of November, 1432, and assuredly his will indicates an estrangement from his grandson. It is clear that women possessed no attraction for Gilles de Rais. His observed indifference to the lively ladies of the court at Chinon, an indifference which was ascribed to a quite erroneous cause, is another indication of what I am saying. The heretical Joan of Arc appears to have had some influence over him. It is likely that Gilles' superstition, of which I shall speak directly, was stirred by this woman's claim to the possession of a divine mission.

I left the employ of the lord Gilles de Rais in the year 1427, at the time when he first went to the wars under the protection of Ambroise de Loré. My knowledge of his later life is therefore hearsay. However, I may state that none who knew him early could be altogether surprised by the reputation which he came to have as a man. It was round about the summer of 1434 that the stories began. This was also the time when Gilles was given money by the King to fight against the Duke of Burgundy, but preferred to send his brother René instead. It came to my ears that he had lost all pleasure in soldiering, but liked to practise cruelties upon boys in private. A furrier named Guillaume Hilairet told me about this time that he had heard a certain Jean du Jardin, who lodged with Messire Roger de Bricqueville, say they had found a barrel full of dead children at Champtocé. From the same source, I learned that a woman on the Rais estates, whose name I do not know, had made public complaint of her child being kidnapped and taken to the castle of Machecoul.

In later times I had only one direct encounter with Gilles de Rais. This was in May of 1436 when he took his revenge upon me for publishing on the door of my parish church the royal edict against him. I was then already a priest at Angers, as I am still, and had close connections with the university. Passing through the town, my old pupil took it into his head to break into my house on impulse, and to carry me off as his prisoner. I was kept in a dungeon first at Champtocé and then at Machecoul. It is my opinion that Gilles by this time considered himself above the laws of God or man. However, our mother the Church has weapons with which to save her own. The Bishop of Angers, the university and the municipal authorities all protested, and the lord de Rais was obliged to release me. Although I saw no evidence of his crimes, I experienced for myself in his dungeons the horror of being in his power. Had I been some well-favoured chorister, and not a crabbed old priest, I have no doubt that my fate would have been final.

I know several clerics who have served the Marshal de Rais. All of them have spoken of him with fear and trembling. That he has been able to carry on his career of vice and debauchery for so long a time might be attributed in part to his exalted social position, and partly to the disturbed state of our poor country. His astonishing egotism is shown by his great prodigality, especially in the lavish production of theatrical performances. Then we must note his superstitious character, as indicated by his attempt to call in the assistance of demons, and his design of making atonement for his crimes by the foundation and endowment of a religious institution. Communication with spirits, by the strict observance of certain rites, is of course quite possible, and in no way to be looked upon as an insane delusion. I submit that Gilles is not mad. What in other men would be madness is the vilest of pleasure to him. Though I have no direct knowledge of any murders he may have committed, yet I have no doubt whatsoever that the common report and belief that he is a murderer of children must be true. I knew him in youth for a contumacious spirit, swollen with pride, and in later years for a vengeful and violent man, who thought nothing of raising his hand against a priest of God. Although as his original tutor in the faith it does me no credit and can give me no pleasure to say it, I must also declare that I consider Gilles de Rais guilty of both the sin and the crime of heresy. I shall pray for his soul, as I am bound to. I have no doubt he will not pray for mine.

PERRINE MARTIN, *known as La Meffraye*

My name is Perrine Martin. I am sixty years old. I was born at Parthenay in Poitou. I was baptized at the parish church at that place. I know my *Pater* and my *Ave*. My parents were not rich. Up to the time I left them I followed the plough and sometimes minded the cattle in the fields. Also I did the usual duties of women, such as spinning, and other things. Up to my going to my husband, I never obeyed any one or worked for any one but my father. My husband was Pierre Martin. He was a squire to Guillaume de la Jumelière, who was in the service of the Sire de Rais. My husband died five years ago. At the same time Guillaume de la Jumelière left the service of the Sire de Rais. He had been with him about eight years. I do not know why he left. It was at this time, when otherwise I would have starved, that Messire Roger de Bricqueville first asked me to look for children for the Sire de Rais. I was chosen for the task because I was a woman and sometimes the children would come with me to the castle when they would not have come there with a man. I was told that the children could be either boys or girls,* but that for preference they should have fair hair and be clean-limbed. The Sire de Rais liked best for the children to be between eight and twelve years old, but there were a few that were younger and some that were older. The youngest I found was about seven, that would be one of the two sons of Guillaume Hamelin; his brother was about fifteen, he came too. Wherever we went I was to look for children for the Sire de Rais. Sometimes he would see a child he wanted, or Messire de Bricqueville would notice a pretty child in the fields or at Mass when we went to La Suze; then it would be my task to collect the said child for the Sire de Rais. I took with me little cakes and pastries in a basket, and comfits, and apples. Sometimes I gave them poppy-seed to drink to make them sleep. Then one of the others would come, either Griart or Poitou, and carry the child to the castle in a sack or a bag. Messire de Sillé told me that the blood of the children was needed for a black book of magic which our master was writing. Someone else told me

* *tam mascullis quam femellis* in Friar Jean Blouyn's record.

early that the children went to the English to pay for a great ransom to free the brother of Messire de Sillé. I do not think that was true. I never saw what happened to the children. My task was to collect the children and bring them to the castle. I can name two others that I found and brought to the castle since it was said that they were needed for a sacrifice to the Devil. This was Jehan Barnard of Fort Launey and Jamet Brice of St Etienne-de-Montluce. I think that their throats were cut and they were sacrificed to the Devil. I often saw the Sire de Rais at Mass. I heard him once swearing to God that he repented of his sins, and vowing to become a monk or go to the Holy Land on pilgrimage, begging his bread from door to door. One All Saints' Day I found him washing the feet of three poor men at the gates of his castle and serving them with food and drink. But another time I saw him with blood on his beard. I was never in the room when murder was done. I was never in the room when any act of impurity was done upon the children. I do not know for certain what happened to the children. My task was to fetch and bring the children to the Sire de Rais. I was not present when any child, either boy or girl, was violently and unjustly done to death. I know nothing of heresy. I know of no sacrilege. I believe that the Sire de Rais might be possessed by the Devil. I saw him once with warm blood on his beard and on his hands. When the church bells ring, I have seen him kneel down and make the sign of the cross. To hear blasphemies upon the name of Our Lord troubles him. Many times when Griart or Poitou swore or blasphemed before him, I have heard him reprove them. As a rule, no one in the castles of Tiffauges or Machecoul ever dared to swear or blaspheme before him, for fear of being reprimanded. He would have no women in his service, but myself. I never saw what happened to the little children, either living or dead. I never had a son or daughter of my own. If I had had a son or daughter of my own I would have flown to the ends of the earth to hide them rather than give them up into the hands of the Sire de Rais. I commend myself to God and all the saints, and throw myself upon the mercy of the Church.

XXIII

EXCOMMUNICATION

Now it is Saturday the eighth of October, 1440, and we are
again in the great echoing hall of the Castle of Nantes. The
preliminary hearing – with its limited terms of indictment – is
already a thing of the past, so far as Gilles' judges are
concerned. As they file in and take their seats under the
presidency of Jean de Malestroit, with the Vice-Inquisitor Jean
Blouyn beside him, you can be sure that their heads are full of
the depositions and confessions of those first witnesses. There is
Messire Pierre de l'Hospital, the small, energetic figure in the
fur-trimmed surcoat belted tightly round the waist, a little bit
bow-legged, walking in with a definite strut. He is here to
represent the secular authorities today, though soon he will be
presiding over his own court. Forty-five years of age, with a
fresh complexion and eyes as clear and mild as a glass of water.
He smiles rather fatuously at the Vice-Inquisitor. Jean Blouyn
does not smile back. What is he thinking? He fingers the
amended act of accusation, widened to admit the charges of
murder and offences against nature. The Vice-Inquisitor is a
little, wiry, twisted fellow, tough as wire, with thin black
eyebrows tilted in a kind of agony at everything he sees before
him in the court. He sets down the papers of the indictment,
and folds his hands together like mating birds. Never was man
more utterly smileless. Friar Jean Blouyn is at the pinnacle of
his profession, a pincer-jaw of heaven, an extirpator of error.
He is certainly no saint, as his clever eyes will tell you. Those
eyes have looked on too much human malice for the mind
behind them to be altogether comfortable in its skin.

Now, just for a moment, the officer of the Holy Inquisition permits his wounded gaze to rest on me. I am crouched beside Prelati in the cage. I wear the *sacco benedetto*, the blessed sackcloth which Friar Jean has awarded me as a sign of my desire to repent and be reconciled, a short yellow tunic bisected by diagonal bands forming the cross of St Andrew. I bow my head and beat my breast with my clenched fist for his understanding. He looks away as the trumpet sounds for Gilles.

My lord is dressed in a suit of pearl-grey silk, with a crimson belt around his waist and white boots on his feet. Diamonds flash on his fingers as he salutes the Bishop of Nantes. The other judges he acknowledges with the slightest of bows. It is clear that the presence of the Vice-Inquisitor as yet means nothing to him. From where I am, kneeling in the cage, though, I can see that Friar Blouyn is well aware of Gilles. His hands, which were mating birds, are now a white-knuckled knot.

The Bishop of Nantes addresses the prisoner before him:

'Gilles de Rais, you must know that while this court will concern itself principally with the charges of heresy and sacrilege brought against your person, certain witnesses who have given evidence before Friar Jean Blouyn of the Holy Office have accused you directly of other crimes repugnant in themselves and relevant to the matter here in hand. While you will be answerable to the civil court when it comes to sentence for these crimes, nevertheless I should warn you that they have now been added to the act of accusation against you here. Master Chapeillon!'

Before Gilles can react, the Public Prosecutor steps forward and recites the indictment in full. My lord hears him with mounting fear and fury. It is clear that he is aghast at this new development. Did he expect the filthiest of his deeds to be forgotten? or the terms on which he was arrested to be ignored? Who can say what ever passed through the head of

Gilles de Rais? Having lived for so long in a dream-world, a world where his will was king and each day and night was shaped to suit his appetites and fancies, I suppose it is possible that some part of him imagined that his judges would not really dare to accuse him of murder and sodomy. In this, my lord was like a child who shuts his eyes when confronted by anything he does not want to see, convinced that darkness inside the eyelids means invisibility. Now, though, Gilles' eyes have been opened for him, and he stands accused.

My sometime master's response is a roar of anguish and rage:

'I deny all! Nothing in all these charges against me is true, I tell you, nothing! I have always been, as I am now, a perfect Christian!'

The Vice-Inquisitor speaks:

'Perhaps the Marshal de Rais would care to read over certain of the depositions made against him by witnesses who have appeared before the Holy Office? There is one in particular, by the woman called Perrine Martin . . .'

'God's wounds!' shouts Gilles. 'Has it come to this? Is a Marshal of France to be condemned by the word of a crazy old woman? Am I, the King's friend, to be dragged in the dirt by my servants? I demand that I be tried by my peers, not by this court. You have no competence to judge me!'

My spiritual lord Jean de Malestroit is shaking his head sadly. The other bishops look less tolerant. As for Jean Blouyn, he is picking his teeth. A moment's whispered conference, with the civil Chief Justice Pierre de l'Hospital crowding forward importantly to listen, and the Bishop of Nantes is ready to pronounce.

'Let it be entered in the record that we overrule the prisoner's plea as frivolous, and that in view of the gravity of the charges against him we have no choice but to consider his frivolity much worse than foolish. We remind the Sire de Rais that it is the Church and State alone, and not the culprit, which has the power to appoint judges. At the same time, let it be recorded that we again offer the accused a sight of the evidence against him, and perhaps a few days in which to think over its implications.'

'Evidence!' Gilles is purple-faced with anger. 'I would not use your documents to wipe my arse!'

Master Chapeillon now rises rather wearily to his feet, smiling his half-faced smile, flourishing his eyeglasses, promising to speak the truth and eschew all bias. This is the formal oath which has to be taken. Having sworn it himself, the *promoteur* demands the same of Gilles. Gilles remains silent. Again, the Public Prosecutor demands the oath. Gilles still says nothing. Twice more, a total of four times, Guillaume Chapeillon requires the swearing of the oath from Gilles de Rais, pointing out finally that a refusal to swear could involve him in excommunication. Gilles has gone white now, but he hangs his head, dumb.

What is happening here is this: Gilles knows what Master Chapeillon knows, that the oath is an invocation of the divine name as witness to the truth of a statement. It is an act of the virtue of religion and, if the statement is in the form of an undertaking, its fulfilment is binding under the obligation of religion. Perjury – that is to say, the confirming by an oath of a statement which the swearer knows to be false – involves not just lying but a very great insult to God. When committed with full deliberation and knowledge it is always a mortal sin against the virtue of religion. Anyone giving perjured evidence before an ecclesiastical court incurs a personal interdict. And from an interdict to excommunication is but a step.

All this must be chasing through my former master's brain as he stands before the court, furious but speechless. At last, the Bishop of Nantes has mercy on him, and adjourns the proceedings.

'This court to meet again on Thursday the thirteenth. Meanwhile, let the Sire de Rais know that there are still more witnesses to be heard by the Vice-Inquisitor. Also that next Tuesday he will be called to make a formal appearance before the civil court at the Palace of La Bouffay.'

No doubt, now, the members of the tribunal retire for refreshment, since custom requires that they must have fasted from sunset of last evening, so that their minds are clear when they enter this hall of judgement. Whether Gilles in captivity clouds his mind with anything like the customary heavy ration of wine I rather doubt. As for me, I am content with the frugal bread and water I deserve.

Tuesday, October the eleventh, this is the day set for my lord's appearance before Pierre de l'Hospital presiding over the civil court. Since I was not present there, I must rely upon the record I saw later for my account of it. But, first, consider Gilles' predicament now. The reading of the full indictment must have come as a profound shock to him, and all his wits will be sore taxed to discover the best means of meeting this fresh, if not wholly unexpected, emergency. Should he admit his guilt and throw himself upon the mercy of his judges, or trust his rank and position, and a brazen denial of the charges, to carry him through? The quandary has to be complicated by his uncertainty as to how much his judges really know, or how much weight they can attach to the testimony of such a one as La Meffraye. All the same, to my eyes, knowing him well, he was already in despair in those long spellbound moments when he stood before Master Chapeillon unwilling or unable to repeat the words of the oath.

In fact, when three days later he appears before the civil tribunal, his mind might be observed to fluctuate in the most uncertain manner. Ultimately he seems to gamble on an extreme course, perhaps because he hopes that will show him at his best without definitely revealing any of his guilt. According to the verbatim record, he begins by demanding, in his most authoritative style, that the proceedings should be expedited as much as possible, as he is anxious to devote himself to the service of God. Before the court has recovered from its surprise, he follows up this statement by declaring that it is his desire and intent to bestow large sums of money as gifts on each of the churches in the city of Nantes, and to give the greater part of his fortune to the poor. But if my lord hopes thus to hoodwink justice by a pretence of charity, he is grievously disappointed. Here in the record is Pierre de l'Hospital's response: 'If it is right that the Sire de Rais should think of his soul, it is necessary that he should satisfy the justice of man as well as the justice of God.'

At this point, as will be seen, Gilles stands in grave danger of excommunication, a thing which must weigh heavily on his mind and soul. The use of excommunication as a form of Christian discipline is based on the precept of Christ and on apostolic practice. In the *locus classicus* upon this subject (1 *Corinthians*, v, 5) St Paul refers to the excommunicate being 'delivered unto Satan for the destruction of the flesh that the spirit may be saved in the day of the Lord Jesus'. Contrary to popular belief, the act of excommunication cannot therefore be interpreted as a final cutting off from the hope of salvation, since Paul extends that hope for the last day; all the same, nothing can be more terrible to the believer than that possibility that he is to be excluded from the communion of the faithful, with the lighted candles violently dashed to the ground and his soul extinguished with them. The word used in the New Testament to describe an excommunicated person is *anathema* (1 *Corinthians*, xvi, 22), which is the Septuagint rendering of the Hebrew *herem*. Amongst the ancient Jews, to be *herem* was to be set apart from God and man; amongst Christians, to be *anathema maranatha* is to be bound for hell. Yet having said that, I remember the dying words of Dom Olivier des Ferrières, that hell may be empty save for the devils. Certain it is that the number of the lost is unknown, and the loss of no individual person has been revealed, not even Judas. Yet even if my lord considered this, such thoughts would have been small comfort in the dark hours of the night. To be excommunicate is to be a spiritual outlaw throughout eternity, delivered unto Satan for the destruction of the flesh. With what Gilles had done already, he needed all the help that he could get, not this pitchforking.

It is Thursday the thirteenth of October, and once more Gilles must face the Bishop of Nantes on his throne in the great hall of La Tour Neuve. Here is Master Chapeillon, with his voice that sounds like a wasp trapped in a bottle, again reciting without emotion the terrible catalogue of his crimes. Does Item XXVII, in particular, strike shame and terror through the heart of the prisoner?

> XXVII. Item: that Gilles de Rais, the accused, sometimes at his castle of Champtocé, in the diocese of Angers, sometimes at his castles of Tiffauges and Machecoul, did kill 140 or more children, in a manner cruel and inhuman; and that the said Gilles de Rais offered the limbs of these poor innocents to evil spirits; and that both before and after their death, and as they were expiring, he committed upon these children the abominable sin of sodomy, and abused them against nature to satisfy his carnal and damnable passions; and that afterwards he burned in these same places the bodies of these innocents, boys and girls, and had their ashes thrown into his cess-pits.

Had I been accused of this, or half of it, and known myself guilty, I would have been down upon my knees in public and begging for them to burn me and scatter my accursed ashes to the four clean winds in hope that I might be forgotten for ever. Not Gilles. Not my master, this heretic, this apostate, this sodomite, as he is stigmatized in the final sentence of the Public Prosecutor's speech. He is standing with head held high as he listens to Master Chapeillon appeal to the judges to punish and excommunicate him in accordance with the laws

of Church and State. The crowded court has listened to the
arraignment with feelings of amazement and incredulity. Now
every eye is turned towards Gilles de Rais to hear his answer
to the charges.

Gilles shouts:

'I would rather be hanged by the neck than submit to you
as judges!'

Jean de Malestroit seeks to calm him. He explains, in
French, the implications of the indictment, which was of
course drawn up in Latin. There is no reason to suppose that
Gilles did not understand it in Latin the other times he heard
it. Hearing it in French does not improve his temper.

'I reject the court!' he roars. 'I will do nothing for you
as Bishop of Nantes!' Then, turning to confront Pierre de
l'Hospital: 'I am astonished that you should allow ecclesiastical judges to accuse me of such infamies.'

Tumult breaks out. Pierre de l'Hospital is heard declaring
that the prisoner is in contempt of court. Friar Jean Blouyn,
sucking his teeth, watches Gilles rave and stamp with all the
detachment necessary to his vocation. When order is restored
the level voice of Master Chapeillon is heard again, asking the
tribunal to ascertain from the accused whether he wishes to
answer the charges in writing or verbally, and which day he
would care to nominate for this performance.

Gilles does not wait for the question to pass through the
Bishop. 'I tell you again,' he snarls, 'I have nothing to say!'

For all his patience, Jean de Malestroit looks weary and
pained. He consults with the Vice-Inquisitor, then calls on
Gilles, by name, four times in succession, demanding a reply
to the key charges on the indictment. 'How do you plead to
the sacrilege? The murders? The heresy? The sodomy?'

Gilles shouts him down before the words are out.

'I do not plead! I have nothing whatsoever to say. Do you
think I don't know the Catholic faith from one end to the
other? Do those who say that I have betrayed it know who I

am and what I am? This court has no power to try me. I reject you all. I tell you again, I am a perfect Christian! I am a good Catholic!'

In vain, the Bishop of Nantes seeks to make Gilles understand that his denials are not sufficient to remove the court's authority. 'The prisoner must answer the charges, on pain of excommunication.'

That single word *excommunication* seems to possess for Gilles a terrible reality which nothing else does. Pressed to the bars of my cage, I watch him take two steps back. His hand comes up to his forehead as if to ward off a blow. Then he says in a quieter voice, biting his lower lip: 'I will admit that if I had committed the crimes just charged against me, then I should have acted directly in opposition to the Church. But I would have avoided them, and I would still avoid them! I do not claim in any way to benefit by an ignorance which is not mine . . .'

Only Jean Blouyn seems interested by these confusions. I suspect that of all those present, he is the only person beside myself who sees that excommunication might seem worse than death to Gilles de Rais. However, even that spiritual terror is not sufficient to keep Gilles quiet for long. Soon he is ranting again, calling the Bishop corrupt and the others fools and knaves, refusing to recognize the court or to take the solemn oath. And through all this shouting, Master Guillaume Chapeillon swings his eyeglasses back and forth on their black silk ribbon and persists in his demand that the judges declare Gilles excommunicate for his manifest contumacy, which sentence to be put in writing immediately and then publicly proclaimed.

Jean de Malestroit sighs, tapping his gold teeth with the pectoral cross. Now he is rising to his feet, and calling for the candles. The court falls suddenly silent as the acolyte lights them, and the Bishop of Nantes stands holding the tall flames aloft. Then he dashes them to the ground in a gesture of doom. 'Gilles,

Sire de Rais, we excommunicate you, in the name of God!'

I see my lord shiver as if his heart must stop. His heart does not stop. But he falls back in his chair, and covers his face with his hands. Quietly, then, Jean de Malestroit declares the court adjourned for forty-eight hours, to give the prisoner time to reflect upon what has befallen him. Jean Blouyn sits staring at Gilles as he stumbles from the chamber. The Vice-Inquisitor's face is like that of an ermine in the snow, whiter than white, waiting for and savouring the moment it will feed upon its prey.

XXIV

WITNESS OF GRIART AND POITOU

I have never been sure at what stage Griart and Poitou decided to give their evidence and tell the whole damning truth about the Marshal to the Holy Office. It could have been now, during the adjournment after Gilles was excommunicated by the Bishop of Nantes, or it could have been a day or two later, following that incident when he was invited to question his servants himself in open court. It might even have been before the drawing up of the forty-nine charges against him, and certainly it could have been prior to their full reading aloud in Latin by Master Chapeillon. This last possibility recommends itself because of that appalling Item XXVII in the indictment. The number of Gilles' victims and the horrible detailed information that the ashes of their burned bodies were cast into his cess-pits – these are things unlikely to derive from general hearsay. I think we may assume that when my lord was made excommunicate it was not only his contumacious shouting down and fighting of his judges which turned the Bishop of Nantes so squarely against him. I suspect that either Griart or Poitou had already confessed his crimes and their part in his crimes to the Inquisition, and that Friar Jean Blouyn had passed on the news to the court. Not, I suppose, that it matters much. The most important thing is that at some stage all of Gilles' friends now turned against him, told the truth, and shamed the Devil, whatever the consequences. Prelati, who shared my cell, was the last to crack. As for me, I never withheld any bit of the little I knew. But I will come to the alchemist's confession, and my own, in due course. First, I'm afraid, we have Griart's and Poitou's depositions to put into the record.

Now, I confess that I have known people who read matter like this, find it disgusting (which it is), and conclude therefore that it cannot be true. Such readers claim that some of the more extravagant demonstrations of the depravity of human nature obtained by the Holy Office are the product purely of torture and the impure imagination of the torturers. Would a racked man not sign anything that his pain might cease? Is it not true that celibates think more of lust than those who endlessly indulge in the commerce of lithe limbs, so that it would not be difficult for the inquisitor to attribute to his victim his own cerebral erotic dreams and fantasies, and say that this evil one *did* what this good one fears he might do himself in a world without constraints?

Admitting the attractiveness of the argument, I must still insist that in the particular case of the depositions of Griart and Poitou I do not believe we are dealing with anything other than the most sober and horrible truth. This is what happened, here is what they did, after all Gilles' fine talk this filth is what you come down to. Consider how these two hideous catalogues of the foulest crimes, minute in their specifications, complement each other. It could be reasoned that this identity between them in trifles, where omissions or discrepancies would be natural, suggests manipulation either of witnesses or of records. I suggest that such reasoning is specious and unnecessary. Here, let us be brave and admit it, is that truth which none of us wants to be true; here are the depths of the human heart; here, the gates of hell. If any doubt remains, later chapters must dispel it. Did not the Marshal himself corroborate and confirm everything said by his henchmen in his own complete confessions?

As to the matter of torture, I do not find that of any great import. It might be considered worthy of note that in these confessions or depositions the customary formula that they are made without fear, force, or favour is conspicuous by its absence. I think we can be sure that the methods of the inquisitorial process were not spared to extract information from Griart and Poitou, and if in fact they resisted that process and did not confess all quickly and voluntarily, but had to be put to the Question, then that would explain the ambiguity involved in knowing exactly *when* they talked. I suspect that the progress went something like this: that at first one or the other or both of them made some sort of general admission of guilt, that gradually one or the other of them was induced by torture to be more specific, and that finally both made full confessions, pouring out the stream of vileness preserved now in Friar Jean Blouyn's archive. That would explain how the charge of child-murder, known from the start, came to assume foul prominence only as the trial progressed. At first, it was easier to press down on the charges of sacrilege and violation of clerical immunity, with murder figuring as accessory to the other crimes to which it was connected. Only when Griart and Poitou broke down and told all, so that the evidence spoke for itself and there was no chance of Gilles being able to deny their testimony, did Master Chapeillon know for certain that he had his man for hanging.

What would have been applied to persuade these stubborn ones was the Question Ordinary, or Question by Water. They would have been bound, hand and foot, and fixed to staples in such a manner as to stretch their bodies as far as possible without breaking them, with a rack or trestle two feet high placed under their backs. The Questioner, with his assistant, then proceeded, the one to hold the prisoner's nose and thus compel him to swallow, the other to place over his mouth a horn funnel. Into this funnel water was poured, generally four *coquemars* or pipkins-full, which is to say about nine litres altogether, but by degrees, and pouring the water through a linen cloth. The patient would then be unbound and allowed to recuperate before the treatment was repeated, if necessary. Under the pressure of the water, the heart and bowels feel like to burst.

Thus were Griart and Poitou brought to confess to Friar Jean Blouyn as follows. The reader whose heart and bowels feel like to burst in reading it has all my sympathy.

HENRIET GRIART, *servant to the Sire de Rais*
  Interrogated: if he would tell the truth.
  Dixit: Your Worships, I know not what to say.
  Exhorted to tell the truth.
  Dixit nihil.
  Told to tell the truth.
  Dixit: I know nothing.
  Required to tell the truth.
  Dixit: My name is Henriet Griart. I was born in Périgord in 1411. I came in my twentieth year to the service of the Sire de Rais. I am his bodyservant. He has others, but I am the principal. In that year of 1431 the Sire de Rais lived at his castle of Tiffauges in company with his cousin Roger de Bricqueville. That summer another of my lord's cousins came to live at the castle, named Gilles de Sillé. In the autumn of that year my lord's grandfather died, the ancient Jean de Craon. Then the murders began. At first I took no part in them. I heard rumours of them. Then I saw evidence. My lord and his cousins would feast long and be drunk, then they demanded children for their pleasure. My lord Gilles de Rais must have been the prime mover in these matters. His cousins did not only act to please him. I heard that they took part in what happened. What happened was that the child, a boy or a girl, would be pampered and dressed in fine clothes. The child would be invited to their feast, and given hypocras to drink. These boys and girls were then made to sit upon the lap of the lord de Rais, or sometimes de Bricqueville, or de Sillé, or there would be several children, one for each of the

257

great lords. The Sire de Rais would then take his lustful pleasure with the children, both boys and girls. Sometimes he would hang them up by the neck with ropes, with his own hand, from a hook. Then he would take them down and pretend to comfort them, assuring them that he wished them no harm, but quite the reverse. Then he would say that he wanted to play with them. Then the Sire de Rais would take his own member in his hand and stroke it until it was erect, or he would make the boys or the girls to stroke it until it was erect, and then he would place it between the thighs of the said girls or boys, rubbing his member on the bellies of the said boys and girls with great delight, and vigour, and libidinous pleasure until his sperm was ejaculated upon their bellies.

Dixit: When the said Gilles de Rais, the accused, had committed his horrible sins of luxury he afterwards killed these children, or had them killed.

Asked: by whom.

Dixit: Sometimes the accused Gilles killed them with his own hand, sometimes he had them killed by the said de Sillé, or by Poitou.

Interrogated: did this witness do murder.

Dixit: Not then.

Interrogated: when did witness do murder.

Dixit: In later years. First in 1437. Before that date I knew of the feastings and the things done to the children and the murders, but I did no murder. Then it was on the evening of the day on which my lord de Rais took back his castle of Champtocé from his brother René, in order to dispose of it to Duke Jean V of Brittany. My lord summoned me to his library. He swore me on the Gospels to absolute secrecy. Then he bade me follow him to one of the rearward towers of the castle. In its bottom dungeon lay a heap of little skulls and bones.* My lord instructed us that these must be removed at

* *ossa innocencium quamplurimum mortuorum* in Friar Blouyn's record.

once to his castle at Machecoul. The Duke's men were due to arrive on the following day, so there was no time to be lost. A boat lay in wait on the Loire near by, with one Perrot Cahn its master. Present beside the witness: Messires de Bricqueville and de Sillé, Poitou, said Perrot Cahn, and another servant called Hicquet de Brémont.

Dixit: the Marshal Gilles de Rais stood as supervisor to the work. Poitou being lowered into the pit, he bundled the remains into some sacks. I stood above with a rope, de Brémont helping me. Gilles de Sillé kept watch. We dragged the sacks to the surface. Then the remains were packed into three large chests, and stoutly roped, and taken to the boat hidden under the willows. De Sillé was for throwing the cargo into the Loire, but my lord de Rais would not agree. The boat was moored before reaching Nantes, and the remains transferred to a cart and taken to Machecoul. Here the contents of the sacks were incinerated.

Asked: when did witness do murder.

Dixit: After that night. At Bourgeneuf. At the inn of Guillaume Rodigo. I was told to befriend a young student named Bernard le Camus. The boy was a native of Brest, where little French is spoken, and had been sent to Bourgeneuf-en-Rais to acquire the language. My lord de Rais had me bring Camus to his apartments at the inn. When he came there, my lord de Rais had me spring out and kill him with the braquemard.

Asked: what is this braquemard.

Dixit: This was a weapon which my lord de Rais had specially for purposes of execution. It was a short, thick, double-edged sword, very sharp. Sometimes the Sire de Rais would cut off his victims' heads, sometimes he would cut their throats, sometimes he would dismember his victims, sometimes he would break their necks with a stick which he twisted in a scarf for this purpose.

Asked: for what reason were the children murdered.

Dixit: Did not know.

Exhorted to tell the truth in this matter.

Dixit: I have heard my lord de Rais say that he took more pleasure in the murder of the said children, and in seeing their heads and limbs separated from their bodies, and in seeing them die and their blood flow, than in having carnal knowledge of them.

Required to say more in this matter.

Dixit: Gilles often took delight in gazing at the heads that had been cut off, and held them up for me to see, or Poitou. He would ask us which of the heads he showed us was the most beautiful, the one which had just been cut off or the one from the night before, or the one from the night before that. Then he would kiss the head which he liked the most, and make much of that head, and this gave him much pleasure.

Exhorted to speak of sacrifice to the Evil One.

Dixit: I know nothing of it.

Required to speak.

Dixit: Prelati said his demons must be propitiated. I was never present when a child was thus sacrificed. But one day, on entering my master's room at Tiffauges, I found Gilles holding a glass vessel containing the hands, heart and eyes of a child whom de Sillé had butchered. The child's body was on the floor.

Asked: did he now repent of his very great sins.

Dixit: Repenting, this witness fell into the pit of his own despair. When the soldiers came with the ducal warrant for the arrest of the Marshal and his accomplices, witness had wanted to cut his own throat. This was without a doubt the Devil's doing.*

Asked: when he became a full accessory to his master's crimes.

Dixit: Three years previous, when Gilles made him swear another solemn oath that he would reveal none of the secrets that had been entrusted to him. This would have been im-

* *par tentacion diabolique* in Friar Blouyn's marginal note.

mediately after the murder of Bernard le Camus with the braquemard.

Question: in what place the said oath was given.

Answer: In the church of the Holy Trinity at Machecoul.

Asked: to speak truth in all he knew about the brother of Cathérine Thierry.

Dixit: He, the witness, had delivered the said child to Machecoul to become a member of the chapel. Said child was yellow-haired and a virgin. At this time witness had heard only the rumours about what happened to the children. At this time witness knew what happened to the children, but had no part in it. Witness brought the boy to Machecoul and delivered him to Gilles' room. After he, the witness, had delivered the said child he went back to Nantes where he stayed for three days without returning to Machecoul. Then, returning to Machecoul after three days, he looked for the said child and could not find him. He was told that he (the boy) had left this world in the same way as the others, and Poitou (Etienne Corillaut, also servant to the Sire de Rais) informed him that their master had killed the boy by his own hand, and that, just like the others, it had served his libidinous acts.

Exhorted again to speak truth concerning sacrifice of children to the Devil.

Dixit nihil.

ETIENNE CORILLAUT, *known as Poitou, servant to de Rais*

I first came to Tiffauges as a page in the year 1427. I was fourteen years old. I was a page to the Sire de Rais for five years, during the period in which Messire Roger de Bricqueville had charge of his affairs. The Sire de Rais had two other pages at that time. Their names were Pierre and Perrinet Briant, brothers. They used to entertain the Marshal with their hymn-singing. The Sire de Rais performed the carnal act upon me not long after I first came into his service. Afterwards he was going to kill me, but Messire de Sillé prevented it. Messire de Sillé said that I was a handsome lad and that I would prove to be a good page. I think that I was the only one except Rossignol who was allowed to live after the Sire de Rais had performed the carnal act upon them. After about five years I became a servant of the bedchamber of the said lord. It was in 1437, when I had been ten years in his service, that I became his secretary. During the time when I was his servant of the bedchamber I once saw two dead children on the floor of that bedchamber. When I was his page the Sire de Rais liked to have relations with me upon my belly. It was later that Messires de Bricqueville and de Sillé commanded me to lay my hands on children and bring them to the said lord. He committed his vices on the children, boys and girls, only once, or twice at most, with each of them. If it was a girl he would scorn the usual orifice. He liked to sodomize both boys and girls. Sometimes the Sire de Rais would commit his vices on the said boys and girls before wounding them, but this was rarely. Other times, and that often, it was after hanging them up on a hook, or after other wounds. Other times it was after he had cut, or caused to be cut, the vein in the neck or the throat so that the blood gushed out. Other times it was when they were dying. Other times it was after they were dead and their heads had been cut off, while there still remained some warmth in their body. The said Gilles de Rais to my certain knowledge practised his luxurious vices in the same way on girls and on boys, disdaining their sexual organs, and I heard him say once that he took infinitely more pleasure in debauching himself in this manner with the said girls, as I told you, than in using their natural orifice, in the normal manner. When the children were dead the Sire de Rais would burn their bodies and their clothes. I had to put them in the fire for him, and Henriet put them in the fire. This was in the fireplace in a certain room kept for his pleasures in a tower at Tiffauges that was kept locked, and in other fireplaces in similar places at his castles at Machecoul and Champtocé. Great logs of wood, and faggots, had to be placed on the dead bodies, and huge fires then lit. The clothes of the children were placed one by one on the fire, and held in the flames with a stick, so that the children burned more slowly and did not make such a bad smell. Then the ashes were thrown sometimes into the cess-pit, other times into the moats or down the drains or buried in other hiding places. Forty children were killed at Tiffauges to my memory of it. Forty children likewise were killed at Machecoul. There was always an interval after the fortieth murder. I do not know why. Sixty children must have been killed in the last years, when I was a secretary to the Sire de Rais. Some of these were to do with the diabolic interventions of the Italian alchemist Messire Prelati. I never saw any demon invoked by that Italian master, but I heard one once on the roof, like a great cat walking, and another time Messire Prelati was beaten about the head by his own invisible spirit, whose name was Barron. I know the Sire de Rais killed children long before there was any magic in it. At first he may have killed the children, boys and girls, to keep them quiet after he had had his way with them. Spurning the natural way of copulation, he liked to rub his member against the thighs and bellies of children, and he committed sodomy with these young boys and girls, and his victims were sometimes alive, sometimes dead, and sometimes even in their death throes when these perversions were committed. Sometimes he sat on their chests while they were dying. Once he tortured and killed one child in front of his brother before doing the same to the other child. Of all of his victims, I found about thirty-six for him. La Meffraye found others, and of course Henriet, as well as Messires de Bricqueville and de Sillé. It was not often that we had to use force in kidnapping the children. There are plenty of children available in these bad times. As to the Devil, I know nothing, and neither does my master serve the Devil. Even those murders which Prelati said were necessary as sacrifices did not succeed in making the Devil come. Nothing ever came, not a name, not a God, not a creature; nothing at all.* These sacrificial murders were associated by Gilles with the supernatural and he called them his 'mysteries'. He would fondle the heads of the decapitated children, kiss them in a frenzy on the lips, calling them his 'dear angels'. Once I heard him cry, over one boy's body: 'Go, go pray to God for me.' All this talk of the Devil was the business of Messire Prelati. For his part, Gilles de Rais took a keen pleasure in slaughtering boys, in watching them languish and die, and seeing their blood flow. Killing he liked, and sodomy, for no other reason than the pleasure which such things brought to his virile member. There was no other reason. There was no reason. He liked to kill.

* Note in Friar Blouyn's record: *The Devil's deepest guile is to persuade us that he does not exist.*

XXV

A CHANGE OF HEART

It is Saturday the fifteenth of October, and here once more is Gilles de Rais striding through a pool of stained light in the great hall of the castle of La Tour Neuve. The Bishop of Nantes and his brother Bishops of Le Mans, Saint Brieuc, and Saint-Lô are already installed on their thrones upon the dais, with Friar Jean Blouyn hovering palely in attendance, and Pierre de l'Hospital whispering in the Vice-Inquisitor's ear. There stands Master Chapeillon, leaning on his spread hands at the red-topped table. That curious half-faced smile fades as he watches the Marshal take his place.

Gilles looks different after this two days' adjournment. All the bluster and bravado have gone out of him. His eyes are downcast, his manner constrained. As if in token of the change, he wears black furs, a grey tunic, and no jewels at his throat or on his fingers. His face is white as hellebore as he bows to the bench.

Jean de Malestroit addresses him:

'Messire de Rais, do you recognize the court?'

A pause. Then Gilles says clearly: 'I do.'

A buzz of surprise from the assembled notaries. The Bishop silences them.

'Messire de Rais, do you acknowledge those here set over you in law?'

'I do. I recognize as my judges you, my lord Bishop of Nantes, and Friar Jean Blouyn, as representative of Guillaume Merici, Grand Inquisitor of France.'

Now there is another rustle of excitement in the court, like a wood when the wind suddenly catches the leaves. Master Chapeillon puts on his eyeglasses to peer at the prisoner. The Vice-Inquisitor sits silent and inscrutable in his carved chair, his face like a death's head. But blinking with satisfaction and surprise, the Bishop says:

'Messire de Rais, how do you plead to the charges against you in the indictment?'

Gilles looks away. His lips are moving, but no sound comes forth. For a moment, while the court holds its breath, those pitiless blue eyes consider Prelati and myself where we are crouched in our cage like animals at a show. He must observe that I wear again the blessed sackcloth of repentance. But the Devil is in Prelati; he sits picking his nose.

Gilles' gaze comes back to the judges. Yet when he speaks his eyes seem turned inwards, as if talking to himself. 'My lord, I admit that I have committed certain crimes, here imputed to me, within the limits of your jurisdiction.' Now his hands saw the air with the sharp and meaningless gestures of a drunken man, and all at once those ice-cold eyes fill up with meaning, and the meaning is tears, and the tears are running incontinently down his cheeks as he humbly entreats the Bishop's pardon for the insults showered upon the tribunal in its earlier sessions.

The notaries catch their breath. Their pens cease scratching. Jean de Malestroit is wiping his lips with a little piece of cloth. When he responds there is compassion and rejoicing in his voice at this first stirring of a Christian conscience.

'We extend pardon without condition, *propter Deum*.'

Master Chapeillon rises swiftly.

'Your leave to proceed, my lord Bishop? In view of the prisoner's change of heart, may I take it that he will now agree to submit to the oath?'

The *promoteur* is holding up the Holy Gospels in his right hand, but immediately Gilles is striding back and forth in front of the tribunal like a partridge roused from cover. 'My lord Bishop, with your leave I would like to make a statement . . .'

I do not know why Gilles adopted this tactic, but then nor can I say what prompted his sudden change of heart. I doubt if at this stage he had any notion of those terrible incriminating confessions offered to Friar Jean Blouyn by Griart and Poitou. It is probable that he realized from my wearing of the sack-cloth that I was prepared to tell the Inquisition all that I knew about him, and indeed he may have counted on this to be just enough to condemn him on certain charges while deflecting the court's attention from the murder and the sodomy. For whatever reason, the statement which he now made in open court was far from frank. Striding up and down, gesturing like a puppet on strings, he admitted all his vain experiments in pursuit of gold, but proceeded to deny just about everything else.

'Nothing is more false than this allegation that I have in-voked demons, or caused others to invoke demons, or that I have offered human sacrifices to them!' Then he was off into a long and complicated account of how he once borrowed the book on alchemy from the soldier in prison at Angers. 'But that was the end of it, and I had my chaplain return the book.' When Gilles said this, he pointed his finger at me where I was kept in the cage, as if my very presence would prove some essential innocence or harmlessness in what he was saying. There was something odd about his protestations, as about his pacing up and down, and I was reminded of his behaviour in the days of his drunkenness. He carried his head high, but he had a look of pain. His hands came up and he clapped them together before his chest as he cried out in conclusion to Master Chapeillon that if it was possible to prove anything more then he, Gilles de Rais, Marshal of France, would offer himself to the civil authorities to be burned alive.*

---

* *tunc in eo casu se sponse obtulit igni comburendum*, in the Latin record.

267

The court, as I remember, was not impressed. Master Chapeillon elected to ignore the outburst, and to repeat his request that Gilles should take the oath. Whilst my lord was being sworn, an officer arrived having in custody Griart and Poitou, La Meffraye, and other servants from Tiffauges and Machecoul who had now been caught in the net. I recall how Gilles stood there staring from one face to another as if these newcomers were ghosts, or figures he had dreamed of long ago. There was silence for a while, then the Bishop of Nantes addressed him:

'Messire de Rais, do you wish to put any questions to these witnesses? If so, we consent to it, and to give you more opportunity we will allow you another day to prepare your questions.'

Gilles made an impatient gesture. 'There is no need for that. I rely upon their truthfulness and on the justice of the court.'

Then, another sensation. Gilles is suddenly down on his knees, weeping and entreating the Bishop of Nantes to remit that sentence of excommunication inflicted on him two days before. All his pride and his pretence of integrity have drained from him in a moment. He is a broken man, twisting and twitching in his agony, cut off from even a sight of the sacrament he dare not eat.

The Bishop's face is written with pity for him. He agrees to accede to the wish. Gilles' sentence is then remitted, in writing, and the fact publicly proclaimed, with the customary private penance imposed. Friar Jean Blouyn sits apart, observing these antics with interest. The Vice-Inquisitor's attitude is almost slouching. He leans his long head on his hand and sighs to himself. As for Gilles, he is kneeling to kiss the Bishop's shoe in his gratitude. I suppose I should have shared in that repentance and that joy. I did not, and I do not. I don't know what to make of it.

I remember that among the new prisoners brought in was

that pathic Rais le Héraut. Seeing him there, the Marshal's double, his facsimile, standing across the courtroom from where Gilles knelt weeping, it came into my head (God forgive me) to doubt my lord's sincerity. Let me say why. Sight of Rais le Héraut put me in mind of how much of my master's life had been a theatre of display. His existence was a drama in which he was the central actor. In company with Joan of Arc, he had lived out the role of soldier. Later the theatre of the world, where he had played a leading part with Joan, was replaced by the theatre of his own establishment, his castles, his riches, his retainers, even those guilt-inspired plans for a religious foundation. Rais le Héraut seemed to me like a key to some secret chamber in my master's soul. What did it mean to have this puppet dressed in his own clothes? Was it not to have a mirror of himself at all times and in all places, so that he could be actor and spectator, seen and unseen? I was reminded that before I ever saw Gilles de Rais, I saw the representation of himself which he had caused to be created for *The Mystery of the Siege of Orléans*. It had suited him always to try to find a role, and then to employ someone else to play it while he watched. What if now he was using the structures of religion to the same end? What if the final role he intended to assume was that of perfect penitent?

These reflections, or some of them, chased through my brain as Gilles de Rais was restored to the communion of the Church. As a result, I was unable to share in that delight which we are told is felt in heaven when a sinner repents and turns away from his sin. Not that Gilles had yet turned away from anything, so far as I could see, except perhaps his more violent pride and intransigence. I admit that in taking this critical view of his behaviour I erred on the side of uncharity. No doubt I was influenced by having the Vice-Inquisitor sitting between my cage and that perfect penitent. When Friar Blouyn saw Gilles weep, he produced a little crucifix from the folds of his robe and held it between his brows as if to protect the brain within.

Though I was never sure exactly when it was that Griart and Poitou confessed, I know for a fact that it was one day after Gilles' change of heart that Francesco Prelati chose to talk to the Holy Office. He knew, I suppose, that silence could do him no good now. He must have feared that his master's admissions of alchemy could soon develop into something worse, and it would have occurred to him that if Gilles wanted to blame someone else for some of the murders then he was the most plausible scapegoat. Messer Francesco's task was to sing as loud as possible to save his own skin. If, in doing that, he made sure that Gilles went to the scaffold, then no matter. As I have said before, the Italian diabolist was an average specimen of evil. Here is his deposition to Friar Jean Blouyn, dated Sunday the sixteenth of October, 1440.

FRANCESCO PRELATI, *clerk, friend of de Rais*

Exhorted to tell the truth.

Dixit: What is the truth? I confess that I, Messer Francesco Prelati, of Florence, am a scientist.

Required to speak plainly.

Dixit: My birthplace was Montecatini, near Pistoia. I was once in the suite of the Bishop of Mondovi. I came to France to serve the Sire de Rais. He relied upon me to establish contact with the Powers.

Required to say what were these Powers.

Dixit nihil.

Required again to speak.

Dixit: If God, as is well known, works miracles through his saints, then it is well known also that the Devil possesses great power and will assist those who do him homage. This was Gilles' reasoning. It is not mine. I am a scientist. I confess to certain experiments. I confess the traffic with demons. I can conjure a spirit. His name is Barron. Barron appears to me in the shape of a handsome young man. I could bring him here before you if you wanted him. I confess that once, in a theoretical or speculative mood, I might have given it to Gilles as my opinion that the offering of boys' members was more efficacious than shedding the blood of cocks or doves. But this is no more than the teaching of Agobard or Avicenna applied to reality. In my opinion a distinction should be drawn between *mathematici* and necromancers. I am of the former way, and that is why I term myself a scientist. All that I might have said or suggested to Gilles was said or suggested in a spirit of research, not precept. He did what he liked, not what I told him to do. As to the killing of children, Gilles had been doing that for years before I met him. I knew nothing of it, except what I heard others say. I am no *malefica*. I use no poison, no waxen images, nor have I conjured tempests with my spells. I am what is called the *striga*, one of those souls for whom the *tabulae fortunae* is spread.

Exhorted to reject his witchcraft as idolatry.

Dixit: The Bible itself speaks of a witch as a person who deals with familiar spirits. Is this not in Leviticus, chapter 20, the twentieth verse?* Stephen of Hungary distinguishes the *striga*, the white magician, from the *malefica*, which is to say the black. John of Damascus likewise. Remember when you judge me that the Synod of Reisbach, in the year 799 of the revelation, demanded penance for such witchcraft, but no punishment in this life. I say the crime is unimportant save where *maleficium* is combined with treason and the person of the King is aimed at – and I have done none of this.

Exhorted to submit to the Church his heresies.

Dixit: I am neither an obstinate heretic nor a worker of evil magics. I can weep and say my Paternoster. I do not walk backwards nor against the sun. Weigh me against the Bible and you will see. I tell you again that I am and have always

---

* Friar Blouyn's note: *But see also Exodus, xxii, 18.* This text reads: 'Thou shalt not suffer a witch to live.'

been a scientist, of the *striga*, and a true and loyal son of our holy Mother Church.

Required to speak direct of the demoniac sacrifice.

Dixit nihil.

Required to speak.

Dixit: The first two children chosen for the demoniac sacrifice were Jehan Barnard of Fort Launey and Jamet Brice of St Etienne-de-Montluce. The victims were found by the woman Perrine Martin (La Meffraye). As far as I know, the task of despatching the two children fell to Gilles' cousin de Sillé.

Asked why.

Dixit: Gilles might at no time require any incitement to slaughter, but to his warped mind there was a difference between murder for the satisfaction of lust and murder for the diabolic rites.

Asked why.

Dixit: It became a question of degree, the one form of brutality appearing less culpable than the other. At the back of Gilles' brain there must linger the hope that his soul might not be entirely blasted so long as he sets some limit to his criminality. He left to me the responsibility of propitiating Barron.

Exhorted to tell on pain of death what he knew of the murders at Tiffauges and Machecoul.

Dixit: It might have been that the sight and smell of blood revived Gilles' obsession with murder. At the beginning of our experiments in alchemy his interest in this mechanism obscured the end he had in view, so now perhaps murder in the interest of demonism induced a fresh outbreak of satyriasis. I might have said that five victims would be necessary, quoting Avicenna on the subject. His lust would have turned it into fifteen, or twenty-five, or even fifty. I know nothing of that. He never needed me to help him kill them. There were plenty more in his household who could assist with that. And I heard that in those days he was no longer content to have his victims

brought tamely to his presence, like innocents led to the
slaughter. I believe that he preferred it if Poitou (Etienne
Corillaut, his servant) could organize for him hunting parties,
which must have imparted to the business an element of sport.
No doubt the running down of the quarry heightened his zest
and appealed to his sense of humour. I heard it said that with
his cousins de Bricqueville and de Sillé, Gilles made expeditions to the loneliest parts of the countryside round about
Tiffauges and Machecoul, first marking his victims and then
pouncing on them like a beast of prey. Young shepherds
tending their sheep were this wolf's favourite quarry. I once
heard de Bricqueville remark that Gilles liked sometimes to
vary the procedure by watching from a distance while his
accomplices seized the unfortunate youth. If the boy struggled,
that would be an added relish for him. Bound with ropes, the
boys were swung across the horses and at nightfall they were
taken to the castle. I never saw this for myself, nor aided in
such detestable work. La Meffraye specialized in procuring
children of tender years, so I understood, cajoling them with
promises of rich rewards if they entered the service of the Lord
de Rais. So did Poitou, and Griart who would always have
sweets for such children. If the children protested, so I heard,
he would pop a sweet into their mouths to silence and con-
found them. I never saw this happen. I never witnessed any
act of murder. Poitou once told me that one boy was bled to
death so that Gilles might wash his hands and beard in the
warm blood. I never attended. There were other details which
came to my ears, but I did not credit them entirely, nor do I
know now if they are true or not. What I can say for certain is
that all such reported butcheries were followed by spasms of
remorse. I have seen with my own eyes Gilles wander alone at
night through his castle, pursued, as he thought, by the ghosts
of the children. I heard him, in this state of mind, fall on his
knees and shout aloud and swear to God that he repented of
his sins, and once he vowed to become a monk or go to the

Holy Land on pilgrimage, begging his bread from door to door. These moods were fleeting, and no doubt but that he returned to his savageries with renewed ferocity after them. As St Paul says, without shedding of blood there is no remission; and who are we to argue with St Paul? The blood is the life. Those magicians who object to the use of blood have endeavoured to replace it with incense. But the bloody sacrifice, though more dangerous, is more efficacious.

Exhorted to say clearly what he meant.

Dixit: I have said enough. There is a saying that when an adept seems to have made a straightforward and comprehensible statement, then it is most certain that he means something entirely different. The truth is nevertheless set forth in his words. It is his simplicity that baffles the unworthy.

Exhorted to speak clearly.

Dixit nihil.

Tied with the ropes, and the beam attached to his feet.

Exhorted and required to speak truth.

Hanging, said nothing.

Iterum pendens tacet.

XXVI

A PROSPECT OF TORTURE

Gilles' change of heart was not so complete as it should have been. Indeed, having persuaded the Bishop of Nantes to revoke that terrible sentence of excommunication, he fell now into a state of mind and spirit in which he seemed indifferent to the deliberations of the court, and careless of his own fate as an outcome. I could not say if his *metanoia* was genuine, or merely assumed in order to achieve a particular result of restoration to the communion of the Church. In the story of the Prodigal Son it is made clear for us that it is *conscience* that forms the pivot upon which the sinner's return to God can be accomplished. The words in St Luke, *when he came to himself*, denote that moment in human life when the heart, sickened by dissipation, becomes self-collected, and is no longer 'beside itself'. Strange, no doubt, that we should begin to think of God with comfort only when with joy and comfort we can think of nothing else. Man surely is a compound of riddles and contradictions: by the law of his nature he avoids pain, and yet unless he suffers in the flesh he will not cease from sin, though it is sure to bring pain and misery upon his head for ever. In Gilles' case, I regret to have to say that he seems not to have fully repented and come to his senses until he came face to face with the prospect of torture.

It happened like this.

At the hour of Vespers, on Monday the seventeenth of October, 1440, a number of further witnesses were examined in the great hall of La Tour Neuve by the Bishop of Nantes, Friar Jean Blouyn, and their assessors. This was subsequent to the confession of Francesco Prelati, and to the depositions of all the other principal figures in the affair. Gilles was present while the Public Prosecutor took statements from witnesses to the sacrilege at St Etienne-de-la-Mer-Morte. These included the Marchese de Ceva, Bertrand Poullein, Jean Rousseau, and a Benedictine monk named Dom Jean de Lante, the Prior of Chemère, all of whom had been witnesses to that atrocity when my master threatened to kill a priest in the very act of celebrating Mass. An enormous amount of evidence was thus being accumulated from various sources on every single charge in the bill of indictment, and all of it black and unanswerable from Gilles' point of view. Yet when Master Chapeillon invited him to cross-examine these witnesses, Gilles declined. He sat sprawled in his chair, one booted foot crossed over the other, staring into space as if asleep with his eyes open. At one point, Master Chapeillon came and stood right in front of him, peering into my lord's face, close-up, with his eyeglasses screwed into his eye-sockets, as if trying to draw the soul out of the prisoner, or seeking to read the truth in him as an augur in ancient Rome would read the truth in the quivering entrails of the sacrificed beast. But Gilles did not quiver, and there was nothing to be read.

Two days later, another fifteen minor witnesses were heard, again in my master's presence, each of them testifying concerning children's bones found at Tiffauges and Machecoul, in his castles there, as well as in the house of Perrot Cahn. These witnesses included a surgeon, Messire Robin Guillemet, and a professor of civil and canon law named Jean de Pencoëtdic. Gilles was again invited by the *promoteur* to question anything they said, and once again he declined, preferring to pare his nails and turn aside to smile.

That day's proceedings closed with the Bishop of Nantes inviting my lord to begin his defence, *ad sui salvacionem et justificationem*, as it is written down here in the record of the trial which I have always kept by me over the years of my exile: 'Messire de Rais, when will you start to defend your-self?'

Astonishingly, Gilles said nothing. He sat humming to himself. The song was wordless, but I knew the tune. It was that curious little song which Rossignol used to sing, about how you cannot speak of ice to a summer insect. That night I remember thinking that my lord must be mad now. If he had committed his murders in a dream, in an orgy of lust in which nothing was real to him, surely the procession of ordinary people declaring his guilt, one after another, decent voices in a public court, must have brought home to him the horror of what he had done, and his mind been destroyed by it? Yet even as I thought this, I knew it was not true. Gilles was not mad. Nor, in my opinion, was he ever possessed by any agent or devil other than his own appalling self. That, in the last analysis, is what there is to learn from his frightful story. Not madmen or monsters do these things. We do. The imagination of man is evil from his youth. The only hope for us is: some do not.

When the court assembled again on Thursday the twentieth of October, the Bishop of Nantes directed Master Chapeillon to read aloud all the salient evidence now given on oath against Gilles in the matter of the major charges both secular and spiritual: that is to say, on the counts of murder, heresy, and sacrilege. This the Public Prosecutor proceeded to do, calmly and quietly, going over each day's deliberations of the court as well. Throughout this terrible recital, Gilles sat silent. I chose to believe, watching him from my vantage point in the cage, that he had recoiled or withdrawn himself from con-frontation with his own wickedness. Yet, truth to tell, his manner was too confident plausibly to allow for that interpreta-tion. He sat, legs crossed, with a doggish sort of sneer upon his face. It struck me that he did not really believe in his own depravity. Incredible as it seems, there was still that blind pride in him. Everyone else in the courtroom knew that his heart's core was a fat and awful worm, but Gilles still loved himself. It was filthily absurd, but that was the truth of it.

When Master Chapeillon had finished, it was starting to get dark. The early dark of late October crept through the hall, and the notaries lit their candles to see their own writings. I noticed the face of the Vice-Inquisitor gaunt in the candle-flames. Friar Jean Blouyn looked pale and drawn at the best of times; now he sat listening like a corpse with live eyes. As the last words of the Public Prosecutor's review of the evidence died away into echoes, the representative of the Holy Office rose curiously on his toes, and spread his fingers, bringing his hands together till the fingertips touched in a gesture of prayer. But he was not praying. He was waiting for his prey.

The Bishop of Nantes leaned forward on his throne.

'Messire de Rais,' he said, 'you have now heard all the evidence against you, and the depositions of many witnesses on solemn oath. You do not need reminding that in both body and soul you are in the gravest peril. You have offered the court not the slightest word in observation or rebuttal concerning any of this evidence since you took that oath yourself. Before I declare the case for the prosecution closed, I must ask you again what you have to say in your own defence.'

Gilles considered a while. Then rose slowly to his feet. He bowed to the Bishop, then, turning, he bowed also to the Vice-Inquisitor.

'My ghostly fathers,' he murmured, 'I have nothing to say.'

Jean de Malestroit shook his head, unable to understand the prisoner's attitude.

'You have nothing to say to murder?'

'Nothing, my lord.'

'Nothing to say to heresy and sacrilege and sodomy? Nothing to all these acts of evil which Friar Jean and Master Chapeillon have proved over and again that you most surely have committed?'

Gilles shook his head, and shrugged.

'Nothing,' he said.

Now Master Chapeillon stepped forward angrily, spurred to action by a whisper in his ear from the Vice-Inquisitor. 'My lord Bishop,' he said, 'I suggest that in the light of the accused's continuous refusal to plead, and in order to elucidate and scrutinize the truth the more clearly, it is my bounden duty to apply to the court for the only remedy.'

He paused a moment, swinging his eyeglasses on their black silk ribbon, then catching them in the palm of his outstretched hand.

'I mean, of course, the rack!'

In the absolute silence which ensued I realized that it must have started raining. I could hear the little drops falling quick upon the roof. In those moments, too, the gloom of the great hall seemed to deepen and thicken, while the candles burned more crisply in their holders.

The Bishop of Nantes turned to the Vice-Inquisitor.

'Does the Holy Office agree that the rack is necessary?'

Friar Jean inclined his head.

'Both necessary and expedient,' he declared. 'The court will know the *Directorium* of the Inquisitor Nicolas Eymeric: that torture is to be ordered by a judge only when every other means of getting at the truth is exhausted. That would seem most definitely to be so in the present case. Eymeric also directs that such aids to the truth should be employed only when what he terms some 'semi-proof' of guilt has already been established. Again, in my submission, that is emphatically the case that we have here.'

His voice trailed away. He gazed with bright eyes at the prisoner. Gilles had this glad, half-frightened smile upon his face. It was that incomprehensible smile which convinced me, also, that the rack was needed if my lord were ever to tell the truth. It was almost a gargoyle smile, as if carved half-grotesque in glossy stone. I listened to the rain, and prayed for him. I listened to my heart, and prayed for his victims.

The Bishop of Nantes turned to the other judges.

'My brother of Le Mans? Saint Brieuc? Saint-Lô? How do you say? Should the prisoner be tortured?'

One by one, the Bishops held up their croziers in assent. Pierre de l'Hospital, as representative of the civil tribunal, listened acutely, his head on one side. Then he too, without enthusiasm, raised his hand.

I looked at Gilles. He had the same queer smile on his face, and a gleam of concentration in his eyes. I knew that he was outraged by their proposal. At the same time, he seemed different, suddenly made vulnerable. All the sway of his pride was subsiding in him, like a ship on a sea that grows still. His face, which had been closed and cold, was open now. It looked like the core of a naked flame.

Jean de Malestroit spoke:

'Gilles de Rais, you have heard the court's decision. We decree that tomorrow morning, at the hour of Terce, you will be put to the Question!'

Gilles favoured his judges with the merest nod. Then the court was adjourned, and he was led away.

I think that my lord had never bargained for this. Consider: he knew now what Poitou had told the court, and Griart, and the other witnesses. He had heard some of it direct, and the rest read out by the Public Prosecutor. He had denied nothing. He had not cried out or protested when the details of his crimes were enumerated. On oath, he had declared that he would say nothing in response to any of their accusations. This, he must have reckoned, was as good as an admission of his guilt.

Evidently Gilles hoped that he could be judged on that tacit admission. Again and again the Bishop of Nantes had asked him if he had anything to say in his own defence, and each time my lord had kept silent or replied in the negative. I believe that he wanted to be sentenced without awarding his judges the satisfaction of his own confession. Why? Never underestimate the pride of Gilles de Rais. That pride was a mortal sickness, a fever in the soul. Was he not sprung of the noble stock of Montmorency and Craon, grandson of the renowned knight, Brumor de Laval, grandnephew of du Guesclin, of kindred with the Constable Clisson, and allied with all that was illustrious in France? Did not his barony of Rais render him the head of the whole baronage of Brittany? Had he not been the richest man in the kingdom, and had he not served a woman who was like an angel of the Lord? In all his days, both of glory and of infamy, no one (I am sure of it) had ever laid a violent hand on *him*. He even had that great one's luxury: the morbid horror of being touched at all. I suspect that it never occurred to Gilles that they might put him to the Question. But now that it was definite that they would, what did he think that night?

We can never know for certain, but this is my reading of it, based on knowledge of what the Marshal had told me of his life and on what I saw for myself in the matter of his death. I believe that three things must have made him sweat that night. First, there would be the simple prospect of pain. Gilles had been a student of pain all his life. If there was one thing he believed in it was pain. This, which had once made him brave when he fought beside Joan and then again cruel later in the indulgence of his lust, must now have made a coward of him. Those who take most pleasure in inflicting pain might well be the greatest cowards when it comes to suffering it. Second, there would be the less simple prospect of Joan. Despite all that I came to discover about what Gilles did in the years after that good woman was burned at Rouen, I believe that in some way I cannot understand he remained bound to her memory. As much as he believed in pain, he believed in Joan. And that belief would have extended to seeing her again when he joined her in the fire, and after. At some hour in that long night I believe that either a vision of Joan of Arc, or intellectual concentration upon her example, came to my master's assistance in the process of his salvation. Third, and most complicated to say, it seems to me that there might well have been something about himself, or something about Joan, or even more likely something about himself and Joan together, which Gilles de Rais was unwilling to confess. If he went to the rack, he knew enough about pain to know that he would talk eventually in answer to every question that Friar Jean Blouyn might put to him. Already I had seen for myself how keen the Inquisitor was to have Gilles in his grasp. Could my master have observed the same, and feared it? As to what this secret might have been – which Gilles preferred to take with him to the gallows, leaving to me the eventual task of trying to make sense of it all – I did not know what it was then, nor do I know what it is now. All I can say is that I think Friar Jean Blouyn wanted to extract that secret from my lord. I think he was much disappointed that he never had the chance to compel certain answers from my master's lips, and I feel miserably sure that he knew (which I do not) what questions should have been asked to obtain such answers. The Holy Office was cheated of strange knowledge. But in my opinion there is some knowledge which we are better off without. Until of course, in God's own time, God chooses to reveal it.

Now it is a few minutes before the hour of Terce, nine o'clock in the morning of Friday the twenty-first of October, 1440. I saw this for myself, for I was there. Along with Prelati, I was awoken early and taken from my cell, and put in the cage. Then Griart and Poitou were brought to join us. I think the idea was that the presence of all those who had testified most damningly against him would make the Marshal's submission to the rack the more extreme. Either that, or the inquisitors decided to reward us for our confessions by letting us watch our master as he was broken.

But Gilles was not broken; not his bones, at least. On coming before the Bishop of Nantes, he goes down on his knees. Head bowed, teeth chattering, he makes humble supplication, *humiliter supplicavit* as it says here in the record of the trial which I have by my side.

'My lord Bishop, I beg you to defer my torture for one more day.'

'Why so?'

'Because I would deliberate in such a manner upon the crimes and offences with which I have been charged that I will be able to content you fully.'

Friar Jean Blouyn, seated at the right hand of the Bishop of Nantes, looked at Gilles slowly, without speaking. It seemed to me that he looked down on him, in every sense of the word. He whispered something which I did not catch. The Bishop averted his face.

Then Jean de Malestroit said, speaking in his laconic, measured way that still had kindness in it: 'We are still men, Friar Jean. We are not beasts altogether.'

But although he had evidently resisted the Vice-Inquisitor's demand that they proceed apace to put Gilles on the rack, the Bishop sat musing indecisively, not willing either to agree to my lord's request for another twenty-four hours' remission. Seeing this, where he kneels before him, Gilles then cries out again:

'My lord, give me only to this afternoon.'

'What then?'

'Then I will make my confession.'

'Confessing all?'

Gilles buried his face in his hands. There was dead silence in the courtroom. I remember the smell of fear coming off from Griart and Poitou where they were crammed beside me in the prisoners' cage. I remember the look of eager pity on the face of the Bishop of Nantes, and the snarl that disfigured the features of Friar Jean Blouyn.

Then Gilles said, his voice almost a whisper:

'I will confess all. But let it be to the Bishop of St Brieuc and Messire Pierre de l'Hospital. And let it be in some place far from the torture chamber.'

The Vice-Inquisitor sniffed, two spots of colour hectic in his cheeks, and shook his head angrily.

'It is not for the accused to make conditions . . .'

But Jean de Malestroit was already consulting with Jean Prégent, the Bishop of St Brieuc, and with the Chancellor of Brittany, Pierre de l'Hospital. Having heard their murmured remarks, and those hissed by the Vice-Inquisitor too, he blew warm breath on his babyish hands, stood up in the chill morning light of the courtroom, and announced his decision.

'The court agrees that the Sire de Rais be given one last chance to confess his crimes before we resort to the rack. For this purpose, the Bishop of St Brieuc and Master Pierre de l'Hospital will attend him at two o'clock this afternoon in his own chamber in the castle. However, the court decrees further that the instruments of torture be set up ready for use in the room adjoining, for our patience is exhausted and if the Sire de Rais does not fulfil his promise of full and frank confession of all his crimes then he shall be put to the Question without delay. *Gloria Patri, et Filio, et Spiritui sancto.*'

I heard Gilles' voice joining confidently in the rest of this brief hymn of praise:

'*Sicut erat in principio et nunc et semper et in saecula saeculorum. Amen.*'

Then I knew that my lord Gilles de Rais truly intended to damn himself.

XXVII

THE CONFESSION OF
GILLES DE RAIS: I

Or save himself, depending on how you look at it. The fact is that nearly a week had now passed since Gilles made his humble submission to the court's authority, and begged for that sentence of excommunication to be lifted from his shoulders. During that time, I have no doubt, he must have been preparing the statement he was now to make. Alone in his cell, high in La Tour Neuve, with only the difficult ghost of Joan of Arc for company, he must have spent night after night on his knees. There was no possibility of acquittal: that must have been clear to my master from the moment he knew the witness of Griart and Poitou. Their words condemned him to death as surely as they put the noose about their own necks. There was no hope of salvation here on earth – therefore the time had come to prepare to face judgement in the next. While refusing to view other than with scorn and contempt my lord's favourite description of himself ('a perfect Christian'), I cannot be so uncharitable or unjust as to deny that he was sufficient of a Christian to know what he should do.

Gilles proved that now. The time had come to make his peace with himself and others before he went before God. He knew that in the next world he would once again be called to account for his actions, and required to purge his sins; and that his fate in that world would depend on the manner of his passing from this. Only our mother the Church could help Gilles now. Without her, he must die in total despair.

I was not present when Jean Prégent, my spiritual lord the Bishop of St Brieuc, and the sturdy Chancellor of Brittany, Pierre de l'Hospital, came to Gilles' room in La Tour Neuve at two o'clock that afternoon. The judges, however, were accompanied by two notaries, one for the ecclesiastical tribunal and the other for the civil, whose task was to take the record of all that was said. From Master Jean Petit, who took down Gilles' words for the Bishop's court, I know two things beside that actual verbatim account. The first is that the *greffiers* had carried out the strict instructions of the Bishop of Nantes. In a chamber adjoining the apparatus of the Question was set up: trestles, funnel, ropes, and water-cans for the Question Ordinary; the rack itself for the Question Extraordinary. The door was left open so that Gilles could see this grisly tackle. Whether it would be needed was entirely in his hands. The second additional detail which I heard from Master Petit was that before beginning his statement Gilles flung himself down on his knees and asked a blessing from the Bishop of St Brieuc. When he had been blessed, he then cried out in a loud voice, saying:

'Men are the swords that spirits fight with; no one sees the hands!'

I consider this to be so much Cathar nonsense. It raises the point: how much did Gilles de Rais know of the Albigensian heresy? That sect, of course, was the one modern revival of the Manichaean teaching which would have it that all flesh is evil and all spirit good. The Albigensians deluded themselves that certain of their own initiates, called 'the perfect ones', had attained a level of being beyond all others. These 'perfect ones' were encouraged to commit suicide in proof of their perfection. Now, Gilles was fond of applying that word 'perfect' to his own Christian state, and I suppose that the cynical could say that he was now about to commit suicide by submitting his confession to the Church, as surely as if he plunged a penknife into his own black heart.

What do we know of the tenets of the Cathars? That they believed that Satan is god and lord of this world, of the things which are seen and are temporal, and especially of the outward man which is decaying, of the flesh which holds us captive under the law of sin and desire and death. Their task, as they saw it, was to escape from this prison house of the flesh. Our lord Jesus Christ, in their teaching, was a life-giving spirit who had shown them the way to such escape, and the *boni homines*, the 'good men', as the Cathars called themselves, were his ambassadors. They believed in a spiritual baptism with fire. Their ordained priesthood, the so-called 'perfect ones', were women no less than men. Their only prayer was the Lord's Prayer; they believed that everything that is sexually begotten is impure; and they refused to take oaths.

Thus far, perhaps, it might be possible to imagine that Gilles de Rais knew something of the Cathars, or as I have also heard them called the Bogomils, Patarenes, Concorricii, Paulicians, or Albigeois. I hope he knew no more, for Pope Innocent III preached crusade against their wickedness, and the Church has since decreed severe chastisement against all laymen suspected of sympathy with the heretics (Council of Narbonne, 1235; Bull *Ad extirpanda*, 1252). So far as I know, France has been clean of their filthy dualist doctrines for more than a hundred years now, thanks largely to the vigilance of the Holy Office. I cannot believe that Gilles, for all his vileness, was an Albigensian. Still, that outburst before confession was a Cathar cry, no doubt.

The rest of what Gilles said is here on the record. This confession, technically speaking, was made outside the official court proceedings, and is to be distinguished from the second, fuller confession which he made the next day. However, it is not hard to imagine the drama in that room where the open door stands pointing to the rack. Gilles spoke, so they say, freely yet composedly, *sponte et libere*, like one ridding himself of a burden, yet without once raising his voice. What did

Master Petit think, in writing it all down, this direct record of a human soul's depravity? We do not know, but he was a decent scribe. The atmosphere must have been tense beyond belief in that little room. The record breaks twice out of Latin and into French, as testament to that tension, at points which I shall mark for the reader's study.

GILLES DE RAIS, *his first confession*

I, Gilles de Rais, confess that the things which are charged against me are all of them true. It is true that I have committed the most ugly offences against many innocent ones – children, both boys and girls – and that over the years I have kidnapped or caused to be kidnapped a very great number of them – the exact number, even more shamefully, I do not know – and put them to death by my own hand, or caused them to be killed by others, and committed with them many crimes and sins. In these foul deeds I was the prime force and mover, though I name also as murderers of children my cousins Roger de Bricqueville and Gilles de Sillé, my servants Henriet Griart and Etienne Corillaut, *alias* Poitou, my other servant Rossignol, and little Robin, who alas is dead. I confess that I killed these children, boys and girls, by various kinds and modes of torture: some by the amputation of their heads from their bodies, using daggers, *poignards*, and knives; others with sticks or with other implements for striking, by beating them on the head with violent blows; others again by tying them with cords and ropes and hanging them over doors and rafters until they choked. I confess that I took pleasure in such hurting and such killing. It was my joy to destroy innocence and to defile virginity. I delighted in strangling little boys even as those boys discovered the very first pleasures and pains of their innocent flesh. I liked to apply my own male member to the bottoms of little girls who did not yet know what their other parts were for. With these children, boys and girls, I spent my seed even while they were languishing.

This is not the end of my execrable crimes. I always delighted in dying and in death. The children whom I abused when they were living, I desecrated even when they were dead. After their death, sometimes, I took delight in kissing them on the lips, and in gazing intently at the faces of those that were the prettiest, and in playing with the limbs of those who were the most beautifully formed. Also, I cruelly opened the bodies of those poor children, or caused them to be slit open so that I might see their interior. In doing this, my motive was my pleasure. I lusted after their innocence and their death. Frequently, I confess, while these children were dying, I would sit upon their stomachs and take great pleasure in their throes of agony. I liked to have a boy die under me, or to watch a boy or a girl buggered and then murdered by my servants. I used to laugh heartily at this sight, in company with the said Corillaut and Griart. As for the corpses of my victims: I caused these afterwards to be reduced to ashes by the same Corillaut and Griart and others. This took place first at my castle of Champtocé, then at Tiffauges, then at Machecoul, both in my castles there and in other private places. Once I had started catching and killing children, I could not stop. Some I kept captive for a little while, flattering and cajoling them, teaching them sinful pleasures of the flesh. I liked to make these boys and girls respond against their wills, so that they cried out with pleasure even though what I did to them gave pain. I shut them in the dark and beat them hard. Coitus only excited me when I could prick the object of my desire until the blood came. Even then, I would reject the usual orifice, in the case of the girls, and spill my seed on their bellies or in their arses. Stabbing and sodomy were my principal pleasures with these children. I chose only young and pretty ones, and as a rule ascertained before doing anything to them that they were virgins. I liked to play the role of the father chastizing his children. I would take them over my lap and smack and spank them. This gave me great sexual pleasure and caused erection of my member. One day, after being chastized in this manner, a certain little girl asked me to look at her pudenda. But I refused the invitation as this view did not interest me in the least. At first, I might say, I only killed these children to stop them talking. But soon enough I was killing for the sake of killing. I liked to see blood flow; it gave me pleasure. From an early age, as I recall, the greatest pleasures seemed to me outrageous. That is to say, apocalypse was all that interested me. I believed in hell before I could credit heaven. One grows tired of the commonplace. I began killing out of boredom, and went on because I liked to discharge all my energies. On a battlefield man never disobeys and the whole earth soaked in blood is an immense altar on which everything living is endlessly immolated, until the very death of death itself. Death became my divinity, my sacred and absolute beauty. I have been living with death ever since I became aware I was breathing. My supreme game is to imagine myself dead, and gnawed by worms.

Concerning the charges of heresy, I have never understood this. The facts are as follows: about two years ago I despatched one of my chaplains, Dom Eustache Blanchet, a simple man, who knew nothing of my crimes, to fetch for me an alchemist out of Italy. He came back with Francesco Prelati, from the county of Florence in Lombardy. This man, whom I know as François, soon became my friend. He informed me that he had discovered in the country whence he came certain means of conjuring up a spirit by the aid of incantations. This spirit had promised him, François, that it would cause a demon called Barron to come to him whenever he might desire it. I declare and confess that the said François certainly made several invocations of the demons in compliance with my command. I never was in the room when the demon came. As to the connection between these invocations and my murders – I once told François that I would give his demon Barron whatever he might wish to receive, except my soul and my life, providing the devil would then grant me whatever I would ask. It was my intention thus to ask and acquire from the same devil knowledge, and riches, and power, by the possession and aid of which I would be able to return to my former state of dominion and power in this world. In response to my offer, François told me that he had conversed with the devil and that among other things he required and wished that I would present to him the hand, the heart, and the eyes of a child. This was done.

That is all that I have to say, save that for these sins and crimes committed by me and here confessed, I, Gilles de Rais, humbly and in tears beg mercy and pardon of God.

When Gilles had finished speaking, according to the record, Pierre de l'Hospital asked: 'Where did you begin to commit your practices of sodomy and murder?'

'At Champtocé,' Gilles answered.

'How long ago?'

'I cannot say in what year. All I can say is that I had already begun at the time of my grandfather's death.'

'Who gave the idea to you?'

'No one,' said Gilles. 'My own imagination drove me. The thought was my own, and I have nothing to which I attribute it, except for the pleasure and gratification of my senses, and to fulfil my own desire for the knowledge of evil.'

Pierre de l'Hospital evidently found this difficult to accept. He again asked Gilles who had influenced him, and why he had committed such appalling deeds, reminding him that the fuller his confession the more sure he could be of earning Our Redeemer's pardon.

But Gilles, for his part, must have been racked by the shame of his disclosures, and anxious to end the ordeal. The following exchange is recorded in French:

Gilles: Alas, my lord, you are tormenting yourself, and me with you!

l'Hospital: I am not tormenting myself in the least. I am astonished at what you have said, and cannot simply be content with it. My only desire is to have you tell the truth concerning the cause. All I am asking is the simple truth (*la pure vérité*).

Gilles: Truly there was no other cause, no other end or intention, save what I have told you. I have already told you enough to destroy ten thousand men.

The Chancellor and the Bishop accepted this, and the interrogation ended. Prelati was then summoned to the chamber. I imagine that the judges were concerned to establish some link between the murder of the children and the invocations. From the foregoing, it is obvious that Pierre de l'Hospital, in particular, found my master's motives quite incomprehensible. Also it is probable that he felt the prosecution's case would be complete if he could reinforce the charges of heresy and witchcraft.

Prelati, questioned, confirmed Gilles' statements concerning the invocations, but denied specifically that he had himself done any murder. Gilles had provided him with the limbs and the blood of a child, the Italian said, but he had never butchered any child himself. He repeated his rigmarole definitions of the kind of magician he claimed to be, white rather than black. He claimed again to be a scientist, and a true and loyal son of the Church.

The Chancellor then ordered Prelati back to the cell which he shared with me. As the guards took him to the door, the Marshal stepped forward with a cry. Tears poured down his face as he embraced his fellow criminal.

Gilles cried: 'Farewell, François, my friend! Never shall we see each other again in this world!'

How the alchemist reacted is not recorded. I think we would not be at variance with probability, and his known character, if we imagined a certain sly indifference in those eyes of vair. Prelati was already occupied in saving his own skin, to the exclusion of anything else. In that occupation he succeeded, as you shall see. As to feeling for his master, I doubt if he ever possessed any, although on one occasion Gilles had seemed to save his life.

Gilles went on now, beseeching Prelati to cast himself on the mercy of God. Again, his words are recorded just as he said them, by the pen of Master Petit:

'*Je prie a Dieu qu'il vous doint bonne pacience et cognoissance, et soyez certain, mais que vous ayez bonne pacience et esperance en Dieu, que nous nous entreverrons en la grant joye de Paradis!*'

Which is of course to say: 'I pray God that he may give you good patience and understanding, for be certain, providing you have good patience and hope in God, we shall see each other again in the great joy of Paradise!'

For all the evil of the occasion, and the vileness of their crimes, both together and apart, I have always found these words of my lord's quite extraordinarily moving. Neither Gilles nor his friend François *deserved* even a sight of the glimmer of the glow of Paradise from where they had elected to place themselves, far from the presence and the mercy of God. But Christians are rewarded better than they deserve. That is the whole point of Christ's sacrifice. And, but for Christ, which of us could bear to have the great unblinking moral eye of God's justice fixed upon him on the final day?

Then Gilles said to Prelati: 'Pray God for me, as I shall pray for you!'

It is not recorded that the alchemist answered him.

And so they parted.

XXVIII

THE CONFESSION OF
GILLES DE RAIS: II

I remember now that it had been my intention to put my own confession into the record here. That no longer seems to me worth doing. There is a sense in which the horror of my master's confessions cancels out anything which any of the rest of us, who were only his disciples, can ever have to say. The shadow of de Rais blots out all other shades. Things hasten towards the close. The reader, I feel sure, would rather have the rest of the story in Gilles' own words, and in the words of the verbatim account prepared and kept by the notaries of the Bishop's court and Pierre de l'Hospital's court in La Bouffay. However black and vile the content of these documents, they contain the heart of the matter, and nothing else can substitute for them. My own confession, in any case, was small. In fact, from the moment I was taken into custody at Nantes, I lost no time in co-operating fully with the authorities, both ecclesiastical and secular. I told them all I knew, which was little enough. The reader can take it that my confession was strictly and utterly truthful, but much less detailed than I have written in this book. They did not need my word to convict Gilles de Rais. So I said enough to convince them that what he said was true: namely, that I am a simple priest, and that I had for most of the time known nothing of his crimes, and participated in none, and that when I had suspected what might be happening, I ran away – and only ever came back against my will.

We hasten, as I say, towards the end.

That first confession of Gilles' was termed *extra-judiciare*, and the next day he was called upon to repeat and confirm his previous statement, supplementing it by any details that it lacked. No greater humiliation, I suppose, could have been imposed on the once proud and mighty Lord de Rais, and no doubt he spent the night praying for strength to sustain his spirit.

When he appeared on the stroke of nine in the great hall of La Tour Neuve, Gilles looked haggard and drawn. His extreme pallor was intensified by the black damask pourpoint and hood of black velvet that he wore. A densely packed court awaited him. The Bishop of Nantes began proceedings by asking the prisoner if he had any statement to make.

'No,' said Gilles de Rais, muttering, head down, but this surprising negative can be taken as the last dying word of that demon of pride which had possessed him for so long and to such dire ends. In the next moment the tears were running freely down his cheeks and he burst out in a loud voice, crying. 'Yes, yes, yes!' cried Gilles de Rais. 'I confess before God and this court: all the charges against me are true! all I said yesterday is true! My lord, if you will have my confession already made read aloud by Master Chapeillon, I will correct any errors in it and reveal to you still more of the truth of my crimes against God and God's commandments!'

There was silence as the Public Prosecutor rose to read aloud the record of Gilles' interview with the Bishop of St Brieuc and the Chancellor of Brittany. When he had finished, Gilles asked that his own confession might be repeated in French, so that all present could be in no doubt concerning his wickedness. 'By these confessions,' he said, 'and by others which I intend now to make, and by the shame that you see written on my face, I hope the more swiftly to obtain grace from God and the remission of my sins.'

This was done, to mounting horror amongst those in that courtroom who had not understood the full import of his self-accusations when they were couched in Latin. Then, enjoined by the Bishop of Nantes to further proclaim his guilt, Gilles began the recital of his crimes in a voice that trembled. It was, I daresay, a terrible ordeal, and the sweat ran down his face as he talked his way through it, but the Marshal seemed determined now to spare neither himself nor his hearers any of the truth concerning what he had done and how and why he had come to do it. His murders and violations, his perversions of the body and the spirit, the agonies of his victims and the ugliness of his soul, all were defined exactly. His auditors held their breath, until the frozen silence of the court was shattered by the scream of a woman, perhaps the mother of one of the murdered children. Even the priests sitting in judgement, their nerves tempered by the fires of the confessional, shuddered as they listened to what Gilles had to say.

GILLES DE RAIS, *his second confession; as taken down by D. Alneto, J. Parvi, G. Lesne, notaries to the court of Jean de Malestroit, Bishop of Nantes, on Saturday, the twenty-second of October, the year of Our Lord 1440.*

I am, my lord, those things which I have been accused of being: a murderer and a sodomite, one who has dreadfully offended against God and his fellow men. I owe what I am to my own self, and to no other. I am the least of men, and the greatest of miserable sinners. Yet must I say that if I have so much offended against the light, I owe it, in part, to the evil lack of direction I received in my youth. I went, at that time, with the reins slack upon my neck, free to pursue my pleasures as I liked, and I did not see fit to withhold myself from anything. I always took delight in any illicit act. For this reason, my lord, I beg those present who have children of their own to instruct them better than I was instructed, and to teach those children in sound doctrines and to create habits of virtue in their youth and childhood. As for me, my whole youth was spent in luxury, and misspent in vice. I was subject to nothing but my own caprice. Nothing was sacred to me. All the evil that I wished to do, I did. This may sound little enough in the catalogue of my sins, but I assure you it was not. Consider: it was to the execution of evil, and evil alone, that I devoted my best hopes and thoughts and care. Only the prohibited and the unseemly ever held my interest for more than a moment. I say that I began in grievous error.

My lord, it is my belief that cruelty arises from the very heart and loins of man. Compassion, in contrast with it, is a secondary if blessed manifestation, and acquired late. We need faith to teach us kindness, where the vile passion of unkindness comes as naturally to some of us as sap in spring. I tell you that I knew early that there is a hideous pleasure which is produced by intense and forbidden impressions and fatal sights. To those who have once indulged themselves in this direction, coarseness and bluntness of the spirit become like second nature. In such men, pity is silent. So it was with me, so did I grow, but I have worse to tell.

I am one of those for whom all that is connected with death and suffering has a mysterious sweet attraction, a terrible downward drag. I will not say that this was irresistible, only that I could not resist it. Whatever inward opposition I might have felt, had I been better instructed, I admit that in the end all would still have been as it was, for I was in the grip of a wicked impulse and could not do otherwise than to occupy myself with such forbidden things. I was born, so I think, with an innate desire to humiliate and hurt, to wound and even to destroy others in order thereby to create a sexual pleasure in myself. That lust and cruelty often occur together is a fact that has long been recognized by philosophers and observed by students of the human animal. It seems to me that I am different only in degree, not kind, from others who have given themselves to these savage desires. The example of the degener-ate Caesars comes to mind. While still a boy I read in the pages of the historian Suetonius how Nero and Tiberius and the other Roman emperors took delight in having youths and maidens slaughtered before their eyes. Why do such horrors fascinate? Why does evil glow? I cannot say, only that it does, they do. These imperial excesses haunted my dreams and excited me vilely in my waking. It was from reading those descriptions of the orgies of Tiberius and Caligula that the idea was formed in me of one day locking children in my castles, and torturing those children, and killing them. I confess that both in the prospect and then the commission of these acts I enjoyed an inexpressible pleasure. If I could otherwise express it, I might never have sinned. I did what others dream. I am your nightmare.

As a child, my lord, I never myself knew correction. I ran my heedless ways; I did what I liked. When I grew older, I seemed always above the law – above or beyond it – there were never such limits for me. I exhort all parents here present to look to their duty and not to spare the rod where it is needful – not in cruelty but justice, lest their children should grow up crooked, and fall into the abyss where I am fallen.

(At this point, according to the notaries, Gilles cried out loud in his contrition and grief: *cum magna cordis contritione et amaritudine, cum magnaque lacrimarum effusione*, as it says in their record. It will not be fanciful, therefore, if the reader imagines his tears before passing on.)

I am a damned man [the Confession continues] and a measure of ruin. I am the great archangel of the house of the dead. Yet am I only Gilles de Rais, a man of no meaning. For this, in tears, I beg mercy and pardon of God. And now, my lord Bishop, in addition to those murders and outrages which I have confessed already, I wish to set it in the record against me that when recently I was a petitioner at the court of our sovereign lord and prince, the Duke of Brittany, in the canton Josselin, of the diocese of Maclovia, so little was I in control of my own passions that I caused to be killed several young boys who were found for me by my servant Griart. Some of this was to do with witchcraft, but most was not. I did my deeds for blood's sake, not for the Devil. I confess that most of my murders have been the outcome of lust, and not necromancy. As to the manner in which I put those boys to death, I have described this already, and it seems to me that to repeat or to dwell on such details now would be an exercise in vain sensation. Unless the court so decrees, therefore, I shall not speak again of *how* my victims were done to death, neither the male nor the female children. My methods were unspeakable, my lusts ungovernable. I killed because nothing else but killing could ever quiet my lust. I note the fact, my lord, in tears, and beg God's forgiveness for it, as I beg humbly on my knees for the pardon of the parents of those children I have killed. There is nothing I can utter which will explain to you, or to myself, or to God, why I have done the wicked and wanton and abominable things which I have done. Not explanation, but confession is my burden. I confess before God and my judges here that I have done murder upon murder and committed sodomy upon sodomy, and that I know I am not worthy even to ask for your mercy or then to suffer punishment at the hands of decent men. In truth I am an outcast. I belong to the outer dark.

Once more desiring to be specific, I confess and declare that after the last festival of St John the Baptist, a handsome youth who stayed with a man named Rodigo, dwelling in Bourgeneuf-en-Rais, was one night brought to me for carnal usage. I was then a visitor in the same place. This youth was picked out and fetched for my pleasure by my servants Henriet Griart and Etienne Corillaut. I confess that during that night we all three committed sodomy upon the person of this boy, and that I then caused him to be killed and his body to be burned near my castle at Machecoul. Again, my lord, at the time of my last stay at Vannes, in the month of July of last year, a man named André Buchet delivered over to me in the dwelling-house of a certain Jean Lemoine a very young boy whose name I do not know. I used this boy in a manner I have previously described, and it was my cruel libidinous delight to watch my servants use him in similar fashion. When we had done, and the lad was dead, I caused the same Corillaut to throw the boy's body into the privy of a residence belonging to a certain Bretden. These names and habitations are mentioned by me not to incriminate others, but to make real and exact those nameless boundless horrors which I have done.

I could go on, my lord, but let this stand. I believe I have told you enough, and more than enough, for you to judge me. What others have told you concerning my manifold sins and crimes is true, as I have heard their witness read out here in open court, and I admit it. What I have added to you, and to my lord the Bishop of St Brieuc, and to Master Pierre de l'Hospital, is also the truth. I can only beg you and all the faithful to pray for Christ's mercy on me, who deserve it less than anyone who ever lived since the beginning of the world.

My lord, truly the nature of my sins and crimes is such that without the protection of our holy mother the Church, the Devil himself will carry me body and soul to hell! [At this point the record notes that Gilles again threw himself down upon his knees, and cried out in anguish.] O my God, my Creator, my beloved Redeemer, I implore your mercy and forgiveness on my ruined state! And you, parents and sisters and brothers and friends of the children I have so cruelly murdered – you, whoever you are, whom I have sinned against and injured, whether here present or elsewhere – grant me, oh I beg you, grant me, as you are Christians and the faithful of Jesus Christ, the succour of your prayers for Gilles de Rais!

When my lord had delivered himself of this speech, there were

ome in that court who stared at him stony-faced, seeing only
hat what he had confessed he had done made it inevitable
and necessary that he be put to death. However, there were
others who knelt and prayed for him, with cries of Christian
pity and forgiveness. It should be said that before his confessions there were many in Nantes who would have been
prepared to throw him before wild wolves to meet his end;
indeed, the people of the city would most likely have been
capable of tearing him in pieces with their bare hands, had
they been given that opportunity. Now, though, the more
charitable among them perceived Gilles to be a miserable
fellow sinner facing death, prepared to confess his sins, needing
their prayers. The notaries do not record how many prayed
for him. Nor do I know it, for I was among that number.

When I looked up the Bishop of Nantes was saying:

'Pray that the anger of the Most High may be pacified,
Messire de Rais! Pray that your contrite tears may purify the
soul of your being!'

Then Master Chapeillon rose and asked the court to announce a day for delivering judgement.

The Bishop of Nantes consulted with his brother Bishops,
and with the Vice-Inquisitor. Friar Jean Blouyn sat beady-
eyed and baffled in his chair, content enough with the prisoner's confession, no doubt, yet with his long face grown
somehow sharper and more ratlike, as though disappointed. I
never understood this look of the Vice-Inquisitor's. It was a
scholastic look, a look of pure scepticism. Yet he evidently
concurred with the date which Jean de Malestroit proposed.

The Bishop of Nantes fixed Tuesday the twenty-fifth of
October for the day of his judgement, giving himself and
Gilles three days in which to prepare for it.

Before that day came, the rest of us had to come up for
sentence.

First, on the twenty-third of October, the secular court
heard the confessions of Griart and Poitou, which were

identical in almost every detail with the ones they had already made before the ecclesiastical court. Both were condemned to death by hanging and burning.

The next day, Prelati and I appeared before the Bishop of Nantes. The alchemist, cleared of the charge of murder, but convicted of heresy, sacrilege, diabolism, and apostasy on his own admission, was condemned to life imprisonment. In respect of his clerk's tonsure, this sentence was to be served in a prison of the Church. Passing it, the Bishop made clear that he required Prelati to be kept in solitary confinement, on a diet of bread and water, and with regular scourgings by his gaolers. As it happened, Prelati was not in prison long at all. This is because he found another noble patron interested in alchemy, namely René, Duke of Anjou, who had also served in arms with Joan of Arc. Undoubtedly there is a chain of coincidence here which I never understood. On the face of things, the Duke of Anjou seems to have been impressed by Prelati's alchemical powers, as revealed in the course of the trial. For whatever reason, the Duke succeeded in having him removed from the ecclesiastical prison and attached to his own household. There, doubtless, the diabolist would have seen that cup in Anjou's possession, which some claim might have been the Holy Grail. I never saw it, but one who did once told me that it bore this strange inscription incised in its rim:

> *Qui bien beurra*
> *Dieu voira.*
> *Qui beurra tout d'une baleine*
> *Voira Dieu et la Madeleine.*

Which is to say:

> *He who drinks well*
> *Will see God.*
> *He who quaffs at a single draught*
> *Will see God and the Magdalene.*

And do not ask me why this sticks in my head. For some reason, it is there with Rossignol's song of ice and summer insects, the children's rhyme about Gilles the wolf, and that song about the man of double deed. If I knew why these things chimed, then I would be wiser. If I were wiser, I would never have written this book.

Prelati did not die in the service of the Duke of Anjou. He succeeded in getting himself appointed in due course as governor of the village of La Roche-sur-Yon, but then one day he had the imprudence to seize Geoffrey le Ferron, Treasurer of Brittany, who happened to be passing through La Roche. Declaring that le Ferron had been responsible for all his misfortunes since the unfortunate affair at St Etienne-de-la-Mer-Morte, Prelati flung the Treasurer into a dungeon and tried to extract a ransom for him. The Grand Council got hold of the matter, and the Italian's true identity was revealed. Despite his ducal patron's attempts to save him yet again, Francesco Prelati was condemned to death and hanged on the second of May, 1456, a year and a half ago, a few weeks before I began this writing, though at that time I did not know of the event.

As for me, I was fined three hundred gold crowns and condemned to be banished for life. Since exile is a fit definition of the mortal condition, and I never was truly at home anywhere I found myself in this world, it may be said that I got off lightly. So be it. I will say no less myself. God and the Bishop of Nantes were merciful, and Friar Jean Blouyn was not ungrateful. I got off lightly.

XXIX

THE VEILING OF THE CROSS

The woman they called La Meffraye hanged herself in her cell below La Tour Neuve before any sentence could be passed on her. I did try to pray for her soul, but the words would not come.

Now it is Tuesday the twenty-fifth of October, the year of God's merciful sentence on mankind 1440, and once again it is the hour of Terce, nine o'clock in the morning, and the scene is set in the great crowded hall where the Bishop of Nantes has conducted the Church's trial of my lord Gilles de Rais.

Gilles stands before the bench in simple clothes. I will confess it, I cannot remember anything he wore, neither texture nor colour, nor its cut. Thus, for perhaps the first time in his trial, my master achieved a moment of proper humility and anonymity. Previously, even when appearing as a penitent, he had dressed himself up in some spectacular black stuff, directing the eye of the beholder outwards from the man to the apparel, just as he could be suspected of playing a role in some drama that was of his own making. Now Gilles just stands here, head down, broken, nothing in his costume in any way remarkable, a guilty man awaiting his due sentence.

There are, in fact, two sentences to come. The first, in the name of the Bishop of Nantes and Friar Jean Blouyn, must deal with those crimes which Gilles has committed within the jurisdiction of the Holy Office. The second, in the name of the Bishop alone, will deal with those crimes which fall outside it.

Pale at the nose with anger, the Vice-Inquisitor delivers the first sentence. He stands and says, reading from a paper:

304

'In the Holy Name of our Lord Jesus Christ! We, Jean, Bishop of Nantes, and Friar Jean Blouyn, Bachelor in Sacred Letters, of the Order of Friars-Preachers of Nantes, being delegate of the Inquisitor for heresy for the City and Diocese of Nantes, in judgement assembled, and having before our eyes nothing but God Himself; with the advice and consent of our lords the bishops, jurisconsults, doctors, and professors of Sacred Letters here present; having examined the depositions of all the sworn witnesses summoned in our name and in the name of the Public Prosecutor by us deputed, against Gilles de Rais, our subject and justiciable; having ordered these depositions to be recorded exactly in writing; having heard his own confessions, made spontaneously in our presence; and having carefully weighed and considered every other reason affecting our decision:

'We pronounce, decide, and declare you, Gilles de Rais, summoned before our tribunal, to be shamefully guilty of heresy, apostasy, and the evocation of demons, for which crimes you have incurred sentence of excommunication and all other penalties determined by the law; and we declare finally that you must undergo punishment and correction therefore, as the law requires and the holy Canons demand, as a heretic, as an apostate, and as a trafficker with demons.'

Gilles, stunned, sinks to his knees like a bull awaiting the *coup de grâce* in some Spanish bull-ring.

Which the Bishop of Nantes now delivers, standing in turn, reading from another paper, declaring Gilles guilty of unnatural crime against children of both sexes, of sacrilege, and of gross violation of ecclesiastical immunity.

Gilles stares at his judges, speechless, nodding. In that moment I realized that, as with Joan of Arc before him, it was the sentence of what seemed like final excommunication which struck him to the heart. Convicted and on his own admission guilty of such monstrous crimes, he could still not believe that the Church would cast him out. Perhaps the most charitable understanding would put it thus: since the Church is by definition a society of sinners, the greater the individual sin then the more does the sinner need the Church. Gilles could face death and ignominy, but being excommunicate he could not bear.

Now, still on his knees, hands outspread in supplication to the Bishop and the Vice-Inquisitor, he is protesting brokenly that he has never understood the nature of heresy.* Nor does he know that he has ever committed it, but that since the Church has declared this to be so, he begs the Church to restore him to her communion.

Jean Blouyn breathes on his nails and gazes elsewhere. But the Bishop of Nantes ignores him, and offers Christ's charity: 'Gilles, do you now, detesting your errors and your sorceries, and those other vile crimes which have severed you from the Catholic faith, desire to be received once more into the bosom of the Church our Mother, and to return to her?'

'In the name of God, I do!'

'Then, in the Holy Name of Jesus, be it so!'

The Bishop steps down to embrace Gilles, and to draw him to his feet. But my lord will have none of it. Still kneeling, he implores Jean de Malestroit to extend this pardon also to cover the sacrilege at St Etienne-de-la-Mer-Morte, which similarly involves his excommunication. With only the briefest of glances at the representative of the Holy Office, the Bishop grants his prayer. As for Friar Jean, I do him an injustice by implying that his own acts of Christian charity might never have extended quite as far as this. Whether he would have found it in his heart to extend to Gilles the words of God's forgiveness and reconciliation, I simply cannot say. Perhaps it is as well that Gilles did not ask him. As well for Gilles' sake; also for his own.

Then, shaking with a sudden convulsion, like pain, Gilles

---

* *se nunquam scivisse quid esset*, as the official record notes.

begs the Bishop for a confessor to shrive him before he is executed and goes into the presence of God for further judgement. My lord knows, of course, that sentence of death is now inevitable, though it will be left to the civil court to pronounce that which no ecclesiastical court may say.

The Bishop of Nantes thereupon commands a certain Carmelite, Friar Jean Jouvenal, to attend the condemned man for that purpose this very noon. Then the court rises for the last time. The Church's trial of Gilles de Rais is over.

But the law has not finished with my master. This same evening he must face the civil tribunal, to answer the murder charges and be sent to his doom. Since I was not there present, I shall not speak as though I was. All the same, I should here declare that I have read the whole record of the proceedings before the civil court, a manuscript of more than one hundred pages, written down in plain French, and that it occurs to me to remark that the Gilles de Rais who appears in its final reckonings might be said to be a different man from the Gilles de Rais now being led by armed guards from the court of the Bishop of Nantes. Why so? How so? What other cause can there be but the fact that between the end of one ordeal and the beginning of the other, Gilles made his last confession to the Carmelite? What was said and how it was said is not for us to know. It cannot have been much different from what my lord had confessed now both extra-judicially and then in open court. But what was different is that Gilles would be talking direct to God, with the confessor present as his overhearer. By the time that he made his final appearance before Pierre de l'Hospital that evening, Gilles was a changed man in the absolute sense. He had confessed his sins to God, and he had been given a penance and then sacramental absolution. The battle was over, and we might say that the Devil had lost.

I shall pass quickly over what happened at La Bouffay. The court there had received copies of the evidence before the

Bishop's court, along with my lord's own confessions, which made its task straightforward. However, its special business was to deal in formal fashion with the murder of the children, and, quite correctly, as is clear from the record, Master de l'Hospital had decided that this should be faced without shrinking.

Therefore he invited Gilles to state again the details of his guilt, reminding him that the shame of such public confession would help to mitigate his suffering in the cleansing flames of purgatory. And Gilles, as the official record says, now hastened to obey him, *liberallement et sans contraincte*, freely and frankly, and with *grant contricion et desplaisance*.

It was when my lord came to the worst of the horrors he had twice before admitted to the judges of the Church that Pierre de l'Hospital stood up and veiled the crucifix behind him. I have always found that gesture deeply revealing. To the outward eye, the Chancellor of Brittany was much more a man of this world than either the Bishop of Nantes or the Vice-Inquisitor, and of course he had already heard Gilles speak of his crimes at his first confession when indeed the Chancellor had even been able to question him as to *why* he had done them. That veiling of the cross seems to me the reaction of the common man to the story of Gilles de Rais. I do not say that the common man is wrong. At the same time, I point out that the problem for the common man is to find some answer to the question: how is it possible for anyone possessing so profound a religious sense as Gilles undoubtedly possessed to be capable of the acts for which he was convicted? The chief paradox of Gilles' life, and the main difficulty of any effort to unravel it, is that he was both a Christian but withal he was utterly unmoral. To the common man, the two states may seem irreconcilable. Yet it is by no means so uncommon a phenomenon as it appears.

I have heard it said that Gilles' parade of religion was that of a common hypocrite, but I do not believe this to be true.

Not all his vice or his murders managed to eliminate his longing for God, and nothing ever affected him more deeply than Joan's burning and then his own excommunication. So long as he could maintain any form of contact with the divine, he must have felt that he was not entirely lost. Somewhere, once, I heard my master say, 'I am redeemable'. I cannot remember the context, but the remark is striking. Of all the men I have known, Gilles de Rais seems to me the one whose life and death testifies most strongly to the truth of the redemption. That is to say, there is in my lord's story clear indication that man having been created in a state of original justice by his sin forfeited the friendship of God and became enslaved to the Devil. And that Christ by His death on the cross, in which He became a substitutional victim for the human race, paid the price of our redemption, or buying back; by His satisfaction he blotted out our sin, and by His merits He won for us the restoration to the grace and friendship of God. This is the doctrine of the redemption as traditionally taught. It makes the cross the shape of human lust. That is why Pierre de l'Hospital did wrong to veil it when he was sickened by the worst of Gilles' confession.

That my lord would receive the death penalty was a foregone conclusion, and the verdict of the civil court was unanimous. Not all his judges were agreed as to the manner in which the sentence should be carried out, and this was debated at some length as he stood before them. Some favoured beheading, but finally general agreement was reached that Gilles should be hanged and burned. Griart and Poitou would be executed with him.

Pierre de l'Hospital stood to announce this verdict. In order, he said, that Gilles might implore the mercy of God, and dispose himself to die in good estate, and in penitence for having committed such crimes, the sentence would be carried out on the following day at eleven o'clock.

At which Gilles thanked God and our lord the President for

having notified him of the hour of his death. And then he asked a favour of the court.

'Since,' he said, 'Griart and Corillaut, my servants, were my followers in life, may I beg that I be allowed to die before they do? I am the cause and beginning of their fall. I can sustain death and speak to them of their salvation at the moment of passing. I can expressly show them how to die. If it is otherwise, if my servants do not see me die, they may fall into despair, imagining even that they alone are expiating our joint crimes, while I, who drove them to such things, might yet escape unpunished. Give me this favour, for I hope by the grace of Our Lord that, after having been the cause of their fall, I shall by my words and example be the cause of their salvation.'

I think of all Gilles' deeds known to me, this is the only one that shines with any light. It proves, if nothing else, that his remark, '*I am redeemable*', should not be interpreted as bespeaking merely a passive faith in Christ's redeeming power. Standing there before the civil court, listening to his learned judges debate the hour and the means of his death, it had occurred to Gilles to think of how it would be for those other two evildoers. He had realized that if Griart and Poitou preceded him to the scaffold it might cross their minds that some elaborate charade was being played, and that they were paying the full price for the crimes of the three of them, while he, presumably because of his privileges of birth and power, might yet be allowed to escape with his life intact. He did not want them even to entertain such cynicism. And he hoped by his example to give them what comfort he could. This act, I say, was the act of a decent man. I do not say that Gilles would have been incapable of it before his confession to Friar Jean Jouvenal. I do say that it is no blame that it came after.

Pierre de l'Hospital instantly saw the merit in what Gilles was proposing. In the name of the court, he agreed that my lord should die first. In consideration of the spirit of repentance shown by the condemned, the Chancellor even added one favour more. 'I grant you that your body, before it is burned, shall be taken from the flames and buried in whatever church you choose in the town of Nantes.'

Gilles said: 'I should like it to be buried in the monastery church of our Lady of Mount Carmel.'

This was entered in the record. Then, as the court rose, Gilles begged a last favour, as much for his fellow criminals as himself. 'My lord Chancellor, may I request that you approach the Bishop of Nantes and ask for a general procession through the city before the hour of execution?'

'Why?' asked Pierre de l'Hospital.

Gilles answered him: 'So that any Christian who is so minded may pray to God that I and my servants die firmly in the faith of our salvation.'

This being agreed, the trial of Marshal Gilles de Rais was over.

This is the place to discuss very briefly the one objection which I ever heard to the conduct of that trial: namely, that my lord confessed to his crimes only under the threat of torture. To suppose from this that he might have been innocent is of course ridiculous, yet it can be argued that Seneca once pointed out *Torture forces even the innocent to lie*, and that the blessed St Augustine himself recognized the fallacy of torture: 'If,' he says, 'the accused be innocent, he will undergo for an uncertain crime a certain punishment, and that not for having committed a crime, but because it is unknown whether he committed it.' (*De Civitate Dei*, bk. xix, c. 6). At the same time, and in the same great book, St Augustine makes it clear that he regards certain limited forms of torture as excused by the necessity to know the truth.

Now, Gilles was *not* tortured. So what broke him? What made for his sudden change of mind and heart? What made him recognize the court when at first he had refused to? What was the cause that impelled him to make such full confession?

As I have said, we can never be sure regarding any knowledge of the matter. If we are honest men, we will allow for the possibility that this soldier was at heart a coward, and that the prospect of the rack loomed uppermost in his mind when he started to confess everything that afternoon to the Bishop of St Brieuc and Pierre de l'Hospital. Similarly, as I have suggested, we must allow for the probability of an even greater spiritual fear at work inspiring him, and that the prospect of final excommunication was more terrible to Gilles than anything else.

Keeping both fears in mind, I still claim that something better was responsible, and that this something was a someone, and that this someone was the blessed Joan of Arc. I ask the reader to consider in this regard not just my own devotion to the idea of her, which was what led me first to the Marshal's service, but everything I have told you in this book as coming from Gilles' lips on the same subject. It is my contention that all Gilles ever did in his life, after a certain date, was as the direct result of Joan's inspiration, however fatally he misinterpreted that grace. Therefore, I say, at some point Gilles was inspired by Joan to confess his sins, to tell the truth, to return again to God. Joan came to him, in some way, at the turning point in his trial. There can be no other explanation for how he changed.

Still, sometimes I think I have missed the whole point of the story. Take only the fact of the braquemard: what did that mean? There was this sword, with the scenes depicted on it which Gilles allowed me to interpret as relating to Joan of Arc. Then, at the trial, it came out that here was the very weapon he had used to despatch his victims. There is some mystery here I cannot grasp. The facts are as I have given them, that's all. If the reader can make more sense of them than I have, then I would be glad to know it before I die.

The nearest words come to the truth, perhaps, is this. We all of us have small names for the eternal verities. For Gilles, the various names of hell were Joan, Joan, Joan; the various names of heaven were the same.

XXX

EXECUTION DAY

Now it is Wednesday the twenty-sixth of October, the year of
Our Lord 1440, and in one hour's time it will be eleven
o'clock. The weather is cold and bright, with a frosty sun.
The great Cathedral bell has been tolling since dawn, slowly,
remorselessly, like a hammer striking nails into a coffin. Now,
one by one, but in unison, all the bells of the churches of
Nantes join in to follow it. The narrow streets of the city shake
with the sound. On the stroke of ten the huge studded doors
of the Cathedral are flung open. Priests emerge from its
darkness in black funeral-copes, followed by monks with
lighted candles in their hands. They walk behind a tall black
crucifix, reciting the seven Penitential Psalms which are said
for the dying, beginning *Domine, ne in furore*:

> *O Lord, rebuke me not in thine indignation: neither*
> *chasten me in thy displeasure.*
> *Have mercy upon me, O Lord, for I am weak: O Lord,*
> *heal me, for my bones are vexed . . .*

Chanting, praying, the sound of many voices rising above the
tread of many feet, the procession makes its way through the
streets of Nantes. It circles the city, passing the Castle on its
way to the place of execution. From his cell in La Tour
Neuve, no doubt, my lord Gilles de Rais can hear the waves
of sound. For certain, he has heard the bell since dawn.
Perhaps, as his funeral passes below him, he can even make
out the words being chanted against those seven sins he found

more deadly than most, particularly the words of the fourth psalm, expressing his own penance for his lust:

> *Behold, I was shapen in wickedness: and in sin hath*
> *my mother conceived me.*
> *But lo, thou requirest truth in the inward parts: and shalt*
> *make me to understand wisdom secretly . . .*

With the ordinary plain people of Nantes, merchants and nobles and peasants, walking behind the priests and the monks and the nuns, their voices raised to join in the general lamentation, those familiar words which take on new and terrible meaning for this day:

> *Make me a clean heart, O God: and renew a right spirit*
> *within me.*
> *Cast me not away from thy presence: and take not thy*
> *holy Spirit from me.*
> *O give me the comfort of thy help again: and stablish*
> *me with thy free Spirit.*
> *Then shall I teach thy ways unto the wicked: and sinners*
> *shall be converted unto thee.*
> *Deliver me from blood-guiltiness, O God . . .*

Asking for the solemn procession, Gilles asked for this. If, in his cell in the tower, behind the barred windows, he does not hear the words of the psalms and see the incense rise prayerfully from the swinging censers, then let it be because he is crying those prayers himself, down on his knees, in that state where a man does not need incense.

Now it is Wednesday the twenty-sixth of October, the year of Our Lord 1440, and in half an hour's time it will be eleven o'clock. The procession has crossed the bridge to the isle in the Loire which holds the place of execution. There, in the meadow of La Madeleine, three gibbets and three pyres have been prepared. The procession coils about that death site like a snake. There, on a raised platform, sits Jean V, the Duke of Brittany, with his suite below him. On another platform, opposite, the judges of both Tribunals are gathered, together with their officials. The Bishop of Nantes is shivering, perhaps from the cold. The Vice-Inquisitor has a look of complete absorption. As for Master Chapeillon, his eyeglasses are screwed in, and he wears his hood up. Pierre de l'Hospital stands on a little stool. The psalms complete, the Litany of Recommendation for a departing soul has now begun, imploring the clemency of the Holy Trinity and crying to the loving Mother of God, to angels and archangels, patriarchs and prophets, apostles and evangelists, monks and hermits, martyrs and confessors, priests and levites, all the saints of heaven, to plead and intercede for these three sinners who are already drawing their last hour of breath:

Kyrie, eleison.
Christe, eleison.
Kyrie, eleison.

And to one of these petitions, as again my lord Gilles de Rais knows very well, the soul of every guiltless child murdered either by Herod or by him, in Jerusalem long ago or just recently at Tiffauges or Machecoul, will be responding in paradise in behalf of its assassin:

All ye holy Innocents, pray for us.

The three gibbets are lofty and strong. The three unlit pyres are of brushwood faggots, sprinkled with tar. The public hangman, Monsieur de Nantes, stands by his apparatus, dressed in scarlet. His voice joins in the litany as he tests his ropes:

Be thou merciful, spare us, O Lord.
Be thou merciful, graciously hear us, O Lord.
From all evil, good Lord, deliver us . . .

At the edges of the meadow, the aspens are shedding their gold leaves in the rising wind. On the other side of the river a great flat patch of oak-scrub is red like gore.

Now it is Wednesday the twenty-sixth of October, the year of Our Lord 1440, and in fifteen minutes it will be eleven o'clock. My lord Gilles de Rais, accompanied by Henriet Griart and Etienne Corillaut always known as Poitou, is being marched over the little bridge to the place of execution. The three have been brought from their cells under strong armed guard. The route they have taken has enabled Gilles to cast a look at his own Hôtel de la Suze, the scene of many great gatherings and of some of his worst crimes.

All three men wear simple grey tabards and tunics, and their hair has been shaved from their skulls. The voices reciting the litany cease as the amen is reached. Now there is only the sound of the marching men coming, and a curlew calling over the river bank. The public hangman has a crest of snow-white hair. It shines in a shaft of the sun as those approach whom he is to execute. As they draw nearer, you can hear the voice of Gilles de Rais. He is exhorting his companions to be of good courage and to trust in the mercy of God. Now, beneath the gibbet, he continues this comfort while his judges strain to hear him.

Gilles de Rais says:

'There is no sin so terrible that God will not forgive it, if only the sinner has great repentance and contrition in his heart, and he asks forgiveness with good hope. God is readier to pardon than the sinner is to ask. Thank God with me for this manifest sign of His love – that He now allows us to die in possession of our strength and all our faculties, without punishing us suddenly for our wickedness.'

Both Griart and Poitou are wet with fear. Their eyes go everywhere except the gibbet. Gilles, while he still speaks comfort to them, looks nowhere else.

Gilles says:

'Do not weaken, I implore you! Persevere in prayer but a little more, the time is not long. Have such a regret now for your crimes that you do not fear death, which is such a little hing, and without which we cannot see God and His great glory. How much ought we to wish to be out of this world where there is only misery. Together we have sinned, and immediately our souls are separated from our bodies we shall meet with God in Paradise.'

Then Griart and Poitou thank their master, in tears, and cry brokenly likewise to return his comfort. The three men stand for a moment, hand in hand, motionless, spellbound, like creatures given up as prey. Across the river, the bells in the churches stop tolling, then the Cathedral bell stops. The curlew cries. The wind is still rising. A red leaf blows against Gilles' shirt and sticks there, just below the heart, like a drop of blood.

Now it is Wednesday the twenty-sixth of October, the year of Our Lord 1440, and in a few moments it will be eleven o'clock. Gilles kneels and begs God's pardon in a loud clear voice. Then, rising, without any gesture, he addresses the great crowd, who listen in silence.

Gilles de Rais says:

'I am your brother in Christ. You who are present – you, above all, whose children I have murdered – I beg you, one and all, by the Passion of our Lord, to pray for me. Forgive me with your hearts the evil I have done you, as you hope yourselves for mercy and pardon from God.'

Kneeling for a last time, Gilles addresses himself to the holy apostle St James, and to St Michael, provost of Paradise, who once had Joan of Arc in his earthly care. After praying to these saints, asking their succour to assist him *in extremis*, he addresses himself again direct to God. 'Lord Jesus Christ, son of God, have mercy on me, a sinner.' Then, the death warrant being read aloud by Pierre de l'Hospital, and Friar Jean Blouyn holding up the crucifix before his eyes, Gilles strides like a soldier to his gallows. He ascends by the ladder to a high stool. His hands are bound. The noose is fitted around his neck. Monsieur de Nantes steps forward and lights the fire.

A moment later, the stool is kicked away. Gilles' body drops. He hangs free at the end of the rope.

Now it is Wednesday the twenty-sixth of October, the year of Our Lord 1440, and the time is eleven o'clock. The flames of the pyre curl round the half-strangled figure. Poitou cries out: 'Now is the time to be a strong and valiant knight in God's love!' Gilles does not struggle. He is dead before the rope catches fire. Now the rope breaks, sending his body crashing into the flames. When it is sure that the fire has completed the work of the gibbet, the remains of Gilles de Rais are dragged out and given to certain ladies of high rank.

Henriet Griart and Etienne Corillaut are then hanged and burned, and their ashes thrown as powder to the wind.

EPILOGUE

No more do I dream that I have to go back to the castle. No longer do I spend my days and my nights remembering that time with Gilles de Rais. The writing of this book has served its purpose.

Beyond that simple act of exorcism, I see a deeper meaning, a more profound achievement. In trying to marry Joan of Arc and Gilles de Rais – to make sense of the confluence of good and evil – I have come to realize that the key to evil is its being immaterial. Gilles, in the last analysis, does not matter. He is certainly less to be reckoned than any of his victims. The best to be said of him is that by the time of his death he knew as much himself, and acted accordingly. If that is so, then I say that he came by that knowledge through Joan's intercession. And so have I, who knew that astonishing woman only through him. My mind is now fixed on the figure of Joan of Arc.

I have been one who tried to know the sun by close attention to the shadows cast by a blighted tree at night at the winter solstice. God is that sun. Joan was God's mortal moon, showing His light to us even in these bleak benighted times. Gilles was the crooked tree who did not comprehend the moonlight that had fallen on him. Too long have I sat in his shadows, trying to make sense of them. Now, even if there is more sense to be made, I beg leave to be excused from that responsibility.

Joan, the moon herself, is a different matter. It is my belief that in her we have burned a saint. This opinion is perhaps heretical. Let it stand, none the less. I believe that one day, unlikely as it may seem, this peasant girl from Lorraine will be canonized. Saint Joan! I beg the reader not to laugh, or dismiss the idea. I think she may already be a saint in heaven. It will take the Church here on earth a little time to recognize the shining fact, that's all.

I spend my days and nights now studying all there is to know about her. I have copies of the documentation of her trial, and likewise of the many depositions which formed part of the evidence for her rehabilitation. I have several other bits and scraps as well. In truth it is amazing what you can deduce if you are sufficiently assiduous and impassioned. It has been said, for instance, that nothing now exists which will enable us to imagine Joan's physical appearance. Yet I can estimate that she must have been five feet two inches tall from the length of fabric ordered for the *huque*, or dress, of green which was made for her on the command of Duke Charles' Treasurer after the victory at Orléans. I prefer this hard evidence to what Gilles told me. At the same time, I have also no doubt that she was dark haired, having seen a single strand of her hair pressed into the seal of a letter. That hair was black.

She was not a 'shepherdess'. It was only the noblemen of the royal entourage who thus qualified her, since to them all peasant women are more or less the stuff of such quaint poetry. 'Up to the time she left her parents she followed the plough and sometimes minded the cattle in the fields. Also she did the usual duties of women, such as spinning, and other things' (Jean Morel, of Greux, her godfather). 'She employed herself at home with many duties in the house, spinning hemp or wool, following the plough, or going to harvest, according to the season' (Béatrix Estillin, of Domrémy, her godmother).

The only point on which the memory of her childhood companions singles Joan out as extraordinary concerns her piety. Her friends recall having teased her about it. 'We told

her that she was too pious' (Mengette Joyart, her friend).
'Often she was bashful when others reproached her with going
too devotedly to church' (Hauviette Syonne, another friend).
She made confession frequently and heard Mass as often as
she could.

Now entertain the paradox of destiny. For this simple
peasant girl, of great piety but little else, is suddenly called to
assume the vocation of war. 'All the combatants admired her
courage,' says Thibaut d'Armagnac, who fought beside her.
And as a further complication: she talked well. I think it is by
Joan's words that we know her, what she was. Let me call up
just a single instance from her trial. Asked by one of her
judges the impossible question of whether or not she was in a
state of grace, she made reply: 'If I am not in the grace of
God, may God place me there, and if I am may God keep me
there, for I would be the unhappiest person in the world if I
knew I was not in the grace of God.' This seems to me a
sentence of the purest and sweetest and strongest inspiration.
The speaker is *there* in her words, and the words ring true.

Even the title which she gave herself tells a high history:
Joan la Pucelle, Joan the Virgin. This virginity, of such
importance in her life, was twice affirmed: first when she was
examined at Poitiers, and then when she was examined at
Rouen under the direction of Anne, Duchess of Bedford. Its
import, I should say, goes deeper than mere physical abstinence from pleasures of the flesh. There is no special virtue in
virginity, unless it is chosen directly for God's sake, and for no
other reason, in order thereby to belong to Him and to serve
Him utterly. This was indeed the case with Joan of Arc
('From the first time I heard my Voices, I dedicated my
virginity for so long as it should please God'). Virginity draws
attention to the sex in a very special way. It might be said
that under her knightly dress, Joan was the Lady, *la Dame*,
the inspiration of love, whom men approach with trembling
and for whom love is inseparable from worship. Adoration of

321

this kind is not forbidden. Under the name of *dulia*, we may afford it to saints and angels and other express vehicles of the glory of God. Such is the feeling which Joan inspired in her companions in arms. 'On the way, Bertrand and I slept every night by her – Joan being at my side, fully dressed. She inspired me with such respect that for nothing in the world would I have dared to molest her; also, never did I feel towards her – I say it on oath – any carnal desire . . . I had absolute faith in her. Her words and her ardent faith in God inflamed me. I believe she was sent from God' (Jean de Novelemport, knight, called Jean de Metz). The same sentiment was felt by the Duke of Alençon, who attests to the chastity of this girl who more than once had to camp and sleep with soldiers in the field. One of those soldiers explained what was felt by common men in regard to her purity: 'I heard tell from several of Joan's intimates that they never experienced any desire for her. That is, occasionally they had felt carnal desire but never did they dare abandon themselves to it, and they believed it not possible to be able to.' Another testified: 'I remember well that at the time I was with her, never did I have the desire to do ill.' I know Joan's purity is still communicable.

And what are we to make of what she called her 'voices', or her *'conseil'*, that divine inspiration which first came to her one summer mid-day in her father's garden in her thirteenth year? ('I heard this Voice to my right, towards the church; rarely do I hear it without its being accompanied also by a light.') All I can say is that this source of knowledge and instruction was more real to Joan than the world itself. It is a fact that she never herself gave any other explanation for her acts or her mission. On every page of the record of her trial there is the same resounding affirmation: 'If I were in a wood, I could easily hear the Voice which came to me. It seems to me to come from lips I should reverence . . . I have done nothing except by the command of God and His angels . . . Nothing in

the world that I did was done except by the command of God
... I have said it to you enough, that I did nothing except by
the command of God! ... The Voice comes to me from God
and I do not tell you all I know about it; I have far greater
fear of doing wrong in saying to you things that would
displease it, than I have of answering you ... My Voice is
good and to be honoured!'

One of the rare clerks with courage to resist the pressures
exerted upon him, Master Jean Lohier, retired from her trial
in order not to be implicated in injustice. He declared, much
to the point, in an examination of Joan's statements: 'If she
had said "it seems to me" instead of "I know for certain", it is
my opinion that there is not one man who would have been
able to condemn her.' But as another assessor, the sceptical
Jean Fabri, said: 'She insisted on her revelations too much.'

The world could not forgive her that. So the world burned
her. I find it hard to forgive the world therefore.

But here is Joan to have the last word herself: '*I will say willingly what I know, and yet not all. I am come in God's name; I have
nothing to do here; let me be sent back to God from whence I came.*'

May he, who is able to understand, understand.

As for Gilles de Rais: he is no more my lord, and I am even
less his man than I ever was. I think seldom now of his death,
of his life never. May the same be so for you have read his
story.

I, Dominus Eustachius Blanchet, priest, sometime canon
regular of the diocese of St Malo, in Brittany, began this work
at the monastery of Subiaco, on the seventh day of July, in
the year 1456 of Our Lord, and completed it tonight in the
Great Hospital of Milan, on the Feast of the Holy Innocents,
the twenty-eighth day of December, Our Lord's year 1457. And
I pray you all that have read my book to pray for me, as I do
pray for you and all other good readers on earth or in hell.

THE END

NOTE

This book, though a work of fiction, is based on the following primary historical sources: the original account of the canonical trial of Gilles de Rais, drawn up in Latin, to be found in the Archives of the Loire Inférieure (No. 9175); the original account of the civil trial, to be found amongst the communal archives of Thouars; the basic biographical study, the Abbé Eugène Bossard's *Gilles de Rais Maréchal de France dit Barbe Bleu 1404–1440* (1886); the *Procès de condamnation et de réhabilitation de Jeanne d'Arc*, edited by Jules Quicherat (1841); Alain Bouchart's *Les Grandes Croniques de Bretagne* (1514); Alain Chartier's *Histoire mémorable des grands troubles de ce Royaume soubs le roy Charles Septiesme* (1594); Mourain de Sourdaval's *Les Seigneurs de Rais* (1845); Armand Guéraud's *Notice sur Gilles de Rais* (1855); Guillaume Couginot's *Chronique de la Pucelle* (1859); Noel Vallois' *Le Procès de Gilles de Rais* (1913); and the Abbé Bourdeaut's *Champtocé, Gilles de Raiz, et les ducs de Bretagne* (1924).

It is to be noted that Bossard does not include the more explicit passages concerning his subject's sexual deviations even in Latin, so that his record of the trial is incomplete. For the full text one must consult either the facsimile edition published by the École de Chartes (Volume XXIII, 1862) or the modern French translation in Georges Bataille's *Le Procès de Gilles de Rais* (1965).